SHADOWS OF RUIN

THE BROKEN PROPHECY BOOK 2

ANNA APPLEGATE

HELEN DOMICO

CONTENT NOTES

This book contains content that some readers may find triggering such as:

On-Page Violence
Threats of Violence
Torture
Kidnapping
Grief
Death
Death of a Parent
Mental Health Struggles (Anxiety, Panic Attacks)
Profanity
Open-Door Intimate Scenes

Read with Care <3

For anyone who had to find the strength to keep going when you didn't think you could.

*And to **Chumbawamba** for creating "Tubthumping." It's not only our personal anthem, but our characters' too. "I get knocked down, but I get up again. You're never gonna keep me down."*

BROOKMERE
Broham
Larkslary
Uppington
Ellevail
Logan Lake
Valeford
Lomen Forest
Starhaven
Southern Forests
Demarva
Briartown
Hemlock
Crimson Forest
Canyon City
Mount Legion
Firestone
MYSTHAVEN
Ridgemont
N

ATHERIA

BLOOMS OF DARKNESS RECAP

Here's a quick reminder of where we left off:

- Princess Illiana "Lana" Dresden is the sole heir to Brookmere, who just happens to be the only Fae born without magic…and it's a total secret, known only to the few she calls friends.
- Vivienne Nazar, the royal seer, gave Lana a prophecy when she was a few months old, which to her dismay, has followed her every day. Because of a mysterious illness plaguing the king (aka her father, but not really her father—her uncle, something she didn't learn until the end of *Blooms of Darkness*), he enacts the ancient tradition of the marriage trials to fulfill her prophecy and secure the crown.
- Meanwhile, a darkness is spreading across the kingdom. Fae are wild, crazed, and have stronger than normal magic. Lana, posing as "the Hidden Henchman" along with her friends, go behind the king's back and provide resources to the towns

plagued with this new evil. Ian (her BFF and Captain of the Royal Guard), Leif (a kitchen worker), Corbin (a stable worker), and Kalliah (Lana's lady in waiting) all play their respective roles to work the drops and help the kingdom.

- During the marriage trials, eight Fae come forward to fight for Lana's hand in marriage. One of those contenders just so happens to be Kade Blackthorn, a mysterious shadow-wielding Fae, who held a knife to Lana's throat during one of the drops and gave her a nickname she hates (but also kind of loves), Little Rebel.

- Three trials are held for Lana's hand. However, things go wrong in all the trials, contenders die (RIP Lord Thatcher, Frederich, and Edmund), the darkness creeps closer, and certain contenders (Casimir) seem to be in cahoots with the evil royal advisor, Andras Braumlyn, a man who tortured Lana for years under the guise of coaxing out her magic. Lana also lost Elisabeth, the palace healer, who was like a second mother to her, in the midst of the trials.

- But like all good love stories, Lana starts to fall for Kade. Neither can ignore the spark between them. But amid the absolute chaos during the final trial, when the dark ones attack the palace under Andras's command, Lana finds Kade murdering the king. When the king remains alive, Kade uses his shadows to end the man's life while he's lying in Lana's arms.

- It didn't end there though… Ian comes in, seeing it all, so Storm knocks him out, leaving him behind in the attack.

- Kade, along with his friend Storm, kidnap Lana

for their own agenda and take her to Mysthaven, a
land that doesn't exist…or so Lana thought.

With so many questions left unanswered, our story begins…

PROLOGUE
KADE, SEVEN YEARS AGO

The crowd gathered for today's execution stared gleefully at the bleeding man, trembling on his knees.

The show hadn't even begun, yet blood stained the cobblestone of the dais in the courtyard beneath him.

"Those who stand against Mysthaven will be swiftly brought to justice." The king's brash voice echoed through the jagged mountains surrounding the palace courtyard. "Traitors are the reason the darkness spreads in our lands. With their lies, they seek to control you."

My hands tightened into a fist watching the large man, broken at the feet of the king. The involuntary twitch garnered the king's attention, and his eyes narrowed on me.

This execution was the third this week alone. The plots against the king, against our kingdom, seemed to be increasing. I nodded toward the king, his black velvet robe billowing behind him in the wind, just like his black hair underneath his black glittering crown.

Always black.

Dark.

Perhaps on someone else, the crown would look beautiful.

The dark material shimmered in the sunlight. On him, it merely amplified the cold cruelness stored within.

"Traitors must therefore be punished accordingly." A sinister smile curved his lips upward as the king gestured to the two guards holding the latest *traitor* at his feet. "Kade." The king summoned me forward.

My shadows pooled at my feet, swirling around me. My power had increased significantly in the past year, the shadows developing a mind of their own. Usually, I wielded them as a deadly extension of the king's will, but lately an internal battle between my shadows and me flared. Rare in the grand scheme of using my powers, but enough for me to take notice.

They hated the king. Their reluctance to follow my commands around him had been the first sign that perhaps somewhere deep inside me, I didn't like the monster I'd become.

The Monster of Mysthaven.

The king stepped back, as murmurs from the crowd hummed around me. Their bubbling excitement at the public displays of violence disturbed me. It hadn't before, but now… something didn't feel right.

"Storm," the king shouted, pointing at one of the guards holding the man.

Storm. He hid our friendship well. He glanced at me, barely acknowledging my presence. It reminded me of eight years ago when he spoke to me in annoyed grunts, requesting we train together.

No one spoke to me, except this man. A man who dared to befriend the shadow-cloaked monster.

He stared at me now while he drew his sword and presented it to me with an exaggerated bow. We both knew this was a damn show. A show of the king's power through us, his Guardians.

The king inclined his head toward me, giving his *monster* space to work. "This is what happens when you choose to defy your king," he roared to the eager onlookers. Their shouts of excitement filled the air as their arms punched the sky in heady anticipation of the impending execution. I chose to ignore the disgust building at their enthusiasm.

I flipped the sword in my hand and briefly met the traitor's gaze. His eyes didn't hold wrath or anger. They didn't even contain spite.

For one moment, I hesitated.

Instead, the man on the stone ground watched me with something that made my skin crawl.

Hope.

As if I would somehow do the right thing and defy the king's orders. I could barely tell right from wrong anymore. Not that I ever admitted that out loud.

King Dargan approached me and placed a hand on my shoulder, squeezing tightly. Dread coiled in my gut. I knew he noticed my hesitation. The gesture wasn't in comfort or reassurance, like he wanted others to believe. His voice dropped. "You do as you're told, when you're told, or you will face punishment as well."

He squeezed my shoulder roughly once more and took two large steps back. I clenched my jaw, wishing the traitor would look away as I sliced the sword forward hurriedly through the man's neck, but not completely. And his gaze never left mine. Blood spattered as the crowd cheered. The man's head clung to his body in a desperate attempt to remain attached.

Nausea churned deep within me, and I pulled my arms back and swung again. Harder. Faster. With one more clean swing over the man's neck, his head rolled from atop his body.

The *thud* on the ground as it fell turned my stomach. Gasps from the crowd tittered around us, but none of them dared to run.

"Remove the body," the king ordered the additional

guards lining the courtyard. He prowled toward the shadows, returning with a leather whip in hand.

The whip wasn't new. Bringing it out in public was though. My body tensed, freezing in front of everyone.

"Kneel before your king," he said, dramatically pointing the whip at my face.

I felt Storm flinch, but I didn't look at my friend, who stood just a few feet away from me.

"It seems my Guardians need a reminder. Disobedience at any level, Guardian or not, will not be tolerated."

My lip curled as I met the king's hateful glare, but I schooled my expression, refusing to give him any satisfaction. Unbuttoning my shirt, I shrugged it off, kneeling before him, hands on my knees.

He grinned. "Face them."

I lifted my chin, turning and kneeling before the people of Mysthaven. How had we become a kingdom of people who cheered and enjoyed public punishments? A kingdom so terrified of their neighbors that they turned on each other, praying the king stopped the spread of evil and dark ones in our land.

The more the king unleashed me to destroy these so-called traitors across Mysthaven, the more I learned about them. The more inconsistencies appeared in the narrative spun by the king. The more I *felt* like a monster. Not the righteous hand of the king, but a weapon wielded by evil hands.

"No one is above the king. No one is above Mysthaven. Anyone who believes they are will be held accountable. For allowing so many traitors among us as of late, my Guardian will accept this reminder of my might and my mercy by retaining his life."

Crack.

The whip lanced along my back as the king finished spewing his lies. He held himself above all else.

Crack.

The leather split my skin. The familiar sting across my back tingled across my spine. He'd drawn one of his special whips for this display. The king had a collection of torture devices containing some sort of magic. Magic that somehow made my punishments harsher.

As pain flooded my body, I let it fill me with rage. I kept my hands on my knees, unflinching, refusing to give him the satisfaction of breaking me.

After all, I've had years to get used to this particular form of punishment.

I lost count at thirty lashes, and once the last *crack* rang in the courtyard, the crowd had gone silent.

When the punishment stopped, the crowd quietly shuffled away. Most of the other Guardians left too. Dismissed by the king perhaps? Or maybe just done watching their leader, the king's most trusted Guardian, be whipped for so long.

I finally let go of my control, falling forward as my body trembled, shadows nowhere to be found.

The king's polished black boots appeared in front of my face. He leaned down. "You will remember your place. You will abide by my orders. Hesitate again in my presence or at an order, and I will destroy you."

I lay on the cool cobblestone, wishing it would swallow me whole. *Monster.* I'd remain his monster, or I'd die.

Maybe dying wouldn't be so bad.

Feet scuffed along the stones, but I didn't raise my head to look at who approached.

"The winds, they whisper a solemn tale. One fated in nature, calling to you. Magic swirls in unrelenting waves, crested in light." Our seer, the strange woman who always cared for me, spoke in her riddles as she kneeled beside me.

"Are you flirting with me, Cassandra?"

She squeezed a piece of unblemished flesh. "Hush, boy. Hush."

A warmth radiated along my back. Cassandra's skills were

unrivaled. How she held such strong healing gifts while also being a seer made no sense. No one knew how deep her magic ran.

No one but me.

She'd been healing me for years. The king didn't pay enough attention to know when Cassandra had taken over my healing from the palace healer, Nadia.

Or if he knew, he didn't care.

The wounds on my back wept blood. Suddenly, my shadows whipped out of me, called forth either by Cassandra or after my own natural healing abilities kicked in. I couldn't heal others, but I could assist my own Fae abilities and bolster them to quicken the process myself.

When I finally pulled myself from the ground, bloody droplets, more black than red, ran down my rib bones.

Slow. Steady.

Cassandra didn't stop her ministrations, swirling her hands in sweeping motions. Sparks emitted from the tips of her fingers, and her eyes narrowed in concentration.

"I think my magic is abandoning me," I said to her, confiding in the woman who had stood by my side since my mother died. "Or fighting me."

"Your magic will guide you if you let it."

I shuddered. "I'm the Monster of Mysthaven. My magic should obey."

"Obey who?"

I didn't respond. I didn't need to. She knew everything, even the darkness inside of me. The one I tried and failed to fight so many times.

"This is not your path, Kade Blackthorn," she hummed. "You forget my words, but I never will."

She spoke reassuringly as she continued healing me, her speech coherent, in a way it so rarely was.

"I'll speak them once more for your weary soul." Her

hands continued removing the pain from the lashes decorating my back.

I knew the words she'd speak, even if they didn't make sense to me yet. She believed in me. Believed I'd figure out this damned prophecy. Cassandra's assurances to convince me the prophecy was mine drowned out my protests long ago that it might be for someone else.

Her voice changed, coming out as if she spoke the words of a lullaby as she finished mending what the king had so enjoyed breaking.

"Rebels rise where darkness lies,
Not one but two must break the ties.
Across the void, a queen you must seek,
Trust freely given, for one alone proves too weak.
Though evil will free and be bound no more,
Fate still awaits one final war."

CHAPTER I

IAN

"The king is dead!"

"Murdered!"

I attempted to force open my eyes, but they were so damn heavy. A throbbing pain radiated from a hundred different places over my body. The gasps and cries around me barely registered past the intense torment raking over my skin.

"After such a sickening act of betrayal, your princess fled. Queen Roxana remains so stricken with grief she cannot even be here to tell you herself of the atrocities committed today."

My head bobbed once as I struggled to compel myself into a conscious state.

Lana? Lana fled?

No. Bile crept into my mouth, but I swallowed it down, ignoring the acidic taste it left behind. She would never. I must get to her. Find her, fight for her.

A cool breeze flitted through the air, dragging with it the coppery smell of blood until it permeated my senses.

I am the damn captain of the guard. I'm better than this.

I cannot fail her. Not again.

Inhaling took more energy than I could muster. I choked against a thick rag. Fuck, I was gagged as well.

This time, I focused more on breathing through my nose slowly, refusing to give in until I succeeded. Once a breath filled my lungs, I focused on what I could remember.

Where had I been before now?

Thoughts raced through my mind.

Storm had knocked me out right after I found Lana and Kade beside the king's body. The king's *dead* body.

No. Fury pulsed across my numb arms, hungry for an outlet. Questions bubbled to the surface, each one trying to command my attention. How much time had passed since Storm and Kade's betrayal? Where was Lana? The others? Was I hearing a crowd around me? Who in the damned Fates' names is bellowing to them?

Then, one thought took over completely. *If I ever see Kade Blackthorn again, I will slit his throat.*

With a renewed sense of vengeance fueling my desire to escape whatever situation awaited me, I finally cracked open my eyes.

Well, shit.

Andras stood a few feet in front of me, gold-lined robes tattered, blood dripping to the ground from an unknown source. He brandished a bloodied sword in his hand while shouting at a crowd of scared Fae.

Where were the dark ones? How had Andras won?

"Princess Illiana Dresden is a traitor! She promised Lord West her heart if he would siphon all the king's power into her. She is not only a traitor, but a liar!"

My head throbbed as I desperately tried to fully regain my senses. Surely, no one would believe Andras's lies. How had he even gathered such a crowd after the attack during the trials?

"Princess Illiana has no magic, she has never had any magic. She has lied to you for her entire life. Her deceit and treachery know no bounds."

Anxiousness filled the air so thickly I tasted it on my tongue. Whispers, gasps, and screams echoed in a chorus orchestrated by Andras. A master manipulator. No doubt using his magic to influence the minds of those around him.

How could his influence be strong enough to turn the citizens of Brookmere against their beloved princess?

A groan reached my ears, and it took me a moment to realize it was my own.

The fog in my head finally cleared enough for me to process more of my surroundings. I looked down and realized the throbbing stemmed from the rose vines strangling me against a stake. Blood seeped from each prick of the thorns against my skin. Unable to move without the thorns digging deeper, my attention returned to Andras and his filthy mouth.

"After Lord West refused to siphon from the king, Princess Illiana murdered her own father in an attempt to steal his magic for herself. But she didn't act alone. When Lord West threatened to bring her to justice, she fled the kingdom with the thief, Kade Blackthorn. A male with no ties to nobility, no heritage to speak of. An imposter."

The crowd shouted among themselves as Andras continued spewing his filth. "A criminal trying to steal the crown and rule this land, alongside the princess betrayer, for their own selfish desires." He spat on the ground. "We must rise up together. We mustn't let her treacherous acts ruin Brookmere's good name. The queen lives! And I—" His sword clattered to the ground, and he sighed, placing a hand over his heart. It almost sounded as if he wept. "I will aid her in every way I can. I vow my life to protect her now."

My gaze shifted to the Fae in the crowd. Disappointment tasted bitter. Andras had spilled Lana's secrets for them to feast on, and they'd turned on her. Just like she always feared they would once they knew her secret.

Lan.

"Though it pains me to think this could happen, we have a

duty to justice. If any Fae, near or far, lays eyes on Princess Illiana Dresden or Kade Blackthorn, you are to notify one of the Royal Guards immediately."

Double shit.

I needed to escape these chains of thorns. I must find Lana. She'd never have fled with Kade. It wasn't possible.

He must have kidnapped her. I refused to believe she'd go willingly with the man who'd murdered her father.

Each twitch of my body coming back to life forced the sharp thorns deeper into my skin. Escaping without causing significant harm to myself felt impossible.

But I'd heal.

"Fear not, citizens of Brookmere. Not all of us have faltered like your princess. I will protect you!" His weepy theatrics were gone now. Replaced with the conniving arrogance he'd always exuded. "I will lead us to safety. I will rebuild our kingdom, safe from the dark ones. The very same dark ones Princess Illiana used to infiltrate the palace, *our* palace. I will aid our people to rise back to the glory we have always been destined to achieve. I will rid our lands of these treasonous traitors."

I yanked at the vines. *Enough.* Enough of his vitriol.

Andras met my eyes, and a sickening smile, hidden from the crowd just for me, spread over his elongated face. "Traitors like our weak, pathetic captain of the guard, Ian Stronholm."

Unaware my body could become any straighter, it shocked me when it did, freezing rigidly. Guards stepped closer with their swords drawn. I'd take them down one by one if I could escape this disaster. They'd die before taking me away without knowing Lana's location.

"No!" someone shouted. "He's no traitor!" Voices rose from the crowd, coming to my defense.

The sea of Fae shifted, restless. Hearing Andras lie about Lana without her here was an easy manipulation. It didn't seem to work quite as well when I still stood before them.

Angry shouts continued to fill the air as their support for the hatred Andras spouted faltered.

"Enough." Andras's voice rose above the crowd. He bowed his head. "I trusted him, too," his voice broken in a way which would never ring true. "But the king is dead. Captain Stronholm stood witness to the entire event."

Heavy, deathly silence overtook the crowd instantly.

The leaden reality finally sank in.

I raised my head higher, my mouth so dry, I could not even speak. Desperation tore through me to find someone to reject Andras's lies. One of my eyes was swelled, a stabbing pain directly in the cheek underneath it. Beads of sweat pooled at my hairline and rolled down my face.

There.

Corbin's and Leif's faces appeared through the crowd directly in front of me. Leif's leg, though wrapped, continued to bleed through the gauze. I quietly thanked the Fates they'd survived the siege with so few injuries.

Corbin met my gaze.

His eyes burned with too many questions, mimicking my own. Did he know if Lana had fled to safety? Or if what Andras said was true instead? I tried to ask, through raised brows, praying he understood what I was trying to convey. Willing my thoughts to him, wishing desperately for just one moment alone with my friends.

The slightest shake of his head was the only indication he understood my question from afar. He didn't know her location either. I slumped, giving in to the vines as they twisted harder.

"I never thought I'd see the king destroyed, especially by his own daughter."

The faces in the crowd were wary, waiting for whatever might come next.

"I will ensure justice be brought to Ian Stronholm." Andras's voice echoed over the crowd of Fae who now grimaced toward me. Turned by pretty words and lies.

"And when we've taken care of his treachery, we'll hunt down Princess Illiana." He paused, a sinister smile spreading across his face. "She will pay for her crimes against our kingdom."

CHAPTER 2

LANA

I am Illiana Dresden, and I am stronger than the darkness within me.

After all, I'd survived torture as a child.

I survived the panic attacks in the aftermath.

The never-ending barrage of pain and grief.

I survived by reminding myself of what I knew. What was real. Now, all of it crumbled at my feet, threatening to pull me under for good.

Holding on to reality? Now that would be impossible. My *truth* was all a lie.

It seemed as if everything, my entire existence, had been built on a throne of lies, exacerbated by the king of Brookmere.

The king. My father...or who I *thought* to be my father.

For now, the distinction between king and father would have to wait. As would processing the remaining shattered pieces of my heart crumbling inside me, and the other revelations his last words ushered. There were more pressing matters at hand.

Like how I could possibly be standing in a desolate,

drained, mist-filled land where the border of Brookmere, a vast ocean, had been not a second before.

I turned to the infuriating male standing stiffly beside me, seething. "Mysthaven?" I repeated the name he'd said.

Slowly he turned to meet my gaze. Kade Blackthorn pursed his lips, his brow furrowed almost as if *he* were the one in pain. But I knew better.

Kade Blackthorn's betrayal ran as deep as the rest of the lies I believed.

Storm cleared his throat. "Technically, Mysthaven lies on the other side of this lovely monstrosity."

Kade ignored him. "Welcome to the void, Little Rebel. The space between our worlds. A space no one may enter without being blessed by our king."

Storm, his loyal sidekick and friend to the betrayer, snorted.

"*Our* king is dead thanks to you," I seethed, spitting the words at him.

Kade's stormy grey eyes held my own. "Your king may be dead, but my king is still very much alive."

My mind reeled. There was another world. A place nobody knew about. Well, no one in Brookmere at least.

Another world with its own king.

"And I suppose you are one of the king's chosen few then. Blessed with such powers to cross?" My eyes rolled in condemnation.

Kade's lips twitched ever so slightly, like they always did when we fought, tipping his head as his only response.

My heart pounded in my chest. The ball of nerves in my stomach grew into something vile, forcing its way down to the soles of my feet and tips of my toes. My breath stuttered, panting in and out in short bursts.

For the first time, I'd allowed someone into my life. Someone new, beyond Ian and my few friends. Someone whom I believed worthy. A man I thought would fight for me and our kingdom. But in an instant, the dream my heart had begun to craft brutally broke into a thousand pieces.

The life I'd dared to imagine, where Kade stood by my side as king, had deteriorated to nothing when I found him standing with a knife in my father's chest.

And if that weren't enough? He'd used his powerful shadow magic to finish the job by snapping the king's neck as I held him in my arms, begging for him to live.

That was the man I thought I could trust with more than my secrets.

My heart.

He'd ripped it from me unapologetically.

I pushed away the painfully fresh memory. Shoved every last emotion into a small box deep within me and locked it. Swallowing hard, as if I could seal it away.

Wallowing would get me nowhere. Being out of my element wasn't a luxury I could afford right now. So I cleared my throat, steadying myself to take in the void, as Kade called it. I had no other option, since the two of them allowed me to walk on my own but never let me out of their sights.

The land around me lay dead. Shriveled like powerful magic sucked every ounce of life from the soil.

A loud roar scattered the tiny pebbles across the ground as I braced myself, feeling the world shudder beneath my feet.

"What in the Fates was that?" I hissed.

Kade met my gaze, his normally grey eyes dark, black in a way I'd only seen a handful of times before. His jaw clenched as he kneeled before me, taking hold of my leg and running his hand upward until he gripped my thigh.

I jerked, trying to pull away. "What are you doing?"

"I hardly think this is the time to make things up to her," Storm snorted.

I shot him a look.

"Bastard," Kade muttered under his breath, yanking something from his pack.

I wobbled, not ready for him to be on his knees before me. His other hand gripped my hip and steadied me. Thankfully, this time Storm kept his thoughts to himself.

Kade moved swiftly, not looking at me once as he wrapped my sheath around my leg, securing it forcefully before placing my dagger inside.

"Stay with Storm if anything happens," he said.

I reached for him, grabbing his shoulder before he rose. I couldn't help the movement. "What are you talking about?"

His hardened face masked any emotion. Most likely on purpose, but I didn't know why. He took my arm, standing and pulling his blade over his head from where it rested on his back. "This place was created to separate our kingdoms long ago. A powerful sacrifice created it. It's not just the land that's dangerous, but the beasts inside. We must travel through, and quickly."

The roar sounded again. This time I noticed a cawing tapering off at the end of its cry. Like the beast lurking in the mist grew excited. Almost as if it knew it no longer remained alone. The echoes of its song bounced off the jagged rocks and cracked earth.

Kade's shadows twisted around us. I didn't miss how his body trembled, darkening the shadows closest to his skin.

This other kingdom apparently sucked.

Before the echoes of the beast died down, a fresh round of screeching ricocheted through the air, this time so close it forced Storm to grab my arm and tug urgently. "Run," he commanded. "Now."

Not wanting to meet this beast, I obeyed, keeping pace with Storm, allowing him to release my arm.

"Dagger," Kade said, his voice gruff and tight.

I unsheathed my weapon, trying to keep my own fears at bay. This couldn't be happening. Not only had Kade kidnapped me, but he brought me somewhere even more dangerous than where we were before. Somewhere the mist originated. I hadn't missed the way it leeched from the void before we crossed.

The same strange mist that appeared around dark ones, spreading the darkness throughout Brookmere. The reason my biological parents had died. The reason Andras, the king's horrid advisor, had grown so powerful.

Kade brought me right in the middle of it all.

The two men slowed, whispering between themselves. We shuffled through the rocky terrain hastily, the sounds of the beast not heard again.

My thundering heartbeat pounded in my ears, this time for a different reason than fear from the mysterious roars of a creature in this place. This time, it pounded with an idea. An idea that may kill me but would give me a chance at going home.

I clasped my dagger tightly in my hand, grateful for the mistake Kade made returning it to me, and a smile spread over my lips. The mist hid our surroundings, but we hadn't run far enough that I couldn't turn back.

The second Kade spoke again to Storm, I turned and sprinted back the way we'd come.

"Lana!" Kade shouted, fear tinging his voice.

His fear wasn't enough to deter me. I ran faster than I'd ever run before. The mist thickening before us, but I didn't care. I pushed forward.

Whispered sounds whipped around me, forcing my heart to beat faster and faster, but I would not be afraid. Not now, when this may be my best, and only, chance to break free.

A cool breeze stirred around me, caressing the damp skin on my neck. I almost had a chance to savor the moment before something slammed into my side, knocking me to the ground and taking my breath with it.

This time, the roar echoing through the void blasted directly into my face.

I stared into the spittle-filled mouth of a horrific-looking creature. Three rows of sharp fangs jutted out from its gums, as well as a maroon tongue larger than my thigh. Three times my size, the creature reared back onto its hind legs for a moment before hovering over me once more.

I screamed, stabbing my dagger into the creature's side, only for it to bounce off the beast's hardened, scale-like exterior. The iridescent hues of blues and blacks along its scales melded perfectly into the mist.

Shouting, I struggled beneath the weight of the creature on my stomach, thrashing back and forth in an effort to garner enough space to swing the blade with a more forceful momentum. It hissed in my face again, the stench of its breath overpowering my senses. I drew back my dagger, readying myself to slash into its neck instead.

The beast opened its maw, tongue curling back, ready to bite into my neck.

Pitch-black shadows engulfed the creature, freezing it mid roar, instantly snapping its body with a loud crack. The *snap* echoed around us almost as long as the beast's caw.

The weight of the animal lifted as it rolled off me, but the way the creature had attacked me, forcefully knocking my breath from my lungs, left me struggling for air. I scurried backward on the ground while trying to sit up.

"Did it bite you? Lick you?" Kade slammed down in front of me on his knees, running his hands over my face, my hair. "Did any saliva touch your skin?" His hand traced my neck.

I whimpered, jerking back. "What was that thing?" My body shook, the fear I'd shoved down while running decided to make a grand, inconvenient entrance now.

"Lana!" he shouted. "I need to know. I don't have enough antidote—"

"No," I answered, finally getting a full breath in. "Nothing. It just slammed into me."

His shoulders sagged, but his labored breathing didn't ease.

"What was that thing, Kade?" I asked again. I gritted my teeth, shoving my hands to the dirt so I could stand.

Kade's shadows wrapped around my waist, holding me in place, even as I tried to back away. In my periphery, Storm's body solidified more clearly through the mist, poised and ready to catch me if I somehow escaped Kade's shadow hold.

Storm spoke while Kade tipped his head back, closed his eyes, and breathed deeply. "We call them voidlings. They don't exist outside of this place. Their venom will kill you in minutes."

"I told you we had to move quickly," Kade said, ignoring Storm's explanation, "and you thought *now* was the time to run?" His shoulders heaved along with his ragged breaths.

I opened my mouth to put the arrogant prick in his place, but he took a step toward me.

"No, you will listen to me, Little Rebel," he continued. "I will not lose you to the void. I will not lose you to these beasts, to any monster, any dark one, any fucking Fae that threatens you—" He stopped, eyes widening frantically for the briefest moment before he snapped his mouth shut. "You cannot cross the void without me. Trying will get you killed."

He didn't release his shadows' hold on me but turned his back to face Storm.

"We run," Kade said. "Stay with her, I'll scout a few feet ahead."

The mist thickened, making Kade almost invisible as he left us behind. I forced myself to push down the panic triggered by his absence. Even if Kade had been *blessed* by his king, part of me worried for his safety. I hated it.

Storm came to my side and grabbed my hand. "Sorry, but I'll be holding on this time. I think if you get lost in here, we'd be at risk of him destroying both of our kingdoms to get you back."

"Your assumption about his feelings for me are ridiculous." I swiped with my free hand at the dust layering my body. My failed escape attempt hit me hard, and a shiver of fury ran through my body, causing me to physically shake. "Just get me out of here."

Storm's grip tightened marginally, but he didn't have any retort for me. I hated being coddled, but I wasn't stupid enough to try to escape his grasp. Not until I could at least see all my surroundings with my own eyes.

We jogged after Kade, Storm maintaining a steady pace.

It immediately reminded me of my training with Ian. Running with my best friend. Fates, I'd run every moment of every day to be back home with him and know he was safe. To know they were all safe. Even if that likelihood was merely wishful thinking.

Ian.

Tears formed, daring to break free, but I discreetly wiped them away on my shoulder before they could fall. Both Storm and Kade assured me Ian wasn't injured by whatever Storm had done to him at the palace. Trusting them didn't seem possible, no matter what they said. Yet I couldn't keep from asking again.

"Swear to me you didn't seriously injure Ian?" My voice cracked.

Storm's head whipped toward me. "I used a very old magic my grandmother taught me. It merely knocks a Fae out momentarily. I'm sure he's already awake and cursing my name."

I believed him, even before he squeezed my hand reassuringly.

I didn't want to trust Storm, but for some reason with this, I did.

"How much farther does this place go on for?" I asked.

"Not very. The void is small. A sliver of evil in the world."

He didn't say anything else, but sure enough we slowed only minutes later, Kade's figure formed in front of us so abruptly we almost slammed into him.

As soon as we stood by his side, the mist lessened, and my racing heart slowed marginally.

Kade put himself between Storm and me and took our hands before surging us forward. This time I knew we were leaving the void instantly as the mist faded and the tugging sensation returned.

We stumbled through and I caught myself, yanking away from Kade's firm grip as soon as I knew we were free from the void's hold. His shadows finally slipped away from my waist, allowing me to stand on my own.

I let out a sigh, relieved to be free of the void. I brushed at my clothes and stared ahead, and my jaw dropped. The sight before me looked nothing like Brookmere.

In the distance, ice-covered mountains poked through dark storm clouds. Lightning flashed among them, illuminating the dark and beautiful jagged peaks and slopes.

A rumble in the distance to the east of the mountains showed a blaze shooting skyward. Like fire erupting from a funneled mountain. I'd never seen anything like it before.

Vicious. The scenery appeared vicious and powerful. Just like the Fae next to me.

Nearby, rocks and dirt in hues of crimson protruded from the ground in massive clusters. Sharp-looking shrubs of greenery poked from the dry land. Pink florals bloomed from a bush nearby, but its pointy leaves warned there was more to their charm. The diversity of the land between the dry, cracked ground, the luscious florals, and the mountains painting the distant sky hardly made sense.

It was the opposite of home in every way, and yet it thrived with a terrifying beauty.

Words failed to come to me. How could somewhere so vastly different exist in the same world as Brookmere?

A growl, more human than beast, reverberated from a cluster of nearby rocks. "I'm armed with more damn weaponry than the king's entire armory."

Kade grabbed my arm, yanking me closer to his side.

I gripped my dagger as the deep voice bellowed again.

"I swear to the Fates, come forward now from the mist or I'll slaughter you before you take your next breath."

CHAPTER 3

LANA

A dagger landed next to my feet, slicing into the ground with ease.

"Fucking assholes," Storm grumbled.

Kade's grip tightened on my arm, and he closed his eyes, wincing.

Two figures emerged from behind the rocks, and I bent my knees, trying, and failing, to yank my arm from Kade's grasp.

"We're the assholes?" the man said, moving fast. He pounced onto Storm, sending him toppling over. "You've been gone for *months* with no contact." He swung at Storm's head, but the fire-wielding warrior dodged, rolling away to keep himself from being pinned by the stranger. "No word. No, 'Hello, my dear friends, everything is going according to plan.' Nothing."

Storm leapt to his feet, crouching down, and wielded a flame. The grin on his face made no sense as the two roughhoused like children instead of grown men fighting each other. I yanked again at Kade's grip, attempting to free myself in case this rendezvous became too dangerous, and he finally relented.

A woman, just shorter than me, flipped a dagger in her

hand, walking forward to pick up the additional blade, which landed at my feet a moment ago. She shoved her shoulder into Kade's chest as she stood. "Oops," she said.

A rumble sounded low in Kade's throat.

"Don't growl at me, you prick," she said. "What the hell is wrong with you? Do you have any idea how many times we've had to cover for you?"

"You could have simply said you missed us." Storm leaned over and clasped the male's shoulder after helping him up from their tussle.

"It's not funny," she snapped, glancing in his direction before returning her gaze to Kade. She didn't even bother acknowledging me.

"It's not as if we've been playing tea party, we've had pressing matters to attend to," Kade said, stealing a glance toward me.

What in the Fates is this about?

The female's lips curled as she finally studied me. "Well, he isn't pleased. In fact, I wouldn't be surprised if he meant to punish you for your extended disappearance and lack of duties. His list of traitors has grown tremendously in your absence."

"So, no different than any other time we return." Kade rolled his eyes, stepping around the female and taking a few long strides away from us as he scanned the horizon.

The unknown man with Storm snorted. "Right, except the tagalong you've brought with you might not fare so well."

Kade jerked his body around to face him, shadows billowing outward. His eyes narrowed.

The man held up his hands. "Be as angry as you'd like. You better know how to explain your absence—and her, whoever she is. Actually…" He strode toward me and took my hand in his, kissing my knuckles. "Seeing as you've been in their company for so long, I can only imagine the lack of respect and dignity you've been afforded. How about I show you how a real man of Mysthaven treats a lady?"

"*He* will not touch her." Kade's menacing threat came out low and eerily quiet. "And neither will you."

The behavior made it seem like these people weren't friends, and yet they spoke like they knew each other.

"Kade?" Storm asked, taking a step closer to his friend.

The black in Kade's eyes shifted from his normal beautiful grey. His darkened pupils growing so large, he looked more beast than man.

Something wasn't right. Though his eyes had darkened like this before, the added tremor of his shadows was new.

Despite my hatred toward him, Storm's concern only solidified that Kade's rapidly shifting demeanor meant trouble.

"Fuck, not now," Storm grumbled. He walked over, shoving the new man from my side.

As he stumbled, he threw up his hands and stood close enough for me to see the dramatic eye roll aimed at Kade. "I'm not going to hurt her. I merely thought you needed a reminder of who we're dealing with now that you're back—"

The shadows around Kade darkened into pitch-black night, shuddering with what could only be rage.

"Kade?" I asked.

Though deep, his breathing choked out erratically, each time forcing the shadows to take up more and more space around him. The escalating situation made me fearful *for* him instead of angry *at* him for the first time since everything that happened in Brookmere. Whatever rage took root in Kade right now refused to let go.

I tried to step closer to him, but Storm grabbed me forcefully, holding me back and taking me by complete surprise.

Kade's snarl rattled around us. "Get away from her."

"Get yourself under control and I will." Though firm,

Storm's tone held a compassion so unlike their hardened warrior exteriors.

The shadows around Kade intensified, not just in height but in density, their tendrils exploding in all directions.

"Shield!" the female in the group shouted.

Storm yelled Kade's name as magic exploded. His shadows swirled around me, ripping me from Storm's side before hovering around me in some sort of cocoon.

"Don't you dare." I slammed my hand through their haze, but the barrier they formed remained. "If you're protecting me from whoever those people are, I don't need it. I don't need or want any help from you."

"Get to her now," Storm's voice sounded from outside.

For some reason, logic abandoned me and the thought of Kade's shadows coddling me in some kind of fight infuriated me.

Good. The angrier I remained at him, the easier the hate building inside of me could flourish.

I tried whipping my hands through his shadow magic, but I couldn't see a damn thing. A male shouted in pain. Tits and daggers, were these friends or not? Why wasn't I allowed to see what the hell they were doing?

"Let. Me. Go," I said, emphasizing each word. "You dragged me here and I will not be kept in some sort of shadow prison."

The shadows dissipated moments later.

"How dare you—" My words fell short as I stomped toward the last place I'd seen Kade.

Except, he no longer stood menacingly in front of the group. Instead, he kneeled hunched on the ground, propped on his hands. Tremors skated over him and his breaths came in ragged, rapid pants.

My reckless heart hurt at the sight.

Storm and their two "friends" were crouched behind a ring of fire, clearly coming from Storm's fire magic. I'd seen him wield his fire magic before as we fought the dark ones in Brookmere. The flames receded slowly, and the man I didn't know stood from their midst, clutching his arm to his chest.

It was only then I noticed the charred surroundings we found ourselves in. The few trees hadn't been vibrant before, but they were charcoal now. The little bit of greenery burned. Everything surrounding us had been destroyed. Even the reddish tinted ground had a cracked grey look to it.

A few remaining shadows retreated from my feet toward Kade, leaving that same charred wake in their path.

All the dead earth, the damage—it stemmed from him.

This was Kade's power. In all its glory. A power unfathomable, and, well, unbelievable had I not witnessed it now for myself.

Wielding that amount of power hurt him though. Or so it seemed. Frowning, I watched the still hunched figure of Kade on the ground.

Unsure of what set him off, I stepped closer to him and away from the strangers. Storm could handle them for all I cared.

Kade's head snapped up, his gaze scanning me with an intensity that made me feel exposed. "Are you hurt?" A sheen of sweat glazed his furrowed brows.

Why would I be hurt?

I looked back toward Storm and the others. While he didn't seem at all concerned by anything, the others gawked at me.

Though furious at the shadow-wielding prick at my knees, this hesitant behavior was so unlike the man I knew. The man I *thought* I knew.

"Fates above," the strange male muttered through a sigh. He watched me, looking over me from head to toe like I shouldn't be standing here.

What the hell is going on?

I narrowed my gaze to him. "Why are you staring at me like you're surprised I'm not dead?"

"Well, while I'd like to keep from ruining our friendship before it begins, to be blunt," he said, "you *should* be dead."

I frowned. "From what? His little temper tantrum?" I pointed at Kade. "Unfortunately for you all, it'll take more than that to kill me."

He blinked a few times before his shock morphed into amusement and he laughed. The deep sound was filled with pure joy, so much so that I fought my own smile. Laughter made the least sense in this moment.

But here we were.

The male laughed again, unable to stop himself it would seem, standing and letting his arm fall to his side, twirling it. The destroyed leather showed his skin beneath, turning from purplish blue back to his natural golden-brown color.

"Lana?" Kade rose from the ground, taking my hand and pulling me toward him. He cupped my face, capturing me with his stormy grey eyes, normal once more. He stared at me expectantly.

His nearness soothed the wretched pain of grief ripping me open. I let it wash over me, not caring if I hated myself for it later, as I momentarily took stock of him. His breathing steadied and the pain from earlier didn't seem as prevalent.

"I'm fine," I said through gritted teeth before pulling my face from his touch. I forcefully reminded myself of my fury. Anger made it easier to stay away from him. This man had murdered my father and kidnapped me. This feeling in my heart that wouldn't catch up to my logical mind had to be quashed. I shoved a finger into his chest. "I don't need your protection. I'm not some weak helpless thing. Don't you ever wrap me up in your damn shadows like that again."

"If he hadn't wrapped you up in his shadows you'd be as decimated as the land around us," the woman's voice drifted toward me. She stood with her arms crossed, glancing between Kade and me. "Quite frankly I thought he was killing you inside of them. We all did."

A knot in my stomach twisted. Like jealousy. What did she know about his shadows? About his power?

My body tensed, jaw clenching. No, that was asinine. Kade could be around whatever woman he desired. My time with him was done.

Which made her words stand out clearer. "Killing me?"

"I would never hurt you." Kade's retort was quiet, softer and reminiscent of the male I'd met in Brookmere. The response was meant for me, even if everyone else could hear.

But that was a lie, wasn't it? He had hurt me in ways even Andras hadn't managed during the years trapped in the dungeons.

An awkward silence stretched taut between us before Storm sighed too loudly, running a hand over his face.

He stalked toward Kade and gripped his shoulder. "Better?"

Kade nodded to his friend and turned his back on me, not meeting my studious gaze. Walls that hadn't existed in him before, now erected before my eyes. His distant demeanor surprised me, especially directed at Storm.

Hadn't Storm previously told us during our drop that Kade acted differently in Ellevail? Kade had told me during our dance at the bonfire that who he was with me was who he wanted to be. I didn't know what truths would come to play here in this new land. However, something about the Kade Blackthorn I knew had vanished since crossing the void.

The thought turned my stomach.

Kade's voice broke through my thoughts. "I'll figure out how to explain her presence to the king on the way."

Right. They had a king. *Here.*

Kade and these Fae must work for him. My mind raced, desperately trying to piece together why he'd brought me here.

Which was hard to ascertain when I lacked any details and didn't even really know where *here* was.

"As exciting as this reunion has been, you've got some explaining to do. If we don't get back to Mount Legion hastily, we'll probably all be dead soon," the man said. He approached me, holding a hand to his chest and bowing slightly. "I'm Jax. The polite, attractive, well-mannered male of this lot. So you're in good hands now."

A low grumble came from Kade's direction.

"You wish for death, Jax," Storm muttered under his breath.

I stared in quiet shock, processing the sudden reverent introduction. I wondered if he knew my title or if this simply served as the typical form of greeting here.

"Lana," I said, bowing my head but not mimicking the hand gesture.

"That's Raya." Jax smiled, a dimple popped on his cheek, giving him a boyish look underneath his mop of sleek, curly black hair, completely at odds with the dark stubble and strong jawline. He stood slightly shorter than Kade and Storm, and yet still a few inches taller than me.

Raya nodded, appraising me. I took the time to size her up as well. She started it, after all.

The female's entire physique screamed predator. Her braided strands of hair were pulled back, woven into a bun on top of her head. Her dark skin shone with sweat underneath her leather tunic. I caught sight of the same inky mark I'd seen on Storm and Kade disappearing at her collarbone.

Raya was all warrior. Her face showed no hint of emotion. Hardened. Unshakeable.

"We need to move," she said, her gaze flitting away as if she'd discovered nothing of value in me.

"Where were you holed up?" Storm asked the new Fae.

Jax rubbed his neck. "Sleeping on rocks just half a mile

west. The screams of the beast sent us running this way. I've got plenty of antidotes if anyone needs—"

"We're fine," Kade cut him off. He moved wordlessly in the direction Jax pointed.

What crawled into his shadows?

Raya and Jax followed behind Kade closely, but Storm stayed still, watching me.

"Being here is hard for him. He—"

"Stop," I said, abruptly cutting him off. "It can't be harder than watching someone you lo—" I stopped myself this time. Adjusting. Love was *not* what I had felt for Kade. "Someone you trusted kill your father and take you from your home against your will."

I looked back at the void we'd passed through. Somehow, I had to get away from them and find a way back to Brookmere. If I went with them traveling around their world, how would I ever know how to make it home?

"You'll need him to cross it again." Storm's voice made me jump. He remained beside me, a small smile playing over his lips.

I scowled, hating it. Hating that he thought we could continue to develop the companionship we'd begun to forge.

"Don't," I said. "We aren't friends anymore. I don't want your fake smiles. You successfully deceived me, so you can drop the act now."

His shoulders slouched. "It wasn't an act."

I turned on my heel, reluctantly moving in the direction of the others, but paused. "If I get home and something is wrong with Ian, I'll slit your throat and feed you to the beasts of this void myself."

"One day, you'll care for me just as you care for Ian, Princess. I wouldn't mind another fiercely loyal friend." He bowed his head and moved, taking the lead as though he knew I'd made up my mind to go with them. Maybe he had been babysitting to ensure I didn't run.

But where would I go?

The void wouldn't let me through alone, and I doubted I'd be a match for these four Fae.

Still, I looked back over my shoulder once more. The painful questions I tried to ignore thrust themselves to the fore, spilling into my mind.

What happened in Ellevail? Did Andras get captured or did the dark ones take over?

Had my mother survived?

Kalliah? Leif? Corbin?

Ian?

I stifled a whimper.

I'd get back across the void to my home. Back to the people I loved, or I'd die trying.

Kade Blackthorn had no idea the agony I'd inflict on him should I be kept from Brookmere much longer.

CHAPTER 4

IAN

My escape plan was currently fucked.

I'd been hanging from these chains for hours. Hands tied over my head, complete with shackles around my feet. Not vines like Andras used outside, but thick steel chains.

"Still with me, Captain?" Andras chuckled as he rolled his neck languidly in front of me.

Somehow, despite the exhaustion and pain shooting through my body from the various fists accosting me, I managed a cheeky grin. "Don't tell me you're tired already?"

The vile man grabbed my cheeks with one hand, shaking my head. "That mouth has always been your downfall." He squeezed hard, then took a step back, rolling up his sleeve. He withdrew a dagger from a velvet purple pouch.

As he removed it, the edges and tip glistened with a black liquid-like substance.

I had seen a blade like this once before. Lana had been stabbed with one similar, years ago in this same room.

I refused to reveal any sort of recognition of the weapon before me.

"Do you have memories of the last time I used this

particular blade?" Andras purred, twisting the weapon in front of his face as if admiring it.

I cocked an eyebrow. "I make it a point not to dwell on anything you do, Andras. None of it being very memorable."

Andras stepped forward and the sharpened blade's cold steel traced along my neck. He dragged it just enough to sting. I didn't look away from Andras as he continued the surface-level scratch he inflicted. A warning.

"All this mock bravery when I know you'll break, Captain," he said. His eyes widened in glee as he looked me over. He jerked, pulling back before he slammed his ringed fist into the side of my face. It wasn't his first hit, but this time, he split skin.

"That hasn't worked for a few hours now, I would have thought you'd try something else." I spit, noticing the tinge of red on the floor.

That cruel smile spread over his face. "Always pining after her. Doesn't it bother you that your unyielding love is misplaced in a woman who would never return such affections?"

I matched his cruel grin with my own. Andras didn't understand. If he thought acting as though I wanted Lana as a lover was the way to torture me, he must be desperate. "A bit childish of a tactic for a man wishing to be king, don't you think?"

Andras gripped the blade and slashed it down the length of my arm, deep. I clenched my jaw, refusing to make a sound.

He clicked his tongue. "Already weakening, and I haven't even unleashed all of the power gifted to me yet."

"Magic can't be gifted," I said. Blood dripped down my shoulder from the open wound. The first sign my body had weakened after the hours I'd spent down here—my healing power was significantly lessened.

Something in my arm burned. A pain far sharper than

what a normal blade should produce. I tried to hide the agony as it grew.

Andras tilted his head back, laughing. "You think you know so much, Captain. You were kept in the dark by the king about what's happening in Brookmere, and yet you somehow think you're enlightened as to what true power is capable of doing. A war you know nothing about has been brewing for centuries."

True power?

I jerked at the restraints, filled with a primal need to switch the narrative and hold him at knifepoint to learn more.

He lifted the blade, pointing its tip at the edge of the laceration on my arm and pushing it into my flesh, digging before twisting it around inside the open wound.

"The king was the most powerful Fae in all of Brookmere. You pale in comparison," I said through gritted teeth. "Is that why you're so upset? Why you need Lana? Trouble getting the Fae to follow a weakling?"

He dug in again, deep enough to feel the rush of more blood and damn it, I couldn't hold back an audible hiss.

"The king was *not* the most powerful Fae in Brookmere." He scraped the knife along the cut, like he'd actually decided to skin me. Nausea clawed at my throat, but I forced it down. "My power, my *rights* come from someone far more adept."

I had to keep him talking. Whatever nonsense he believed could hold the key to what he planned, even if he did sound deranged. No Fae had been more powerful than the king.

His face fell into a blank stare as if he'd expected me to have slipped up and revealed something by now. "Where is Kade Blackthorn from?" Andras asked.

I'd riled him, and now he tried to hide it. He nodded to the two guards who'd accompanied him down here, and they moved to either side of me.

"You should ask him yourself," I answered.

A hit from the right struck me in my gut. The guard

snickered. Andras flipped the knife in front of me. "Ah." His lip curled. "So it's not merely the incompetence of my people. You didn't find anything on him either. Interesting."

I didn't bother acknowledging the jab. I knew all too well there was nothing to be found about Kade or his power. Another piece of this puzzle I'd figure out as soon as I freed myself from this cell.

He nodded, and I took two blows in quick succession, one to my gut and another to my face.

Andras reached forward, ripping my shirt down. I jerked against the restraints, desperate to attack him with some part of me. To destroy him. He twirled the tip of the blade above my heart, letting it prick my skin as he did.

"Where would she have run to? Any name, any place she knew of will do."

"Wouldn't you like to know," I spat.

He stabbed the knife in, breaking the skin and dragging it down. I shouted, unable to bite back this time from the injury.

"You will talk. One way or another."

I shook my head, the pain ricocheting through my entire body. At some point they'd be forced to bring in a healer.

I continued taunting the man in front of me, even through the pain. It served as the distraction I needed to hold on to my sanity down here.

"It must be infuriating knowing a woman with no magic bested you." I smiled, taking another punch to my jaw. It felt like almost nothing after the gashes the knife had inflicted. "A woman you deemed inferior."

Another punch.

This one hit too close to my ribs, knocking the air from my lungs, but I refused to stop. "A woman you thought you broke."

Crack.

That hit broke my nose.

Andras held up his hands, leaning down toward my face.

"Your princess left you next to her dead father. She fled. Without you."

His words held no power over me. I would rather he broke every bone in my body than give him the satisfaction of my reaction.

"She ran off with a man she knew for a few weeks instead of staying by the side of the man she's known her entire life. Your loyalty, Captain Stronholm, is grossly misplaced."

With a nod, the guards standing by used me as a punching bag. I lost track of the hits. The pain morphed into a near-constant, blinding sensation, taking over all of my senses. When Andras raised his hand to halt their punishment, I could only see out of one eye.

Despite the bruises sure to mar my body and the blood cascading along my skin, dripping in too many places, I smiled at him. "She will have my loyalty forever," I wheezed, spitting blood at his feet. "No matter what you throw at us, you've never broken us. I won't break now or ever. You'll lose."

"We'll need Maria to handle speeding up the healing process so he can be questioned again," Andras said to the guards. "Leave his feet bound but take off the chains."

They jimmied the lock at my wrist, and I collapsed in a heap onto the floor.

"Until next time, Captain Stronholm." He turned, storming away from my cell.

Time passed in unmeasurable quantities. Maria hadn't come yet.

The flickering lights of the torches remained illuminated, never dimming thanks to the magic in them. Was it minutes or was it hours I spent in solitude? I had no way of knowing.

Eventually, I inched away from the bloodied spot they'd left me in. A flicker of magic within me stirred to life, seeking out the worst of my wounds.

I would heal. I would live. I would face Andras with Lana by my side, destroying him once and for all.

Sensing movement in the shadows of the cell, I tensed. Turning my head slowly, I faced the darkest corner. My blond hair covered my face, practically black now with matted blood and grime.

A sharp *thud* cracked on the stone, and a spiky tail emerged before the rest of the body appeared. Lucien wagged his deadly tail as he pranced toward me on his stubby legs.

How he traveled throughout this palace unnoticed always remained a mystery to me, but right now, his eerie abilities had me feeling grateful.

"Lucien." I held out my hand and the pugron came over immediately. He nuzzled his head into my side, puffing out a hot steam of breath. Thankfully, fireless.

"Am I glad to see you," I whispered.

The beast looked up at me expectantly. "She's not here," I told him. I might be the only one who believed Lucien understood us, so I'd be damned if I ignored what years of watching him with Lana had revealed. "If you ever loved Lana, you have to help me get out of here."

A small puff of smoke erupted from the pugron's snout. Like he agreed with me.

"Is Kalliah in the palace?"

The small puff turned into a volcano of smoke.

"Do you know where Lana is?"

This time he blew a stream of fire to the side, his eyes drooping like a lost animal.

Smart boy. Smoke for yes, fire for no.

I frowned. "You must find Kalliah. Find a way to tell her where I am. See if she can help."

Lucien backed away, spewing steam. His gaze never left mine as he trotted toward the wall, disappearing from my sight.

"Please, let the pugron do as I said," I whispered.

In the meantime, I had to plan. To plot. Not just an

escape, but where to run. Somewhere I could use as a base to begin my search for Lana.

I closed my eyes, leaning against the cool stone of the inner wall of my cell.

It was a different game down here than before. This time, I was the main attraction.

Andras may be powerful, but he'd underestimated me like he always had.

How I'd escape, I didn't know. But when I did, the Fates themselves would pay. They might play by their own set of rules and prophecies, whispered and told in secret passings for only the blessed to hear.

But I, too, could play by my own rules. Bound by nothing and no one except for the loyalty to the ones I loved.

So if playing dirty was what it would take, then Fates be damned.

For I'd stop at nothing to win this cursed game. Not a soul would stop me.

And every last Fae, Fate, and speck of nature would pay tenfold if Lana was harmed before I got to her again.

CHAPTER 5

KADE

"Why did they think your shadows would kill me?"

Lana's damn body threatened to kill *me* at the moment. The bite in her words did nothing to deter my wayward thoughts. Instead, her fire drew me in further, which wasn't ideal seeing as she'd taken over too many of my senses already.

I gripped the horse's reins harder, not caring that it caused my forearm to tighten around her hips.

"I told you before, they don't play. They destroy." I exhaled, failing to mask my smile as I recalled a very memorable evening in her bedroom when she teased me about the deadly magic I commanded.

Silence fell between us. Knowing her, it wouldn't last.

We rode in front of the others, steering the four horses toward Mount Legion. *Four* horses, even though Jax and Raya both knew the whole purpose of crossing into Brookmere was to fulfill the damned prophecy. A prophecy calling for a queen, which meant clearly we'd need five horses upon our return.

I rolled my shoulders, feeling Lana stiffen as my body pressed against hers. No doubt she could feel exactly what her ass rubbing against my fucking cock did to me. There was no give, no space between us. Desperate to keep her from feeling uncomfortable, I tried to think of anything else. My father. Cassandra wearing that horrifically sheer silver dress at the Festival of Swords six years ago.

My desire shriveled. Now I just needed to keep it together from here on out.

Fates, Lana should have ridden with Storm. Or Jax. Hell, even Raya would have been a better option. Should have, but I knew myself enough to know it wouldn't have gone well. A vise tightened around my chest at the thought of her pressed up against Storm or Jax in this way.

What the hell was wrong with me? I stretched my neck, somehow believing that might snap some sense into me.

But I was beyond common sense when it came to my Little Rebel. Besides, no part of me felt comfortable with her anywhere except close to me now that we were in Mysthaven.

"Why am I here, Kade?" she sighed, breaking the quiet as I knew she would. "Why bother to take me at all?"

It took more willpower than I cared to admit not to brush a thumb along her thigh to provide her with some sort of reassurance. Even if I was the last man she'd want to accept it from right now.

"I have to see someone before I can give you the answers you are looking for. I do not want to say the wrong thing or mislead you any more than I already have."

"Say the wrong thing?" Lana huffed incredulously. "You are content with killing my father, hurting Ian, kidnapping me, but you are worried about saying something that might, what? Hurt my feelings?"

"Illiana—"

"No, don't Illiana me. You are a monster." She huffed loudly. "I need to get back to Brookmere. Regardless of what you think *you* need me for, my kingdom needs me more. I must see—"

Her words died, and my fucking worthless soul split at the tremor she tried to hide. The sound of her heartbreak dug into me worse than the king's damn whip.

I wanted to comfort her, *needed* to. But with what? I had no idea what her real purpose was in the grand scheme of things. *Fucking seers and their prophecies.*

"I have to put eyes on my mother. And Ian," she finished her earlier thought. Her comment was said more to herself than to me.

"We should talk about what you thought you saw with your father." Dread pooled in my gut, knowing there was a very real possibility nothing I said would garner her forgiveness. "Please let me explain."

Lana whipped her face around, smacking me with her hair as she turned. "I don't *think* I saw anything. You killed the king. My father. I *know* what I saw. Your dagger in his heart. Your shadows around his neck while he lay in my arms. What more is there to talk about, Kade?"

"You need to listen to me. Your father came to me, he wanted to protect you—" I stopped. If I went down that road, she'd blame herself and live with more guilt than she already carried. "He knew Andras would try to have Casimir siphon his magic. He knew—"

"No," she whispered.

"I know this is hard to hear, but you have to let me try." I tightened my hold on the reins once more, drawing them closer, merely to feel like I could hold her while explaining. My shadows curled around her hips, resting on her legs as if they could help her through this.

She didn't make a move or show discomfort at their touch. *Thank Fates.* It gave me a second, a selfish damn second to feel warmth spread through me. The strange sensation I only felt around Lana. I didn't realize how desperately I craved it until I'd gone a mere couple of hours without it.

"Your father didn't want them to siphon his power. He

asked me to do it, to end his life so they wouldn't get his magic—"

"Stop," she commanded. "He wouldn't do that."

"His focus was on protecting the kingdom," I pressed. "If they had obtained his magic in his weakened state, even briefly—"

"My father would never have asked for death over facing an enemy." Her body shook, and I didn't know if it was from anger or grief. "You make him sound cowardly."

"Cowardly?" I sighed. "No, he may be the bravest man I've ever met."

"I can't do this," she whispered, now shivering in front of me. My shadows thickened where they held her legs, like they were trying to pour into her somehow.

I didn't think there was anything left to break inside of me, yet my chest tightened with anguish.

"I can't imagine how hard this is, but you have to understand. You have no idea how sorry I am. I wish I could take it back. I wish there had been another way, another moment to think."

"But there's not. Because you murdered him in my arms," she shouted, breaking the quiet around us, her voice cracking on the final word.

She let out a painful sob before she shoved her elbow into my stomach. Wheezing, I gripped her thigh, falling forward.

Lana huffed. "This is only the beginning of the pain I plan to inflict on you, Kade Blackthorn." She briskly wiped her hand across her cheek, whisking away the tears there. "Mark my words."

"Stopping here for the night!" Raya shouted, halting the line of horses.

Lana jumped from the horse without hesitation before I could say anything more. Jax grabbed the bags mounted to the animals containing our supplies and threw one to Lana.

Inclining his head, he and Lana left the horses to set up the tents.

Quickly and quietly, we worked to establish our temporary campground for the evening. Lana observed every interaction with a keen eye, no doubt looking for any possible piece of information to hold against us later.

I stood outside my now finished tent, unable to stop studying her. Her entire demeanor exuded wariness. Her discomfort tugged at something deep within. Something I'd long since believed dead. The spark Lana elicited from me had been life-altering, reforming my blackened heart around something else. *Her.*

Being back here in this loathsome kingdom, closer to *him*, threatened to disrupt the pieces of me that had slowly begun mending during my time in Brookmere. Though I could handle guilt and doing things I loathed here, watching Lana look like a prisoner, at my hands no less, wasn't something I could stomach.

She looked at the tent to her right as Raya finished putting up the one they would share. Her body tensed before she shifted, rubbing her arms and staring at the small space. Lana hadn't been alone since the travesty of the final trial, and I could only imagine some time to herself would be helpful. Even necessary. At some point she had to grieve.

As if she were a bloody razorven, I approached slowly. "Here, take mine," I said, waving my hand behind me toward my tent. She needed this space. I couldn't let her go home, but I could try to give her a reprieve from being surrounded by strangers. "Jax and I can share a tent for the evening. But do not try to escape. It's not safe."

Jax approached holding two pieces of bread in his hands. His gaze darted between the two of us, searching for something in that obnoxious way he usually did, always seeing more than any of us wanted.

Lana nodded silently and strode toward the entrance.

"Great, I get to room with His Moodiness—hey!" Jax yelped as Lana swiped a hunk of bread from his hand before escaping to the privacy of my tent.

She jerked the tent flaps closed. An inky tendril of shadow crawled along the ground toward the tent, hovering outside. My shadows weren't burdened with a fear of her rejection. Perhaps I could feed from their confidence and pray to the Fates she would forgive me one day.

I yanked at the magic, willing it to return, but it failed me. Instead, they stretched farther from me as I gave up and moved to the campfire Storm had created. Part of me screamed to stay with the shadows and say something to her, but the guilt threatening to overtake me wouldn't help.

I needed to focus. Away from Lana and this ache inside of me.

"Do you have spare clothes?" I asked Raya. "A cloak, something. She's not dressed for traveling. We had to leave Brookmere unexpectedly."

Raya narrowed her gaze at me, her lip curling, but stormed off, retrieving a dark cloak and throwing it in Lana's tent before she returned.

Inhaling deeply, a small moment of relief settled into my bones as I sat before the fire. I was finally back with my friends. The few I could trust implicitly. While I knew we each had stories to tell, I savored this one moment of normalcy before the chaos of fulfilling the prophecy continued.

Slowly, each of my friends gathered, reunited again for the first time in months.

A soft snore filled the air, reaching us from Lana's tent as we sat in silence, chewing the days-old bread, until Jax finally broke the quiet.

"So, brother, are we going to talk about the princess snoring in your tent, or shall she remain yet another mystery to solve?"

Storm chuckled from across the fire.

"What are you laughing at?" I snapped.

"Oh, I'm more than happy to tell Jax and Raya all about our adventures in Brookmere. I think they will be particularly intrigued to know about your escapades these last few months."

Raya sat silently, shaking her head, already annoyed. She always had little patience for our banter, just wanting the facts as quickly as possible.

"Well, friends," Storm began, leaning in, "let me tell you a tale of a land far away, where we met a fair maiden in the woods. Kade held her at knife point, and then tried to win her hand in the deadliest marriage trials I've ever heard of. Trials that would have led to Kade becoming the King of Brookmere."

Jax had taken a swig of water and promptly spit it everywhere. "*Marriage* trials?"

"But it doesn't stop there," Storm continued.

Sparks flew toward the sky in an impressive display as Raya rolled her eyes at Storm's theatrics.

Jax flicked the knife he had been using to cut the bread in his hand, waiting. "Come on, what happened next."

"You're a child," Raya huffed.

Storm laughed, some of the tension from the day fading away. "The icing on the honey cake from our time away, besides me having to hunt him down after he spent the night with our dear princess, had to be watching him attempt to flirt. It's been eons since he has tried to woo a lady, and it was…awkward as fuck. Disastrous."

"Apparently not disastrous enough to keep them apart." Jax grinned.

I growled. "Enough."

"Yes, enough," Raya said sharply. "If you're going to take all day to get to what matters, I'll start on our end. You have been gone too long and our list of excuses ran dry weeks ago. We must return to the palace."

The humor faded instantly, drying up to die, like the land around us. Returning to the palace was unavoidable. My eyes darted toward my tent where Lana slept, shadows pulsing, wanting to keep her far away from the king. Raya's chocolate eyes bore into me until I met hers.

"I know we do," I said. "I'm sorry for the pressures you were left with."

"There is going to be hell to pay since you haven't been here to enforce the king's psychotic laws." Raya stared deep into my eyes. "It's getting worse."

"I already apologized," I said a little harsher this time, refusing to break Raya's stare.

Storm cleared his throat, apparently sensing the mounting violence filling the space between us. "I am going to train with Lana. We need her sharp, ready. Ian taught her well, so it will not be hard to hone her skills further."

"Train her so she's more capable of stabbing him?" Raya pointed exasperatedly at me. "All while we're also fighting against the king? Brilliant plan, Storm."

"She's already able to stab him," Storm said. Raya frowned at the comment and Jax shook his head in silent disbelief. I merely shrugged.

Storm stretched his arms over his head, cracking his back and staring me down. "He wouldn't even fight back at this point."

My jaw twitched as I clenched it hard. "Your point?"

"She needs to know everything. Including why you killed her father."

"What?" Raya gasped.

Jax stared, mouth agape.

I glared at my best friend, knowing full well he was not only going to make me face my guilt, face Lana, and handle this, but also ensure our friends knew exactly what happened in Brookmere. All at once.

"He begged me to," I said, clenching my hands into fists as

dark shadows built around me, like they could somehow protect me from my own guilt.

"Which you need to tell *her*," he insisted.

"I tried."

"Try harder," Storm countered, unwilling to accept my retort.

"Fates save us." Jax ran a hand over his face.

Storm's menacing gaze broke from mine, softening as a smile spread over his lips. "The princess says 'tits and daggers' when she curses."

Jax whimpered, clasping his chest. "It's perfect."

"You're not to train her," Raya said, once again interrupting the two with a simmering anger. "She'll kill him."

Storm's eyes flicked toward me. History told us all there would be no winning this battle tonight; Raya rarely backed down when she was in a good mood, let alone in her current state.

"It's not up to you," Storm said quietly before he rose, trudging back to his tent. He waved Raya off as she stood next to the fire, hands on her hip. I didn't miss her bending down toward a pile of rocks.

Storm was right about one thing, Lana needed to train in order to survive here in Mysthaven. Selfishly, I wanted to be the one to train her. My shadows stretched taught, hovering toward my tent, demanding to be near her. They would want to train with her, too. Impossible to do if she wouldn't talk to me. Which would clearly continue if I couldn't find a way to tell her about her father.

"Have you been able to bolster the rebellion?" I asked Jax.

He grunted. "Without the Monster of Mysthaven around, people have seemed more willing to listen."

I sighed, lowering my head. "They need to be willing to risk it, even upon my return if we have any hope of them being brave enough to stand up to the king."

My questions ceased when Raya stilled, dropping the rock

she had picked up to throw in Storm's direction. Her head hung low, and when she raised it once more, her eyes reflected a shimmering white hue.

"Fuck, not now," I muttered.

Raya stiffened, her entire body frozen for a few moments more, before her eyes returned to their normal chestnut brown. Her gaze connected with my own.

"He knows you've returned." She swallowed a deep breath before continuing. "He's made the decision for us."

Jax rose as well, nearing Raya's side. "What do you mean, made the decision for us?"

"We've been ordered to go to Canyon City before returning to the palace. A group of traitors were discovered creating a plan to cross the void. The king wants the leader dealt with. Now."

My mind spun, working the pieces together like we always had done when instructed to deal with traitors. I should have known coming back here would mean an immediate task. "We'll go at dawn," I said grimly.

Raya didn't relax her gaze, appearing uncharacteristically nervous. "Publicly, Kade. He wants it done in the city square."

Jax cursed under his breath before walking toward the tent we'd share. I closed my eyes, steeling my emotions, locking them away as Raya moved to her own space. The man I'd become in Brookmere couldn't exist here. The man Lana allowed me to be wouldn't help us.

I inhaled slowly, opening my eyes and snuffing out the campfire with my shadows, just like I'd smother the part of me that had sparked alive these past few months. It was the only way to allow me to unleash the side of me lying dormant so I could become the monster the king had created me to be.

The monster Illiana believed me to be.

The Monster of Mysthaven.

CHAPTER 6

LANA

A sliver of moonlight shone through the crack of the tent flap as I awoke several hours later from the truths haunting my dreams.

A scream threatened to escape my lips, but I bit down on the fleshy part of my hand to not wake the others. Tears streamed down my face in a waterfall of emotion.

The dreams of my father's bloody chest weren't nightmares at all. They were real.

I swallowed a sob. And now? I was alone.

The grief of that loneliness surrounded me like a dark inescapable pit, worse than my nightmares.

More horrific than the terrors of the dungeon all those years ago.

The all-consuming thoughts doubled me over with a phantom pain inside of my gut, threatening to drive me mad.

Losing Elisabeth and then my father—alone, these two tragedies would have sent me into a spiral, but being taken here to a land that shouldn't have existed? Away from the only two people whom I could rely on to pull me through such overwhelming grief?

It felt impossible to get through this.

I was being buried alive by this heartache with no outlet. No way out.

Only a few days ago, Kade may have been the one to help dig me out of this endless pit of despair. A chance that only existed for a damn heartbeat before he killed the first man I ever loved.

Now nothing would save me.

And yet... Maybe I didn't need to be saved. Maybe the woman I'd become while tunneling out of my own grave would save herself and destroy anyone and everyone who dared to stand in her way.

Kade and his friends were the enemy, and if I could hone my hatred for them, I knew I could keep the loneliness at bay.

I am Illiana Dresden, and I am stronger than the darkness within me.

Wiping my tears, and renewed in strength, my rapidly beating heart returned to a steady pace. The desire to scream into the mountaintops subsided, slightly.

A throb in my hand pulled my attention. Small droplets of blood glistened on my skin in the moonlight. A stark reminder of my lack of magic and healing ability. In a flash, what little determination I had conjured now escaped.

All of my failures boiled down to my lack of magic. I'd lost Elisabeth and my father because I couldn't save them. How many times would I rise from my grief, only to plummet back into it again?

Resigned, I curled into a ball on my open bedroll, Raya's borrowed cloak falling around me. The flaps of my tent fluttered in a breeze, and a familiar warmth tickled my feet. Kade's shadows hovered, tucking me back in before whisking a fallen piece of hair behind my ear.

Before I could turn and shout at Kade, his shadows, with one last squeeze, retreated. Kade was nowhere to be found.

Several more minutes passed as I tossed and turned, unable to calm my racing mind. Lying here served to make everything worse, so I rose to exit the tent, patting the pocket where my father's letter rested. Perhaps reading his words would help focus me. Besides, staring at the stars would provide some comfort. Walks in the middle of the night had always cleared my mind before, hopefully it would work tonight.

Fates, I hoped Mysthaven had stars.

Upon first glance, Kade and his companions were nowhere to be found. Embers from the earlier fire dwindled, but still offered an endless supply of warmth, no doubt from Storm's magic. A small rock formation lay a few feet away, beckoning me as if it knew it offered the perfect place to stare at the sky.

I sat down and looked upward. The stars shone just as brightly in Mysthaven as they did in Brookmere. I searched until I found my favorite constellation, following the trail of four stars that led into an arrow, one belonging to a warrior maiden who chased away a deadly serpent a few stars to the right.

The patterns they made felt like home.

Home.

I pulled out the letter. No one else knew the secrets it contained. I had no intention of sharing them either. Not now.

Even with the brilliant moonlight, I could barely make out his elegant writing.

My mission contained in my father's words.

Illiana, you are the key to Brookmere's survival.

Your mother asked she be buried with a journal she kept, passed down from each generation in the royal family. She needed it secret. Safe. You must go to your parents' home and find it. I ensured her request was met. In it, she always believed you'd have everything you needed to save our lands.

A clear objective, spelled out by my father's hand, lay before me. Go to Valeford to find something my birth mother had left behind. What could she have possibly hidden of such importance in a mere journal? It rattled me knowing the key to our kingdom's survival remained hidden in such a small town, in a grave no less. But the king's words were clear.

I reread the letter, this time in full, which revealed who the king and queen actually were to me. That they'd stepped in to raise me after my real parents were murdered by the dark Fae infesting Brookmere twenty-two years ago. The third time through, the resolve settled in me again, this time rising stronger than before.

Having a purpose would give me a reason to go on. Strength. Strength *and* courage to move past the grief over Elisabeth and my father. To avenge their deaths in any way possible. Nothing else mattered.

"How do I get out of here?" I whispered to the stars, asking like they'd whisper their secrets back to me.

I shivered, the frigid temperature freezing my skin. I wished I'd brought my blanket to keep warm.

Murmurs hummed through the night, and I stilled, turning my head in the direction of the noise, beyond the small gathering of rocks around me.

As they continued, I rose quietly, tucking my letter back into my pants pocket. Walking around the rocks past a few trees, I peeked past my hiding place.

Kade and Storm sat side by side facing out toward an ominous-looking mountain range.

"Want to tell me why you let it overtake you so spectacularly earlier?" Storm asked.

Kade shook his head. "I know Jax was merely running his mouth as usual, but the thought of the king knowing she is here—" He paused, picking something up and tossing it forward into the night.

They're talking about me.

"And?" Storm prodded.

"The thought of him using her, hurting her," Kade sighed. "I couldn't stop it."

Silence fell between them, but only for a moment before Storm sighed. "It sounds like your own magic destroyed it, overcame it even as it escaped you. Your shadows made sure she was safe."

"Don't." Kade's voice held a warning toward his friend. "It's stronger here. She isn't safe with me. And we damn well know she won't be safe with him."

Him. Kade continuously referenced *him.*

The king.

"This was always the plan. We needed a queen for whatever purpose Cassandra foresaw."

A prickling sensation stirred in me. Foresaw? It sounded too familiar. Too much like a prophecy. Hadn't Kade mentioned a prophecy when we were fleeing? I thought it had been mine, but what else did Storm mean?

I needed to hear more. Needed to know what I was doing here. I stepped forward to hear better, and a dried twig snapped beneath my eager feet.

The men startled, but before they could catch me, I fled.

I barely made it a few paces before shadows wrapped around my waist, followed quickly by a pair of arms.

Kade tsked. "Spying is so unbecoming, Little Rebel."

I backed a step away from him, shocked he let me. "What were you talking about with Storm? I heard you. I'm not safe here. Who is Cassandra?"

Kade's eyes narrowed, those beautiful grey swirls standing out against his skin in the moonlight.

"Taking your time to fabricate another lie?" I pressed. "I guess I shouldn't expect anything honest from *you.*"

"I never lied to you." Kade's gaze flitted to my mouth, staring as the grey in his eyes twisted with black, which seemed more prevalent here.

My jaw twitched. "How can you say that? You lied to get me to sleep with you and—"

He took the one step remaining between us, my back hitting a deadened tree. "I *never* lied to you," he growled. He braced a hand on the side of my head while grasping my chin in his fingers, forcing me to meet his gaze. "And I didn't coerce you into what we shared. Don't you dare twist what happened between us."

My lip curled as I snorted, yanking my head from his grasp. "Yes, well when you said you were in Brookmere for a queen just to get me in bed, I didn't think you meant you'd be kidnapping me."

He leaned in so close that I felt his breath against my skin. Fury radiated off him as his shadows pulsed. We stood barely an inch apart as his chest pressed against mine, rising and falling in rhythm with my own.

I needed to move. Now. Otherwise, my traitorous body might do something like lean into him. My eyes prickled, damn it all. Damn *him*. He wouldn't get any more of my tears.

But Kade saw it all.

Every flutter of emotion.

He leaned down, almost like he wanted to kiss me, but instead grasped a strand of my rose-gold hair between his fingers. His eyes cleared to grey as he swallowed, not breaking eye contact.

"You believe many things about me, Little Rebel," he said softly. "And the longer we stay here, the more you'll learn. The more you'll hate me. But I meant every word I said to you." Kade dropped my hair and skimmed his knuckles across my cheek tenderly. "Every touch. Every pleasure-filled sound. Every damn moment between us was real. I may have hidden truths from you, but I never lied. Except that night, when I told you I was there for a queen." His voice trembled over the last few words.

I stopped breathing, watching as Kade pulled his hands away, and his shadows.

"I was only there for you," he whispered.

He turned, walking away and leaving me alone.

I shivered from his absence. As much as I hated him, every time he retreated, something in me broke further. It shouldn't be possible, seeing as everything I loved had been taken from me. What else was possibly left to feel such pain?

Kade Blackthorn's presence should have filled me with fire, with a rage so fierce, it would warm me until he died just like my father.

Instead, his absence triggered a horrible sorrow. This festering, wretched pain I couldn't work through lessened around him, which must be his shadows or magic keeping emotions at bay when he was near. That was the only explanation as to why the stabbing ache in my chest returned full force as soon as he disappeared from sight.

I fell to my knees, reliving the death of Elisabeth, of my father. Watching the nightmare in my mind of losing Brookmere. I'd conjured horrors in my head at what happened to Ian, my mother. No news of the palace meant no way of knowing what Andras had done.

Instead of fighting harder to destroy Kade myself and return to my people, my remaining family, I kept losing my nerve. I craved the respite from the pain his nearness brought, yet all of this was his fault.

I breathed deeper, heavier, as I let that hatred consume me. Hating myself for my body's reactions to him was enough to fuel that fire for now.

I planned on using it to hurt him the second he let his guard down. If he remained distracted talking with Storm or the others, instead of watching my tent, I'd have a chance to sneak away.

Tomorrow night, I told myself. Tomorrow, I'd prevent Kade

from following me, and then I'd return home. No matter what.

CHAPTER 7

IAN

D*rip.*
Drip.
Drip.

The dripping hadn't stopped in years.

No matter how much time passed, the noise still haunted me. The echo in the frigid dungeon as the water splashed against the cold stone crawled along my spine. Not because of fear for myself.

No. The dripping meant she needed me. It meant she was hurting.

But I was no longer a young Fae. This time I was older, stronger.

I knew what it took.

I was not some pawn. Certainly not his pawn despite the way he ranted on and on in front of the Fae of Ellevail.

My body twitched against the cold stone. I blinked, letting my eyes acclimate to what my mind already knew—I remained in the dungeons.

Images flashed one at a time, but in the same repeating loop. This room and the torture Andras had bestowed on Lana.

Fates, Lan.

I had to get out of here and find her.

I balled my hand into a fist at the thought of the betrayal she must be experiencing. I'd failed to protect her when she needed it most. All of us duped by Kade and Storm, their friendship a farce for a bigger plan we couldn't possibly have seen.

Never again.

The darkness of the dungeon didn't reveal much, but I knew all too well I'd been thrown into the same cell we had always been tossed into after being tortured.

Andras's anger over my lack of information had caught up to him too many times now. I had lost track of the ways he inflicted pain on me. The last round, he tried to skin the flesh off my back with a whip. But nothing would make me talk.

Maria's tears were almost too much as she'd tried to heal me after the last time. Her jaw tightened when I reminded her to stay strong, and her hands stopped trembling enough to succeed in her ministrations.

It was thanks to her I knew Kalliah was safe. As safe as she could be, hidden away with the queen.

While Andras spoke true of her mourning, she wasn't looking for revenge on Lana by his side as he'd made the Fae of Ellevail believe. She was a prisoner in her own palace. I discerned that much from the guards as they did rounds past my cell.

I rose onto my arms and twisted until I faced the metallic bars holding me captive. Thankfully they could bear weight again after being tied up for so long yesterday.

I reminded myself staying awake and alert mattered. Lucien might make an appearance, and I needed to ask more questions of the pugron.

Great, I thought. My entire chance at escape boiled down to trying to communicate with an animal who came and went as he pleased.

Distant footsteps grew louder. The distinctive click of the heavy-booted heel gave away his element of surprise. Andras was here.

"I will give you one last opportunity to spill your secrets before the real fun begins. Whips and sticks may break your body, but I can break your mind, Captain." Andras seethed as he came into full view in front of the cell. "Where is she?"

"As I've told you before, I. Don't. Know," I spit toward the coward of a man. "And even if I did, I would *never* tell you. You are a disgrace to this kingdom, Andras. You will not win this war you've waged."

Andras's lips twitched and he waved his hand, roughly slamming my body forward against the metal bars, pressing me against them forcefully.

"You choose pain and suffering? Why am I not surprised? You always were a martyr. Always pining for the affections of a princess so far beyond your societal rank. You worthless, insignificant nobody."

My body seized suddenly. I felt him. *Felt* Andras clawing at my mind. Inside my damn head. *What the fuck?*

"Tell me where the princess hides and you'll live," he purred. "Continue to lie and I'll take my time skinning you alive."

"How could I possibly know where she is when I've been trapped here for days?" The strength it took to keep the talon-like object out of my head made my voice quiver. I didn't allow the fear to consume me, determined to stay strong.

"Still not talking?" A voice came from the shadows beyond Andras.

Lord Casimir West stepped into view. My lips curled back, seeing the pathetic excuse of a man. Lana never would have chosen him. I didn't bother suppressing my grin at the thought.

"I'd wipe that smirk off my face if I were you, *Captain*," Casimir taunted. "I'm on the hunt for your pretty little princess, and I *will* ensure she comes back home. You don't want to be on my bad side." He paused. "For Lana's sake."

I scoffed. "Doubtful you are up to the challenge, or I wouldn't be bored to tears with Andras's questions asking me of her whereabouts."

Andras still magically held my body pressed against the bars with such incredible strength, I knew there'd be bruises. Casimir stepped forward, his hand lunging out, wrapping around my throat.

His white teeth glistened as he grinned, gripping me tighter.

Andras held his index finger forward as though pointing at me. An enormous onyx gem rested garishly atop a gold setting. I swear if he told me to kiss his ring, I might vomit on it.

"I don't have all day, Casimir," Andras hissed.

Unlike the first time Casimir had siphoned magic from me during the marriage trials, I realized his intentions instantly. He grinned as he took hold of my magic.

I tried to fight, thrashing against his hand while he continued to pull my abilities, zapping them from me effortlessly. As my magic left me, my body slumped forward. Andras released the magical bindings on both my body and the assault on my mind all at once, and I fell to the ground. My face collided against the bars, bouncing back painfully.

I didn't react. I refused to let them see weakness, taunting me now that my magic had been drained from my body. I couldn't let them think they were winning.

Casimir touched the ring, and it smoked as the air around it pulsed and glowed.

What the fuck?

Andras's head shook wildly, lending a deranged air to his already unhinged demeanor.

"I feel it," he said. "It's working."

Finally, the pulsing magical glow settled into the ring.

"It will be nice to question him without all of that bravado hiding behind his meager power," Andras said, sounding bored. He held up the ring in the dim torch lights of the dungeon. "And to do so with his own magic working against him."

Andras pulled me toward him again with just the flick of his wrist.

This time, the hold he had on me felt insurmountable. How was this possible?

He grinned. "Ah yes, the power is there."

Grabbing my arm through the bar, his fingers elongated. His nails became pointed and sharp, almost like the claws of a hawk. Andras cocked his head to the side, then twisted my arm.

The *crack* of snapping bone would have been more prominent had I not shouted in agony.

He released my arm, touching my forehead, and a searing pain radiated throughout my body, throbbing over the pain of my broken arm. "Your defenses will be nothing now," he whispered giddily.

The agony in my head lessened almost immediately.

"No," he snarled, pulling his hand back. I collapsed to the floor again. "No, it's gone already."

He slammed Casimir into the wall. "Figure out a way to make it stay. I know it works." He pulled Lord West toward him and then slammed him back again. "He told me it would work."

"Yes, Your Grace. I will not fail you again," Casimir promised, bending on a knee.

"You're disgusting, groveling before a mad man." I grimaced through the pain, refusing to let them keep me down.

Casimir stalked toward the cell again, squatting in front of it. "When I discover where your princess is, I'll have my fun with her. Did you hear that, *Captain*?" He smiled, licking his lips. "I can't wait to taste her. To see what you and Kade were so worked up—"

"I'll kill you," I shouted, raging against the bars between us. "I'll get out of here, wrap my hands around your neck and enjoy every second of watching you beg for mercy if you even think about looking at her."

Casimir didn't say a word, just wriggled his fingers in a wave and walked away.

"No!" I screamed again. I was losing. Failing at all of this, with no way to protect Lana.

Especially not when Andras had some plan to siphon others' magic. It hadn't worked today, but what was to keep them from finding a way to make it last? How unstoppable could he become?

With Casimir on the prowl, searching for her, I prayed she hadn't left Brookmere by herself. I didn't want her with Kade and Storm, those traitors. But if she were with them, it would make it more difficult for Casimir to capture her.

I refocused my breathing, refocused my mind on surviving. Gathering what I knew in order to use everything against the man still standing in front of me. I might be failing Lana right now, but I wouldn't forever.

"It was I who gave the blessing for him to do what he wishes with Illiana," Andras said. "As long as he ultimately brings her to me for my uses."

I clenched my teeth.

"I do love to watch the hope fade from my playthings," Andras chuckled. "Now the real fun can begin."

A shout from down the corridor forced Andras's attention away from me to acknowledge the intruder. A flurry of whispers, too quiet even for my superior hearing to pick up, passed quickly before Andras returned from the shadows.

"Prepare yourself. I'll be back later for some *quality* time together."

I grasped the bars and shouted at the man receding down

the hall. "You will never be king. I will make sure of it. On my father's grave, I swear I will kill you."

Andras stopped midway down the hall and laughed. An evil, sinister laugh. "You have no idea what I'm capable of, boy. I'll be king before the year is up either by using the queen or forcing Illiana to ascend by my side. Once the crown sits atop my head, I'll destroy her. And you. Just you wait."

The click of Andras's shoes slowly retreated. I remained kneeling on the cold floor. Alone again.

He'd never get to her. I wouldn't allow it. I needed to escape from these dungeons. Somehow.

Shuffling scraped on the stones down the hall. More than one pair of feet made their way toward me. I stared into the darkness, watching until Corbin emerged with a cup of water and a tray containing bread and soup. Guards flanked him, one on each side.

Finally, a familiar face. I scrambled to the bars.

"Corbin," I said, unable to keep the relief from my voice despite the guards. Knowing he survived instilled hope that the others were okay too.

One of the guards stiffened at his side. Corbin clicked his tongue. "Don't bother speaking, Captain. Our friendship ended the minute you chose those filthy traitors over your kingdom."

"What?"

"You heard me," he snarled. He shoved the tray through the small opening in the metal bars, designed for feeding prisoners.

"What are you talking about?" I demanded.

His cold eyes met mine. I frowned. It was impossible. Corbin would never follow Andras. Even without knowing the details of what the monster did to Lana, to me, he'd never betray his friends.

"You would do well to obey, Ian," he said, his voice sharp

and condescending. "The sooner you accept you will never succeed, the sooner we can all get on with the inevitable."

The guards at his sides snickered.

"Oh, how the mighty fall, eh, Corbin?" The man to Corbin's right nudged him in the ribs, like they were sharing a joke between old friends.

I stared dumbfounded at the man I thought I knew. My stomach twisted in defeat, hope shriveling in my chest at his words. His demeanor. "How could you, Corbin? I trusted you."

What happened to my friend?

Corbin's eyes darted to the tray before meeting my gaze. "Enjoy your meal. Who knows when you will be allowed food again, traitor."

The guards laughed, and before I could respond, the three of them marched down the hall to leave. Andras *must* be using his mind magic to influence Corbin. There was no other explanation. None I would accept at least. He would never say such things otherwise.

If he'd gotten to Corbin, had he gotten to Leif as well? Kalliah? I swallowed the bile rising in my throat.

Escaping this prison had been a necessity before, but it was even more critical now. There was more than one person who needed saving. Andras's brand of insanity would poison the entire castle otherwise. I'd already witnessed him poison Ellevail with such lies, turning the Fae against Lana. That shit would spread, quickly too, given how powerful Andras's magic seemed to be getting.

I didn't remember it seeming so insurmountable before.

Frustration overtook me, and I shouted into the darkness, screaming until my throat went raw. Stumbling back from the bars, I let myself fall to the cold floor beneath me.

How had things gotten so fucked?

I let go of the bottled-up reactions once the door shut, growling out my frustration and the pain.

I lay on my side, facing the space where Lucien had appeared the previous night. Blinking slowly, fighting passing out from the unrelenting pain, I watched the corner.

A feminine gasp echoed in my mind.

I frowned.

"Hello?" I asked. At least, I thought I did, but my mouth didn't move. I tried to sit up and groaned.

A foreign presence lingered inside my head, somehow here with me. I wasn't alone.

Had Andras's magic finally infiltrated my mind?

"Who's there?" I tried again, knowing I was most likely talking to myself, presence or not.

I refused to believe I'd gone mad. *Think.*

"I know someone is in here. What are you doing?"

No response. A figure lurked in my mind, not at all hateful like the talons. No, this feeling was the opposite in every way. Something familiar, though, seemed impossible. I squinted, as if somehow I could see whoever, or whatever, was here.

After a few moments of continued silence, I gave up, choosing instead to give in to the dreamlike state completely and let my body mend itself. Rest would trigger my magic to heal. Maria would have less to worry about when she arrived.

No one was in my head. Even accepting that fact, it didn't stop me from whispering into the recesses of my mind.

"Tell Lana I'll find her."

CHAPTER 8

LANA

"You!" A rage-filled, deadly female voice broke the silence of the camp early the next morning.

Raya stormed toward me with one finger outstretched. "What the hell kind of magic did you use on me?"

I frowned, shocking myself slightly that I didn't feel the least bit scared of the raging warrior before me. I dragged my gaze over her from head to toe and turned back to continue folding the blanket from the tent. "I don't have magic," I responded coolly.

It felt strange to say it out loud, but with everything else going on, it seemed pointless to pretend here. These weren't my people.

She knocked the blanket out of my hand and onto the ground. "Don't you lic to me."

I reached for the dagger at my thigh and yanked it out. "Get away from me."

Raya laughed. "You think you stand a chance against me?"

"Raya!" Kade shouted, striding toward us.

He moved to stand between me and his friend, but I shoved him. "I don't need you to run interference."

Jax laughed off to my right. He tossed an apple in the air before taking a large bite. "Get her, Princess."

"Stay out of this," Raya snapped at him. She turned her attention back to me. "How did you put me into someone's mind? Tell me now or I swear I'll—"

Kade growled. "You'll what?"

Raya met the arrogant asshole's gaze, and her vengeful posture lost a smidge of its bravado. She held up her hands. "I want to know how she put me into another's mind without my knowledge. If she has that capability, don't you think we should know?"

Kade glanced at me, then back to Raya. "Illiana is telling the truth. She has no magic."

I gave her a smug smile, but Jax's breathy expletive stole Kade's attention away from Raya and me. His gaze narrowed on Jax.

"How could she possibly be of use to us with no magic?" Jax questioned.

Worthless.

Nothing.

Andras's voice filled my head, ringing in my ears. *No, not now.*

A warm hand on my forearm snapped me back to the here and now.

Kade pulled me close to his side as he stared down Jax. "Watch it."

Why was he bothering to defend me?

Raya ignored them now, speaking again, with only nominally less vitriol. "I've never…" She paused. "I control whose mind I enter. But last night, I was in a dungeon. Inside a man's mind. A stranger's."

I froze, swallowing the lump in my throat at her words. Raya had mind magic.

Like *Andras*.

Warning bells triggered inside of me. Another powerful Fae at Kade's side, and this one had mind magic.

"Why do you think I had anything to do with your disgusting mind magic?" I hissed. She didn't necessarily deserve the spite thrown her way, but I couldn't stop it from spewing out of me.

She narrowed her eyes, studying me.

"Could it have been the king?" Kade asked her.

She kept her gaze fixed on me and shook her head. "It has something to do with her." She pointed. "I only escaped when the man said, 'Tell Lana I'll find her.'"

I sucked in a breath. Ian. It had to be Ian.

She said the man had been in the dungeons?

I wobbled, and Kade's shadows immediately circled around me, steadying me before his arm wrapped around me.

"Was he hurt? How do you know he was in a dungeon?" I asked. When my legs steadied, I took a step toward her, but she moved into a defensive position.

"I don't know. I felt it. He's badly injured."

Without meaning to, I let out a whimper. Kade sucked in a breath.

"Can you talk to him? Can you get back into his head?" I grabbed her and she swung a fist at me, attacking.

Kade pulled me back before she hit more than just my arm. I thrashed, fighting him as his grip around my waist tightened. "This is all your fault."

He didn't let go. I only stopped my battle with him when I noticed Storm standing near Jax. Lunging from Kade's arms, I ran toward his friend, shoving him as soon as I stood close enough. "It's your fault too. You left him defenseless. They have him in the dungeon. If something happens to him, I'll kill you."

I slammed my fist into the side of Storm's face but wasn't

expecting the pain to radiate up my wrist. *Tits and daggers*, how the hell did he have such a rock-solid jaw?

Storm didn't fight back. "I'm sorry. Lana, I'm sorry." He held up his hands.

"Take me back," I said, some of the fight leaving my voice now that I'd gotten a solid punch in.

Storm glanced over my shoulder, toward where I knew Kade stood. When I looked to the man in charge, his mournful expression did nothing but keep my wrath simmering. "Take. Me. Back."

"We can't," Kade said. "Not yet." He ran a hand through his dark hair. "The sooner we get to Mount Legion, the sooner everything will become clear. Then I'll return you home."

"Ian might not have that long," I argued.

"Ian isn't my problem right now. Our two kingdoms are." He didn't spare me another glance, instead barking orders to the others to clean up the camp.

Storm leaned toward me, ignoring Kade's directives as I stood, lost in this stupid place. "Ride with me?"

I glared at him. "I don't know which is worse, you, him, or the other two I don't know."

"Well, Raya would throw you off the horse. Kade would kill Jax because he'd use you to tease him." He pulled the top half of his dark shoulder-length hair back into a bun. "Your choice is me or Kade."

Kade tensed, pausing as he loaded his pack. He wanted me to ride with him. I knew it from the possessive way he hadn't given me a choice yesterday. Which made my choice easy, even if I hated Storm right now too. "You."

"Lana." Storm touched my arm. "When we have what we need, I will come with you and ensure Ian's safety. He's strong and unbreakable. I'll make sure you get to him."

My jaw clenched. "I'll hold you to that."

We traveled for almost an hour in silence, except for Kade and Raya, whispering to each other. That did *not* bother me.

At all.

Even if it did, I worked to destroy those feelings immediately. Because I didn't give a damn about the man. My heart would catch up to my mind eventually, seeing as it had already been ripped to shreds thanks to him.

A tension filled the air, waiting to explode at a moment's notice from our earlier outburst. I didn't trust Raya as far as I could throw her, which perhaps wasn't far given her clear strength. Kade's shadows pooled around his stiff body as he led the group of us forward.

His anger radiated backward, enveloping the rest of us.

When I had chosen to ride with Storm, I didn't miss the flicker of sadness reflecting in Kade's eyes. It lingered for only a moment before setting itself into rage.

My hand still ached from smashing it into Storm's jaw. He, however, was unfazed. Storm hummed quietly to himself as we rode through the ragged grounds of Mysthaven, careful not to touch me more than necessary.

Where Brookmere thrived with lush greenery, forests, and florals, Mysthaven stretched out, dry and ragged. The red dirt kicked up around us as the horses trotted along the worn trail. Dead-looking plants randomly stuck out of the land with no rhyme or reason. The twigs, which once presumably held life, looked ready to snap if touched.

Brittle.

Every so often, tall, looming trees held the slightest bit of color, breathing the tiniest bit of life into this depraved world.

Yet, in the distance, tall, sharp rock formations rose, demanding attention. Though dry, there seemed to be a different kind of beauty in this place. The opposite of

Brookmere, but still brimming with a cold, harsher version of nature.

"So," Jax interrupted, turning to face Storm. "What's the count?" He ran his fingers through his curls, pushing them out of the way and throwing me a wink. His locks just long enough to tuck behind his ears.

Storm chuckled. "1,681."

"And what about you, oh fearless leader?"

Kade's jaw clenched. "1,679."

Jax could hardly contain his excitement. The sound of him slapping his hand on his knee echoed throughout the valley where we rode. "He bested you? My, my, Kade, what did Brookmere do to you?"

"I don't know if I'd tease him at the moment," Storm said, his voice mirroring the smile he wore.

"What's the number about?" I asked.

Raya turned in her saddle, grinning like she'd scare me into silence. "Dead bodies."

I stiffened.

"They all deserved it," Storm added.

"Does that number include my father?" I gritted my teeth. I didn't care if my current mood destroyed their banter.

"No." Kade's voice reverberated, but he didn't turn as he said it.

I thought back to his words, to what he tried to tell me on the ride yesterday. How true could they be? I couldn't imagine my father ever asking for death. He'd fight. For me. For my mother. For Brookmere.

Something in my gut hadn't been able to ignore the few words Kade did get out about what had happened though. Maybe that was his goal. To make me question what I know I saw, and then use me for whatever purposes he'd concocted.

Turning over my thoughts led me to Ian. To Raya's fury at seeing Ian somehow. *Mind magic.* I'd thought it was an ability only Andras possessed, but she had it too. Which meant she could use it against me.

This was dangerous. All of it. All of them.

I closed my eyes, stuffing down the sorrow of my father's death, the fear for Ian's life, and the unknown of my mother and Kalliah. If I didn't distract myself, I'd wither. I sat straighter, a better thought than withering coming to mind. Distracting myself by getting information about who I traveled with could only help me in the long run.

"How did you all meet?" I asked, breaking the tense silence I'd created.

"We're all Guardians," Jax said, flashing me a smile. "Soldiers for the king. I met Storm when I was younger, riding his coattails as he rose in rank."

Storm snorted.

"Storm has never feared anything," Jax continued, "which is why he was the only one brave enough to approach that one." He pointed at Kade's back. "Apparently, he asked him to train every day for a few weeks until Kade finally gave in. Then of course we learned that the monster of—"

"I proved myself ten times over from those younger years of needing him, and now have bested him in our count," Storm interjected, cutting Jax off from whatever he'd been about to say.

I frowned. Swallowing, knowing I needed information about *all* of them. "And you, Raya?"

She went rigid in her saddle, riding next to Jax. "After being abandoned as a child on the steps of the palace, the king decided he'd like to hone my—what did you call it?— *disgusting* mind magic. I met this lot when I became a Guardian."

My heart softened, marginally. I doubted she'd give me any additional information, but she'd obviously been through hell if the king, who they all clearly despised, had a hand in training her.

The need to apologize became instantly overwhelming. "Someone very—" I swallowed. "Someone who hurt many people I love has mind magic. He controlled what I could see. What I believed to be real. It was the only time I've encountered it beyond cautionary fairytales. His torture lasted for years, and his betrayal to our kingdom ran deep. I apologize for making a judgement without knowing you," I said quietly.

She glanced over her shoulder at me. "Well, I don't have illusion mind magic. Up until now, I've only ever been able to mentally communicate with the king. Don't worry your precious princess head."

Kade grumbled something toward her in warning but didn't engage her further.

Raya looked away from me, and I wondered if her attention would cease altogether.

"Don't feel bad," Jax laughed. "Raya doesn't like anyone."

I returned to taking in the road before us. Not that there was much of a road. The vast openness made it impossible to miss anything.

"Where are we going?" I asked Storm.

"The king requested we take care of a problem on our way home," he answered.

"Canyon City," Jax sighed. "I haven't been there since Alvira Synclair broke my heart."

Raya reached out and punched his arm. "You slept with her sister after telling her she might be the one for you, you cad."

Jax rubbed his arm. "In my defense, Opal's mead had to have been a stronger concoction that evening, because she looked just like her."

I pursed my lips together, holding back a memory-pained smile as I thought about how close they appeared. It reminded me of Ian and Kalliah. Of Brookmere. How would I ensure he lived? If he had been thrown in the dungeons, where were the others? Leif? Corbin? I inhaled, shaking slightly.

Storm let go of the reins with one hand and squeezed my shoulder, but he didn't say anything.

Kade's shadows fell over his horse in the front, snaking back to us.

"Fucking Fates." Jax shivered. "What are they doing?"

His shadows had almost reached me when, at Jax's comment, they snapped back toward Kade, immediately restricting themselves to hovering beneath him.

"They do that now," Storm said.

Jax shook his head in disbelief, all while Kade remained quiet. Refusing to turn around and engage, not even with his friends.

"What problem are you handling for the king?" I asked, continuing to prod until otherwise shut down.

"We're soldiers, what do you think a problem entails," Raya said, as if that would end the conversation.

Jax snorted. "To be fair, the question has merit. Especially since we know very well the problem isn't a real traitor. It's merely someone innocent the king wants to—"

"No." Kade tugged on the reins, turning and stopping our journey. "Not another word."

I frowned. "So, I really am a prisoner? We let *you* into our fold in Brookmere. Happy to see the same courtesy isn't extended here."

"You have no idea what it's like here," Kade argued.

"Whose fault is that?"

Kade's horse neighed, though seemed not to react too much to the shadows swirling around its hooves. "Mine. I know. I'd make this same choice every damn time though. I will not give him a reason to do anything to you. I refuse."

"That's enough," Storm said quietly from behind me.

Kade's gaze flicked toward Raya, and he inhaled a breath.

"It doesn't matter if the mark is guilty or not. We're under the king's orders. We ride."

With that, Kade jerked the reins on his horse and led us once more, this time increasing the pace.

"What is going on?" I asked Storm.

"More than we can tell you right now. But Lana, please, when we get to Canyon City, do as you're told, when you're told," he answered, voice lowered more than before.

On the horizon, the outlines of buildings appeared, breaking the monotony of the red valley around us.

We had almost arrived at our destination and hadn't undergone a single attack from beast or Fae. In fact, we hadn't seen anyone at all.

"Are there dark ones in Mysthaven?" I asked, suddenly aware that apart from the attack in the void by the creature, there didn't seem to be a soul around this place but us.

Storm grunted in confirmation behind me. "Not nearly as many as we faced in Brookmere. The ones who attack here do so closer to our cities."

"Which means everyone needs to stop talking and be on alert," Kade snapped, turning slightly from his horse. I met his gaze but immediately looked away. I didn't want to try to understand the pain I felt at his hollow stare.

"Let's get this over with so I can find Opal," Jax said. "Now that I brought up her mead, I'm going to need to bring some home."

"This isn't a pleasure trip. We know the rules," Kade said.

Raya snorted, pulling her horse to ride beside Kade again. "Do *you* remember them? We're not the ones who have been gone for months."

I saw his shoulders stiffen, even from here. "I remember."

The silence that fell over the friends now held a somber air.

The view of the city cleared the closer we rode. The name made sense as we approached; a huge canyon ran along the left of the outskirts. Up north in Brookmere, there was something similar, much shallower, and with a stream cutting through it. I wondered if this one contained something so beautiful, or if the bottom was dry like the land.

The buildings of the city weren't tall, made up of rough white exteriors with clay-colored roofs. The homes on the outskirts had yard space containing livestock, surprising given the climate. We passed through until the structures became larger, built much closer together, with business fronts sprinkled in between the homes.

Shouts echoed in the streets, and a buzz of noise surrounded us. Still, the group stayed quiet, riding through.

A few Fae noticed Kade, and shrank into the shadows of their homes, some even slamming their door before hiding.

I glanced over my shoulder at Storm, but he didn't acknowledge me. Instead, his steady gaze focused ahead as his jaw ticked. When I faced forward though, his mouth came to my ear. "Whatever you see, stay with one of us at all times. Do what you're told, no matter how you may feel about what you witness."

My heartbeat stuttered and breath hitched. Why in the Fates did Storm feel so anxious that he needed to prepare me in such a manner? If the man truly wasn't a traitor as Jax had insinuated, shouldn't this detour be simple?

We broke through the scattered buildings and approached a very crowded center of town. The architecture surrounded a large open area, the city radiating outward in a circle from this bustling epicenter. Fae laughed, others bargained, noises rising around the market square in a symphony of chaotic sounds.

Yet as the Fae noticed our arrival, the hustle of the city center ceased.

Everyone stared at our party as the haunting silence hung thickly over us.

A few stray souls braved making a noise by whispering in tones of disbelief, but I didn't see where they came from.

I thought I caught the word *monster*.

Kade slung his leg over his horse, shadows flinging outward. The Fae standing closest to us, backed up hurriedly. He clasped his hands behind his back, slowly making his way toward the crowd, until they *couldn't* continue their retreat.

"Someone has been causing problems for the king," Kade shouted. His voice, the one that teased me by calling me Little Rebel, swearing to the Fates as it caressed my body in bed, sounded so hard and different now. Goosebumps pebbled along my skin.

"And unless you all want to die"—he lifted his hand, and his shadows erupted outward as the Fae in the front gasped—"you'll tell me where Richard Draven is. Now."

CHAPTER 9
LANA

Every cell in my body remained frozen in place on the horse, even as Storm slipped off behind me, stalking toward Kade in the wake of his shadows.

Storm gripped the hilt of his blade, unsheathing it while Jax and Raya dismounted, following close behind.

"I believe you were given a fair ultimatum," Storm said, running his hand over his blade.

My heart thumped so hard in my chest, it hurt.

The reaction to Kade, to all of them, made no sense for soldiers who were meant to be Guardians. Their own people didn't trust them. They outright feared them.

I slipped off the horse, remaining close to the beast in case I needed to flee. Not like the group wouldn't catch me, but the thought tempted me.

Kade curled a shadow up and over a man trembling in the front of the crowd. A crowd huddled together like animals being herded for slaughter as more time passed.

"Tell me now," he said as his shadow circled the man's throat. "And live."

The man raised a shaking arm, pointing toward a

retreating figure at the edge of the square. Upon seeing he'd been outed, the figure turned to run.

Kade's shadows lashed outward, flashing past everyone and darkening the square in their wake. They grabbed the man from behind, lifting him at the waist and dragging him back to the center of town as he screamed.

"I've committed no crime," he spat at Kade.

I inched closer, observing the purely vengeful look on Kade's face. Shivering, I wrapped my arms around myself.

"We'll see." He grinned at his captive. Surely he'd listen to the man though. Especially if Jax thought him innocent.

A small wooden platform backed up to a building wall to the left of the square, and Kade…well, Kade's shadows set the man down on it, wrapping his arms and legs in the inky-black magic.

The crowd parted, refocusing their attention from our group to the platform. Raya startled me, approaching hastily, and hooked her arm around my side as she led me to stand between Storm and Jax. She remained behind me.

None of the group looked at me.

Kade paced back and forth in front of the wooden platform. "Richard, you have been accused of conspiring against the king, aiding dark ones, and spreading their poison."

"It's a lie," the man cried out.

Kade whipped another tendril of shadow to cover his mouth. My eyes widened, and I wiped my palm against my thigh.

"It's not your turn," he hissed. "Where was I?" He tapped his finger against his chin.

His words from last night filtered into my mind.

The longer we stay here, the more you'll learn. The more you'll hate me.

"Ah yes, you've been accused of conspiring against the

king. Is there anyone who can speak on behalf of Richard? Anyone at all?"

The crowd cowered, no one making a sound. No one moving.

It was as if they remained rooted in place, unable to do anything but stare at Kade. Which had been the truth? This man terrorizing Fae with his mere presence? Or the man who'd begged for me not to die. The man who made my soul feel at peace.

Kade tsked. "Looks like they agree that you're a traitor." An evil grin spread across his lips, although it didn't seem right to call it that. I met his gaze, his dark, colorless eyes, and gasped. The black stood out so much more than it had in Brookmere.

Storm put a subtle hand on my back as I involuntarily shifted.

My breathing shallowed, quickening as I waited to see what came next.

"You didn't work alone though, did you?" Kade said, pacing again. "Your wife, what is her name again?"

Kade looked back and Jax lifted his chin. "Bridget." His voice, too, was cold, and he smiled back at Kade.

Terror gripped me. They were all insane. Taking pleasure in this? It didn't feel right. Why this show if the man wasn't truly a traitor?

The shadow loosened from Richard's mouth. "No, please. She had nothing to do with this. She's done nothing. I've done nothing."

"Silence!" Kade roared. He nodded toward Jax.

The crowd parted as Jax walked through them, and my stomach twisted. No one defended the man, and no one did anything to protect a woman who cried a few rows from the wooden platform.

Jax grabbed her arm and escorted her forward. This time, when my stomach heaved, I thought I might vomit.

Tears streamed down her face. No, Kade wouldn't do anything to her. He wouldn't. Harming a woman seemed so out of character for even this level of crazy.

A shadow scooped under her chin. The shadows that had made me feel safe, now wreaked terror on the Fae here.

"Would you care to explain your choices before you die alongside your husband?"

"No, Kade," I yelled, stepping forward.

Storm grabbed me, holding my arms behind my back.

I struggled against him. "What do you think you're doing? Get off me."

"Shut up," Raya seethed angrily behind me.

"You said they weren't even—"

Storm silenced me, covering my mouth with his hand.

I fought against his hold. He'd told me to stay quiet, and there had to be a reason, but logic was the furthest thing from my mind right now.

"Please," the woman said. That's all, one word.

Kade's shadows tied her up around her shoulders. "You should have thought about the consequences before betraying the crown." He lifted her in the air, putting her next to her husband. He didn't prevent the woman from grabbing onto her husband as they huddled together, looking out.

"We never aided the dark ones," she shouted at Kade. "We've protected our people from them. From the king. From you monsters," she yelled louder.

Was he really going to do this? This couldn't be happening.

Kade merely stared at his fingers, brushing them on his shirt before looking back at his prisoners. "Anything else you have to say? These words will be your last."

"I hope you die alongside the king, Monster of Mysthaven."

Kade grinned. "I would say I grew tired of teaching

traitors lessons." He looked to his group, Jax smiling, and I assumed Storm and Raya were doing something similar, but I couldn't see them. "But I'd be lying. It brings me great pleasure to show you what the crown thinks of those who disobey."

Storm still covered my mouth and gripped me with unmovable strength, forcing me to watch the torture before me. I couldn't look away from the woman holding her husband on the platform.

Kade turned to the crowd. "Let this be a reminder of what will happen if you defy the crown."

His shadows hurtled toward the couple on stage, and they disappeared.

I screamed behind Storm's hand, as he kept his hold on me, pulling my arms together with one hand. "Stop it, Illiana. Now."

I bit down, hard on his damn hand, but he didn't relent. Didn't even flinch.

The smoke cleared, and I gagged when Storm finally moved his hand. One look at the ashy particles floating in the breeze near a cloud of shadows where the couple stood seconds before had me spilling my stomach on the dusty ground.

Kade had killed them. Even though Jax and the others believed they were innocent. He murdered them.

I heaved, tears pouring from my face.

He killed them.

"Carry on." Kade waved a hand toward the crowd. "Opal," he shouted.

A thin woman, donning a worn floral apron and long wildly braided red hair, shuffled over. She hung her head, hands clasped in front of her.

"We need two rooms for the night. You'll accommodate us or share their fate."

She bowed, retreating with the rest of the crowd.

The town square emptied, Fae fleeing until only the five of us remained.

I wanted to run toward Kade and stab him in his lying heart. Everything *had* been a lie. Everything. A man like that couldn't love. Not that what we shared was love—I refused to accept that. An infatuation, an intense pull, I'd admit to those. But I couldn't believe I'd love someone who murdered so easily. Regardless of what the king claimed they'd done, they hadn't even had a chance to defend themselves. No trial. Nothing.

He approached me, unafraid of my reaction, and took my chin between his fingers. "You run, and I'll find you. No matter where you flee, even to the other side of the void, my shadows will find you, Little Rebel. Do you understand?" He searched my eyes, an unyielding determination glinting in his own. "Stay with Raya." He looked at her and cocked an eyebrow. "Can I trust you to handle her?"

"I'll handle you, you lying *monster*," I spat.

His brows furrowed. "I'd tell you to look deeper than what you see, but we both know you won't listen to the words of a *monster*." His shoulders slumped, despite the tilt to his chin. Then he walked away with Storm and Jax, back toward the cloud of shadows that had destroyed the supposed traitors.

"Are you coming with me nicely, or will I get to use a weapon on you?" Raya said, a corner of her lips lifted.

"I will kill you if you touch me."

I meant it too. I followed Raya with a new resolve to do exactly as I'd intended to the other night—flee. Now I just needed an opening to get away from these psychotic killers.

Because there was one thing I knew for sure now: the Kade Blackthorn I thought cared about me didn't exist here.

If he ever existed at all.

CHAPTER 10

LANA

The door across the hall slammed as heavy footfalls thudded inside.

A few murmurs followed as the door in the hallway shut more quietly the second time around.

I glanced at my new warden, but Raya ignored me, sharpening her blades with the stone in her hand. The steady grinding of the metal hitting the rock's surface didn't falter, even with the commotion of the others returning.

We'd been here for almost an hour and she'd said nothing to me since leaving the center of town.

"Feeling left out?" I asked, not sure why I thought taunting her made sense. She hated me already. Not that I cared.

She cocked an eyebrow, avoiding my gaze. "Typical behavior of a spoiled princess, throwing around childish taunts to get attention."

I gritted my teeth.

A knock at the door forced her to stop and answer it. Jax whispered something to her, and she looked over her shoulder. "Kade is in the room across from us and will know if you try to leave. The rest of us are heading downstairs; one of us will bring your dinner up shortly. Stay put."

She shut the door before I could think of a retort.

"Stay put," I mimicked once she left. I paced around the small room, letting out an agitated huff.

I glanced toward the door. If Kade waited alone in his room, and the others were downstairs in the tavern, now would be my best chance to flee. There had to be an exit from somewhere other than the front door. I'd get to the horses and return the way we'd come. Kade couldn't be the only person in the kingdom with the blessing from the king to cross the void. I wouldn't accept that.

If I could escape back to the void, I could find a way. I knew about the voidlings now, too, and would be more prepared. I *would* find a way.

Stepping from the bed and keeping as light on my feet as possible, I tiptoed to the side of the room where I'd discarded Raya's cloak and threw it on. Twisting my hair into a quick braid, I hid it inside the hood. I inhaled, slowly, quietly, before opening the door, thankful the hinges didn't squeak. As I entered the hall, I stopped, standing rigid outside my room, holding my breath. No sounds came from the room across the hall. If Kade was in there as the others said, I couldn't hear him.

To the left, a small window sat too high to reach. I doubted I'd fit through it even if I managed to reach it quietly. The stairwell to my right presented the only option.

My escape route.

I tiptoed down the hallway, glancing over my shoulder only once. The door to Kade's room remained closed.

My heart pounded in anticipation of my escape, and I prayed the raucous noise of the tavern below covered the sound. The opening at the bottom would be hard to pass through without being seen, but the hallway did, in fact, continue. My freedom depended on this moment.

I peeked around the corner of the opening once I reached the last stair, searching for the others. In the back corner, opposite me, the three of them sat at a table. A tall blonde woman blocked Jax from my view, but none of them faced my way.

A burly man rose from a table closest to the hallway like a damn gift, and I took the advantage of his saunter toward the bar to sprint across the opening.

I threw my back against the wall, waiting one heartbeat. Then two.

The noise from inside the tavern didn't dull, and no one chased after me through the opening. I exhaled slowly, allowing relief to calm some of the anxiety flooding my veins, before facing the end of the hall. Two doors stood there, unmarked and exactly the same. I reached for the one closest to me, sending up more silent pleas to whomever might be listening.

Locked.

"Damn," I muttered. The palms of my hands dampened as my nerves increased, distracting me from the task at hand. I was so close.

I forced myself to take a deep breath, careful to do so as silently as possible, before focusing on the other door. I gripped the tarnished handle and turned. This time, the door swung open easily.

The smell of ale and old wooden crates accosted my senses as I snuck into the dark room. Multiple boxes and barrels crowded the small space, stacked far too high. I let the door shut quietly behind me and made my way through the maze of a storeroom. I forced myself to maintain a semblance of steady breaths, still trying to calm my racing heart despite my success thus far. Sneaking past Kade and his cadre was one thing, but escaping the tavern completely was another.

The only window in the room barely let through enough moonlight to see what lay directly in front of me. My toe hit an unmovable solid barrel, and I clenched my teeth, holding back a yelp of pain..

Shuffling through more slowly, I moved until I escaped the taller crates of supplies and made out a door in the corner. Perhaps the Fates hadn't abandoned me after all.

I opened the door, moonlight illuminating a back alley to the tavern. Grinning, I ran to the end, looking around for the next step. I spied the bay of horses, tied up along a wooden post, bales of hay stacked in front of them.

An excited hysteria ran through my body, knowing I'd made it. I approached the horse I'd ridden earlier. "Hello again," I cooed, reaching for the stallion's nose. He flicked his head up, swatting my hand away. The horse pranced in place, looking like he wanted to make more noise than I could afford.

"Shhh." I reached for the stallion, but my hand was brought up short.

I shouted as my body pitched backward, a damn shadow covering my mouth.

I twisted uselessly in his shadows as Kade's eyes shone in front of me. A smile tugged at his stupid lips. "I suppose you think you're clever, Little Rebel."

"Get your hands off of me." I tried to yell, but the words muffled against his shadows, coming out as a slew of angry nothings.

Kade wiggled his fingers in my direction as I continued to fight for release from my shadowy captor. "Technically they *aren't* on you." His sly smile widened in excitement. "Let's change that."

Faster than should be possible, he lifted me over his shoulder, and I had to brush the hood back so it didn't block my view. This time his shadows did leave my lips.

"Put me down right now," I seethed.

He didn't listen, holding me firmly in place despite my fists pounding against his back. This time, we didn't enter the tavern through the storage room. No. The bastard marched me through the main hall itself.

Despite my protests, my curses, Kade merely laughed. The tavern quieted briefly, but returned to the rowdy atmosphere almost instantly. Not a single patron appeared to care at all about a woman being manhandled by the Fae who had tormented and killed some of their own earlier.

Jax's unruly laughter sounded from behind me, and I held up my middle finger in his direction.

Kade strode through the crowd, undeterred by my fists as he marched us back up the stairs. He slammed the door to his room open before tossing me onto the bed.

I rebounded, jumping up, fists clenched. "I will never stop fighting to escape you," I hissed.

Kade crossed his arms, cocking an eyebrow at me. "And I will always find you."

I wondered briefly if I could actually harm Kade to get my freedom. I closed my eyes, drawing up the memory haunting me. Forcing myself to see my father die in my arms by Kade's shadows. To relive the murders I'd witnessed earlier.

My breathing deepened, heavy as I ran my fingers along the blade at my thigh. Oh yes, I could do this.

I'd hurt him just like he hurt me, and so many others.

Kade's eyes dropped to where I brushed the dagger, and he smiled.

He fucking *smiled*.

I launched myself forward, flinging myself at his chest while whipping my dagger from its sheath.

Kade stumbled, his momentum pulling us both to the ground. A thought briefly flickered through my brain that he'd purposefully let us fall. Like he believed I had no chance to take him by surprise. But it didn't stop my fight.

I wrapped my legs around his center and forcefully thrust the palm of my hand upward, hitting the underside of his nose.

Blood gushed from his nostrils. A perfect shot.

Kade snarled as he tried to control the bleeding with one hand while blocking me with the other.

I embraced the relentless need to cause this man pain. His healing abilities immediately sprang into action though, and the blood slowed to a trickle faster than I would have hoped.

"Lana—" he grunted, blocking another one of my punches with ease.

He didn't fight back. Instead, he merely protected himself, which only fueled my blinding rage.

"If you don't stop, you're going to hurt yourself," Kade said, shoving aside my fist headed for his jaw like it was easy.

"Fight back!" I shouted at him. "Fight me, you coward!"

Kade had the audacity to laugh. "Oh, Little Rebel. Haven't you learned by now? Violence doesn't deter me. Now, are you going to let me talk or are we going to continue this lesson in fighting?"

"If violence is what you want," I muttered, mostly to myself, "violence is what you'll get."

I wrestled my legs free, repositioning myself and my unsheathed dagger. As I settled on top of him, I gasped at how hard he was beneath me. Our fight clearly a turn-on as I felt his impossibly thick length through our clothes. Despite myself and my desire to cause him pain, my eyes flicked to his.

A breath caught in my throat, and I forced my fingers to grasp the handle of my dagger more firmly. All of the shifting in his lap and his *excitement* sent an electric shock up my spine. I would not be distracted just because my body liked the feeling of him beneath me.

Without any further hesitation, I brought my head closer to his face.

I pressed my knife into Kade's neck, but not so hard that it drew blood. My erratic breathing only increased as his shadows wrapped around my waist, holding me in place, not fighting me.

He lay firmly in my grasp. All it would take was one move

and he would be incapacitated, certainly enough so I could flee.

Yet I hesitated. My breath came in ragged pants as I so desperately attempted to summon the courage to end this battle of wills.

"Finally going to let me explain myself?" he asked, his voice rough.

I growled under my breath. I hated that he didn't fight back. I wanted him to make this easier. I *needed* him to show me the man I hated. To fight. Letting me take what I wanted made the possibility that he spoke the truth far too real.

He cocked his eyebrow, patiently watching me as his shadows continued to slither around my waist.

I huffed out a breath. I still held power here. "Right, because I'm feeling extremely trusting while your death shadows hold me hostage."

Kade blinked once, then his shadows loosened from around me instantly. I didn't move my knife. In fact, I pushed harder until I saw a pinprick of blood pool at the tip of the blade.

His eyes darkened, but not with that black swirling ink. Not in anger. No, this time they darkened for the same reason my thighs clamped harder around his waist. A sound from the back of his throat almost distracted me from what I wanted.

Almost.

"Tell me what happened. And know this is the only chance you'll get." I didn't let up on the grip of my dagger. Kade didn't attempt to move it away either.

He stared at me, meeting my gaze, unflinching. "Your father knew his time had come. You saw for yourself Lord West can siphon others' magic. The king believed—truly believed—the plan was for Lord West to steal his magic. If that happened, no one would stand a chance against the dark ones and whoever led them." Kade's lip twitched. "Andras in particular."

He took a breath, his eyes flashing with a deep, devastated look. *Pain.* That couldn't be right.

"I said no, Lana. I told him I couldn't. He begged me to do it. He said they'd take you—" Kade stopped, clearing his throat. "The dangers of letting them have him, his power were too great. He made me promise to make sure he couldn't be brought back. Then he told me to look out for you, and I vowed to, with my life. When I hesitated to go through with his request to end his life, he helped me guide the blade into his heart."

My hand trembled as my lip quivered, but I swallowed it back. Grimacing, I steeled myself against the emotions. Emotions had done nothing for me before. They hadn't saved anyone I loved.

Kade didn't take the opportunity to move, even as my body shook in anger, loosening the foothold I had pinning him to the ground. He stayed under my blade, even though both of us knew it wouldn't take much for him to gain control. "When you came in and he somehow remained alive, I finished it because I promised him I would. I wish there had been any other way. I wish I could take away the pain it caused. To never, ever have done something to hurt you so deeply."

"Why would you agree to protect me? Or do anything my father asked? You've never spoken highly of the king," I asked, needing the answer.

"I was wrong about your father. He's one of the bravest men I've ever met," Kade said firmly. "And you know I'd give my life to protect you, and not just because of the vow I made to your father."

"Don't," I commanded, finding the strength I needed. I *wouldn't* go there with this man. "How do I know you're telling the truth? This could all be an elaborate lie, and I'd never know because the only person who could corroborate it died."

"You're right. I have nothing to offer to prove myself. I

swear to you it's the truth. While here, you'll find many things about me that you didn't know. But it won't change this truth, Little Rebel."

We stared at each other, and his unyielding gaze seemed so convincing.

The grey in his eyes called to me, begging me. Something deep within me thrummed to life processing Kade's words, urging me to believe him. Even though I didn't want to.

"Your father died to save you—and his mate."

I dropped the dagger, the breath from my chest gone. "What did you say?"

"There's no way he should have been able to say it, except for a blessing from the Fates themselves at his sacrifice. But in the end, he spoke with conviction of the queen being his mate. I—" He exhaled. "I thought you should know that he loved you as much as he loved his *mate*."

Tears pooled in my eyes, and I slumped forward onto Kade's chest. The hate and anger I'd desperately clung to dissipated. He seemed so sincere. It made everything worse. I didn't want his words to make sense, but if my mother and father had been mates, it did.

I had been *so close* to trusting Kade with my entire soul, to loving him. To giving him my heart. Yet he killed my father, then killed the people in the square without a moment's hesitation. How could the man who stole my heart and the murderer be one and the same?

I wanted Ian to be here. He would know how to navigate the onslaught of information. He'd be here to catch me as I free-fell from the overwhelming feelings this brought. He'd help me discern the truth.

Emotions overtook my common sense, my body shuddering with a sob. Kade moved slowly, like he thought he'd scare me away with his movements, before he brought his hands up to me, wrapping his arms around me. The gesture snapped me out of it long enough to scramble off of him.

"Don't touch me," I cried, suddenly desperate to regain my controlled facade.

I had to get away. I wouldn't be vulnerable. *Couldn't* be vulnerable. Not with him. Allowing him to comfort me would betray my father. Good reason or not, this man killed him. And many others, based on today's ordeal.

The jumble of thoughts in my head banged around so much I wanted to scream.

"Please," he whispered. "Don't hide from me. Let me help."

"You've done enough." I stood, embracing the sharp twisting pain separating from his touch brought, and ran from his room, stumbling into my own.

I needed time. Space.

The king and queen had been mates.

The love I'd witnessed my entire life, the love I pined for, had been the truest form of love. A love that shouldn't exist. And my father loved me with that same fierceness.

The man who took me in without hesitation and raised me as his own.

The man who gave his life to keep me safe.

I fell onto my hands and knees inside the room across the hall and screamed, letting the wretched noise force itself from me.

I crawled to the bed, pulling myself up before I collapsed in a heap. A useless lump of a Fae, stuck in this Fates-forsaken world with this Fates-forsaken man and his followers.

I needed my friends more now than ever before. I needed my mother. Fae I could trust implicitly, who I knew could help me process this entire disaster.

I lay in silence for minutes, an hour, maybe longer. Time meant nothing to me. I rolled, staring, my gaze transfixed upon the wooden beams above me.

The eerie quiet did nothing to calm my mind or its racing thoughts.

I knew it was only a matter of time before Kade's shadows appeared. I felt their presence before I put eyes on them. They had a mind of their own, and I liked them far better than I liked Kade himself right now. Their weight soothed a deep part of me, allowing me to breathe in my desperate search for respite. Even if I couldn't stand to allow myself to be with Kade in this moment, I would greedily take the relief his shadows brought. Even if they'd murdered the people in the square.

What the hell was wrong with me?

They creeped from the door, slowly building, until they completely enveloped me.

I wanted to push them away, but I couldn't. It felt right being in them. I lost the ability to care what that meant.

They were a comforting weight, a blanket, soothing my breaking heart. Easing the tension from my very soul.

I didn't need to wait to know if he was near. I just spoke. "I planned to hurt you tonight. Hurt you so I could escape and return home. Flee so I could save Ian and the rest of my friends."

He waited before he responded. "How many times do I have to tell you? You wouldn't have been able to enter the void without me, let alone survive it."

"Why? Because whoever your king is hasn't deemed me worthy enough to enter that land? Hasn't felt it necessary to bless those who wish to return to their home?" I sneered. Anger was a living, breathing being inside of me. My cheeks heated, burning with the feeling of it.

Kade stepped into my room, walking toward me cautiously. His shadows receded slightly so I could see his face. Concern was etched into his brow as he kneeled beside the bed.

"Blessing is the wrong word, even if I did say that before," he murmured, "but no, you have not been *blessed* to enter the void."

My breathing turned more ragged, more panicked. How would I ever escape? How would I ever be able to fulfill this quest my father—no, my king provided for me?

"Illiana, breathe," Kade whispered. "We cannot return yet. There is something I have to do. Someone I must see first. Someone you need to speak to as well. Cassandra—you heard Storm and I talk of her. She's a seer like Vivienne." He sucked in a sharp breath. "After we speak with her, I promise you I will return you to Brookmere. I will make sure you get wherever you wish to go, unharmed. I will fight for Ian, your mother, whoever needs it." He brushed a hand over my hair once, then pulled away. "Whatever you ask of me, my heart and my sword are yours to command."

Tears pricked my eyes once more, and I was thankful for the darkness surrounding us. Hiding at least the last bit of dignity I had left.

"Why?"

His fingertips brushed the tears from my cheeks, even as more fell. So much for hiding. I should have known. "Because watching you break at my hands is something I cannot endure again. Something I will not endure again."

"Why not just let me go now?"

"The king knows I have returned, and he will stop at nothing if I ignore a direct order again. It is why we shifted our course today. Having you at the palace will already be dangerous enough, so I will not risk you getting caught in the crossfire of his rage and punishment at my disobedience."

Kade reached out and let his hand wrap around my face, his thumb stroking softly over my skin.

"I don't trust you."

"Oh, Little Rebel," he murmured. "I would hardly expect you to trust me after what I've done. Let alone right now."

He stood up, reaching forward, but hesitated. His jaw ticked and his hand fell back to his side, clenching into a fist before he turned to walk away. His shadows lifted from my body, trailing behind him, and the loss of their weight left me chilled.

"Trust or not though, I vowed to your father to keep you safe. No matter the cost. I swear to you, Illiana, I intend to keep that promise, until my dying breath. My life is yours. Whether you want my protection or not."

CHAPTER 11

IAN

The clanging chains reverberated down the long hall toward my cell.

Clink.

Thud.

Clink.

Thud.

It felt like days since I had seen anyone other than a Royal Guard shoving half-moldy food through the small bars. I didn't know whether to be worried or mentally preparing for another round of torture from Andras. Chains could mean any number of things.

Things I didn't want to think about anymore.

Lying in the corner of the cell, I left my back to the door, uninterested in seeing who stood before me. The metal tray scraped along the stone as it settled through the slot. Gentler than on any other occasion.

"Ian," a soft, delicate voice whispered.

Her voice faltered and cracked as she said my name. Yet I didn't move. I wanted to, but my limbs ached, the soreness of my body weighing me down.

"Ian, get up." Her voice was a little stronger this time.

Groaning, I rolled to lay on my back as I twisted my head toward the cell door.

Kalliah.

Pulling every last ounce of strength from the Fates themselves, I forced myself onto my knees, gripping the wall like it would provide any sort of assistance.

"If you know what's good for you," Corbin spat, "you'll walk over here and pick up this gracious meal."

I flinched at the sound of the man I'd trusted with my life. With Lana's life. What happened to one of my truest friends? How could he have turned so vile so fast?

Slowly, I pulled myself into a standing position and shuffled the short distance to the cell door, leaning on the wall the entire time. Panting, I waited for one of them to speak again.

A few moments later, Kalliah broke the silence. "Ian, you have to agree to work with Andras. It is the only way you stay alive. Lana is gone—vanished. Your loyalty to her and to the dead king will get you nowhere."

"Be reasonable, *friend,*" Corbin sneered, barely giving me a moment to process that Corbin wasn't the only one who had given up on Lana. "Andras has taken over the palace. The dark ones answer to him. He is set to be the next ruler of Brookmere. The queen is locked in the eastern tower along with this traitor in chains." He nudged Kalliah, and she banged into the cell. My hands clenched into fists at my side. "And if rumors serve true, the queen is refusing to speak. Andras will marry her, or he will have no choice but to find Lana and claim her as his."

Everything turned red. My vision shifted, and fire boiled in my veins at Corbin speaking about Andras claiming Lana so casually.

I lurched for the cell bars. "You disgust me," I spit at him. My body protested the sudden movement. I barely recognized my gravelly voice.

Laughs from the shadows sounded, and two additional guards came into view. "You're right, Corbin. He's so easily riled when she's mentioned."

Corbin grinned, but Kalliah said nothing. I noticed the chains around her ankles and wrists. Those were the sounds I'd heard. Not chains for me, but chains *on* her.

Yet she still insisted on siding with Andras?

"Kalliah, what happened?"

Her eyes widened ever so slightly before she shook her head.

This couldn't be happening. After all we had been through. For everything we had set out to accomplish together and for the two of them to turn so quickly destroyed the hope I remained clinging to. A soul-crushing pain flared in my chest.

"He'll never find her if she does not want to be found." The sentence took far too long to speak with my still-healing ribs from last night's "entertainment."

Corbin snickered. "She has nowhere to go. Nowhere to run. Without you or any of her other friends by her side, she will have no choice but to come crawling back. Begging to be saved."

I shot my arm out, grabbing him through the bars, smashing his face against the cool metal. "How *dare* you speak about your princess that way. She called you a friend, and this is how you repay her kindness?"

My heart beat erratically, my cheeks flushed in anger. I could not believe the words coming out of his mouth.

"Ian," Kalliah said sternly, "take your food and think about what I said."

The guards grabbed her by the shoulder and started forcing her back down the hall.

I released my hold on Corbin. "Kalliah, it will be okay," I tried to shout, but it came out as a wheeze. "Be strong for Lan."

"Shut up. I liked you better when you were unconscious." Corbin sneered again. "Might I recommend the soup? One of your personal favorites. Perhaps that tongue of yours will burn so we won't have to listen to your nonsense anymore. Perhaps it will help you to remember who our true leader is."

Corbin turned on his heel and didn't spare me a second glance as the footsteps receded down the hall.

With the temporary rush of adrenaline gone, my shoulders dropped. I stumbled and collapsed to the ground. How had things gotten to this point? Where the fuck was Lana?

Wallowing would do me no good. Rotting in this cell would not be the way I died. I needed my strength if I had any hope of fighting back. Even if it came in small packages like these pathetic excuses for meals, if one could even call them that.

I reached for the tray, holding a single cup of soup. The container released no steam, which made my stomach turn, thinking about eating it cold. The likelihood I could keep this down was a longshot.

Fates, there was nothing I hated more than vegetable soup. That asshole knew that too.

Vegetable soup.

I frowned, pausing.

Fucking. Vegetable. Soup.

Corbin knew I hated it more than life itself. Hell, we provided vegetable soup at all of the Hidden Henchman drops, just to try to get it out of the palace walls. Often joking about how we would rather battle a strox than eat another bite.

Without hesitation, I grabbed the bowl off the tray and sure enough, there was something underneath. A small slip of paper.

I immediately grabbed it and put it in my pocket, knowing

I only had a few more minutes before the guards returned to collect the tray.

I gulped down the soup as fast as I could, holding my nose and reminding myself to be thankful for any sustenance. My healing magic worked faster after a meal.

Just as I finished chewing on the last chunk of potato, the guards returned and collected the tray. Laughing at the mess I had made down my shirt.

I didn't care.

Once the final door slammed shut for the evening, I pulled the paper from my pocket.

My eyes widened as I read its contents.

"HH not here. Plans might not be our strong suit, but trust us. Be ready."

I couldn't help the smile teasing across my lips.

My friends hadn't abandoned me. Or Lan.

I *was* going to escape. Then I'd bring Andras to his knees for ever daring to think he had power over us.

Sleep came easily that evening, knowing I needed as much rest as possible. An excited energy thrummed in my veins, like I'd so often felt when plotting Hidden Henchman drops. Purpose drove me forward in all things.

A whisper in the night pulled me from my slumber.

"Ian, darling."

My eyes flew open at the voice that shouldn't be down here. Fear and disbelief collided inside of me, my body instantly on high alert.

"Your Majesty?" I rose, finding movement less challenging than it had been earlier. Whether through my resolve or forcing that Fates-awful food down, my abilities were finally returning to their normal state.

I bowed as soon as I got to my feet.

"Stop that right away. Come here," she beckoned, reaching her hand toward me through the bars.

Her cold touch surprised me, and I wrapped my other hand around hers to try to help warm the queen. "It's not safe for you down here." I kept my voice low, just as she had.

"Oh, Ian, you look… What have they done—"

"Don't worry about me, Your Majesty," I interrupted, cutting off her concerns. She had enough on her plate without worrying about me. "Please tell me why you're here. You've put yourself in grave danger."

"Do you know where she is?" The queen's voice cracked. "Is she alive?"

I squeezed her hand between mine. "I have to believe we'd know if she wasn't. Though I don't know what happened or where she'd go."

She nodded, and her body shook. "Losing them both—" She raised her other hand to her mouth, closing her eyes. "Well, there wouldn't be much left for me if I lose them both."

"Don't say that. They'd want you to be strong. The king would want you to fight."

She whimpered, then fell forward, letting go of my hands and clutching the bars.

"Your Majesty?" I asked, frantically trying to see if she had an injury I'd missed. I reached through, touching the cloak she wore.

"Ian, you must escape. You must find her." The queen's delicate fingers traced over the bars as her voice grew more distressed. "Illiana is the key to our kingdom's survival. Alister insisted she return to Valeford should anything ever happen. He made me swear to it over and over. Especially in these last few months as his health deteriorated."

Her lips trembled and she winced. I reached for her hand, needing to reassure her somehow. To do something. Anything, because right now, it appeared the queen was fighting an adversary I couldn't see. And losing.

Her once brilliantly optimistic and kind eyes met mine. They'd deadened, and the sight of it hit me harder than I expected.

"Do you understand what I'm saying, Ian? Illiana *must* get to Valeford."

"Why Valeford? What must she do? Does she know?" A thousand thoughts raced through my mind as Queen Roxana shivered again, violently.

She needed to get out of this dark, damp place. Lana couldn't lose her mother too.

Queen Roxana shook her head. "I do not know. He couldn't tell me specifics." She cried out. "I just know there is something she must do, and it begins in Valeford." She finished the sentence through gritted teeth.

Her body convulsed and a tiny amount of blood formed beneath her nostrils.

"Your Majesty! What's happening?"

"Andras's mind magic is strong." Her voice came out barely a whisper. "Fighting it is getting harder. Too hard. I must go before I am caught out of my chambers. Remember, my sweet boy, she needs you. I need you. This kingdom needs Illiana. By royal decree, I order you to accompany Princess Illiana to Valeford, Captain Stronholm."

Nodding and placing my hand over my heart, I swore, "With my dying breath, I will ensure Lana accomplishes what she needs to. We will save this kingdom, Your Majesty. We will save you."

One last breath, one last look, was all she gave me, before she turned and fled into the darkness of the night. I listened to the whisper of her slippers on the stone floors until they disappeared up the stairs before I took my next breath.

She had given me a royal decree, and I would be damned if I didn't follow it until my dying breath. Just as I'd sworn.

Lana would make it to Valeford if it was the last thing I did in this world.

CHAPTER 12

LANA

My entire body rebelled as the morning light cascaded into the room.

It couldn't be morning. I hadn't even slept an hour with the unnerving sensation of Raya watching me through the night. I swear the hyper-focused Fae slept with one eye open.

And unnerving was putting it mildly.

Beyond the sensation of my jailer's watchful gaze, I couldn't stop replaying what Kade had told me about my father and his death. It was a *choice*. A choice he'd made for me, if I were to believe Kade. It certainly didn't feel like a lie last night. Or now.

Then, even more shocking than his request for Kade to kill him, my father had a mate. How many times had they told me mates didn't exist in this world? The strongest bond in every fantasy, every myth in our libraries, and he sacrificed it for me. How much pain had his decision caused my mother? Would she forgive me once she discovered the truth?

The weight of his love, of his final moments, felt like too much to truly comprehend.

I peeked over my shoulder, Raya's back to me for the first

time all night. Since she didn't seem to be in a hurry, I rose, tiptoeing to the tub hiding behind a thin curtain in the corner of the room. The water remained unused last night, which meant it'd be freezing.

I dipped my pinky finger below the surface, shivering, but quickly stripped myself of my dusty clothes anyway, dropping into the tub. I'd be a fool to pass up an actual bath for the first time in… I didn't even know how long it had been anymore.

"What if I had saved that water for myself?"

Raya's cold voice made me jump, the soap flying out of my hand. I grimaced at her as her head poked around the tattered curtain. She burst out laughing. "Hurry up. I'm washing too. And not in front of you."

Grumbling under my breath, I cleansed myself as best I could under the circumstances. Even if it only lasted for a few moments, feeling clean lifted my spirits.

Raya and I changed places in the makeshift washroom so we could each have some semblance of privacy. Just as I finished putting on my tunic, a quick rap on the door sounded. As I opened it, Storm ushered me into the hall.

"You talked to him."

I frowned, finishing a fast braid in my hair. "Since that isn't a question, I'm assuming you two were gossiping late into the evening?"

Storm smiled. "I'm just grateful he told you something."

"Why?" I pushed. "Why do you care?"

Storm put his hands on his hips, sighing before he shook his head. "I've known him for years. He carries a heavy burden, and with it, he thinks he has to protect everyone. He—"

The door slammed open and Kade stood in the frame, glancing between the two of us. When his gaze stopped on me, something flickered in his eyes. Hope? No. I couldn't quite place it, but it disappeared in an instant.

"Are we ready?"

Storm snorted. "I just walked out of the door a moment before you." He shook his head again. "I'll obtain our horses from Opal."

He stalked down the corridor, leaving Kade and me alone in the hall.

It seemed strange after the horrors of yesterday that anyone would do this group a favor. Letting them stay, caring for their horses—it all seemed like a lot to give when Kade had murdered two people yesterday. Unless fear drove their compliance.

I wrapped my arms around my waist, nausea churning in my stomach as I thought about the execution we'd witnessed —what Kade had done. Too much guilt lay wrapped up in allowing myself to feel the overwhelming pull toward him.

Kade's shadows lingered, inching closer as we stood awkwardly in the hall.

"I'm surprised anyone would help you all," I said, forcing the harsh words to convince my heart of what my mind believed to be true.

Kade's face softened. "Lana." He took a step forward but immediately stopped himself. He'd been doing that more and more. "We'll be downstairs when you're ready."

My heart squeezed, a painful weight in my chest at the thought of the Kade I'd known versus the person I'd seen here.

I nodded, recoiling from the different feelings this man brought out of me, but followed close behind.

We'd barely hit the first floor of the tavern before Raya's footsteps sounded hurriedly behind us. Jax leaned over the counter, talking to the owner of the tavern, who handed him a large brown sack.

"Until next time, gorgeous." He winked at her and strode toward us. "Horses are saddled and ready."

Upon entering the stables, it became all too apparent I would be riding with someone else, again. Why I thought they could have procured another horse overnight, I do not know. But I'd stupidly hoped.

Jax and Storm mounted their enormous chestnut stallions and moved toward the main road, discussing something in hushed tones. There was absolutely no way in this world, or any other, I would ride with Raya, in fear for my very life. Which meant, reluctantly, I joined Kade next to his steed as he mounted.

A calming whisper of shadows fluttered down my arm. I hated how soothing they were. How much I wanted them close.

I can do this.

Kade reached for me, swinging me up onto the horse. His hands braced my hips, the position forced me flush against his body.

I swallowed. Fates, being pressed up against him wouldn't help my clashing thoughts. His shadows swirled around me and whipped playfully through my braid. I tried swatting them away, without success.

Kade leaned closer, wrapping his hands around the reins. "Hold on. Onyx is a feisty ride." His whisper in my ear elicited a full-body shudder before he spurred the horse into action.

Damn him.

The relentless pace of the group, combined with my stiff posture to keep from colliding with Kade, made the ride brutal. We moved swiftly throughout the dead lands. I took in our surroundings again, unable to comprehend how someplace so lifeless could be so beautiful.

Kade's silence allowed me to replay the events of the past few days over and over in my mind. From the moment I told him my secrets and shared my bed with him, to my father's death, and then discovering Mysthaven. All of it. After hearing him out about my father, regardless of whether he would earn my forgiveness or not, there was still one thing I couldn't come to terms with.

The action I couldn't get over.

The fact that Kade had killed those Fae in the streets and looked as though he enjoyed doing it.

It ate away at the dark recesses of my brain. Something inside of me screamed that I didn't know the full story. That there could be some "perfectly reasonable" explanation for their deaths too, like my father's. Were they actually traitors to the crown or was something else happening? From each person's comments, I couldn't be sure what was the truth.

My father's saying—*Never trust something is as it appears at first glance*—scratched at the back of my brain.

But Kade's eyes had been so black. Dark, almost in the way the dark ones back home looked.

The horses slowed from our canter, Storm calling for a small reprieve for the animals.

I shifted, but Kade enveloped me, tensing as though he thought I planned to jump off the horse. "Don't even think about it," he whispered in my ear.

I leaned forward, pulling away from him, trying to escape how completely he overtook every one of my senses. "You should have used some of your precious time last night to bathe. You smell as if you rolled in garbage."

He didn't though. At least not enough to mask the scent I was beginning to crave whenever he wasn't near me. He smelled like my favorite mornings in Brookmere, when rain faded and left behind the promise of a new day. Crisp morning air and nature, completely satisfied and filled with hope.

I hated him for it.

Kade's dark laugh stirred that thing deep inside of me I had yet to figure out. "You interrupted those plans with your lackluster escape, Little Rebel. Now you can suffer the consequences."

The spark between us trailed up my spine, as if it enjoyed his teasing. My body was a traitor.

"You know," I said, my voice cracking from pushing my desire away to focus on more important things, "out of all the fucked-up things that have happened to me recently, I cannot get over you killing those Fae yesterday. Were their crimes so heinous it warranted their deaths? Publicly like that? Especially when your friends questioned their guilt?"

Kade stiffened behind me.

Jax scoffed as he trotted closer to Onyx. "For someone he loves, you sure do act like you don't know him at all."

I gaped, my mouth wide at the insinuation. *I* didn't know him? Jax didn't know his friend at all if he thought Kade Blackthorn loved me.

"You have no idea what you are talking about," I said, sitting straighter. I needed distance from the warmth caressing the skin at my back.

Jax stared me down, narrowing his eyes before shaking his head. "He didn't murder those Fae."

"Jax." Kade's voice held a warning.

Jax held up a hand toward his friend. "No, I know you think this is safer, but she's going to need to trust us where we're going."

"I saw it with my own eyes. Those Fae died. Snuffed out by his shadows. Over what?"

Jax growled, "You saw what you were meant to see."

Kade tensed behind me.

Raya snorted. "Don't worry, Princess, they don't tell me anything either. I'm too much of a *liability*."

That gave me pause. Raya seemed an integral part of their group. Why wouldn't they tell her? "I don't understand."

"The king has too much access to me," Raya explained, surprising me that she responded herself. Or at all. She clucked and encouraged her horse forward, the rest of us following suit. "He molded my mind magic to what he wanted me to be as a child."

Kade's shadows settled around me, and I let them.

"I wasn't born in a palace," she said. "Certainly not surrounded by family and loved ones."

Jax snorted. "Are there such things as loved ones in the palace?"

Raya snickered along with him. "Fair point. As I said before, I was dropped on the doorstep, inside the royal gates, abandoned by my worthless parents. I had to fight every day to survive there. When the king discovered I had the ability to connect through minds, he didn't hesitate to use it to his advantage. Forcing me to enter life as a Guardian, to train not only my mind but my body as well. I rose in the ranks quickly and became one of the elites, just like the rest of these fools."

"We are all elite of course." Jax held out his arms, spanning them over his outfit. "The Guardians of Mysthaven. The best of the king's soldiers." He winked.

Raya rolled her eyes, something I found her doing often when Jax spoke. "Whatever the king did in our private training sessions altered the way I use my magic. Through his training, he has access to my mind at any time. Over the years, I have learned how to shield him from seeing everything, but without the ability to safely test some of our theories, we don't know what the king can and can't see through me."

I gasped. "The king is that powerful?"

"Yes," Kade said from behind me, and I didn't miss the way he shifted his hands on me, tightening his hold. "He can wield several other elements too—air and fire. He is powerful, as was your father due to their royal bloodlines."

I glanced back toward Raya. The king's power aside, that level of intrusion, especially from such a young age? It was awful. The king, so far, sounded far from a good and just ruler. The fear the others had of him was palpable.

She cleared her throat. "So while I know some of the

dealings occurring in our group, and help however I can, I am not privy to everything."

"Help with what?" I questioned, but Kade spoke at the same time.

"Raya, you know we do it just as much for your protection as ours. We trust you, we just can't take any chances that he will find out about anything we're doing. It would ruin all we have worked toward. All that we hope to accomplish."

"You don't think I know that?" Raya snapped. "Of course I do, but it doesn't make it any easier to be left on the outside."

A strained silence surrounded the group as we trudged along. Raya and I were more alike than she realized. I could empathize with her feeling of being left on the outside because I had felt it my entire life.

It's why I fought so hard to establish the Hidden Henchman. Watching others take on risk, take on life while I remained safe in a guarded palace had never sat well with me. It still didn't.

As a warrior, it would be difficult. As a Guardian, that feeling must be tenfold.

If what Jax said was true, and Kade didn't really kill those people, what happened to them? Where did they go? An explanation lay within reach, but any hope I had of obtaining those answers in Raya's presence remained slim.

We moved through a tunnel of leafless trees, their branches forming an interconnected archway above us. Thorny bushes lining the edges made it impossible to escape the well-established trail without our skin being torn to shreds.

Kade shifted in the saddle and his arm loosened, though still resting on my hips. The hair's breadth between us did nothing to calm the electric current of energy sparking as it always did. His presence wrapped around me. If Jax and Storm spoke the truth, then perhaps I had been too harsh a judge.

Though he'd made it impossible to continue trusting him blindly, I could at least refrain from assuming the worst immediately.

While I would never be over the death of my father, maybe, just maybe I could grant Kade a bit of a reprieve from my loathing. Right now, I needed one moment not to worry about the warring emotions inside of me. So I'd use him in the same way, all for a second of peace and the possibility of returning home quicker if I cooperated.

At least that's what I told myself.

"I'm too tired to fight this anymore," I said, as I stopped resisting the lull of riding in front of him and nestled my back against his chest.

Kade sighed. A strange relief fell over me as our bodies connected. One he must have felt as well, if his sigh served as any indication.

"I'll take any excuse you need to give if it means touching you again, Little Rebel." His whispered words brushed over my skin. This might have been a bad choice.

I tried to keep those thoughts at the forefront, but Fates, the comfort his arms provided—*no!*

I needed a distraction. "How much long—" I started to ask as we exited the tunnel of trees, when Onyx reared on his hind legs, neighing in fear.

Kade's shadows burst outward over the ground, and I saw what startled the horse.

Dark ones.

A horde of them.

I cracked my neck, preparing for another battle. Apparently, the Fates took my need for a distraction literally.

Storm dismounted, sending a massive fireball toward the incoming attackers, creating a space for us to gather ourselves.

Jax and Raya paired up together instantly, working on slaughtering the assailants to the left side of the tree tunnel. The two slashed their blades from their horses with ease. It was clear why they were Mysthaven's elite Guardians in the way they moved.

My gaze remained transfixed on them and their deadly dance of swords and magic.

Jax moved as if he knew exactly where Raya would be next. The two proved to be an absolutely lethal combination.

Kade, Storm, and I shifted to the right side of the tunnel.

I went to unsheathe my dagger as Kade produced a sword from the horse's pack, thrusting it into my hands.

"Show them what you've got, Little Rebel," Kade said with a wink as he dismounted in a smooth movement. Shadows swirled around his feet, billowing into clouds around him.

His arrogance really did know no bounds; we were being attacked, for Fates' sake, and he managed to wink. My skin warmed at the gesture, which felt much more like the Kade I knew. A weight clearly lifted in him after telling me the truth about my father last night.

He pulled his sword from his waist and then, with his right hand, conjured shadows into the shape of a sword. An actual sword.

A freaking shadow sword.

My jaw dropped as the shadows thickened, matching his other blade, becoming less and less transparent.

"Is it bigger than before?" Jax shouted, stabbing through a dark one while still on his horse.

Storm grunted. "Definitely more solid. Harder and longer too."

"Hopefully he knows how to wield it," Jax laughed.

"Shut up, you idiots," Raya scolded, cutting off Storm and Jax from continuing their teasing.

A dark one screamed and stole my attention, running toward me. Crouching slightly, I welcomed the attack. I would prove to all of these Guardians I could hold my own too.

Kade's shadows exploded outward from his body,

knocking out a group of ten dark ones before my feet even landed on the dusty ground. From the corner of my eye, I saw fireballs fly through the air.

Rushing forward, I took the opportunity to deliver the killing blow to a dark one Kade was battling. Slicing into the man's stomach, I hummed in satisfaction as blood gushed from the wound while he fell to the ground.

Without a moment's hesitation I turned, moving on to my next target.

A caress skimmed over the length of my back. Kade's shadows. At first, they lingered, but as I approached the next attacker, the shadows formed a solid cover over my body. Like armor.

Shadow armor.

Well, that was kind of cool.

"You were holding back in Brookmere," I shouted over my shoulder.

Kade chuckled behind me but didn't answer.

Using the techniques Ian taught me, I skillfully took down two more dark ones without receiving a single scratch.

He would be proud of me. The thought stuck in my gut, and a void hollowed out inside of me. I missed him desperately.

Jax and Raya left a pile of bodies in their wake as they moved swiftly through the onslaught.

Kade moved off to the side to deal with another group of dark ones, while Storm backed himself closer to me.

Back-to-back, we battled a few more charging around us. Storm was an incredible fighter, and his fire magic was entrancing. If Ian could ever forgive Storm for knocking him out, together they could be unstoppable.

A figure to my left caught my eye, but I didn't have time to look as I took on a particularly large man. Though twice my size, I refused to back down, meeting my attacker blow for blow.

When another appeared from behind the one I fought, he lunged, slamming me away from Storm. I stumbled. Before the dark one could swing his blade down over me, I rolled, swiping at his ankles.

I caught him, a howl ripping from his throat. To my left, the figure from before—a large, dark catlike creature—took form and prowled before pouncing on the attacker whose ankles I'd sliced.

"What the hell is that thing?" I shrieked at Storm, wielding my blade against my first attacker since the one who'd shaken me to the ground remained preoccupied with the panther.

"It's Jax," Storm shouted over his shoulder. "Show off."

"Tits and daggers," I hissed, sinking my blade into my assailant's gut.

The man fell to his knees, eyes rolling, as Jax growled. I turned, checking to ensure his safety when a gurgling shout drew my attention from behind.

Before I could raise my weapon to defend myself, the dark one on his knees lunged forward with his blade. Storm jumped in front of me, pushing me out of the way, as he plunged his dagger straight into the dark one's chest.

"Not tonight, asshole." Storm ripped his weapon from the dark one's body.

"There's nowhere to hide. More will come. So many more." The dark one laughed as he choked on his own blood, falling to the ground for good this time. Even now, he wheezed, "We're stronger than you could ever imagine."

Pulling myself up from the dirt, I turned to thank Storm but shouted instead.

A small dagger stood lodged into Storm's upper thigh. Dangerously close to a main artery.

The adrenaline from the battle must have dampened whatever pain he felt, because it wasn't until I screamed that Storm looked down and saw the knife protruding from his leg. He fell to his knees.

"Storm, no!" I yelled. "Kade!"

With a final blast of his shadows, Kade knocked out the few remaining dark ones near him and ran over to Storm and me, panting heavily.

"Lana, it's fine, I'll heal." Storm winced.

The adrenaline at seeing the dagger in Storm subsided. Just because I lacked healing abilities, didn't mean these Fae did. Ian had healed himself plenty of times from injuries. Storm would be able to as well. I breathed deeply as relief calmed my original fear.

Jax shifted back into his Fae form and approached, standing beside Kade.

"I got it. It's taking you long enough, you oversized baby," Jax said as he reached down and removed the knife from Storm's leg.

"It's been some time since anyone broke skin," Storm countered.

Kade ripped a piece of cloth from his tunic and tied it above the wound to slow the bleeding.

We stood in silence, breathing heavily, waiting for Storm's natural healing ability to kick in.

"Well, that was fun." Jax grinned. "Not too bad, Princess."

I huffed, handing the sword from Kade's pack back to him.

"Told you she has been trained well," Storm said, taking a step forward. His leg wobbled, causing the others to hesitate.

The flow of blood had slowed, but now, black circles peeked out from the makeshift bandage.

"For fuck's sake, what is that?" Raya asked.

Storm untied the fabric from his leg, wincing.

"Kade, are you seeing this?" Jax asked. "His skin is turning…turning black."

My heart stilled and the sinking feeling inside of me worsened as I noted Jax's expression laced with worry.

Slowly looking up and meeting Jax's gaze, Kade spoke.

"We need to get to Mount Legion, and fast before it spreads any farther."

I jerked my head toward Kade. "He is going to be okay though, right?"

Storm shook once, and he swayed, suddenly unsteady on his feet. "I have you, brother," Kade said. He looked grim as he picked up Storm and carried him toward the horses.

He pushed Storm up onto Onyx to sit slumped over, and as soon as he had, I grabbed his arm. "That blade was meant for me, Kade." Tears welled in my eyes. "He has to be all right."

Kade's jaw tightened, but before he could speak, a hand shot out in front of me. Raya offered the reins of Storm's horse. "Looks like you're on your own for this stretch."

Nodding, I grabbed the reins. I swallowed, watching Storm's body, swaying still from atop the saddle. Kade stood next to me, grasping Onyx's reins in one hand.

He brushed his thumb across my cheek but didn't offer me reassurances. He let a shaky breath escape before turning to his friend.

"Do you need to lean against me?"

"I'll stay seated. Get on, you overbearing ass," Storm mumbled back.

Kade mounted Onyx behind Storm, glancing at me with a fear I'd never seen in his eyes.

"We need to ride. Now." Kade's voice faltered. "If we don't get him to a healer soon, we could lose him for good."

CHAPTER 13

LANA

We rode hard through the barren land.

The pathways twisted and turned through more of the wild, wind-shaped trees.

Storm rode with Kade, barely sitting upright as the horses galloped faster and faster. Kade's shadows worked overtime holding him in place.

Not once did the horses falter as they blazed their way through the terrain and into the mountainous region of the land, leading straight into a city. The city I could only assume my companions called home.

No one spoke, too scared to think about losing Storm to the poison. He groaned every so often, and Kade quietly whispered to him each time.

Tears formed in the corners of my eyes as the wind whipped around us. My hands raw from holding onto the reins too tightly for so long.

Kade shouted over his shoulder. "Stay behind us when we get to the palace, Little Rebel. Don't draw attention to yourself."

The air racing past us whipped my acknowledgement

away, and when Kade looked over his shoulder, his eyes held a desperation in them I wouldn't ignore.

"Please," he yelled.

I nodded, trying to give him a reassuring smile.

A few hours later, we passed the first sprinkling of houses along the outskirts of the city. What I beheld amazed me. The homes were built from beautiful gray and black stones. Even with the monochrome colors, the beauty astounded me. Light danced along the smooth glassy black portions of the stones, blinking as if showing off. The trail we followed arced upward, taking us into the mountains. The longer we rode, the more the buildings seemed erected as if they were extensions of the mountains themselves.

We climbed higher still.

After riding on the stone street, passing homes and curious gazes from the crowds throughout various points of the ride, large giant gates loomed before us. While the homes and buildings of the city were made from rocks and stone, the entire fortress of a palace protruded from the very mountain itself.

It screamed danger and power as turrets and stone walls jutted from the mountain, like the palace had always been a part of the stone and rock.

Raya, Jax, and Kade each rendered a salute of sorts, touching a fist to their shoulder and bowing their heads as they approached the guards at the gates. The two men standing at attention dipped their heads, and the steel gates opened just enough for us to pass through as we continued up the road to the palace.

Where the palace at Ellevail stood bright, filled with large windows to observe the gardens, this palace in Mysthaven was dark. The windows were smaller, and the glass appeared blacked out, tinted in a way I had never seen before. Columns of stone further accented the fact that parts of the walls seemed to be made of the mountains themselves.

We slowed the horses to a trot as we approached the massive staircase leading to the entrance of the palace. The intricately carved doors, lined in a metal I didn't recognize, opened with a slow creak.

Reaching the edge of the stairs, Jax leapt off his horse and disappeared through a smaller side door hidden under the stairs. He moved with steady purpose to retrieve a healer for Storm.

A group of Fae emerged from the front of the castle, descending leisurely down the stairs. One man stood a head above the rest, dressed in all black. A strange power emanated from him, as my feet unconsciously slid back a few inches, before I realized who stood before me.

The king.

His long black cape billowed in the crisp breeze and a glittering obsidian crown sat upon his head. Guards in bright red dress uniforms flanked him on either side and marched down the stairs, stopping every couple of steps and assuming their positions as the king slowly made his way down toward us.

We dismounted, and Kade assisted Storm to his feet. Storm's arm slumped limply over Kade's neck as he barely maintained the ability to stand. My chest tightened as the formidable warrior appeared so weak in Kade's arms. Blood soaked through his pants and dripped down his leg onto the ground. The wound must have opened again on the ride, or perhaps it had never truly begun to heal in the first place. A lanky man adorned by a robe a size too small lifted his chin haughtily. "Announcing King Dargan." He waved his hand and bowed, scrambling backward as the king descended the remaining stairs.

Kade, Storm, and Raya bowed their heads as the king reached the bottom step. I instantly followed. The last thing I wanted to do was upset a king when I so desperately needed to be able to leave this land. None of those gathered on the steps in front of us bothered to look in my direction though.

Kade tensed beside me as we waited for the king to speak.

"You finally decided to grace us with your presence." The king's deep voice echoed, filled with barely restrained rage. "You have kept me waiting."

Kade said nothing, keeping his head bowed. Weren't there more pressing matters than the king belittling his soldiers? Like one of his elite Guardians bleeding out in front of him. The others followed suit after Kade, remaining bowed, as did I, watching through my eyelashes as best I could.

"Waiting for *months*," he seethed. The ice in the king's tone sent an eerie chill racing down my spine. The king sucked in a breath. "In your absence, the traitors of this kingdom have run rampant. Your cadre was left to serve as the enforcers, for which they are clearly not equipped."

He walked toward Kade and circled him like a razorven. A predator through and through, stalking around Kade as if playing with his prey, waiting to strike. I shivered, unaccustomed to the heavy magic lingering in the air around the king, raising the hairs on my neck. I didn't dare lift my head to take in the scene more.

I'd never felt a magic like this before, but with it came an additional sensation. Something dark and foreboding slithering off him. A warning radiated outward, threatening and imposing.

The king stroked a pewter-colored amulet around his neck. "Disobeying me again will not be tolerated. Ever. Lest I remind you of how you will be punished. We do not want another public display, do we? I thought you'd grown tired of it, but perhaps my lessons didn't sink in if you think you can disappear and neglect your duties for so long."

Kade's restraint weakened and his shadows slowly spilled from his fingertips, pooling at his feet. Out of the corner of my eye I saw him raise his head and stare at the king, who now stood directly in front of him.

My heartbeat quickened watching Kade appear so submissive. Except for his shadows, ready for a fight.

I wasn't the only one to notice that either. The king grinned as Kade's shadows grew exponentially.

"We'll have to get that magic back under control, won't we?"

I raised my head enough to see Kade's face. His eyes darkened, that blackness taking over as he watched the king.

Kade dipped his chin. "Storm has been injured and we need to get him to Nadia right away. Dark ones attacked with some sort of poisoned weapon that's preventing him from healing properly."

The king cocked an eyebrow and took a step back, flicking his wrist in a gesture I assumed meant we could stop bowing since the others finally lifted their heads.

Murmurs sounded behind us, and I turned, seeing people standing on the other side of the gates we'd passed through.

My neck ached from keeping it bowed for so long, but I could finally take in my surroundings better. A tingle trailed my spine, the familiar warmth of Kade's presence soothing my anxious soul. I glanced down, noticing it had been from a quick touch of his shadows along my calves.

The king stared at each Guardian, making no move to hurry despite Kade's report on Storm's injury, and the obvious pain of the injured Guardian before him. His strength faded with each moment we stood here.

Finally, King Dargan's gaze landed on me, and a cruel smirk eliminated the warmth I'd felt a second earlier. "And who, may I ask, is this fair maiden? I don't remember picking up strays being one of your missions."

"We found her along our journey and Storm took a liking to her," Kade answered without missing a beat.

Storm nodded in agreement. Even in pain, he winked at me. Though he moaned when he turned his head back.

What the hell are these two doing?

The king's eyes narrowed. "And you think she is welcome here? In my home?"

Kade's jaw ticked.

The king hummed. "I trained my Guardians to be stronger than that. Your soft hearts will get you killed." He looked me over purposefully, lingering on my chest before taking in the rest of my body. His gaze violated my space. It made me feel…less than. He clicked his tongue. "I suppose she's pleasing to the eye. The Guardians already treat my palace like a brothel, so what is one more whore to add to their never-ending list?"

Kade's power radiated off his body as he tried to restrain himself. His shadows flittered like they were itching to escape, pulsing on the ground around him. I knew better than to say anything smart in response, and not just because of Kade's warning. The last thing I needed in this moment was another Fae's attention on me, let alone a king's.

The king gave the four of us one more sweeping glance, halting his studious appraisal at the sound of footsteps running toward us.

Jax returned, trailed by two women.

Kade made a move to pull Storm toward him, but the king grabbed his arm. "You will be dismissed only upon my command."

"He's dying," Kade said, the menacing words flaring the king's eyes.

"Our people are watching. I suggest you do as I say." The king dropped Kade's arm before plastering a sickening smile on his face. He stepped up two of the smooth obsidian stone stairs, grinning at his people.

Then he raised his hands to the crowd, waving, as their cheers filled the air.

I was going to vomit. This King Dargan was cruel, yet compelling. His demeanor was so unlike my father, who loved every single man and woman. He never would have delayed the healing of an injured Fae. Especially one of his own warriors.

"It seems we have something to celebrate, my people," the king said. He spoke now for their benefit, ensuring his words echoed out into the space behind us. His eyes flitted around the crowd, searching, taking everything in. Almost too quickly.

The circular amulet hanging around his neck swayed. I swallowed, watching more closely. It wasn't mere pewter. No, inside, the gem billowed with dark grays, purples, and blacks, swarming. Moving. Even with my lack of magic, I *felt* the thing. I shivered.

"Not only is our beloved Festival set to take place in two days, but the blood moon will also rise that evening. The first time in three years, which means the Fates have deemed it the perfect time to prepare ourselves for a sacrifice. To claim these lands as ours, to keep Mysthaven from collapsing under darkness, and to prove your allegiance to your king. Your faith that I, King Dargan, rule these lands with a just and mighty hand will be rewarded. Two days from now, not only will we hold our annual Festival of Swords, but we will also invoke the Blood Oath." His lip curled up so far, it would haunt me as he took in the gasps and surprise in the crowd. Some clapped, some cheered, but most silently stared. "Warriors, prepare yourselves. For only a few will be found worthy to join the ranks of the Guardians."

An eruption of cries echoed throughout the crowd. Kade, Storm, and Raya stood stiffly beside me, seemingly unnerved by the king's proclamation.

I had no idea what a Blood Oath or a Festival of Swords was, let alone a blood moon serving as the inspiration to hold both. However, one look at my companions and I knew whatever it entailed would not be wholly pleasant.

I shifted toward Storm, whose head bobbed as the pool of blood grew at his feet. I needed to keep him with us, so I whispered, hoping the conversation would keep him conscious. "These people are going wild. They seem pleased. Is the Festival of Swords a celebration?"

Storm's face paled more so than it already was, and he swallowed, but before he could speak, the king turned and began walking toward the steps to return to the palace.

The two women with Jax rushed forward to Storm, grabbing his arms as Jax assisted in holding him up.

Kade's eyes met mine as he passed his friend to the women, and a frantic feeling hit me in the chest. He shook his head almost imperceptibly and turned away from me.

The king, once higher up on the steps, turned back again and waved at the crowd, who grew louder at his attention.

Finally, he beckoned Kade with his hand. He hesitated only slightly before he took the steps, standing two below the king. His shadows sank into his skin, into his being, hiding away fully for the first time since we'd entered these lands.

The king stopped him. "A joyous time indeed for all with the celebrations, knowing our prince will be a part of it."

My stomach rolled, recoiling. Prince? *Prince!*

Kade turned, avoiding eye contact with me altogether, nodding to the crowd alongside the king. Then he raised his hand to wave.

This man wasn't just the king. He was Kade's *father*.

The king gripped Kade's shoulder. "Come, my son, we have much to discuss now that you've returned home."

CHAPTER 14

LANA

Imagining Kade Blackthorn at the end of my blade made training effortless.

Deliciously, violently effortless.

Thud.

Each swing pulled forth more of my internal rage against the Guardians I was now stuck with. They'd left me alone in a room, with no updates for hours. Waiting in a strange place with *nothing* and no way to communicate with them.

Shouting, I swung my blade forward, arcing it against Storm's.

Trapped in this miserable world away from those I loved most while surrounded by a group of liars. And, apparently, a damn prince.

Block.

The latter of whom I could hardly trust. Especially since he'd withheld his royal status. Another lie. Another secret.

Clash.

Deceitful, arrogant ass.

Storm brought his sword down on me in a new parry. The two women Jax had retrieved had immediately disappeared with Storm after the announcement from the king, and I hadn't seen him until this afternoon, when he knocked on my door and insisted we train.

Block.

Sweat covered my body as Storm attacked relentlessly, using each of my successful blocks as fodder for the next attack, never faltering in his movements. For someone so gravely injured yesterday—poisoned, no less—he absolutely did not show it.

"Come on, Lana. I'm technically still recovering. You can do better."

I muttered under my breath as I swung for his now healed leg.

"Oh, low blow, Princess," he said. His blatant smile took away from the jab. "I'll tell you what," Storm teased, circling me. "You knock my blade from my hand in the next five moves and I'll tell you my first name."

"It's not Storm?" I asked, surprised.

He cocked an eyebrow, shaking his head.

I hated the grin spreading over my face as I charged this time, laying down a few solid blows, but not disarming him. My five moves quickly came and went.

"My name isn't enough to inspire your training?" He held his hand to his chest. "I'm wounded. Where's the Hidden Henchman? I'm starting to wonder if Ian taught you anything."

The mention of Ian snapped me out of the fun I was having with Storm. "Don't talk about him!" I spat. I twisted, knocking the sword out of his hand with one final swing. The blade landed on the dirt floor of the ring, dust billowing around it as it settled on the ground.

Both of us stood staring at each other, panting. "Halfway decent, I suppose." Storm smirked, moving first.

I wasn't sure how they healed such a serious wound so swiftly, but all that remained now seemed to be a slight limp. Without a doubt, the magic used to heal him had been extremely powerful. The healer on staff must be as good as Elisabeth. I swallowed a sob as memories of our time together played in my mind.

"That is with me only being at about half capacity. You should absolutely be able to defeat me right now. Even without magic."

My lip curled as my sadness dissipated with his words. I'd spent the last hour channeling all my anger into our training. His mouth shifted my focus from training to him. Never mind that before the healers took him away, I silently begged for him to survive. Despite everything, I couldn't quite hate the man.

No, he'd slithered under my skin just like his *prince* had. "Whatever, Storm."

His smirk disappeared. "Listen to me, Lana, you need to be prepared if you are to survive your time here. Ian taught you well, but there is so much you still need to learn. We need to train. It's the only way to ensure your safety."

I ran a hand through my hair in utter frustration. "All I want to do is get back to Brookmere and save my friends. Save my mother. I will not be here long enough to train." I kicked at the dirt. "Besides, how am I to trust any of you? Every time I turn around, there is another secret being revealed. Another lie to discover. Kade's a damn prince. Funny, he conveniently left that out of every conversation we ever had."

Storm grabbed a pitcher from the side of the ring, filling a glass of water before approaching me with it. He held out his hand, offering me the cool liquid. I grabbed it and downed the glass in a few gulps.

"I know this is *a lot* to take in, but you must know Kade is only doing what is best for his people."

"And kidnapping a princess and bringing her to another world justifies his actions because it's what's best for *his* people? What about *my* people?"

Storm opened and closed his mouth a few times, unable to find the words to counter my fury.

"My turn, Little Rebel."

My attention jerked toward the training ring entrance behind me. I tried to ignore how my stomach fluttered as Kade strode into the ring. I hated how attractive he was, even with the evident rage etched on his face.

"Do you have a death wish?" I asked, raising my weapon.

His smile wiped away all the concern and tension from his face for a brief moment. "At your hands? I wish for everything."

He reached over his shoulder, drawing his sword from its sheath at his back, and stepped into the ring.

Storm walked by him, throwing me a grin over his shoulder. "Make him pay."

"Gladly," I said, bending my knees into a defensive stance.

The second Storm exited the ring, Kade's shadows exploded out of him, exactly like I'd seen when we'd first entered Mysthaven.

"Fucking hell, Kade," Storm shouted, but he was trapped behind the wall of black circling us.

Kade stalked forward, that earlier grin now stuck on his face.

I lunged, attacking first and putting all my energy into perfectly orchestrated offensive strikes. Kade blocked them easily, much to my disappointment.

"Something on your mind?" he asked.

I grunted, blocking a strike near my waist. "A million things are on my mind." I turned, swinging my sword toward his dominant arm.

"Am I one of them?" He grinned.

"Yes." I turned, trying to land another strike. "But only because I'm rested enough to want to fight you again."

His laugh echoed in the room and curled down my spine as he blocked me. Again.

We danced around each other before I used everything I could recall from training with Ian, along with a few additional moves Storm forced me to learn earlier. My breathing grew heavier, while Kade's eyes shone like this was all a game.

I let my anger get the best of me though, throwing too many emotions into my attacks until they were hardly accurate at all.

He swiped his sword forward in an easy motion, but as I dodged the blade, he crouched, sweeping me off my feet. I hit the ground. Hard.

"You lied to me," I exhaled sharply. "Again."

He pounced on top of me, his body pressing mine into the ground. "I like to think of it as failing to mention."

I felt every muscled groove of his body, as my eyes fluttered closed, relishing the contact despite my fury. He knew it, too. The arrogant bastard's lips twitched up as he witnessed my heady inhale.

My body trembled in pure desire, and I loathed it. *Loathed* my reaction to him.

"I know you have something to say, Little Rebel." His voice softened as he leaned down, drawing a dagger from his boot. He traced it slowly along my side and up to my neck. "Give me your anger."

"You deserve every ounce of it," I said, struggling ineffectively against his weight.

He snorted. "I do. But since the only way you seem to have a real conversation with me is when one of us is holding steel, I'll wait right here until you're ready to let it all out."

I shifted my hips, a poor choice because it only served to settle him more firmly between my legs. I arched.

Stupid lust.

"I gave you the deepest parts of me," I conceded. If letting him know my wrath would get him off me, I'd give it all. "Secrets only known by those I love. And you gave me nothing." I swallowed, watching his eyes take me in, processing my words.

"I trusted you with pieces of myself I've never trusted anyone with. You didn't have the decency to return even the tiniest bit of it." I knew struggling would get me nowhere, but I had to fight. He slid his blade down, resting his forearm on my chest, reminding me I couldn't escape.

"You lied about who you are, what you are. You killed my father. You took his life in front of me. I hate that I had started to forgive you and then another hidden truth is dropped in my lap. I hate that you turn around and do *this*. You tease me, mock my pain. You smirk and smile and twist every feeling inside of me and I hate it. I *hate* you."

He took a deep breath, closing his eyes. When he opened them again, I lost my breath at their vast depth. "You're right," he said. "You opened up to me and I panicked because someone so strong, so perfect trusted me. No one trusts me, except the few you've met. No one loves the monster here."

Monster. I'd called him that. The Fae in Canyon City called him that too. Yet everything I'd seen from him showed there was more to him than that. I knew it. Deep inside of me I knew the destruction in the city had been an act. Jax had confirmed it. I also knew the responsibilities of a crown, and how heavy it weighed. Mine came from parents who loved me; his—I shuddered thinking of his father.

"I should have told you about needing you. Needing your help. I should have told you who I was. Fates, Storm has been insisting I tell you everything for weeks now. I hate being the son of that man. He is everything evil in this world, destroying everything he touches. If he knew for one second I cared for you, he would exploit you to get me to do his bidding. Even more so than I'm already forced to do."

He leaned forward, resting his forehead against mine, and his shadows pooled around us. "I didn't want to be the Prince of Mysthaven around you. I wanted to be Kade. Just Kade, the man *you* allowed me to be."

Tears pricked my eyes thinking about what we'd shared in Brookmere. The fissures cracking over my heart trembled with his words.

"I believe you," I whispered. "About everything. But Kade…" My voice trembled. "I will never be able to unsee it. To forget it."

He didn't say anything, but neither of us moved.

"I'll never unsee it either. I can never take it back. My fear of what might happen to you outweighed everything, and I wish…" He shook, his entire body rolling with whatever emotion racked through him. "I wish I could change all of it. I'll never be able to truly tell you how sorry I am. Because I am—so, so sorry."

The tears slipped out and Kade pulled away, dropping the dagger and cupping my face.

"Hate me, Little Rebel. I deserve it all," he whispered.

He loosened his hold enough so I could push him away. He met my gaze, and for a moment, nothing else mattered. I believed everything he said. I believed his apology, his pain. But it didn't mean I could trust him.

Kade shook his head, breathing in a few short pants before rising to stand fully. He looked over his shoulder, body tensing again, and held out his hand to me.

This time I took it. We stood there, holding hands until he gave me a sad smile and squeezed mine once.

The shadows dissipated around us, and Jax and Raya rushed forward into the ring, chaos ensuing.

"What the hell, you can't block us out like that. What if she tried to kill you?" Raya shoved Kade.

"I just needed a damn minute," he retorted. "One minute."

Jax brought his hands to his waist. "Well, now that we're

all here, perhaps we should discuss how absolutely fucked we all are."

CHAPTER 15

KADE

Of course my own cadre disrupted my brief moment of calm.

Despite knowing I unquestionably could not live without them, they had a penchant for interfering when I needed space.

Lana's walls were finally breaking, crumbling. She believed me. Now I had to convince her to consider trusting me again. I refused to live in this or any other world where that woman did not believe me when I said how sorry I was for the pain I caused.

And the pain I had yet to cause. I knew there would be more, especially being here. The temptation to have remained in Brookmere, to have her choose me and stay there for good almost blinded me from coming home at all. But leaving my people to suffer at my father's hand would have eaten away at me.

I'd been a fool to think I could shut off my feelings for her after taking her. For assuming that being in Mysthaven would alleviate my desperate need. Instead, everything I felt for Lana escalated, reminding me that the more time I spent in her company, the more I wanted to fall at her damn feet. The more I wanted to be *hers*. To give her complete power over me for whatever she wanted with me. Even if what she wanted was to hurt me for what I'd done to her.

I stretched my neck, wincing as the semi-healed wounds on my back pulled too tightly. Nadia had demanded I stay another ten minutes to heal my father's lashes completely, but I needed to see Lana. I'd left her alone for too long. If I hadn't been unconscious in the healer's quarters, I would have been by her side immediately after speaking with my father. I should've anticipated the king's offer for me to take on Storm, Jax, and Raya's punishments as well. He knew I would do it. His desire to put me in my place outweighed his need to hurt them.

Storm frowned, scrutinizing the stiff way I moved. I straightened immediately, but he knew. He always did. My friend shook his head, clenching his fists. Thankfully he wouldn't give away my secret to the others. Admitting to them that I accepted their punishments was never something I would burden them with. They carried enough.

Raya paced abnormally fast, back and forth, a few yards away. Her hands on her hips, exasperated by the entire situation before us. Like so many times before, I felt sorry for her. To be so close to knowing it all yet kept at arm's length. Our relationship with Raya showed my monstrous side in yet another way. Even if the reasons were sound. Even if she understood. It didn't make it right.

"So, who's going to say it?" Jax said, looking between all of us, pausing. "Nobody? Okay, I will. Not only did we make it back in time to battle in the Festival of Swords, but now we must somehow pass the damned Blood Oath."

A heavy silence hung in the air. It had been three years since the Blood Oath was last called, just after we started the rebellion.

"What is the Festival of Swords?" Lana asked. "And the

Blood Oath?" Her hands wiped away the dirt left on her clothes from where I'd pinned her to the ground.

I drew in a breath through my teeth, staring at her. Having her delicious body beneath me, even for those few moments, scattered my brain, making it impossible to think about the vast problems that lay ahead of us.

No—focus, Kade, focus.

"The festival is a battle," Jax offered. "Then a celebratory ball. But mostly a battle. It's a time for the king to pit his Guardians against each other. But also for the *Fates* to allow any man or woman to be called into the arena to fight us. If they do, and survive to tell the tale, they earn a spot in the king's army."

"How does someone win?" Lana's face paled as she asked.

Jax grinned. "Worried about me?" He winked. "To win, you must survive. If someone draws your blood three times, you're disqualified. Although some die because they lose themselves in the heat of the battle."

She swallowed audibly.

"The battle itself is then followed by the Guardians' Ball," Storm continued. "Winners rejoice and celebrate their newfound status in our kingdom. It is a night of revelry and allegiance. Only a few earn a spot in our army. Their families rise to the highest status possible for non-nobility."

"That sounds bloodthirsty," Lana said. Her nose crinkled, displaying her obvious disgust at Mysthaven's traditions. "It's like the marriage trials but on a larger, more frequent scale. And I thought *those* were barbaric."

I couldn't blame her—the Festival of Swords was barbaric. More people died than Jax alluded to. The whole festival was a far cry from the nature-filled gatherings she'd grown up with in Brookmere.

"Is the Blood Oath at the ball? Or the battles?" she pressed.

Her questions were valid, but it didn't make answering

them any easier. The more she learned about us, the more she'd realize the Kade she'd met back home didn't exist here. I hated the thought of her knowing everything. Not just because I thought it might irrevocably keep us apart forever—I had such a slim chance now to win her heart—but because the more she knew, the more danger she would be in.

If my father had any inkling of the way I felt for her... I closed my eyes, breathing in the dusty sweat-stained ring and grounding myself. I couldn't think of what Lana may face here, or I'd be useless to protect her.

I needed to talk to Cassandra. *With* Lana. Then find a way to get her the hell out of Mysthaven.

None of which would happen before the Festival of Swords.

I wanted to kill someone. Hurt something. I *needed* to. The more I thought about this...

Storm punched my arm, snapping me out of my internal spiral. The others stared, and I realized my shadows had darkened, encompassing me as my mood declined.

"The Blood Oath occurs every blood moon," I said, focusing on the thing I least looked forward to Lana experiencing. "The last one occurred three years ago. We swear our fealty to our king by offering our blood as a sacrifice to the Fates. The act symbolizes not only our loyalty to our king and his cause, but to the Fates themselves."

Knowing my father, he'd timed this purposefully. There probably wasn't even a blood moon set to rise. I'd stupidly believed we could slip into the palace, visit Cassandra, and leave so Lana could return home.

If I thought for a moment the king would enact the festival at our appearance, I never would have brought Lana back here. I tensed, letting the ache of my wounds distract me. She was in so much danger here. All because of me.

"Ah yes, but it's not just any offering of blood for your king. The oath reveals who is truly loyal," Jax jumped in. "The magic behind it is said to show the king who is a faithful warrior and who is a traitor in hiding. Traitors are dealt with harshly. Normally by death. Very publicly." His gaze flicked toward me. "At the hands of the Monster of Mysthaven."

"Do you have to be so…you?" Raya asked, waving her hands at Jax.

He shrugged. "What? It's not like we think he's *actually* a monster."

"She does." Raya jerked her head toward Lana.

Normally I wouldn't mind Jax's taunting. I'd grown accustomed to it, and I had done monstrous things. I deserved the reminder. With Lana here now though, I hated it. I didn't need a reminder of how unworthy I was of her. I clenched my jaw, trying to keep my emotions at bay so I didn't lose control of my magic. Again.

Lana's eyes widened as she turned to look at me. I'm not sure if it was fear or disgust swirling in those gorgeous icy blue eyes.

"Which leads us to our very big problem," Storm said, taking over once more. "How can we pass the Blood Oath and avoid our best friend murdering us?"

Lana dragged her hands down her face. Tendrils of her rose-gold hair swayed in the breeze, whipping around her face. I'd had my hands in that hair. I'd been so damn close to having her heart too. She stood so close right now, I could easily reach out and touch her.

My shadows moved along the ground, crawling toward her like they somehow thought they could sneak up on her.

"Why would you not pass the Blood Oath?" Lana asked. She looked at me, noticing the shadows, and cocked an eyebrow.

I couldn't help but smile and shrug, putting my hands up.

The shadows curled around her ankles, not bothering to stop. The only other time they'd reacted so autonomously was fighting me against the king's orders.

Jax blatantly stared at the shadows before glancing at me, wide-eyed. I'd spent so many years concerned about the destruction my shadows might cause outside of actual battles, I rarely let my magic loose. Seeing them interacting with Lana, dancing around her, drawn to her, shocked all of them.

Fates, it shocked me too. With Lana, my magic didn't seem as horrific. It strengthened, daring my preconceived beliefs to shatter and accept that my shadows could be more than just a death sentence.

Storm sighed. "We've spent the last few years as traitors ourselves."

Lana met my gaze, frowning before looking back at Storm and the others. "So what you're saying is that Kade, *Prince* Kade, murders all the traitors in Mysthaven every three years when the Blood Oath is given? And this year in particular will be difficult, since you're no longer loyal to your king?" Lana asked, hands on her hips.

"Precisely!" Raya yelled, throwing her hands in the air from where she'd resumed pacing in the corner of the training ring. Her footsteps carving a figure eight in the dirt.

"That's enough information," I said, earning a furious glare from the woman I'd fallen hard for.

Not just a glare. She took three steps to reach me and shoved her finger into my chest. "You want me to trust you? You want to prove you care at all? That you are sorry for not telling me things?" She pressed up against me now, tapping her finger above my heart to each word. "Then start talking—now."

Damn it, this woman.

I sighed, waiting for her to back down, even though I knew it wouldn't happen. I'd have to choose. My secrets, which kept pushing her away, or my truth. Which could get her killed. I needed to protect her from the evil lurking in this castle. I had seen what my father did to things I cared about. He'd inflicted years of pain on my mother, knowing it would keep me in line. He hadn't had a person to control me with since her death years ago. I shuddered at what he might do to Lana.

"Kade." Storm said my name and I didn't need to look at him to know what he'd insist I do.

"She could die," I growled toward my oldest friend. My first friend, really. One who knew exactly how dangerous this entire thing was.

"I doubt you'd allow that," he said, trying to smile.

My shadows flared along with my temper. I stepped away from her and toward Storm. "I can't be everywhere. I can't lose—" I stopped myself. Stopped and took a breath.

Letting Lana know just how much I needed her would do no one any good. That part needed to stay locked inside. I barely admitted these feelings to myself, I couldn't admit them out loud. Especially not to her when I was the last person she'd ever willingly rely on again.

Storm refused to relent his unyielding stare. Lana still stood a foot from me, waiting for me to disappoint her again.

Damn it. A part of me, a quiet part, agreed with Storm. Letting her in was the right thing to do.

I had to tell her something. Tell her almost everything, most likely. And pray to the Fates that it didn't ruin it all. I blinked once, in time with a deep breath.

"About three years ago, we decided we didn't like the way the king was running our lands," I said. Lana's shoulders relaxed and her face brightened. She hadn't expected me to actually open up. "As I'm sure you've noticed in the brief moments you've seen him, he is dark. There is an evil to him that is unexplainable. We didn't approve of his tyranny. While he trained me, used me as a monster to do his bidding for my entire life, it has escalated over the past few years. Even my magic, my shadows, began to rebel against his commands. So we decided to do something about it."

"No, no, you're leaving parts out," Jax interjected.

I grimaced, shooting him a look, wishing it would shut him up. "What part?"

"Cassandra." He turned to Lana. "You saw her come with our healer, Nadia, to take Storm. Cassandra is our seer."

Lana's eyebrows shot up.

"She gave Kade a prophecy." Jax grinned, wiggling his eyebrows. "Something about rebels, which provided the additional encouragement that our tyrant king should be put in his place."

It took most of my willpower to keep from knocking Jax out. A good fist to the face might remind him to bite his tongue. Storm's smirk didn't help the situation either. He was all for letting Jax run his mouth and tell her everything. How could they not see how dangerous this was for her?

"You better sit, Princess. This is a tale that will knock you off your feet if you're this into it already," Jax quipped as he sat himself along the edge of the training pit, pulling an apple from his pocket. The man never stopped eating. It was like he had a damn tree down his fucking pants.

Lana didn't move. She barely even acknowledged Jax. Instead, she took one step toward me, mouth still open. I cocked my head to the side, watching her. Confusion danced across her face. I wanted to know what made her look that way. She knew of seers—Vivienne lived at the palace in Brookmere. So why the strange look?

I waved my hand at Lana to take a seat near Jax, if it was what she wished to do. She closed her mouth, blinking a few times before she stood straighter and snapped out of whatever had come over her.

Once her back turned to me, I gave Jax a look that said, *you better behave, or else.*

He shrugged, biting into his apple. Storm took a seat as well, but Raya still paced. I'd have to make sure what I said didn't involve more than she knew. Which should be a safe amount of information for Lana. As safe as it could be, at least.

"Now that you're comfortable, Jax, may I continue?"

"Oh, please do," Jax mumbled as he chewed. "I'm dying for more."

I rolled my eyes before returning my gaze to Lana.

"Even though we're Guardians, sworn to our king and kingdom, we took matters into our own hands. With Storm's help, I no longer murdered the 'traitors,' as my father called them. We created a system to keep the illusion that I remained his faithful monster, while also ensuring no other innocents died." I shuffled my feet, uncomfortable at the memory of Lana's horrified gaze during the most recent fake deaths in Canyon City. It had been the worst torture to let her believe what everyone else in this kingdom did.

I cleared my throat. "We created a network of trusted people and began moving the *traitors* to a safe house. We have been harboring them there until I've been able to take them across the void myself." I looked toward Raya, eyes softening now that she'd stilled her pacing. "I cannot say where, so please don't ask. Raya's connection with the king is too strong, so for her safety and ours, we don't speak of it out loud. We cannot risk everything we have built over these last few years."

Storm moved to stand beside me, placing his hand on my shoulder. *Strength.* He knew all too well about the guilt eating at me, not being able to fully include Raya.

Lana's gaze finally left mine to look at Raya. "He can read all of your thoughts?"

Raya shrugged, as if she could brush off the comment, even though I knew how hard this was for her. "I've worked incredibly hard to learn how to protect my thoughts and mind from the king. For the most part, he only sees what I want him to. But…" She looked to me, nodding. "…in an abundance of caution, we limit my knowledge as best we can. I won't risk the only people who have ever cared about me."

She'd been treated as an outsider because of her magic her entire life. But the minute my father's hold on her lessened, I'd make it up to her. I had to.

"We originally came to Brookmere looking for a way to allow our people to integrate into your kingdom," Storm continued, shifting the attention from Raya as she would want, thankfully leaving out the prophecy bit for now. "While there, we heard inklings of the Hidden Henchman, so we figured we'd try to get some supplies for our people who left everything for a chance at life. The supplies we requested from you were for those people. It gave us an opportunity to provide more for those we saved. It also gave us a chance to meet someone who may have been like-minded, someone brave enough to stand up for those who needed help." Storm rubbed his neck. "We wrongly assumed your father ruled like King Dargan, given the hardships our people faced in the border villages of Brookmere. We certainly didn't realize the Hidden Henchman and the princess were one and the same."

I could see Lana trying to process everything, her facial expressions providing a mirror to her feelings within. Horror, sadness, concern. Fates, I could practically see the wheels turning in her mind, trying to comprehend it all.

Watching her process her feelings ignited my own worry. Everything we'd just revealed made her a potential target for the king. The reminder felt like ice trickling through my body. "We cannot and will not tell you anymore. I will *not* put you in any more danger than I already have."

She stared at me, searching for something, or maybe simply deciding whether to keep trying to kill me or not. I didn't think I'd mind the latter since it usually ended with one of us on top of the other.

"None of this helps us get through tomorrow!" Raya jumped in impatiently. "She knows why we're not loyal, but now *how* are we going to pass the Blood Oath? The rebellion had only just begun the last time we took the oath. With only one half-assed save under our belt, we were able to pass. It's been *three years* now. We have committed hundreds of treasonous acts. We have no idea if the magic of the Blood Oath can cut through my careful defenses, let alone if you lot can keep your secrets hidden."

Lana froze, her chest rising and falling rapidly as realization dawned on her face about the rationality of Raya's concern. "If they don't pass, you'll have to kill them."

I nodded, not shying away from her stare. Fates, I wanted to tell her it would be okay. I wanted to get her out of here. Maybe I should forget my prophecy and return to Brookmere. Perhaps she'd let us stay there for a time.

But he'd find us. I'd leave too many defenseless. I had no doubt my father would find new ways to harm innocent people, with or without my help.

"Raya, you are technically still following all the king's orders exactly as intended. You know nothing about where the rebellion is hiding and have never been informed of details because of it," I stated plainly, ignoring Raya's huff. "You should be fine."

"Yeah, it's just the rest of us that are fucked." Jax grinned. Storm lunged toward him, slugging him in the arm, much to Jax's amusement.

"Cassandra oversees the oaths," I said, thinking out loud. "I have to talk to her anyway, so maybe she will have some insight about how we can stay alive."

"And you trust her?" Lana asked.

"Implicitly."

I'd picked up that Lana didn't seem particularly fond of Vivienne in Brookmere. But Cassandra had saved my life too many times to count, keeping whatever darkness lurked inside of me at bay. Though I had no idea if her role in my life was due to her caring about me or ensuring the prophecy was fulfilled.

I glanced up, noting the sun dipping behind the upper

walls of the training pit. "I have a meeting with the king," I sighed. "But I do not want Illiana anywhere near him. Not at any time. Especially should anything go wrong during the oath."

I met Raya's stare first. "You will stay with her. You're the only one we know for sure will pass. She can stay in her room for the beginning of the festival, and then you can escort her to the ball. It would be too strange for her not to attend the finale, but we can at least keep her hidden away for the festival."

"I'm sorry, I'm not staying with her," Lana chimed in. "She's more likely to kill me than anyone else."

I narrowed my eyes onto my ever-argumentative Little Rebel. "You *will* stay with her, and that is final. You are in over your head here."

"I am far from incapable, and you know that. I can take care of myself. Besides, it sounds like you should be more concerned about yourself than me. You forget I've had years of surviving a royal court."

Shadows seeped from my fingertips, my anger fueling their request for release.

"You have survived nothing compared to what you will see here."

She stepped toward me. "If I can survive Andras, then I can certainly survive your father."

A tendril reached for her, wrapping around her waist, panic clawing at me in a way it hadn't since I saw her incapacitated with a blade lodged in her side while fighting in Brookmere. "You don't know what my father is like," I shouted.

Lana stormed closer, standing so close her chest touched my body.

"I will not be treated like some useless pet," she seethed. "You never treated me like I couldn't handle myself in

Brookmere. I'll be damned if you start this overprotective Fae male bullshit now."

My shadows flowed heavier, rising around her. I felt the tension of the others, still not used to the fact that my shadows refused to harm her. I stared directly into her eyes. "This has nothing to do with your abilities and everything to do with how tyrannical my father is. You will do as I ask."

"Tits and freaking daggers! You are insufferable!"

"Is it always like this?" Jax asked Storm. I saw him nod, even in my periphery, to which Jax snorted. "I get it now."

"Illiana, you will stay with Raya. You will absolutely avoid the king *at all costs*," I stated with conviction. "And Raya, you will not leave her side. You will protect her, and you will keep her safe."

Raya threw her hands up in the air again, opening her mouth to argue yet again.

"That is my final word."

I walked off, wrapping myself in my shadows to keep me from hearing Lana's protests and steeling myself to face the king. I needed to calm myself and my magic, because if he had any suspicion, any idea of what Illiana Dresden meant to me, she'd be taken. *Used.*

And I'd burn the entire kingdom in retribution.

CHAPTER 16

LANA

Today was my birthday.

I'd been alive for twenty-three years, and instead of a day of merriment and celebration, I was trapped in Mysthaven.

Not only stuck in Mysthaven with none of my friends, but also waiting alone, in hiding, to hear if a deadly festival and a Blood Oath would kill my only allies here.

Then, after all that, I'd attend a ball.

The prospect of attending the ball sounded dreadful as it was, but it would also be a ball without Ian. The first ever. Plus, I wouldn't have my conspiratory partner in crime, Hale Bardot, either. The thought made my stomach roll, thinking of yet another person I wanted safe back home.

And Ian.

I doubled over, my heart unable to spend time thinking about what terrors he might be facing in the dungeons.

My chest constricted, lungs collapsing to where I couldn't get a breath in. I closed my eyes, desperate to stop my panic from controlling me right now.

I inhaled slowly, tapping my foot nervously on the ground.

What can you see? What can you feel? I let myself hear my friend's words in my mind.

I stared at myself in the mirror, running my hands over the training outfit Raya had procured for me. It matched my Hidden Henchman persona more than the princess side. Thankfully.

The clothing hugged me tightly, and I forced myself to feel the soft fabric touching my skin. I breathed again.

The black-as-night outfit reminded me of Kade's shadows around me. The thought calmed me further. I almost sobbed as the tightness in my chest loosened.

My thoughts about Kade persisted, unable to stop thinking about what he'd revealed yesterday in the pit. He'd spoken of his own prophecy. Another damned prophecy that very obviously dictated things in his life. Same as mine.

Internally, the second he'd said it, I balked, not understanding why he would keep it a secret. Until I realized I, too, had kept my own prophecy a secret.

I'd have quite a lot to say to Cassandra once I gained an introduction. But as soon as we met with her, I'd also have to reveal my own prophecy. Which I should probably fill Kade in on as well, seeing as he was not the only one keeping secrets. Maybe. *Fates, Kade.*

I breathed deeply again.

He was leading a rebellion against his own father, standing up for his people while at the same time being forced to murder traitors. Hearing their story made everything from Canyon City click into place. I'd never seen dead bodies, never saw the man and woman after Kade's shadows engulfed them.

I'd been swept up in those shadows enough to know they didn't always cause harm.

Far from it.

I'd condemned him immediately. Even if that was exactly what they wanted me to see, I still felt guilty. Jax teased Kade about being the Monster of Mysthaven, but I saw what it did to him. He truly believed it. I'd believed it too for a moment.

I shuddered. Thinking of the risks Kade took, the awful things he allowed his people to believe, all in the name of saving others, broke my heart. How lonely it must be here for him. Forced to obey a father who used his son so terribly.

This new information battled the dichotomy of the man I knew, who he was with me, versus the atrocities he was forced to commit. I rubbed at my chest, the ache there threatening to permanently etch itself in place.

No matter how much I tried to hate Kade Blackthorn, I couldn't.

The pull toward him felt too strong. In some moments, my very soul called to him. Wanted him, despite the heartache he'd caused.

I sighed, walking away from the mirror and leaning against the bed. I wanted to curl up in a ball and not move until the world made sense again. Even if I knew that wouldn't solve anything.

Storm had popped his head in about an hour ago, saying I would be by myself for a while and reminded me not to leave my room until Raya came to get ready with me for the ball.

He didn't leave until I swore it no less than five times.

I'd wanted Kade to come. To reassure me he'd talked with Cassandra, and they would all be safe. That he would be safe. He had yet to appear though.

Time dragged by, giving me a taste of what a long, boring day I had in store.

Tits and daggers, there better be alcohol at this ball tonight. I could at least drown my sorrows.

A knock at the door startled me, only until I realized it was probably Raya, sent to be on babysitting duty earlier than either of us wanted. Or Storm making sure I hadn't attempted to escape.

Or maybe Kade had come after all.

I took my time to answer the door, opening it slowly, about to say something rather obnoxious, when I saw who stood before me.

Not Raya. Not Storm. Definitely not Kade.

King Dargan.

I inhaled sharply before remembering myself and curtsied, opening the door wider. Even if I knew only a little about the king, defying him would surely land me on his bad side. I knew my place around a castle, and how to act around powerful men.

"My apologies for the way we first met, young lady," King Dargan said, a smile I'm sure he thought alluring dancing over his face. "When I heard you'd been placed here in the royal guest quarters instead of the Guardians' wing, I was intrigued. Would you care to join me for the Festival of Swords this morning?"

I pressed a hand to my chest, bowing my head submissively, even if my skin crawled doing so. "I've been asked to wait here until the celebration tonight. I'd hate to be in the way of such an important event."

"Nonsense," King Dargan said sharply. "I'll be escorting you to the colosseum, I insist."

Not good.

"I'd be honored, Your Majesty. If I could have a moment to change—"

"Unnecessary." He reached forward, tugging me through the door to his side. It took all my wherewithal not to flinch at the way his hand curled around my waist. "You look perfect for witnessing a battle."

My instincts told me this certainly would be a battle with him, just as much as the Guardians' battle in the ring.

Even though his grip loosened around me, an eerie sensation pricked at the base of my skull. I knew I should not be anywhere near this man, but when a king gave an order, it must be obeyed.

Hopefully Kade would understand I didn't go looking for trouble. I almost snorted at the quick thought.

Two guards fell in step behind us, their persistent presence as heavy as the king's. I lowered my head, tracking the king's footsteps to make sure I followed slightly behind. Appearing subservient would make me seem less threatening.

He led me down the hall, its walls lined with a handful of large portraits of various Fae. All sat on thrones. After reading a few nameplates in passing, I understood this to be a collection of Mysthaven's prior rulers.

Each face contained a sadness I couldn't quite shake. One that didn't make sense to be captured in official royal portraits. The portraits of our prior kings and queens in Brookmere were happy, joyous. Proud. I didn't get that feeling here at all.

The pain in the eyes of these rulers radiated outward. Especially the one at the end. My gaze flicked to the gold-plated inscription: King Jasper Blackthorn.

"My Guardians have lost their manners, it seems. We were not formally introduced, my dear," the king said, pulling my attention away from the portrait. He stood at the doorway at the end of the hall. A guard held it open for him, and he beckoned me to follow into the stairwell. "Do tell me your name."

Calling me a common whore did make it difficult to indulge in the niceties of a formal introduction.

My immediate retort transformed into a slight panic. Kade had spent so much time telling me *not* to be with the king that he'd failed to tell me what to say to him in case everything went wrong. Which clearly it had. I waited until we finished walking down the stairs before responding.

"My name is Illiana." Concocting a lie would be too hard to maintain, especially without discussing it with the others first.

"Well, Lady Illiana, I must assume you hold a title of lady if you're being held in such high regard by my men. It appears you won them over in record time. I cannot recall any others ever being invited to the palace, especially on the eve of the festival."

He smiled at me before grabbing my hand and placing it on his arm. I wanted to flinch at his touch but controlled my reaction. I didn't need the king thinking I was suspicious of him. Instead, I put on my royal princess mask I'd donned so many times before and pretended to enjoy his attention. Even if his evil reminded me too much of Andras. I stiffened, my heart thudding more wildly.

Not now.

He was the last person I should think about at the moment.

The king raised an eyebrow, and I forced a smile. I'd done more in the past few weeks than I ever had in my entire life. I was more than the emotions Andras's cold words made me feel.

If I wanted to be the queen Brookmere deserved, I needed to take back control from those dark memories weighing me down.

My smile came effortlessly as I slipped back into my courtly role. Perhaps I could use this time with the king to my advantage and see what he would be willing to tell me.

"I'm sure I was merely at the right place at the right time. Lonely warriors returning home and all that." I averted my gaze, recalling how many noblewomen whispered about men enjoying mystery and the chase. Fates, maybe the idiotic rules of court might actually come in handy here.

"Lonely Guardians make for poor bedmates. Perhaps you will be by my side for longer than just today, Illiana."

I clenched my teeth, lowering my head, eager to change the subject. "I am honored, Your Majesty. I have never been to Mount Legion before. It is such a beautiful city. Perhaps you could tell me about it?"

"Ah yes, the first time in Mount Legion is always memorable. I'm sure your journey here consisted of my son and his companions gallivanting across the lands, frequenting the seedy taverns he so enjoys. The grandeur of Mount Legion is a stark contrast to what I'm assuming you're used to."

The desire to defend Kade and the others simmered in my chest. "They've been nothing but honorable. You should be proud of your warriors."

The king laughed. "You are a delight. I know all too well what they are truly like. You'll see. Careful of my son especially. He likes beautiful things but tends to destroy them."

I refused to give in to the king baiting me for information on Kade. If he wished to gossip about his son, he'd have to do so elsewhere.

As we exited the front of the palace, we walked left toward a large balcony. I had been so caught up when we arrived, I'd missed it completely. The balcony overlooked a great canyon nestled between two of the largest mountain peaks. The immediate plunge down took my breath away. A fierce flowing river raged below us. Rays of sunlight sparkled off the black streaks in the mountainous rocks. At sunset, this view must be spectacular.

"Here in Mount Legion, we pride ourselves on the more fearsome beauty of the earth surrounding us. It takes bravery to see the beauty in such vicious lands, but it's there."

His pause lingered, waiting for me to say something. "You speak the truth indeed. I'd forgotten how beautiful wild and dangerous things can be."

The king smiled arrogantly. "I, too, enjoy the beauty of wild, dangerous things." His fingers brushed over my shoulder.

I forced a laugh. "I can assure you I am neither of those things."

Yet.

"Oh, I doubt that." He chuckled. "For my son and his friends to bring you along with them, you would have to be"—he paused—"monstrous. Speaking of, we must continue. The Festival of Swords is a grueling treat I am excited to experience with you."

He guided us onward, along the balcony toward a massive, wide entryway. Mountains shot up along all sides, circled around us, and though beautiful, it reminded me of walls, caging me in.

My pulse skyrocketed. Thinking of Andras and his torture in the cages of Brookmere's dungeon would not serve me here.

The king held out his arm, a gesture I was already tired of. With no choice, I placed my hand on top of it again as we descended stone stairs. Archways ran along the top rows of a massive colosseum. Designed with rows and rows of spectator seats, all of which offered a clear view down to the center of the arena.

Fae filled almost the entire colosseum already, watching the Guardians warming up below. The competitors worked in different stages, some running, some sparring, but all preparing for the main event.

The king led me along an upper walkway and down to a marble-floored landing area. A white pergola draped in black billowing fabrics covered a variety of wines and food spread across tables in the back. Parallel with the view of the arena sat rows of chairs raising in elevation behind the front row of obsidian stone seats. The king's place was clearly marked, an obnoxious glistening throne standing a head taller than the other seats at the end of the row, in clear view of all the spectators. Unfortunately for me, there were plenty of seats beside his ostentatious throne.

He ushered me forward, past the others milling about. Most stared at me in disdain. I knew from the haughty looks on their faces that I stood among Mysthaven's nobles here. The divide between nobles and commoners was clear, just as it was back home.

I eyed the throne the king currently led me toward. "Surely the queen or someone more worthy wishes to be by your side for such an important event," I said. I hadn't seen or heard of where the queen might be, but surely she'd be here.

The king's eyes narrowed. "The queen is dead." He gripped my arm tighter, causing my heart to pound frantically.

Shit. A citizen of Mysthaven would know that. "Well, I'm sure she's always here in your heart," I said, desperately attempting to correct the error.

A few moments went by, and the king's posture straightened. His face softened, like he'd caught himself seconds before flying into a rage. "How right. But, Illiana, I told you you'd be beside me, and here you shall stay."

I nodded my head. "Of course, Your Majesty."

The king's sharp scolding that the queen was dead reminded me how much I had yet to learn about Kade. He hadn't mentioned his mother ever. Or his father, to be fair. To have this man as his only remaining family was terrifying.

The king stepped away from me and stood in front of his throne, pointing to the arena below. "There is your Storm now, I believe."

Sure enough I spied Storm, Jax, and Kade grouped together, while Raya remained off to the side, warming up alone. Kade's back faced me, but as if he sensed me somehow, he turned, glancing up toward us. His eyes met mine, and immediately his shadows flared, expanding outward and causing a few other Guardians nearby to run to the other side of the ring. His gaze sharpened, eyes narrowing. He took a step forward, like he'd be able to reach me, even with an entire stadium between us.

Jax touched his arm, and Kade shook his head, shifting his attention to his father. He lowered his chin before sweeping into a reverent bow.

"Interesting," the king mused. He raised an accusatory brow at me. The flare of Kade's shadows, the reaction to my presence in the colosseum, hadn't been missed. "Here I thought you were brought to my palace for Storm. Yet it appears you may have garnered more than one of my Guardians' attentions."

CHAPTER 17

LANA

My body stilled as the king silently stared at me.

A cruel smirk shadowed his face.

Raising my chin slightly, I forced my voice to remain steady. "I'm not sure I understand what you mean, Your Majesty."

His eyes shifted, two catlike slits assessing me, before he clicked his tongue and turned away.

He waved at his people.

I didn't relax, despite his attention being elsewhere. I couldn't let my guard down now.

Kade's shadows were not recovering below, seeping out of him so much that if it continued, he'd black out the view of the arena entirely in minutes. Storm forcibly grabbed him and led him to the side. He spoke until Kade lifted his sword and the two sparred together.

The king didn't give them much time before raising both his arms. "People of Mysthaven, welcome to the Festival of Swords!" he shouted, the echoes of his voice reverberating off the canyons surrounding us, even without magic.

I glanced down at the pit, noting Kade's eyes fully trained on me. Even from this distance, I could feel his fear. See it through the agitation of his shadows. As much as I wanted to reassure him I would be all right, I didn't actually know if that was true; his father had already discovered our lie so easily.

"We gather to watch our Guardians fight, to battle for honor," the king announced. "To witness the select few chosen by the Fates to join my warriors, should they survive." A titter of excitement ran through the crowd.

I closed my eyes, remembering the last time I sat on a dais like this, not too long ago, for the start of the marriage trials. How quickly things changed.

"Once the Guardians have shown why they are the most revered in our land, we'll witness the reaffirming of their oaths, and the oaths of any new Guardians we welcome into our ranks."

My gaze roamed from Kade to Storm, Jax, and even Raya in the back. I hoped they'd made it to Cassandra. I didn't think I could stomach watching any of them die, even if I was still angry with them. With all that had transpired, I couldn't help but feel an attachment growing. To all of them.

My foolish heart.

"Are you ready?" the king shouted, and the crowd roared, rising to their feet. "Let your blades strike true, Guardians of Mysthaven."

I shuddered, wondering why on earth the king would revel in his own warriors destroying each other unnecessarily or hoping their blades struck true. It seemed like such a waste of good men.

"With blood may you reign," he announced. My jaw dropped as the crowd chanted the line. This kingdom's vicious mantra, I realized. So incredibly different from our "May nature guide you" motto.

Suddenly, fire exploded into the air, spreading around the arena in billowing strands. The fight had begun. Below me a flurry of movement took over the arena, and Guardians descended on one another. I jumped back, startled at the immediate intensity of their attacks.

I dared to look at the king, who sat watching with rapt fascination. "Marvelous, isn't it?" he cooed without looking away from the fight.

"I assumed it would be one-on-one fighting," I admitted.

He turned toward me. "Where would be the fun in that? This way, they can turn on each other. Weed out the weak."

Keeping my face as neutral as possible, I watched. The king's maliciousness unnerved me.

In Brookmere, it had been evident Kade and Storm possessed skills, both with magic and blades, far surpassing most of our soldiers. Evidently, the same could be said of the others in Mysthaven as well. Watching them fight, even in such a bloody and extreme tradition, mesmerized me. Then again, the fluidity and grace warriors possessed always held a certain allure for me. Even as a child, watching Ian train and hone his skills had been breathtaking.

Screams echoed around us, a Guardian falling. Clashing swords rang in the pit below. Some purposefully sought out individuals to attack alone, while others teamed up in groups, making it nearly impossible to survive their concerted attack. The brutality of their aggression grew the longer the fight continued. My gaze remained focused on each of those I knew. My hands clasped the edge of the seat in anticipation. Storm, Jax, and Raya were all safe, fighting their way among their fellow warriors.

Though there were those walking to the edge of the ring, merely bloodied, a few bodies littered the dirt floor of the ring too.

I'd never considered myself bloodthirsty, but watching the others move with grace and a ruthless efficiency stirred something inside of me. Especially Kade.

My eyes lingered on his form, his physique. I shifted in my seat. He battled, his sword whipping through the air swiftly, marking other Guardians with three strikes before they even had a chance to raise their blades in their own attack. All the while, he kept his blows shallow, never injuring those he battled more than necessary to disqualify them.

I let out a breath as he disarmed another attacker, one that got far too close for my liking.

"Careful now, Illiana." The king's voice sounded too close to my ear. I'd been so entranced with Kade, I hadn't noticed him shift toward me. "One might think you have eyes for a different Guardian. I do feel obligated to tell you though, my son is off-limits for the likes of you. He has far too many options as it is." The king brought his hand to my knee.

I wanted to rip it off.

"Dalliances distract him from his true purpose. Beyond whoever is selected to be his wife and bear him an heir, he's mine."

His purpose? Slaughtering traitors. At the king's command. What would my life have been if my parents had treated me like this man treated Kade? How was it possible he ever learned to thrive when this bloodthirsty king served as his only example of a man at a young age.

He stroked my knee. "If you're interested in someone outside of *Storm*, do let me know. I have space for an additional consort, even if you are a lesser Fae."

My body chilled. I was through with men touching what wasn't theirs. Right now, every fiber of my being raged in response to his unwanted advances. That rage only burned fiercer as an internal voice screamed that Kade was more mine than his.

And my damn leg the king so eagerly pawed at, my body —those certainly belonged to me as well.

"I suggest, Your Majesty, you remove your hand. I don't appreciate being touched without permission." I cocked an eyebrow, knowing I treaded a dangerous line with my words.

"I have no desire to be a consort. Unfortunately, though generous of you to offer, my heart lies elsewhere."

The king's cold smile grew at my words. He slowly removed his hand, one finger at a time, but his expression seemed far too victorious. He looked nothing like his son. I may struggle to know the true Kade, but I knew that no one owned him.

Including this tyrant.

I clenched my teeth, wanting to run. Or shove the king off the balcony.

A deafening roar from the arena drew our attention back to the fight. A Guardian came up behind Kade, sword over his head as though he meant to kill, not injure. Kade had just knocked a Guardian in front of him out of the competition and hadn't turned around yet. I gripped the railing of the chair, helpless.

Kade twisted at the last minute, easily disarming the man and slashing his blade across the right arm of his attacker. He ducked, then sliced his opponent's leg and opposite arm. Three strokes and it was over. Blood pooled from the minor wounds of the Guardian Kade defeated, his expression hateful even from up here in the stands.

I closed my eyes, loosening my death grip.

"You give yourself away too easily," the king drawled, his eyes still on the ring. "My son bows to my command, whether he likes it or not. If I say you're gone, so you shall be. I'd remember that before you get too comfortable running your mouth."

I raised my chin.

In the brief time I had spent in his company, I knew everything I needed to about this man. Mysthaven may not be my home, but I'd be damn sure I helped my friends with whatever they needed to succeed against their king.

My friends.

Again, the thought struck me. They had every chance to

hurt me yet hadn't. Every chance to command me without including me. They bared their darkest secret to me, willingly. Kade brought me here for a purpose, one he felt strongly about. His hesitation in Brookmere, his words—for the first time I no longer doubted them.

The competition continued below while my focus remained on Kade. He'd had to fight his whole life. What had Storm said about how he acted back home? Cold? Closed off?

Perhaps the man in Brookmere truly was Kade. A Kade free from his father. A man able to experience life without the weight of being the king's monster every second of every day.

Tears sprang to my eyes.

Which meant my father's request, the request to take his life, forced Kade right back into the role of the monster he'd briefly escaped while in Brookmere. I gasped, bringing my hand to my chest. The impossible burden placed on Kade's shoulders even in Brookmere was overwhelming.

Fates.

The king rose, standing and raising his arms again.

Kade's gaze immediately found me as the fighting ceased, and he took a step forward. Like he'd leave the damn arena to come up here. I shook my head subtly. Too many emotions filtered through the pain I'd clung to the past week. The anger dissipated, transforming into something else entirely. A feeling weaving over my heart, my soul. A desperate need to protect Kade Blackthorn in a way he hadn't ever been given before.

I needed air, even though I sat in the open colosseum.

The pace of my breathing increased. I closed my eyes tightly. The entire situation was horrible. In my grief, no matter how rightful, I'd ignored everything he experienced.

"Shall we add in some more fun, my people?" the king bellowed to the crowd's delight. "The time has come for the lottery of Guardians! Cassandra will draw the names from those in the crowd who will be chosen to compete for a place among my warriors."

I opened my eyes. Now was not the time to be caught up in this. There would be time to process everything. Later. Right now, I had to get through the rest of this battle, and hope the others survived the upcoming Blood Oath.

The king lowered his arm, extending his hand toward the entrance to the arena, where Cassandra sauntered out. A deep blue tunic billowed around her body, two sizes too large. Her face donned a smile, and her skin practically glowed despite the dimming sun as she approached a small table set to the side of the arena. On it rested a large cauldron. Black, shiny, it took me by surprise; I hadn't noticed it at first.

She tossed her curly silver hair over her shoulder and waved a palm over the mouth of the pot.

"Guardians for Mysthaven, tried and true. Hearts and minds we seek for you. In the depths of the Fae not yet pledged, bring forth more warriors to fight at blade's edge." Her voice carried through the colosseum, an airy sound flitting around us.

A shimmery gold smoke swirled along the edge of the cauldron before shooting straight up into the air. The spectators cheered at the theatrics, leaning forward and taking in the show.

Cassandra's smile widened as she brought her hands from above her head downward in a slow descent. As she did, the smoke settled from the eruption, following the height of her hands until the cauldron merely steamed with the golden mist.

A man approached her, holding a scroll and quill. She nodded toward him, then the king.

"Begin," he ordered.

Cassandra snapped a finger. A plume of gold mist puffed out in a circle in front of her face, then dissipated.

"Morgan Talley," she said.

The man beside her wrote on the scroll while a group of Fae at the far side of the colosseum shouted, slapping a man on the back as he moved toward the aisles leading to the arena's entrance.

He'd barely made it to the opening when Cassandra moved again.

"Tyson Rivbane," she called out from behind another puff of gold.

The same process happened again. Cheers erupted from various locations in the colosseum, and the potential Guardian moved through the aisles and into the ring.

Cassandra called out more names of both men and women. As soon as they entered the arena, they were handed a sword, mostly procured from bleeding Guardians already removed from the battle in the arena.

Forty or so Guardians stood in the center of the arena, either unmarked like Kade, Storm, Jax, and Raya, or boasting one or two bloody wounds.

I couldn't look too closely at the scattered dead bodies lying on the colosseum ground.

Almost twenty additional hopefuls lined up along the rim of the fighting ring, waiting for their turn to duel.

"And finally…" Cassandra waved her hand over the cauldron once more. This time she paused and tilted her head, frowning before she looked at the crowd.

"Illiana Dresden."

CHAPTER 18

LANA

My heartbeat thundered in my ears as the sounds of the colosseum faded.

I stared down at Cassandra, who watched me carefully, no expression on her face to indicate what the hell might be going on.

So much for Kade trusting her.

Why? Why would my name be called?

Kade strode forward. "She cannot compete, she—"

"Silence," the king commanded. "The magic of our land has spoken." He grabbed my arm roughly, forcing me to stand, and leaned close, whispering in my ear. "I wonder, would you have an interest in a position as consort now?"

He pulled away, standing in front of me, as he ran his hand up my arm.

"Excuse me?" I snapped, immediately attempting to pull away from him, but he didn't relent.

"I wouldn't have my consort compete to be a Guardian, you see," he said. "Care to save yourself? I'd hate to see such a beautiful face bloodied, or worse—dead."

I inhaled sharply as a deep-seated rage boiled in my veins. "As you've said, the magic of the land has spoken."

His eyes darkened, the green suddenly changing, transforming into a smoky black. I'd seen that before.

In Kade's eyes.

I startled, and this time when I stepped back, the king brought his hands down to his side. "I look forward to seeing how long you last."

My body trembled as I fisted my hands, walking toward the aisles leading me down to the arena. Determined to survive, I hoped I could make it out unscathed.

I wondered what the group of hopefuls would do to become Guardians. Killing a woman who looked like she didn't belong might not be a far stretch. Little did they know I could fight too.

I held my head high as I walked through the entrance into the arena. A man with a gash all the way down his arm, splitting his black tunic into two long strands, handed me his blade. "With blood may you reign," he said.

I heard the king's shout to begin. This fight took place in the same way the initial fight had. A free-for-all.

A blade came toward me, and I blocked it. No sooner did I twirl to meet my attacker than a black tendril came and whipped his sword away, slicing him three times across the chest in such rapid movements, I barely had time to blink.

I whipped my head to the side, but Kade fought his own battle.

Idiot. The king would have no doubts now that I meant more to Kade than he'd originally revealed.

"I can fight my own battles," I hissed at the tendril as if it was sentient and could fucking understand me.

The tendrils of shadows retreated, shocking me by obeying, as another attacker came forward. I fought, parrying him with greater ease than I'd assumed I'd have to. Many of these men were untrained. I hit him twice in the arm, drawing blood, before he yelped, falling to his knees. Raya stood from a crouched position on the dirty floor.

"I had him," I said, glaring at her.

"I figured pissing you off would help me pass the time." She shrugged. "It has."

Then we were fighting back-to-back. None of the people I battled seemed eager to deliver more than minor injuries. After knocking two more men out of the battle with shallow cuts, my confidence swelled.

A sharp sting ran along my spine, knocking me to my knees as I cried out in pain. I turned, seeing a man with shaggy red hair lift his blade to strike me again. So much for my confidence and no death blows. His eyes narrowed on me.

"Friendly with the king?" he asked before bringing his blade down.

"Lana!" Kade's voice shouted from somewhere to my left, but I ignored him. Raising my own weapon, I blocked the deadly assault.

"Not at all." I gritted my teeth, rising to my feet.

The man lunged forward, our blades locking. "Too bad. I might have spared you."

I spun, slicing forward and catching his thigh. He roared, reeling back but not leaving the fight.

Shadows swiftly skittered toward me, but I didn't need them. "No," I commanded. They paused, lingering a few feet away.

The anxiety, the fear that so frequently made me hesitate lessened. I'd trained for this. I'd fought. I'd survived multiple battles, and I knew my capabilities.

I may not be the best warrior, but I would survive this day. For now, I believed I was fully capable of handling myself in this fight. I had confidence in myself, for the first time in a long time.

I'd use it, wield it as another weapon in my arsenal.

Our swords clanged, the ferocity of his hit reverberating up my arm, but I countered with my own strength. I noticed a wound on the man's shoulder. He had two hits already. I only needed to land one more.

I smiled, backing up and forcing him to fall forward with his next blow.

He jerked his gaze toward me. "A woman has no chance of defeating me. I've trained for this day," he hissed. "Waited for this moment my entire life."

"Well, seeing as how you were only now selected for the chance at being a Guardian, I'm going to guess you're not trained well."

Fueling his emotions helped me. His movements turned savage. Wild, and out of his control. The man's swings, though harsher, were easier to anticipate.

I heard Kade call my name again but refused to focus on his voice.

This time when I blocked the man in front of me, clashing my blade to his, I knew I'd won. "Enjoy knowing a *woman* bested you."

A pulsing light spread over my hands, and I inhaled, twisting my blade and slicing the man's other arm. He stumbled back, glaring at me with lethal rage.

I almost lashed out due to his use of magic but hesitated. The light rimmed my hands and then disappeared. That was—

Impossible.

"I think not," a voice hissed. I looked up, realizing the man had no honor or intention of leaving this battle despite being down by the rules of engagement.

His rush caught me off guard and I lifted my blade, moving slower than I would have liked.

Before he reached me, a shadowy tendril wrapped around his throat and a blade slammed mercilessly through his gut.

I stumbled back a step.

Kade whipped around, eyes roaming over my body. "Are you hurt?"

I shook my head. "Only my back. It's fine."

He grabbed my arm, spinning me around and inhaled sharply. "We'll get you to Cassandra."

"We're in the middle of this stupid festival, if you hadn't noticed."

"I don't care," he said, gripping the hand that didn't hold my blade.

"Kade, your father—"

As if I'd burned him, he dropped my hand. He closed his eyes and inhaled a few times. My words summoned the tyrant himself.

"Well played, Guardians." The king's voice echoed around us.

Kade and I stared at each other before I glanced at the man's body, dead on the ground. He'd killed him without hesitation.

Everything I'd felt since this morning tumbled through me. Realization, need, and an aching pain collided inside my chest for the man standing in front of me.

Storm and Jax approached us, and the three of them shifted, all positioning themselves around me.

"Not bad, Princess," Raya said at my back. They surrounded me, maneuvering into this formation on purpose in a way that obstructed me from the view of not only the spectators, but the king himself.

"Faithful warriors, your bravery has been witnessed by your king," King Dargan announced as the crowd roared in a standing ovation. "Those unlucky enough to find themselves out will be among the first selected for a station along the outer outposts of the kingdom. You retain your life, but you've fallen from grace. Perhaps next year, you'll earn back a place closer to the palace."

At least they'd live.

"Cassandra will administer the Blood Oath, and then," the king shouted, "my people, we will celebrate our Guardians and another year of their fealty and our strength. With blood may you reign."

A terrifying realization hit me. The Blood Oath. Now that my name had been called, I would be asked to take it. But I wouldn't, especially not to that man. I certainly wouldn't pledge myself to another kingdom when I would always remain loyal to my own. A kingdom that, once I returned, I would save no matter what it took; I would die defending it if necessary.

The king turned from the platform he stood on, parting the crowd greeting him, and made his way down the colosseum stairs. Down toward us.

I swallowed. "Please tell me you spoke to Cassandra," I whispered.

Storm, closest to me out of all of them, dipped his head once. At least she'd keep them safe. I hoped. Though throwing me into the festival didn't make me feel as though she had my best interests at heart.

We hadn't planned for *me* to be in this position.

I wondered briefly how many fake oaths Cassandra could pull off. I may be in deep shit myself, but I needed all of those with me to be okay too.

Even with the knowledge that they'd spoken to her, each of the three men radiated a tangible unease.

Raya stepped directly to my side as the other Guardians shuffled in front of us, all appearing eager to take the oath. Or perhaps they were merely eager to get out of here and go to the celebration.

I peered around the line. Cassandra hadn't left her position by the cauldron. This time, the smokey makeup of whatever lay inside glowed red instead of gold.

The king stalked through the entry way, entering the arena, and stood a few feet to Cassandra's side, looking each Guardian in the eye as they stepped forward.

A hissing noise startled me, and black smoke shot from the

cauldron. A man shouted, crying out in agony. "It's not true, my king."

I gasped, watching a seasoned Guardian in the front fall to his knees before the king. He reached for the king's feet, but King Dargan kicked him back. "You dare touch me? You beg for mercy when the Blood Oath has revealed you to be a traitor?" He slammed his foot into the soldier's face.

The Guardian collapsed in the dirt, and two men came to either side of him, lifting him by the arms and dragging him out toward the center of the arena.

I looked at Kade. He stood utterly still, staring at Cassandra. Except for his clenched jaw, his face showed no emotion.

He'd have to kill him. He'd be forced to kill that man. Even though he most likely wasn't a traitor, or maybe he merely fought against the king somehow like the Guardians currently surrounding me.

Or perhaps worst of all, he simply drew the short stick in this terrifying game of luck.

I shuddered, wrapping my arms around myself. Warmth pricked at my fingers, and I glanced down at my hands. They were as they'd always appeared. No light. Nothing. I must have imagined it. The short-lived spark looked so much like the flare that happened in Brookmere a few times in the past few weeks.

Nature. That's what I originally thought. A blessing from nature in the moments I needed it most, even if it had added nothing to me magically. But how could nature's blessings reach me here? And why?

The oaths continued. A few more men barked out their loyalty when the cauldron found them unworthy. Five stood in the center of the arena, with only a handful left before Jax's turn.

I held my breath, watching the playful shifter approach the cauldron and Cassandra. The king scanned those of us who remained until his gaze fell on me. I refused to meet his eyes, but I felt his stare. Warning bells rang inside my mind, demanding I heed the danger of this Fae.

Perhaps my only hope lay with being honest about who I was, which surely would go over poorly. Though it had to be better than being deemed a traitor with a Blood Oath I didn't feel remotely able to fake.

Kade shifted, stepping back to stand behind Raya and me.

I wanted to ask him what to do, but I couldn't risk anyone hearing. Whatever instincts I possessed, I'd need to trust them. Right now, everything inside of me rebelled at putting my blood in that cauldron.

Jax furrowed his brow as he sliced his hand on the dagger, dripping his blood into the smoking vessel. The red coloring pulsated, and then nothing. No hiss. No black smoke.

Jax passed, walking forward to take his place behind the king.

Storm approached Cassandra next.

I clasped my hand into a fist, unable to stop the tremor racing through me.

He repeated the motion, slicing his hand, and Cassandra did her job once more. Storm passed.

Raya approached next, leaving me standing with Kade at my back.

As expected, Raya passed as well.

I was out of time trying to come up with a plan. I refused to swear fealty. Or even pretend. Kade and the others were in a position where they had no choice.

But I had a choice.

I was Princess Illiana Dresden. And no amount of fear would stop me from denying my family. My title.

Cassandra's gaze hit me, and her wariness pushed me over the line for what I had to do. That one fearful look told me her faking *my* oath would be more difficult than the others.

"King Dargan, I did not choose this fight," I said. "A Blood Oath should be given freely, willingly, not forced."

The king's brow cocked. "The Fates spoke very clearly, and whether forced or not, those who participate in the Festival of Swords must swear their loyalty to their king."

"I cannot take a Blood Oath to you. For my loyalty forever belongs elsewhere."

I kept my voice as quiet as possible so only those closest could hear. Shouting out my refusal of the Blood Oath would have been a mistake. Tits and daggers, *this* might be a mistake too. Cassandra's face slackened with what looked like relief.

I had to do this. I knew it in the marrow of my bones.

The king's sneer intensified as he approached me. "If you dare defy the Fates and their calling, if you are disloyal to your king, you will die a traitor. Simple as that."

Kade stepped closer behind me, and the king's gaze flicked over my head to his son. "I might enjoy making you kill her."

I moved closer to the king, steeling my nerves. "I will not take the Blood Oath to you because I am loyal to my own kingdom."

The king's eyes widened, staring at me. A dawn of understanding washed over him before his face hardened. "What did you say?"

"I am the Princess of Brookmere," I said, voice low. "I do not swear loyalty to anyone but myself and my people."

He stepped back, like my words had a physical effect on him. His wild gaze darted to Kade, eyes narrowing. "I want to watch you take your oath, boy. *Now.*"

I steadied myself. Refusing to let the fear welling inside of me slip out in any way in case the king watched. And oh, I *knew* he did.

Kade grabbed the dagger and cut his hand, holding it over the cauldron while Cassandra stepped back. If the hiss came, the black smoke, I'd fight by his side to escape.

A red flare, strong and convincing, radiated from the cauldron.

Kade passed.

The king's anger enveloped me, making me want to shrink back, but I wouldn't give him the satisfaction. He stared at Kade until that evil smile reappeared.

"Very well, how could we deny the sanctity of royal blood?" He sneered again as he walked away toward the front of the arena and turned to Kade. "Kill the traitors…and make it good."

Kade didn't look at or acknowledge me. My gaze met Cassandra's, but she quickly glanced away.

It was enough to know we were under a microscope. Even more so than before. And there could be no errors.

Kade unsheathed the sword at his back, and then, in his empty hand, his shadows formed his second blade. His blade of shadows and darkness.

He held his head up, facing the traitors, and his eyes darkened along with the shadow blade until all that remained was destruction.

I shivered, and a part of my heart broke for Kade. For the man standing, weapons out, against his own people. People likely to be innocent.

One by one he lashed out, first with his sword, and then with the shadow blade. I didn't look away as the latter left ashes in its wake.

When the last man's body blew away on a phantom breeze in the ring, Kade's shadow blade evaporated. He left the bloodied sword out, hanging by his side.

"And now, we celebrate," the king shouted from the edge of the ring to the excited crowd around him.

Footsteps echoed as the spectators left the colosseum. Guardians walked toward the exit, like this hadn't been devastating. Like they hadn't lost their friends, ones they must have fought and trained beside for years.

I stepped toward Kade, but Raya grabbed my arm.

"We have a feast to attend."

I thought I might be sick. This wasn't like Canyon City. These deaths had to be real.

I looked over my shoulder and stared at Kade until he met my eyes. I poured every ounce of compassion I could into my gaze, but he merely trembled once and looked away.

CHAPTER 19

LANA

I stared at my washed and primped reflection in the guest room mirror, shocked that only a few hours had passed since the Blood Oath.

I'd achieved all the things Kalliah normally would have done if we had been together.

A lonely yet proud sense of accomplishment came over me for what I'd mastered in such a short amount of time. Even if *mastered* was a stretch without Kalliah's brilliant capabilities.

I rubbed at my chest as if that would somehow drown out the ache of worry for her. The ache of missing her.

Surprisingly, Raya had dropped off some beauty essentials on my bed shortly after we returned to the palace. I'm sure she was thrilled to share with me. On top of the supplies, she also left two dresses to choose from.

I selected the sleek fitted emerald-green satin dress. Black lace covered the bodice, wrapping around and zipping up the back. The pleats on the skirt of the dress made it appear as if I was gliding when I walked around the room. The loose skirt also allowed me to conceal a dagger on my thigh. Clearly necessary after the events that had transpired earlier today.

The other option had been an obnoxious pink dress, with

frilly sleeves and a corset back, which was entirely too low. It was probably one of the ugliest things I had ever seen, so picking between the two had not been difficult. Raya presumably thought it funny to leave me with such an atrocious choice.

I touched the braided crown I'd woven atop my head, pinning it just like Kalliah had shown me. It only took me three attempts this time, so my practice had been paying off. Again, I craved her presence. I missed her desperately. Besides needing her expertise in hair and makeup. I missed my best friend. My confidant.

I had no idea if she was okay. I had to get back to her. Back to my mother.

I had to return to Ian.

If Andras had hurt them, I swore on the Fates themselves I would destroy the man in even worse ways than I'd already planned.

I looked up from the vanity stationed in the far corner of the room, out the large arched window overlooking the gaping canyon I'd seen from the balcony earlier.

While this room did not have the homey feeling of my own back in Brookmere, it felt elegant and comfortable, and the view was spectacular.

I jumped when a quick rap sounded at my door.

I braced myself in case Kade stood on the other side, ready to scold me for being with his father. The moments with the king had certainly been an experience I did not wish to repeat.

The sooner Kade accomplished whatever it was he needed to, the sooner I'd force him to take me back to Brookmere. Far away from his father.

He promised.

Steadying my nerves, I took a deep breath and opened the door.

Before me stood the grey-haired seer of Mysthaven, Cassandra.

"May I, my dear?" She peeked around me into the room.

"Yes, of course," I assured her without hesitation. "Come in."

I ushered her into the room, looking down the hallway to see if she had come alone, before shutting the door.

I met her in the middle of the room, and before I could say anything, she grabbed both of my hands. Her eyes appeared to be searching for something within me. They darted back and forth, up and down, and I could not tell what she was trying to find.

"It is a great honor to meet you officially, Illiana," Cassandra said. Her wiry hair reminded me of Vivienne. In any other circumstance, one would have thought they were related. "I don't wish to keep you long, I simply wanted to come by and heal any injuries you may have sustained from earlier. You fought spectacularly."

She gently clasped my hands as if to prove herself. A warmth spread over my back, tingling up my spine as my injuries soothed. I watched our hands, noticing a faint glow of light emitting from her palms as she channeled her healing power into me.

I'd seen it so many times before. When Elisabeth healed me.

My chest tightened, watching the last bit of light fade from Cassandra's hands.

Giving them a squeeze, I smiled at the woman, even if I struggled to give her my full trust. "Thank you. I'm not sure how you knew or if Kade sent you, but thank you."

"Ah, Illiana, it is my job to know. To see. It is the least I could do after the Fates forced my hand today." She didn't let go of my hands, instead gripping them more firmly in her own. "I have lived a thousand years, and when such a light comes before us, we must bask in its glory. Feed it, feed it. Feed the light."

I stared at the woman. She slipped into a nonsensical chatter under her breath, sounding far too much like Vivienne's.

She shook her head and smiled once more at me, our hands remaining clasped.

"Kade wanted to bring me to you to talk—"

She let go of me and brought a finger to her lips. "Not now. Not now, but tomorrow. Yes, tomorrow will do nicely."

She bowed her head slightly and walked to the door. Just as she reached it, she turned back to me.

"Illiana, what you believe you see may be something else entirely."

Before I could even try to comprehend what she'd said, she walked out, leaving me standing in the open doorway, confused.

I shut the door, backing up into the room.

What you believe you see may be something else entirely, played on repeat in my head. Something clawed at the back of my brain. *This is important.*

I returned to the large window, staring into the depths of the canyon below. The sun setting in the background made the stone mountains glisten with the last minutes of daylight.

Gasping, it finally struck me.

What you believe you see may be something else entirely was far too close to my father's saying, *never trust something is as it appears at first glance,* for it to be a coincidence.

A lesson he'd reminded me of since my childhood.

A pang of hurt echoed in my heart. I missed my father. So much. He'd have advice or know what to do. How to act with this vengeful king.

I hated fate, hated prophecies. Especially after living so long in the shadow of my own. Things seemed far too coincidental to believe anything other than the Fates were at play. Cassandra said tomorrow. Kade and I would get the answers we both sought, and then I would go home.

Once I was with Ian and Kalliah and my mother, then I could deal with what had happened. For now, I had to steel my resolve and shove the emotions threatening to take hold of me for good deep within.

Besides, if the Fates wanted to play, then I was ready.

Torches lined Mysthaven's great hall, dimly lighting the room. Twice the size of our ballroom in Ellevail, this space stretched on and on, seemingly unending in length. Dark-colored florals stood in urns scattered throughout the hall, with long dining tables lining the outskirts. The food smelled divine, wafting from the back of the room, and while many people sat at tables eating, others milled about the room enjoying delicacies from silver platters held by various staff walking about.

Others danced to a string quartet's music, and *many* drank. They all seemed happy. Or at the very least celebratory. It was a feast unlike any I had ever seen. Voracious and liberating in a way Brookmere's balls were not.

Raya led me to the back of the room, waving a hand at a seat and diving into the food plated in front of where we sat. Had I not witnessed and been forced to participate in such brutality today, perhaps I would have devoured the dishes before me as well, but my stomach had other plans. A nervous energy shifted inside of me. I wanted to put eyes on Kade. Something in me needed to make sure he remained unharmed.

Raya sat silently, ignoring the world around her as she pushed vegetables and stewed meat onto her plate.

I eyed a man walking by with a platter of drinks and jumped up, grabbing a glass of wine and downing it. My plans this evening included getting a fair amount of alcohol in me to forget about the horrors of the last few weeks.

My twenty-third birthday had been an absolute shit show thus far, so I may as well continue in such a fashion.

The doors on the opposite side of where Raya and I had entered slammed open, and Kade breezed through them. Jax and Storm followed closely behind. They had all cleaned up.

Too well.

I stared at Kade's all black attire. His tunic hugged his chest deliciously, halting on his forearms. He'd rolled up his sleeves to the point where I could see the inky black design of his tattoo peeking from underneath the shirt. The top lay unlaced. His sword didn't rest across his back in its usual place, instead sheathed at his side.

I smirked, knowing he'd attend a ball with it, and grazed my fingers over my own dagger, strapped to my thigh.

"Finally," Raya muttered under her breath. "Thank the Fates."

I couldn't take my eyes from Kade as he moved across the room. His shadows trailed behind him as if he wore a cape. His eyes appeared dark, just like they did whenever he had his "episodes." I wondered what darkness lurked in him to cause such changes.

And why it didn't scare me like it should.

I stepped further away from the table, not bothering to let Raya know where I planned to go. I didn't think walking directly up to Kade right away was smart, but maybe I could get to Storm. Someone more talkative than my babysitter.

I stalked a server at the side of the room, grabbing another glass from the drink tray.

Kade stopped in front of a raised table I assumed the king would be sitting at when he arrived. He didn't bother sitting down. Instead, he grabbed a chalice of something, swallowing it in one gulp. He spun and grabbed the first woman before him, leading her onto the dance floor.

An uncomfortable, sick feeling knotted in my stomach. He hadn't spared me a glance. Not one.

"Arrogant asshole," I muttered to myself as a hand clenched my shoulder.

I turned swiftly, prepared for an attack, but found the king standing behind me.

"I often call him that myself," he chuckled.

"I apologize, Your Majesty." I stumbled with my words, putting the glass of wine down onto the table closest to me before I did something clumsy like spill it all over his robes.

If I drank much more, I might do it out of spite. The hate growing for this man, well, it was vast.

"Not that it's your business, *Princess*, but it is tradition for the prince to dance with all the eligible women at each ball until he is betrothed," King Dargan sneered. "He has been gone far too long, and his time to secure a wife has come. I'm sure you, too, must be required to find a husband."

His words hit their mark, as I'm sure he knew they would. I refused to give him any indication that they had an effect on me. Even if something in me raged at the thought of witnessing Kade paraded around to the women in his court. I didn't know how to respond to the king, so I chose to stay silent.

The king smirked. "My son inherits this throne, Princess. Perhaps you should set your sights on Storm after all. For no Princess of Brookmere would be worthy of the position of Queen of Mysthaven. Not in either of our worlds." He bowed his head mockingly and walked into the crowd.

Instead of heading to his throne, he strode toward the front of the room.

He signaled to the quartet in the far corner to stop playing. Those on the dance floor halted mid-step. A silence filled the air. All the attendees waited with bated breath for the king to speak.

"Welcome one and all to the conclusion of our festivities,

the Guardians' Ball. Congratulations are in order for those who passed the challenge and the Blood Oath, and who are now members of the elite group of Fae known as the Guardians of Mysthaven. My army." The king snapped his fingers, and a staff member handed him a chalice.

He raised it above his head. "To those who pledged their allegiance once more and survived, your king rewards you tonight with this feast. Eat, drink, and dance, for tomorrow our work begins again. Our never-ending battle to defeat the darkness spreading across our lands will find success. We will rid Mysthaven of the evil of this world."

An explosive chorus of cheers echoed throughout the ballroom.

"That is not, however, the only thing we have to celebrate," he continued. His eyes met mine, and that cruel smirk ticked at his lips. "Our prince is home. We have waited many months for his return, some of us more than others." He winked toward a gaggle of giggling women to his right. "Eligible maidens of Mysthaven, tonight is your time to shine, for Prince Kade is in search of a wife. Perhaps you will be our next queen, should you prove yourself worthy to our prince."

The room buzzed as women chattered excitedly. The energy became palpable as the reason for celebrating became even more apparent.

I scoffed and earned a side-eye from Raya, who I hadn't even realized had made her way to me again. She surprised me by pressing another glass into my hand. I tipped it back. Water. I glared at her.

"I have no interest in watching you make a fool of yourself," she whispered. "At least take a glass of water in between your alcohol."

I conceded, finishing the sobering substance like it might somehow calm the anger coursing through my veins.

I looked to find Kade, but he stood smiling with Jax. Looking totally content. Even with his father's words.

He still hadn't so much as glanced over at me. And for a man who was so insistent I not be left alone with the king, that I needed protecting, I had now been left in his clutches numerous times.

The king signaled to the quartet to begin playing once more as he returned to his throne. Immediately, a group of women surrounded his chair, offering him food and drink. One held a strawberry above his mouth, and I scowled, shuddering at the ostentatiousness. Everyone presented themselves as though they lived to serve him. *Disgusting.*

I grabbed a drink from a passing server, debating throwing it back just as I had the first.

"If you don't slow down, you will be on the floor. And I, for one, will not be holding your hair back tonight should you become ill," Raya scolded. "Watching over you only goes so far."

"Oh, don't you worry, Raya. No need to hold my hair back when it's already up. Let's just survive the night, all right?"

She sighed. "Fine. Let's get this over with."

Kade finished his next dance and immediately began dancing with another, sweeping her off her feet. Laughing with her, smiling at her in a way I thought was only meant for me.

Jealousy nipped at me. I didn't know I could ever feel such a way before, at least not like this. Maybe the alcohol exacerbated it. Right, this had to be alcohol. Never mind I hadn't nearly enough to drink yet. My jealousy *wasn't* this strong.

I finished my glass of wine, relishing the minor numbing warmth tingling through my body.

As Kade began his fourth dance of the evening, still without a single acknowledgment of my presence, I conceded he could dance with whomever he wanted. I knew he had to put on a front for the king, but it hurt nonetheless. Despite all we had been through, my body ached at our separation when we were so close. Others touching him, pawing at him, it gutted me in a way that made no sense. While I knew he had much to answer for—lies, deceit, a prophecy—my heart craved him and his shadows.

I wouldn't let this bother me. Not now.

A man with a silver helmet on his head and a blood-red uniform came and stood before us. A Guardian. A cocky one, too, if the mischief in his eyes served as an indication.

"The king would like for you to dance with Prince Kade," the guard said roughly.

I looked over at the king, and he waved his hand at me. A sickening smile graced his face as the scantily clad woman to his right fed him more berries.

"You may tell King Dargan I am fine where I am and have no intention of dancing with the prince since he made it so clear I am less than worthy of his attention."

The guard stared at me, unwavering in his expression. "You will dance with Prince Kade as the king commands it, or I will be forced to take you over there myself. You won't like how I handle you. The choice is yours, girl."

"It's Princess, actually, and—"

Raya quickly stepped in front of me, glancing between me, the king, and the guard. "She will go. No need to threaten anyone, Braum." Raya turned to me. "You. Go. Now."

I wanted to argue, but her hateful stare shut me up. "Fine."

Making my way through the slew of tables, I followed Braum. The entire room stood between us, and Fae lingered everywhere, making it difficult to pass through the masses. Fae stood eating, drinking, and some went so far as to be kissing and exploring each other already. All right here, out in the open. This was *not* the kind of ball I was used to attending.

Kade finally noticed me making my way toward him,

when the king, again, motioned in our direction, indicating his desire for us to dance together. A sinister smile graced his face.

He rose. "As some of you may have heard during today's oath, we have the honor of hosting a visiting dignitary."

I gritted my teeth.

"Princess Illiana Dresden is from Brookmere, a land unable to be accessed by most of us. Never have we had the honor of hosting someone, let alone royalty, since the void keeps us apart from our neighbors. But don't worry, ladies, she is not a contender for our prince. However, as is custom among royals, we will honor her with a dance."

Raya stood on the edge of the dance floor, watching ever so closely.

Kade's dark eyes bore into me as he scanned me, emotionless. As if he looked through me. He pursed his lips, and I took a step back.

He didn't want to dance with me. He looked like he couldn't stand the sight of me.

"Not so fast, Princess." He aggressively grabbed my hand, unlike his normal gentle touches. I almost whimpered as the familiar faint electric current surged in me.

"You heard the king. One dance."

CHAPTER 20

LANA

Kade placed his other hand on my waist and yanked me toward him.

This felt *wrong*.

He stood rigidly as we took the first few steps in the dance. After a few paces, others joined, and the room returned to its lively nature.

Kade refused to look at me though. This dance was so unlike the dances we'd shared before. Those had been consuming, fiery, electric. This just felt…awkward.

I stared at him, trying to catch his eyes as they continued to avoid mine, the swirling darkness having fully taken over.

"Kade?" I asked.

Something flickered there.

"Kade," I tried again. "Why does this feel so…wrong?"

"There is nothing wrong, Illiana," he said. His voice chilled me. "I told you, you may not like who I'd become once we got here."

His eyes barely passed over me, even as he spoke.

The memory of that darkness taking over when we first entered Mysthaven returned. The way he'd flung his shadows out as his magic destroyed everything. My heart beat painfully in my chest.

This wasn't him.

"Look at me," I said softly. Just as I'd been drawn to see if he was okay after his outburst outside the void, I knew I needed to do the same now. When he didn't respond, glancing about the faces around us, I cupped his face with my right hand. "Kade, look at me."

I didn't dare move my hand until he stared straight into my eyes. Slowly, the swirling darkness receded, and his eyes returned to normal. The tension in his body visibly loosened.

Thank the Fates.

After a few more turns around the floor, his body relaxed completely. He pulled me in closer and whispered in my ear, "I should never have brought you here. No matter what I thought I needed, you cannot stay here. You are in danger every minute you stay in Mysthaven."

"We haven't even discussed what you think you need me for," I said. "I can barely process what happened today. Your father knows somehow about us—"

"Did he say something?" Kade pulled back, searching my eyes.

I frowned. "You weren't very subtle with your shadows unleashing the minute you saw me with him today," I whispered. "Then again, neither was I." My gaze focused solely on Kade. My reactions to the king's taunts had been just as damning as his own. The king seeing through our lie was on both of us.

Kade closed his eyes, and his body tensed. "Do not leave Raya's side when this dance is over, do you understand me?"

I stared up at him.

"Please," he begged.

I nodded. "I need you to be honest with me and tell me why you thought you needed to bring me here."

Kade spun my body out and then pulled me closer.

Pushing a piece of hair behind my ear before wrapping his arm around me. "Later, Little Rebel. Too many ears."

"Ah yes, Fates forbid the eligible maidens think you care for someone who isn't them," I said. I don't know where it came from, but the jealousy I thought I'd successfully drowned with a glass of wine seemed to be creeping its way right back up.

He narrowed his eyes.

My mouth wouldn't stop now though. Watching him merely dance with other women set this beast inside of me ablaze. He unknowingly owned too much of my heart, and if I wanted to come out of this unscathed, I needed to harden myself. "I didn't think I'd be lucky enough to witness your own version of the marriage trials. Or at the very least, all these women clawing at each other to get to you."

His face relaxed, brightening. *Why the hell is he smiling?*

"I didn't think you'd have any interest in who might be vying for my hand."

His smile made me want to punch him.

"You're right," I said firmly. "I don't have any interest in who vies for your hand."

He twirled me again, and when he pulled me in, flush against his body, his breath warmed over my neck. "Say it again, but this time try to make it sound like you mean it."

I shoved away from his chest, but he didn't let go of me. "This dance is over."

At my words, he loosened his grip, his face shifting from playful taunting to serious again.

His eyes scanned mine, back and forth, and he rested his hand on my neck, his fingers running along my jaw. "If you told me there was even the slightest chance I could earn your trust and heart again, Little Rebel, I'd get on my knees before you right now and claim you as mine."

My lips parted and I sucked in a sharp breath of air. My entire soul danced, even as my body froze, keeping me locked in place with his hand touching me. Did he mean that? Even if I believed everything he'd told me thus far, his main purpose had been to take me for his own prophecy. Whatever it may be. Emotions, feelings, his heart—those weren't in play, right?

The song ended and I swallowed, taking a step back. He watched me go, not breaking eye contact even when the next eligible maiden squeezed in front of him and began the next dance.

So I turned, fleeing the gaze that saw too much.

I couldn't look at him right now, couldn't watch him dance with anyone else. Even if his eyes were on me.

What was I supposed to say to that? Why did everything feel like such a mess?

My reckless heart unfurled from the cracked and broken state I forced it to remain in, soaking in his declaration.

As I stood helpless on the edge of the dance floor, Jax approached me with a glass of amber liquor.

He offered it to me, and I grabbed it and took a deep sip of it, immediately coughing as I stared at the strong drink.

"Whoa, whoa, easy there, tiger," he laughed.

I gave Jax "the eye," normally reserved for Kalliah and Ian when they had pissed me off.

"How dare he say things to get under my skin and then dance with someone who wants to marry him? *Marry* him. When I was about to pick him for—" I stopped, realizing Jax might not be the best person to confess my deepest secrets to.

"Uhh…" Jax paused. "Let's get you out of the way here, Princess. We don't need any more eyes or ears on you than necessary."

He ushered me toward the end of the ballroom. As far away from the king and Kade as possible.

Raya met us, drinks in hand, as Jax pushed me toward her. "You know, Raya, girl talk was never my forte. Th-this one's for you," he stuttered, putting his hand to his ear. "I think Storm is calling my name."

Jax turned and fled.

Coward.

Raya handed me another glass and I took a sip. Thank goodness it was wine and not the atrocity Jax provided. I'd tasted better liquor in Ellevail's poorest taverns than what he'd offered me. "Aren't you going to drink with me?"

Raya stared at me, her expression emotionless, as she sipped her water. "I do not drink. You know…mind magic and all."

"Right," I said, sighing as I leaned against the wall. "Did you know today is my birthday?"

"Happy birthday," she muttered before taking another sip of her water.

"Yes, happy freaking birthday to me. I had to fight for my life today. It's clear the king has it out for me in some way. Kade is acting like a confusing ass. And I'm here with you, someone who is forced to be my babysitter and won't even have a drink with me. Do you know what I should be doing right now?"

Raya stared at me. "No, but I'm sure you're about to tell me. Fates, I wish I *could* drink right now."

"This morning, I should have stuffed my face with pastries and breads from Thea. She makes the best baked goods in the entire city. Ian or Kalliah would have picked up the special order she gives us every year. We'd devour everything in my room, so we had a hearty base for our annual night of debauchery. This is the one night, the *one night*, Raya, I would have been free of the palace confines and celebrated like a normal Fae. Freedom with the people I love most in the world."

I swirled the wine around in my cup, suddenly wanting to leave.

"Look, I know today has been a hard day, but—" Raya started.

I needed to talk about them. Talk about my friends. I needed to feel something other than the bitterness dwelling in my soul, so I let myself keep going, talking more to myself than the woman next to me.

"Once a year on my birthday, Ian, Kalliah, and I are allowed to go to Duke Street. No sneaking out required. It's in the *lesser* area of Ellevail. But it's my favorite place in the city. Specifically, we make our way to Dukes Pub. It's cozy, away from every single noble Fae, and the barman makes sure we are taken care of."

Tears formed in my eyes as I thought about how simple those times were with Ian by my side.

"Dukes Pub is a small tavern, with only ten tables and far too skinny a bar for the clientele they serve. The leather covering the seats is worn and cracked, but it never mattered. Tommy Soloman, the barman, welcomes us every year with open arms. He can be a bit grumpy sometimes, but somehow Ian and I wormed our way into his good graces when we were fifteen."

Raya handed me a piece of bread slathered with a sweet cheesy spread, and I promptly bit off a hunk.

"Won him over might be a stretch, but I made sure to tip him generously the first few times we went, and he always let us back. Ian and I snuck into the tavern one day when we were *not* of age. We were bored and needed an escape from the drudgery of the palace. The barmaid who worked there at the time was blind. How she could pour ale as well as she did, I will never know, but we were able to get one over on her. We managed to drink a few pints before Tommy figured out who we were."

I laughed, letting my head fall back as I remembered how red in the face he'd gotten when he discovered the princess drinking in disguise in his bar. I had my Hidden

Henchman outfit on minus the mask, long before that became our plan.

"He was none too pleased the princess and her Royal Guard in training managed to get inebriated underage, but he made sure we were taken care of and coherent enough to return to the palace before sending us on our way. Neither of us wanting to feel the king's disappointment that night."

Raya actually smiled at me. "Go on."

"Well, as soon as we became of age, Dukes Pub was the only place we would go. Last year…" I started laughing uncontrollably and had to steady myself before continuing. "Last year was our wildest year yet. Ian managed to convince a small group of musicians to play for me as my birthday gift, and I spent the night dancing on tables and the bar top. Ian stole a tambourine and played along with them, while I convinced Tommy to join me on top of a table. It snapped in two, sending us crashing to the ground. Ian laughed so hard he fell off his stool. Until he realized my bone was poking through skin and I had broken my arm. We ran back to the castle, and my healer, Elisabeth, scolded us for days." I let the tear fall down my face now.

Raya snorted. "Are you sure you are a princess?"

"Who knows anymore," I sighed, fully succumbing to the delicious buzz of alcohol flowing in my blood. "I certainly don't live the life of a princess now. With my father, who's apparently not really my father but my uncle? Plus, some ridiculous quest to go on now, while the people I love remain at home. Yet here I am. Stuck in Mysthaven without my friends. On my birthday. With a badass warrior woman who hates me."

We were quiet for a moment. "I am a badass," she said. "Fates, I want to hate you. But breaking a pub table sounds like a fun time. Jax would love that story." She paused before speaking again. "Is Ian your friend in the dungeon?"

I nodded, daring to ask, "Have you seen him again?"

Cautiously, I looked at Raya, who now leaned against the wall next to me. She didn't back away from my curious stare but shook her head. "I haven't. I'm sorry."

A woman bumped into me, sending me sideways, harder against Raya.

"Watch where you're going," Raya snarled. The woman bit her lip, grabbing the hand of a man and pulling him to the dance floor.

I remembered where we were again and how much I'd divulged so freely.

Anyone could have heard. I swallowed, refocusing on my surroundings. I looked at the dance floor and saw Kade with another new dance partner. They'd made it fairly close to where Raya and I were standing. The woman snaked her arm around the back of Kade's neck and pulled him closer. Trying to kiss him.

Rage overtook my entire being. While I still had to work out my own feelings, since I did not trust him completely, that certainly didn't mean I wanted him touching anyone else. Or allowing them to touch him either.

Irrational. I knew it was irrational, yet I couldn't help but feel like Kade was *mine.* He'd brought me here, and he shouldn't be kissing other women in front of me.

A faint light emitted from my fingertips as the glass in my hand shattered, slicing into my fingers.

Raya jumped slightly next to me. I wasn't even processing the fact that Kade had pulled away from the woman and had *not* kissed her.

"Okay, well, let's—" Raya paused, sighing. "Let's get you cleaned up." A staff member procured a towel almost immediately.

Raya reached for me, but I shook her off. "I'm fine."

Before she could do more than hand me a towel, I turned and hurriedly strode to the archways boasting open windows to a garden beyond the ballroom. I could get away through the back doors.

I passed Cassandra as she came in from outside.

She grabbed my hand, taking the towel, and the cut I had from the glass disappeared. "My dear, do not fret. What did I tell you earlier?"

I shook my head. Tears trickled from the corner of my eye. Today had been too much. The battle, the Blood Oath, worrying for the others. The ball, the king. Kade. Being here. Reminiscing with Raya about Ian. Ian who was in a dungeon while I was here, drinking and wallowing like a spoiled brat.

"Nothing is as it appears at first glance, Illiana. You must trust him."

I froze.

"Who told you to say that?" This time, Cassandra's words didn't allude to the ones my father taught me. They matched it. Exactly.

"I know many things." She put her hands on either side of my face. "I know a father's love, even one not of blood. I know the strength it takes to stand from the darkness of one's past." She let her hands fall, stepping back. "And I know you. You are the light. You must trust in Kade."

Shaking my head, I backed away from her, from the rantings of another seer. I left her standing at the door.

Escaping out a pair of double doors, I entered the back garden. I'd been right to come out here, but nothing prepared me for the dark beauty of what awaited me. Hedges of black roses lined the vast edges, skirting around rows of exquisite florals glistening in the moonlight. Gray and deep indigo botanicals blossomed in full bloom.

Corbin would love seeing these darker colors compared to our bright ones.

I walked toward a balcony not far from the door. Leaning over the marble railing, I tried to catch my breath.

The darkness here hung heavy in the air. Despite the beauty, the dark ruled. It lurked. Suffocating everything.

My heart raced faster and faster.

I tried to gulp in air, as sweat formed on my brow.

I'd lost myself inside. Over what? The feelings for a man who'd lied to me?

If Andras were here, he'd laugh knowing how right he'd been all those years.

Weak.

Worthless.

No, not here. Not here.

Now was not the time for my panic to take over.

I let out a shaky breath. *Come on.* I counted in my head, like I had done so many times before, but it wasn't working.

I gripped the balcony railing tightly, knuckles turning white.

A small tendril of shadow whispered at my ankles, weaving its way up my body, until it enveloped me completely.

"Breathe, Illiana. Breathe."

CHAPTER 21

KADE

I felt her heartbeat through my shadows.

Erratic, frantic.

I came up behind her and she didn't shy away. Inhaling slowly, I touched the small of her back and moved my arm to the front of her body.

"Breathe," I whispered, like I'd done in the palace hallway in Brookmere.

She twisted around in my arms, makeup smudged from tears.

Fuck, this was my fault. Either for bringing her here or for dancing with so many women tonight.

I let my shadows envelop us before taking her hand and leading her into the gardens, away from prying eyes. I didn't need anyone looking out one of the many windows from the great hall and seeing us together. I'd already done a pathetic job protecting her from my father, I needed to be more careful.

I wouldn't do it by feeding the monster and ignoring her. It had been stupid to even think I could. I hadn't accounted for my actions causing her any kind of pain, which made my decision to embrace the role I played in Mysthaven while she watched even worse.

She didn't protest as I leaned her against a cool stone wall and took a few steps back. I let my shadows linger, since they somehow brought her comfort.

Who was I kidding? They'd fight me to stay by her even if I tried to reel them in right now.

She inhaled slowly, watching me, so I didn't look away. She held my stare, finding that strength inside of her as she breathed in and out.

With her silence, I didn't know what exactly had set her off. Sent her running out here. So I waited, letting the silence linger.

Maybe she needed another minute. Or a distraction. I could give her that. I thought back to when I had her pinned down after she trained with Storm. She'd yelled about how she'd opened up and I hadn't. She was right.

I'd been too damn scared to open up to her when we were in Brookmere. One thing becoming clearer and fucking clearer—my Little Rebel owned my damn heart. After her surprising jealousy tonight, I let myself hope, for the first time since killing her father, that we might have a chance.

If I wanted to keep that chance, I'd have to share parts of myself with her that I'd kept secret for so long. Even if I loathed the idea.

"You've seen when my eyes change, when the monster inside of me takes over," I said.

She tilted her head to the side, then nodded. "What is it?"

I crossed my arms, fingers brushing at the sleeve of my tunic. "I don't know exactly. It's a darker part of me." I dropped my hands. "I'm in control of it most of the time, but there are times it's harder to manipulate. It's stronger here in Mysthaven than it was in Brookmere. At least until I met you."

I frowned thinking about how much less it affected me in Brookmere.

She shuddered out another breath. "Why?"

"I don't know," I admitted. "Storm helped me try to control it. It's exploded out of me a few times, which you have also seen. That change developed a few years ago. It's dangerous."

"You never seem to stay that way long though," she said.

Little did she know even with Storm's assistance, we could barely contain it. We'd discovered his fire could protect him and the others from it when it lashed out, but he'd never gotten it to disappear. Not like she did.

Tell her.

I stepped forward toward her. "When you touch me, I feel you through it. The darkness doesn't last, almost like it can't."

Her lips parted. "Like tonight."

I nodded, so close now I could take her in my arms. Fates, I wanted to hold her, touch her, claim her, but not until she wanted it. Not after everything I'd done.

"Giving in to it felt like the only way to get through this," I confessed. "I'm a fool. Hiding everything I feel from the king seemed like the most important thing, because if he finds out how I feel about you, Little Rebel, he'll break me by using you."

"Don't say things like that," she said. Her gaze went to my lips, then back to my eyes.

"Like what? That you mean something to me?"

She nodded. "I can't. I don't know if I can trust you completely. You clearly have other duties here. I live in an entirely different world. It could never work. Besides, you almost kissed someone else."

I stared at her. Was that what made her flee? Did she think I could stand the thought of someone else touching me? "That almost sounds like you care."

Her eyes flared before narrowing on me.

I couldn't help but smile as I lifted her chin with my forefinger. "I don't know why, but your jealousy makes me want to do terrible things, Little Rebel." I took one last step, closing all space between us as her back pressed into the wall. "Delicious things."

She shoved me in the chest, pushing me away. "I should hate you."

Her soft floral scent washed over me, making me instantly fucking hard. I'd noticed it the first time I stood close to her, and now, it haunted me. The intoxicating sweet smell lingering on her skin as if she'd just walked through a damn garden. It reminded me of spending time out here back when my mother was still living.

Lana had no idea the pull I felt toward her, the desire. It was a damn miracle I could function in her presence.

I'd shoved it all down since we fled Ellevail, suffering as I deserved until that spark of hope ignited tonight.

"Having you here, seeing you with my father today, I panicked. I thought maybe I'd show my own indifference. I danced with everyone he wanted me to, hoping it might take his focus from you. I have been fucking terrified thinking about what he said to you, thinking about what happened today. When you showed up at the battle with him, I thought I might destroy the entire colosseum."

She frowned. "Why?"

How could she not see it? Feel this?

I sighed, running a hand through my hair and stepping farther away, giving her more space. "He could hurt you with no remorse. I'm trying to protect you. You don't know what he's capable of."

She shifted against the wall. "Maybe you should have thought about that before dragging me here."

"You're right."

Lana blinked, surprise flittering on her face. "Well, maybe

this birthday isn't total shit after all. Hearing you say I'm right was as good as any gift."

"Birthday?" I asked, horrified at how she had to spend her day.

She nodded. "Twenty-third." She ran her hands over her arms, rubbing them gently.

My shadows crawled up, copying the movements, and she smiled down at them.

"Well, I'll need to get you a gift, obviously," I teased. "What would the Princess of Brookmere want most?"

Leaning her head against the wall, she closed her eyes, worrying her lip between her teeth. Fuck, I wanted it to be my teeth on her lips.

"I want a distraction." She sighed and looked at me again. "To not be in my head and worried or angry or grieving for one minute."

I stepped toward her, willing to do all that and more, but she hesitated. The pause crossed her features, creasing her brow.

"You don't trust me." It wasn't an accusation, merely me trying to gauge how best to give her what she wanted.

She pursed her lips. "I don't know what I feel," she whispered.

I looked at my shadows, still caressing her arms and wrapped around her legs, and smiled. "But you trust my shadows."

She glanced down at them, her frown deepening. "I guess it's— I know it's strange, since they're you, but I think we both know they have a mind of their own."

I retreated to the railing of the balcony and leaned against it, settling in. Willing my shadows didn't take much since they had always been drawn to her. One of the tendrils gliding up her arm shifted into a shadowy hand and grazed up and around her breast, to her neck and into her hair.

Lana let out a small gasp. Her damn perfect piercing blue

eyes stared me down, daggers in their own right. I felt her gaze sear every part of me.

"I have an idea, Little Rebel," I suggested. Fuck, my cock was hard, straining against my pants already, just thinking about what I could do to her. Do *for* her. "Do you want my shadows to give you your distraction?"

Another hand formed and caressed her stomach, while the shadows around her legs teased her dress higher.

She closed her eyes.

"Ah, ah," I said pausing their exploration. In this, we were one, my shadows and me, without a need to fight or battle for dominance. "I need you to tell me you want it. Tell me yes."

She nodded.

"Out loud, Illiana."

Her gaze snapped to mine, and the need reflecting back threatened to bring me to my damn knees.

"Yes."

I swallowed, gripping the railing to keep from getting any closer. I didn't think after everything that had happened I'd ever get to touch her again. This was beyond my wildest dreams.

Even if she didn't fully trust me, the sliver of hope remained that she might one day fully forgive me. She might let me all the way in. But for now? For now, I'd take this as the precious fucking gift it was and give her exactly what she needed. And then some.

My shadow reached behind her hair and pulled it back, exposing her neck. Long tendrils whispered down her skin. A barely there caress. Just enough to send goosebumps down her body at my phantom touch. Fates, her skin was soft.

Lana let out a hushed moan, eyes fluttering closed again as my other shadows rose higher and higher, tracing the inside of her thigh.

"More. Now," she begged.

"Patience, Little Rebel."

I commanded the shadows to slowly circle around Lana's wrists, stretching them above her head and pinning them in place against the stone wall.

Her eyes flew open, as she realized she was now trapped, unable to move.

"Look at me," I said. She obeyed and I resisted the urge to go to her, to beg on my knees before her to listen to my words. "They will never hurt you. *I* will never hurt you. Never again."

She inhaled and exhaled a slow breath, then nodded.

I willed the shadows formed beneath her dress to continue, changing from whispery tendrils into a hand. If it wasn't going to be my hand, then at least my shadows could feel her orgasm around them.

Shifting, I clutched my own thigh, completely off kilter watching Lana give herself over to my shadows.

The shadow hand coaxed her legs apart, and pushed her satin underwear to the side, not like there was much there to begin with.

The cool whisper of the evening air across her entrance elicited the most intoxicating moan from her, and I had barely begun.

This will be fun.

A shadow finger slowly edged its way inside of her. She was wanting and ready, and I shuddered feeling how eagerly she awaited more through my shadows. She watched me, just as I watched her, and a fire sparked in her gaze. This woman would be the death of me, thoroughly, truly, and I couldn't bring myself to care.

I'd give her whatever she wanted and then some. So long as I could be the one she looked at like that.

The finger began to meticulously stroke inside of her, while other tendrils of shadow snaked around her body, massaging her clit as she shook against the wall.

A shiver of pure desire jolted through me. The way my

shadows glided in and out of her so fucking perfectly nearly brought me to my damn knees.

I gripped the marble of the balcony to the point of pain, willing myself to remain in place. If I allowed myself to move one inch, it would send me into a spiral. One I may not be able to come back from.

No, be still. Feel her beneath your shadows. Let her have everything she needs.

I sent more shadows out from me to play with her breasts, all while others still pinned her arms above her head. I grinned in anticipation, remembering just how much she enjoyed when my tongue greedily devoured her nipples, so I sent shadows there, flicking and pinching them. Suddenly, my coil of control over my shadows loosened, and they took over, but we were of one mind so completely, I didn't need to urge them to do my bidding. Giving her the most pleasure possible was the goal. For both of us.

My shadows were unwavering in their need to claim what was theirs.

Claim what was *ours.*

More and more, the shadows stroked, building her to her peak.

"Please, Kade," she whimpered. "Please."

"I know." I couldn't look away as she writhed against the wall. "Stay with me."

My grip remained unyielding, threatening to crack the marble. Fates, the need to touch her, to be inside of her, overpowered my senses. As if detecting my slip in control, the shadow finger left her and she gasped in anger.

I could feel how close she was to finishing. Her rage snapped me back to the present, and before she had time to revel in it, I directed the shadows to plunge inside of her once more, this time shaped more like me, filling her in the way I so desperately longed to. Her moans deepened as she arched her back, straining against the hold the shadows had her in.

"Yes, yes, yes." Her cries were like air, and I needed more. I needed to hear her come.

A few more pumps, and Lana screamed my name, riding out her pleasure on my shadows. I sent a torrent of them around her to muffle the sound from anyone too close to the gardens. This was *mine*.

Her pleasure, her satisfaction radiated through me, through the shadows. All of it, mine.

My cock painfully strained against my pants, begging to be set free. I would have to find my own release tonight. The sound of her coming would be my muse. A sound permanently ingrained in my brain.

Back fully in my control, I released the shadows from her hands and moved her undergarments and dress back into place as she stood there, panting.

Smoothing the fabric of her dress, I could see she struggled to gather her thoughts. I watched as her walls built back up in her mind.

I wanted to keep her here with me, in an unguarded moment, even if that desire revealed how selfish I was.

"Distracted?" I asked.

She left the wall, walking toward me and hesitantly placed her hand on my chest. Warmth spread over me, radiating outward at her contact.

I leaned down, unable to stop myself from placing a kiss on the top of her head. She leaned into me, so slightly I didn't know if she realized she'd done it, but I clung to that feeling. Just as I would cling to this memory.

"Happy birthday, Little Rebel."

She dropped her hand and took a step back, lips parting and then shutting again.

"Good night, Kade," she whispered.

She retreated back toward the ballroom, and I walked forward, collapsing against the very wall I'd held her against, desperate to revel in the scent of her.

We would be okay. I'd make sure of it. We'd go to Cassandra, figure out what to do here with the prophecy, and then—

Then I'd take her to her kingdom, win it back, and spend the rest of my life proving I loved her.

Fates, I *loved* her. More than anything and in ways I didn't even think possible. Which meant nothing would stand in my way of giving her whatever she needed.

I put my hand over my chest, vowing silently to myself. I'd use the monster inside of me in any way, every way if it meant making sure this world would be safe for her again. Safe for us.

No matter what.

CHAPTER 22

LANA

Flames licked at my skin, singeing my hair and pushing me backward.

"Lana!" Ian's scream echoed around me.

The damp stone walls trapped us both here.

Andras chuckled. "She can't help you."

I screamed, trying to jump through the flames, but it was no use.

I saw him.

I saw Ian lying on the ground, reaching toward me. Andras grinned, grasping a black blade over his head and slamming it into Ian's side.

I jerked upward, shouting.

Tears stained my cheeks and my heart fluttered in time with my breaths.

I jumped out of bed, scanning the room for Ian. For Andras.

But I was alone.

Sunlight beamed through the large windows, falling across my skin and drawing my attention to my surroundings

I wasn't in the castle. Not in the dungeons.

But Ian was.

Fates, Ian remained trapped in Ellevail, and I couldn't get to him.

I wobbled, leaning toward the bed before crawling back into it. This time when I'd relived my nightmare, Ian and I had swapped places.

I drew my legs into my chest, rocking. Squeezing my eyes shut, I pretended Ian sat next to me. I was in Mysthaven. This was real. *Real as roses.* I heard his voice, forcing myself to believe I heard it.

It was a dream. I repeated it over and over.

My breathing slowed, my body letting go of some of the tension balled in my shoulders and chest.

Gulping in one more deep, slow breath, I let go of all of it.

I'd done it. I'd soothed myself without Elisabeth's tonic, without Ian. I let myself feel the inner strength I possessed. The triumph blossomed inside of me.

I am stronger than the darkness within me.

I'd need to be strong to rescue Ian, and all of that started today. Cassandra would tell me why Kade needed me here, and then he'd take me home. I'd make Andras pay for everything he'd done to Ian, and my home, in my absence.

I turned my head, looking toward the bright windows with a settled sense of resolve washing over me.

My gaze caught on a beautiful black rose and small silver package on the nightstand. Even in my jealous and then lustful state last night, I'd noticed the immense gardens outside the castle. Black and deep purple roses stretched out past the balcony and into the night. This looked just like those.

I leaned over, picking up the package. A small folded paper lay under ribbons, and I opened it.

Happy birthday, Little Rebel. Since my original gift didn't last nearly long enough.

My cheeks heated. Groaning, I grabbed the pillow and covered my face. I might be ready to face the world, but I wasn't sure I was ready to face Kade.

His shadows were just as skilled as he was in the pleasure

department. I wanted a distraction, and he'd delivered. Tenfold.

And I wanted more.

Idiot, I scolded myself.

Curiosity getting the best of me, I opened the package Kade left me.

Tearing the paper away revealed a crimson-red box, the edges lined with black stone. Opening the top, I gasped. Inside sat a silver necklace with a small oval-shaped midnight-blue stone surrounded by an intricate woven design of silver strands encasing it. Usually, royal jewelry was elaborate, with an excessive number of gems, but this simplicity—it was elegant, stunning.

I lifted it from the box, holding it up and watching as the sun reflected brilliantly off the gorgeous stone. It was too much, and yet I *wanted* it. I hugged it to my chest. My parents were the only people to have ever gifted me jewelry.

I ran my fingers over the design, the stone. *Damn it, Kade.*

Lifting the necklace, I fastened the clasp around my neck. It fell perfectly, resting in the center of my chest.

Heaving myself from the bed, I dressed quickly, determined to find Kade to say thank you and then to force him to drag me to Cassandra as soon as possible.

Running my hands over my training attire, in the mirror I nodded once at my reflection. It would be impossible to hide my dagger at my thigh today, so instead I kneeled, hiding it within my boot.

I would always be prepared.

I touched the necklace once more, deciding to slip it beneath my shirt, just in case the king recognized it. I had no idea how we'd play this now after last night. I'm pretty sure the scene on the dance floor didn't make the situation between Kade and me less obvious.

I'd been housed around the corner of the hallway to

Kade's chambers, so it wouldn't take long to reach his door, but I paused when I heard voices lingering in the hall.

Silently, I stalked the rest of the way to the corner, halting at the brash tone of the king echoing down the corridor that led to Kade's door.

"You will secure a wife," King Dargan said sternly, "now."

Kade huffed. "Marriage seems like the last thing we should be worried about right now."

"You think you know best?" Dargan sneered. "You must produce an heir. You have an obligation to this family, to this kingdom. You must play your role in protecting the people of Atheria."

Where in the Fates was Atheria?

"Have I not done my part? The Monster of Mysthaven isn't enough for you?"

A cough behind me startled me and I jumped, slapping my hand to my mouth to keep a scream from giving away my position in the hall.

"Hasn't anyone ever told you, it's impolite to eavesdrop?" an unknown man said to me.

"I, uh—"

I only took in the stranger for a second. His long flowing robe swished as he flung it behind him. His brown hair curled underneath a strange black cap. Before I could try to place him, he grabbed me by the arm and forced me around the corner to face Kade and the king.

"I found this one lurking around the corner, my king," the man sneered. "Your conversation is no longer private."

I shrugged his hand off my arm, freeing myself from this intruder. "Perhaps having a conversation in the hallway is the problem, not me simply walking to a meeting with the prince and stumbling upon this." I snapped my mouth shut the minute the words were out. *Great job acting proper, Lana.*

"Why good morning, Princess Illiana," the king said with his eerie smile. "Curiosity is not a sin, but..." He took a few steps toward me and reached for me, but I stepped back. His eyes flared before narrowing. "I suggest you heed this warning and not eavesdrop like that again."

Kade's shadows leaked from his palms before he balled them into fists. "Careful, Father. It sounds like you are threatening a royal guest in your home." Kade tried speaking evenly, but there was a slight tremor in his voice, betraying his emotions. "We wouldn't want to be inhospitable. Diplomatic relations and all that."

The king looked between us and smiled that sickeningly saccharine smile once more. "Now, Tomas, what did you need so urgently before our guest interrupted?"

"You are needed in the study, Your Majesty," Tomas announced. "We are late for our weekly meeting with the royal advisors."

"Ah, is it time already?" The king turned to face Kade. "Do listen to what I say, boy. Or I'll bring you to heel as a reminder."

"Come, Your Majesty, allow me to lead the way," Tomas said, bowing his head and holding out his arm in the direction they intended to travel.

Before they left the hall, the king turned his attention to me. "Have a good day, Princess."

Silently, I bowed my head as he passed.

The two scurried down the hall, leaving Kade and me alone.

The man who'd ravaged me against the stone walls of the castle garden seemed a dream compared to the stoic face before me. "We need to go see Cassandra," Kade said, pivoting toward a set of stairs at the opposite end of the hall from where the king had disappeared.

"Wait, Kade." I grabbed his arm, forcing him to pause. His hardened facial features softened as he looked me in the eyes, and my body came alive. Heat crept up my neck. "Thank you."

"For?"

"This." I lifted the necklace from beneath my training shirt. "It is beautiful."

A sadness appeared in his gaze as he stood staring at the necklace. "It was my mother's—Queen Seraphine." He touched the gem with the fingertips. "I only have two heirlooms from her, this and a ring. She was very special to me."

His mother's? I blinked, unsure of how to respond. "Kade—"

He dropped his hand. "Whether you believe it or not, you are too."

"I can't take this from you, then," I whispered.

"You're not taking it," he said. He stepped into me and brushed a strand of hair behind my ear. "It's a gift. A real gift instead of one given secretly in dark corners."

The heat from my neck licked up to my face. I knew I'd turned a shade of pink beneath his gaze and words. The hesitation lingering morphed into something stronger, a feeling that threatened to ruin me. Which was stupid. Anything with Kade would be doomed.

"Don't you want to keep this for your future wife?" I glanced down and fidgeted with the stone in my hand. "Someone more important than me?"

Kade smiled, his shadows forming a warm cocoon around my legs. "There is no one more important than you, Little Rebel." He moved away, but reached out his hand, taking mine. "Come on, we've got a seer to visit."

<hr>

Kade silently led me through the castle halls, our hands intertwined. Fortunately, Cassandra's room wasn't far, and I didn't have too much time to think about how his touch soothed a restless part of me. Or how his words from earlier, and knowing what the necklace truly meant, snapped together within me like a missing puzzle piece.

Kade raised his hand to knock, but before he could, it swung open, and Cassandra appeared in its frame.

"I've been expecting you."

Mischief and secrets danced in her eyes. She seemed more aware now than she had been in my room before the ball. I couldn't shake that the air around her felt familiar.

Cassandra turned, her silver dress spinning out with her movement as she ushered us into a small sitting area to the right of the entryway. The sitting area was located away from where I assumed her main chambers were, through a closed door at the back of the room. Three wooden chairs surrounded a tufted emerald ottoman, holding a tray scattered with black and purple-tinted roses.

The fairly sparse room revealed nothing about Cassandra, not even the smallest detail. Except for the floor-to-ceiling built-in bookshelves lining the far-left wall. The shelves were made purely of stone and strewn with open books, loose papers, and scattered flower petals. A black table sat a few feet in front of the bookshelves and contained various vials and one open book.

"You've been away too long. I've had no one to sit with me for my tea, dear." She patted Kade's arm, tugging him down to one of the chairs. "Though I can't fault you for your distraction." She winked at me.

In no hurry, she poured tea into three of the cups. "Sugar?" she asked me, after preparing Kade's with two lumps of sugar and a dash of cream.

I nodded. "And cream, please."

She hummed, handing me my tea, and removed a black vial from inside the waistband of her dress. She poured it upside down into her own cup, not bothering to offer any to us or reveal what it contained.

Cassandra sighed heavily and leaned back in her chair,

swirling the cup in front of her face as she stared at the bookshelf.

I looked at Kade, who sipped his tea, but he didn't seem confused by the seer's silence. He gave her a few more moments before coughing, clearing his throat to garner her attention. "Cassandra, we need to talk about my prophecy. I must know what it means so I can get Illiana home."

Prophecies. It all came down to these prophecies. I tried not to let out my frustration that the words of seers held more weight than I thought fair.

I swallowed a sip of the sweet tea, forcing my heaviness at this moment away as much as possible. Whatever Cassandra told us would change things. I knew it. Just as my life had changed with Vivienne's prophecy.

"I've been waiting for this moment for years," Cassandra started with a smile. "The time has come. The beginning of the end. Time's afoot, time's afoot." She continued swirling her tea.

I stood corrected at my earlier thought that Cassandra seemed more present. This woman was just as bizarre as Vivienne, slipping in and out of her rambling. She sounded like her, almost exactly.

Cassandra sipped her tea and set it down, leaning forward to touch Kade's face. "Have you told her Fates' words?"

Kade glanced at me and then shook his head. "I trust her, I just wanted your wisdom without imparting my feelings."

She scoffed at him. "The Fates' words include her no matter your feelings, Kade Blackthorn."

His jaw ticked.

"Go on," Cassandra ordered. "Speak it."

Kade huffed. "Cassandra delivered a prophecy a few years ago. She's had a couple of them in her time—" Cassandra swatted his leg, but not angrily. I frowned, remembering how at ease Kade seemed with Vivienne at the bonfire. He hadn't balked at Vivienne's strange behavior because it had been so close to his Cassandra's. "Rebels rise where darkness lies, not one but two must break the ties. Across the void, a queen you must seek, trust freely given, for one alone proves too weak. Though evil will free and be bound no more, Fate still awaits one final war."

I exhaled. Not much of it made sense to me. Minus that part where he dragged me across the void. But I wasn't a queen. *Break the ties? Evil will free?* That sounded anything but pleasant.

"I'm not a queen, Kade," I said softly.

"He acted on his heart, not the words," Cassandra interjected. "Fate is fickle, and my interference could change too much. But I did always tell him to trust his heart."

Kade stared at his tea.

A tingle ran along my skin under Cassandra's stare. I'd lived almost my entire life hating Vivienne's words. The weight I'd felt earlier returned. Maybe it hadn't left at all, it just became more pronounced now.

"Princess," she said. "The time for decisions has come. Unravel your mind."

I knew her words were about Kade. If I'd trust him with a prophecy, she must know already.

It wasn't a question though. Through my wariness, my anger, my out-of-control mind and heart, I knew one thing—I *could* trust Kade. It may take me time to fully accept it, to let him have all the parts of me again, if I ever did. This moment though? This moment seemed too coincidental. Two prophecies, two kingdoms.

The damned Fates struck again. And a terrifying realization settled in my heart.

Vivienne's prophecy about me must be true. Just as Kade's must be.

Cassandra's voice drifted toward me and sealed my resolve. "If you've made your choice, no more secrets."

Kade finally turned his attention to me. "What secrets?"

My palms prickled with sweat, a nervous energy thrumming from my body. I knew the decision to trust Kade was the right one, a conviction stirring from somewhere I couldn't name. But speaking those words to anyone other than my parents, Ian, or Kalliah? It proved difficult.

"I have a prophecy too," I said, wiping my hands along my pants.

Kade's lips parted, but he didn't look away.

"It was given to me shortly after my birth, by Vivienne. It's why my parents enacted the marriage trials. They believed her words so fiercely and lived completely focused on fulfilling the damn thing."

Kade stared at me, arching his brow as if to say, "Go on."

Taking a deep breath, I spoke the words that controlled my life. "Void of magic, a heroine born, destiny calls, though faint and torn. Many will come from across the land, yet only the strongest will win her hand. With lover's touch she shall ignite, without it perish from the kingdom's blight."

Cassandra nodded with her eyes closed and stood abruptly.

She rubbed her hands together before taking Kade's, then mine. Quickly, she pulled our hands together, forcing us to our feet. My teacup landed with a clang against the table, spilling its contents. She dragged us to the center of the room, unfazed by the mess she'd created. She muttered under her breath, words I didn't understand or maybe just didn't grasp for how incoherently she spoke them.

Cassandra brought our hands up and then joined them together. Kade slid his hand into mine, intertwining our fingers just like he'd done earlier. As soon as Cassandra let go, a powerful shock sent waves of energy through me.

My knees wobbled and I could barely hold myself upright, the electric current so strong. Kade's eyes widened, and he gripped my hand more tightly, his shoulders shaking from the unknown magic pulsating between us.

"The Fates are at work." Cassandra's voice somehow echoed in the sitting area.

The current ceased, and the immediate force of her joining our hands faded.

"Are you all right?" Kade asked, his concerned eyes raking over me.

I nodded once. He looked back to Cassandra somewhat reluctantly. "What does it mean?" Kade asked. "It cannot be a coincidence both Lana and I have prophecies. There has to be more. What are we supposed to do?"

Cassandra's gaze flitted between us once more, all with an eerie sense of calm. "Time will reveal what minds cannot. Fulfill your prophecies and spark your destiny."

"That doesn't help get her back to safety, Cassandra. I need you to tell us more." Kade's panicked tone surprised me. His voice rising. He still held my hand. "I have to get her away from him."

Cassandra let him keep hold of my hand but grasped his other hand, kissing his knuckles like a reverent subject does their king. "The Fates have decreed the time has come. I can give you no more than I have right now. But know this, there is no longer a safe place for you until this ends. Not in either kingdom."

CHAPTER 23
LANA

Kade hadn't said much on our walk back to our rooms.

I hadn't either.

He'd mentioned a meeting and said he'd return, and in less than an hour, we walked to the training ring where Jax, Storm, and Raya waited.

Apparently, when not being used by the Guardians, the others felt the training ring provided the only space away from prying eyes. Together, Kade and I recounted the very minimal interaction with Cassandra.

We quickly repeated the prophecy—well, *prophecies* was more accurate, though the others knew of Kade's already.

Raya paced across the ring, deep in concentration once we finished.

Storm put up his hands. "So what you are telling us is that not only does Kade have a prophecy, but you have one too— and they are connected?"

"It appears that way." I sighed, wishing Ian and Kalliah were here. "Whatever the prophecies mean, Cassandra seems to believe fate is at play and the next steps are something Kade and I are supposed to do together." I rubbed my forehead. "Even if there's no indication of what those next steps might be."

"Logically," Jax started, twirling a sword in his hand and moving slowly through footwork that appeared second nature, "one would assume the 'kingdom's blight' might refer to the darkness. To the dark ones?"

"That is the most logical conclusion, yes." Kade ran his hands through his hair, clearly exasperated by the uncertainty of it all. "But how on earth are Lana and I supposed to defeat them? We don't know how the darkness spreads or where they're all coming from."

Storm put his hand on Kade's shoulder. "We will figure it out together. Just like we always have."

Raya, who hadn't stopped pacing, suddenly paused and pivoted toward us, her braided hair whipping around her face at the sudden change in movement. "Did anyone else feel there was something wrong with the dagger during the Blood Oath?"

We stared at her, no one responded.

Her eyes scanned each one of us. "I haven't been able to stop thinking about it. It's not the same as past festivals. When it cut my hand, it didn't feel like a normal cut. Something was not right."

"Add it to the growing list of concerns, Raya." Jax snickered.

"No, I felt it too," Storm added. He ran a hand over his jaw. "I just didn't think anything of it with everything else going on."

"Me as well," Kade stated, looking at Storm. "It called to the monster inside of me, bubbling at the surface. When cut, it was like he tried to take over. It took everything I had to control it."

"So, question." Jax paused his motions. "Is this where you tell us *exactly* what's been going on with you?" His arms crossed over his chest.

Storm and Kade traded a glance between them. A knowing pause. Apparently, trust was going around with no reservations anymore.

"We joke about the Monster of Mysthaven, but it's not merely a nickname," Kade said. The weariness in his voice made me want to reach for his hand, craving the same support we'd given each other in Cassandra's chambers. "For several years now, I have been struggling with a feeling of evil inside of me. It begs to come forward, to take over my body. A part of me feeds off the evil actions we've been tasked with, relishing it. The Monster of Mysthaven is more than just what my father has me do. The monster lives within me."

He turned to me, walking closer, as he spoke.

"What you saw at the void, the explosion—that is what happens when I can no longer control it. The only times I have been able to rein in the monster without an explosion, is when—" He paused, running a hand over the back of his neck. "Is when Lana touches me. At least, that's the only common denominator I've found thus far."

He'd told me this already in the garden. Whatever took over his body hesitated with my touch. But hearing the depths of it, the certainty that I somehow helped him maintain control, stole my breath.

"He had fewer episodes in Brookmere," Storm said, a slight hint of awe in his voice. "I thought it might be from being away from Mysthaven, but it's been more controlled since we've returned too."

Kade nodded at his friend.

"And the *monster* responded to the blade at the oath?" Raya asked.

Kade nodded again.

"So, something about that blade in particular called that side of you forward?" I theorized, not wanting to use the word *monster* in regard to Kade. Not ever again now that I had begun to grasp what it meant to him. The pain it caused.

"Do you think the king is poisoning people? It wouldn't be the first time a poisoned blade would be used by someone evil."

I unconsciously rubbed the scar on my side as my arms wrapped around myself.

Kade caught the motion, and his body tensed.

Storm's face dropped as he rubbed the spot where he was stabbed. "The blade from our journey here was powerful magic. It left a scar." He paused and my eyes flared.

What are we dealing with here?

Storm shook his head, like he couldn't comprehend it. "No, he's the king. He wouldn't…"

"Wouldn't what?" Raya asked as she came to stand beside me.

"You think he is infecting people with the darkness using that blade." I said it knowing that was exactly the conclusion Kade had drawn. One that seemed obvious, given my own history. Had Andras tried to force the darkness into me in Brookmere unsuccessfully?

Raya sucked in a breath. "Or testing if he *can* infect people."

"I don't feel any different," Storm said, his brow deeply furrowed.

"Seems pretty ballsy if you ask me," Jax stated. "How would he have bottled evil? That's essentially what you're saying. Beyond that, what would make him choose to do something so aggressive now?"

"Nothing is out of the realm of possibility," Kade remarked. "We need to think of all of the times we have seen blades like that before." He stopped, frowning. "This isn't the first time he's used something like this." Kade's voice lowered to the point where I didn't know if he meant for the words to be for all of us. "He used whips and other devices on me. When Cassandra used to heal me growing up, my blood leeched black occasionally."

An emotional ache erupted inside of me. He'd been tortured.

By his own father.

The possessive part of me that balked against his father's words during the festival came alive again. I wanted to go to him, to touch him. Instead, I closed my eyes, clenching my hands into fists. I needed to regain control of myself.

Jax and Raya didn't say a word, but Storm turned away from his friend and us.

"I thought it was because of my shadows, but if we follow the train of thought we're on—" Kade waved a hand.

"But you don't act like a dark one," I whispered.

"He does when he can't control it," Storm added. "You've seen a very controlled version of Kade here and in Brookmere, Lana. Before, it…it could be seen as akin to the dark ones."

"Well, we clearly have a place to start. But how do we get our hands on that blade to see if we're right?" Jax asked.

Storm stepped closer to Jax. "Cassandra may know a way."

Storm, Kade, and Jax huddled together, discussing this new revelation. Raya and I remained on the outside, neither of us able to add anything more to the conversation. When their voices lowered, she stepped back. A flash of hurt in her eyes lingered for a moment before returning to their hardened nature.

"It can suck to be the one on the outside," I said. It sounded dumb now that the words were out of my mouth, and not at all comforting.

"Yeah, well. The outside isn't so bad sometimes."

Silence fell between us. I sat down on the outer rim of the ring, hopping up onto the wall.

A few more moments passed, and Raya looked at me, fear furrowing her brow.

These flashes of emotion seemed so unlike her.

She cleared her throat. "I know you're not the biggest fan of mind magic, and I get that, most aren't. But I could try to check on your friend again if you wanted. I can't guarantee it will work; I normally can't get into others' minds like that, especially at such a distance, but I am willing to try."

Her offer caught me completely off guard. "You would do that for me?"

"Yeah, well, I—" She rolled her shoulders, so obviously uncomfortable with the situation, I couldn't help but smile. I barely knew her, and yet I knew without a doubt this generosity was not given to many. "I didn't realize how being stuck with those three assholes my entire life might mean I missed out on some fun, until your tipsy ranting about dancing on a table. I surprisingly, and against my better judgement, didn't mind our talk."

I didn't even try to stop my grin now. "You liked it. You liked girl talk."

She rolled her eyes. "I will end this immediately if you don't wipe that stupid smile off your face. I know your friend is important to you, and if the roles were reversed, I would hope you would do it for me too."

I stared, realizing she had no reason to offer me this other than extending an olive branch. One I didn't know I craved so badly. An elated, tender feeling swelled in me as I grabbed Raya's hand. "Thank you. It would mean everything to me if you could try."

Raya and I moved toward the seats along the edge of the training ring, and she sat. I didn't know what to expect or how long it would take. I clasped my hands together to keep them from nervously fidgeting.

If Raya pulled this off, she could tell me if Ian was okay. Or hopefully discover that he'd escaped the dungeons and was somewhere safe. Anything to ease my fears, even the smallest bit.

Raya closed her eyes, sitting so ramrod straight she brought the nobility of Brookmere to shame.

I didn't know if staring at her would distract her, so I kept my gaze flitting around the room. The men still talked, but Kade glanced toward me and frowned.

Throwing the best reassuring smile I could give, I turned my attention back to Raya.

She inhaled deeply, her body stilling.

Then she collapsed.

CHAPTER 24

IAN

Warrick's fist split my cheek open as spit flew from his mouth.

Fresh blood dripped down my cheek from his attack. His grin made me wish to the Fates I knew how to break free from the chains holding me in place so I could wipe it off with the heel of my boot.

"Not so tough now, are you?" He spit down at my feet.

I should be grateful he avoided doing so in my face this time.

Grinning back at him—at least I hoped it came across as a grin—pissed him off more. And that was before I spoke. "Unhook me from these bindings and let's see who is tough."

Crack.

His fist at my side snapped my rib. Again.

I'd lost track of how many times I'd been broken and healed. Warrick's appearance provided a new way for Andras to get hours of additional revenge using the hands of others. Just another way he kept his hands mostly clean while allowing those with a vendetta to air their grievances.

"I didn't know you enjoyed bondage, Warrick. Is that why none of your companions have stayed around long?"

"Enough." Andras's voice echoed in the cell before Warrick landed his final blow to my bleeding lips. "Go clean yourself up."

Warrick hit the side of my face playfully, bouncing on his toes, and smiled at me. "See you soon."

Andras stalked in front of me. He tsked. "You could have made this easy on all of us, Captain."

"Where's the fun in that," I hissed. I did my best to ignore the searing pain in my side. Breathing hurt, let alone talking. If things continued as before, he'd send for Maria in order to start with a fresh canvas again tomorrow.

"The time for games has come to an end. I grow weary of the violence, even if I do enjoy watching you squirm." The same damn blade twirled in his hand again. He gripped the handle, stepping closer to me, and without warning slammed the tip into my side.

I couldn't prevent the shout from escaping my lips. It burned. The pain not merely from the wound inflicted, but from whatever seeped into it.

I clamped my mouth shut, biting on my tongue to keep from crying out again until I tasted blood.

"Now, Captain," he said, snickering, "I think we will have a much easier time together."

He held the dagger firmly in my side, not saying anything else.

But I *felt* him. Those talons clawed at my mind. Using every last ounce of magic and strength left within me, I fortified the walls the talons so desperately tried to break down.

A sharp prick dug into me. Whether it was my mind or my body, I couldn't be sure, but the pain radiated outward as I muffled my cry.

Andras laughed. "Not long now."

A darkness developed around my vision. I had to fight this. Figure out a way to fight him. Separating myself from the physical pain was useless, because the pain was everywhere. The harder I tried to block out the physical pain, the more the talons pried, attempting to get into my mind.

Suddenly, just as had happened once before, someone else joined me behind the walls I so painfully constructed.

A female voice inside my head screamed.

"What's happening?" The voice startled me, and I twitched. Andras still smiled, his focus not at all deterred by the voice I heard.

What the fuck? At least I hadn't been wrong, and the presence I'd felt before wasn't Andras and his mind magic.

Knowing that did nothing to calm my aching body and mind or understand how someone else managed to be inside of my head.

Perhaps the voice was merely my imagination, a response to the absolute agony my body endured this afternoon, or maybe I'd completely lost my mind.

"Ian?"

No, I hadn't lost my mind yet. There was a distinct something *else* present. A female voice, by the sound of it. One I didn't recognize. Someone was talking to me inside my head. Andras still didn't seem any wiser as he continued to scratch at my mind, grinning his twisted smile.

That's me, I answered, thinking it instead of speaking the words, because how else would one speak to someone within their fucking mind?

The scratch from the talon made the female voice groan. *"What's happening to you?"*

I'm currently being tortured by an asshole. Apologies if it's uncomfortable for you, whoever you are. Had I known you would be joining, I would've attempted to make this more hospitable for you.

Whoever was in here with me remained silent, but I could sense their indignant attitude. It almost made me smile.

She cursed as Andras managed to chip away at my mental wall, slowly crumbling the bricks I'd so carefully laid.

"Fight back," she demanded.

Right, how stupid of me. Fight back. What do you think I'm doing? I don't know how to stop mind magic.

She huffed, muttering under her breath.

A cooling sensation wrapped around my mind and the imminent threat of the talons lessened.

Stop it, I shouted at the female. *What are you doing to me?*

"Helping, you ungrateful prick," she snapped.

Excuse me?

"Fates, I haven't even met you and I already don't like you." The voice sounded annoyed but calm. Somehow reassuring, even through the insults. *"That's a first. Usually, I have to see a person before I automatically dislike them."*

Maybe I had lost my mind after all. Arguing with a voice in my head didn't seem the best indicator for sanity. Although the strain against Andras's attempts to access my mind had all but halted. I blinked, watching the look on his face fade from a smile to unadulterated rage.

He shoved the blade deeper into my side, and I cried out again.

"There's a darkness seeping into your mind. He's using something to make it easier to gain access."

Yes, well, he's currently digging a fucking knife into my side.

She stayed quiet, but the cooling sensation morphed into an overall numbness, as if Andras lost his pathway to gain entry into my head. *"What I did should help for a little while, but you have to keep fighting. I can't guarantee I'll be able to help you again."*

Great, thanks so much for the advice. Being in my head, talking to this mystery guest did help distract me from the pain. Compartmentalizing it was infinitely easier with the distraction. *Who are you? How do you know who I am or about Andras's mind magic?*

"She didn't mention you'd be a nitwit," she sighed. *"Obviously, I have mind magic as well. I understand how to use it. Clearly, since we're talking in your mind."*

That caught me off guard. It also immediately raised my defenses.

You didn't mention who you are. I hoped my voice sounded as cold as I intended.

"My name is Raya. I'm a...friend of Lana's."

I noted the hesitation.

Nope. I don't think so. You can escort yourself out of my head. Now.

She scoffed. The sound skated down my spine. Like something in me enjoyed annoying this woman.

No, the sensation was merely a reaction to this impossible conversation.

"Lana wanted me to check on you. When we discovered I could enter your mind, we thought we'd try again. She is worried about you."

Stop it. I winced as the physical pain crossed into my mental threshold. *Don't bother. If you're with Lana, then you're with the people who took her. She'd never leave willingly. Kade Blackthorn, Storm, whoever else has her somehow. I'm sure of it. And if you're with her, you're with them. Leave me alone.*

"You stubborn ass. You need my help or that torturer will break through and control you. Is that what you want?" A vague picture came into my mind of a woman with long, dark braided hair, pacing back and forth.

I shook the image away. She needed to leave. *I've managed fine without your help so far.*

"This is why I hate everyone."

I said—

The figure stopped pacing. *"Lana told me about her birthdays at Dukes Pub. About the year she danced on a table, and you played with the band."*

I stilled, both inside my mind and out. I didn't know how Andras would interpret it. Fates, was she really safe? I didn't know if I could trust this voice to tell me the truth if I asked.

Suddenly, I wasn't in my mind anymore. I was back in the cell as Andras whipped the blade from me.

"Damn you," he cried. "Your mental shield is strong, I'll

give you that, Captain. You won't survive the next week though." He unhooked me from the chains and left me in a heap on the cold stone floor. "Enjoy the new scar. You can match your precious princess. Oh, and don't bother waiting for Maria. She won't be coming." Andras exited, slamming the cell door shut.

"*Ian?*" The voice bounced around my head. "*Ian?*"

A little busy trying not to die right now, I muttered internally.

"*Dramatic. If you're conscious, you're fine,*" the voice said.

Ah, so if I pass out, will I get to stop talking to you?

The figure formed again, this time crossing her arms.

"*I need to tell Lana something, and mentioning you're being tortured in the dungeons doesn't seem smart. She's just starting to trust us.*"

Is she safe? I couldn't help but ask. I needed to know. Even if I couldn't fully trust Raya's answer.

"*Of course she's safe. You're the one who isn't.*"

Will she stay safe?

This time the pause spoke volumes.

If you hurt her, I will find you. Hunt you. Kill you myself. No matter what aid you just provided.

"*No harm will come to her at my hands. Or from my friends, who apparently are your friends as well. I can't tell you anything in case that freakishly gangly man manages to break into your mind, but she's with people who care about her.*"

Not likely, I said, but some of my apprehension for her safety dissipated at her words anyway. *I don't trust you. You better be right about Lan though. She needs to get to Valeford. I'll meet her there somehow. I will break free. She has to get there as soon as she can.*

"*She's not going anywhere right now.*"

I reminded myself there was reason enough not to trust this Raya woman. If Lana didn't have the freedom to go where she pleased, how could she be safe?

This isn't up for discussion. There's something she needs to do for whatever is to come. Get her to Valeford, Raya, and pray nothing happens to her until I arrive.

242

"I won't tell her what's happening to you," Raya whispered.

Good. Now get out of my head.

"Ian—"

Gathering my last ounce of strength, I shoved her out. Somehow cutting off her access to my mind. I prayed I hadn't just fallen for one of Andras's tricks, an illusion of a friend in a time of need. However, if other Fae were also gifted with mind magic, it was far from comforting knowing they could gain access to my mind so easily.

My body shook violently, out of control. Hopefully, I'd make it through the night.

No, I *would* last the night. I had no choice. Lana would get the message about Valeford.

Together, we'd find what she needed to take back her kingdom.

As my eyes closed, I heard a faint whimper, and a cold, wet nose pressed against my cheek. "Good boy," I whispered, hoping it was Lucien, even if I couldn't open my eyes to see him. "She's safe. She's safe and we're going to go to her soon. I swear it."

CHAPTER 25
LANA

Sleep eluded me.

I lay under the soft black velvet covers of this too large bed as my mind raced. Tossing and turning, unable to shut down my body or the thoughts whirling in my mind after today's revelations.

My body remained stuck in the moment of pure dread from when Raya had screamed, finally conscious again after what felt like an eternity.

She'd been hesitant to tell me anything, but her reservations revealed enough. My best friend had not escaped the dungeons, which could only mean he was being tortured. The pained look on her face told me everything I needed to know, for I'd spent too many nights down there to think Andras would change his ways now.

She'd described the strange magic she sensed being used against Ian. Kade immediately thought it sounded like Andras had attempted to infect Ian with the same substance felt on the blades at the Blood Oath. Though understanding what the poison did remained a mystery. Everyone here felt fine.

But this meant both kingdoms were under attack from the same evil. However, Brookmere didn't even know Mysthaven existed, so it made little sense to be facing the same dangers or using the same methods of spreading evil.

I turned over, curling myself in a ball as my throat constricted. I hadn't thought there were any tears left after realizing Ian remained trapped. Tears didn't do Ian any good though. I needed anger.

I would fight until my dying breath to save him. I would kill Andras. Slowly.

However, there was one good thing that had come from Raya's vision. Kade took one look at how my knees buckled following that news, sending me to the training ring floor, and immediately decided we'd all return to Brookmere.

Despite needing me here, and Cassandra's assignment to solve our prophecies, he agreed to go back. For me.

I didn't know how to process that on top of everything else.

His command led to brainstorming how we could possibly get away from the castle without causing alarm or notice.

Taking me by surprise again at her generosity and willingness to risk herself, Raya offered to try to plant the idea of a traitor into the king's mind. One on the outskirts of Mysthaven, in hopes the king would call upon Kade to dispose of him, putting us near the void and buying us time to move into Brookmere.

It was risky, too risky. But what other choice did we have at this point? I had to get back home, and I needed Kade to be able to cross the void.

Kade.

I needed him for more than crossing the void though. I was tired of fighting it. I craved his presence. Desperate to be close to him, to touch him, to be by his side. The inexplicable draw to feel his shadows around me thrummed in me almost constantly.

Our lives were clearly intertwined by these damned

prophecies. But some moments made it feel like so much more than that.

Thirty more minutes passed of my circular thinking of Ian, plans to leave, Kade, and back to Ian. My torment throwing me between pain, grief, fear, and need. All I had succeeded in was creating knots in my hair and wrinkles in the covers from my constant movement.

I grabbed the black satin pillow from behind me and placed it over my head, screaming in frustration.

A whisper of a breeze rustled the covers down my body. I frowned but didn't remove the pillow.

The covers moved on top of me again, and I jerked up, looking down the bed to find I wasn't alone.

Kade's shadows were here.

They pulled the covers off, whipping them back. I cocked my head to the side. Were they playing?

Would it be absolutely ridiculous if I tried to pet them?

I let out an incredulous breath. *Get it together, Lana. They are shadows, not a damn pugron.*

That thought only reminded me of Lucien. A smile played on my lips thinking of my brave, ferocious pugron waiting for me at home.

Kade's shadows moved up the bed and snaked behind me, pushing me to the edge of the mattress.

"What are you doing?"

They stalled momentarily before pushing harder, pressing against my back and wrapping around my front.

They called to me. Wanted me for something.

Quickly, I grabbed the pair of training pants strewn on a chair next to the bed and shoved my feet into the flat brown shoes I'd taken to wearing here.

The shadows tremored urgently. The dark pool of them slipping under the door worried me, turning what I thought playful fun into an anxious need to get to Kade. The distance from Kade's room to mine must be stretching their limits. I'd never seen them extended so far away from him.

I opened the door, slipping out and following their trail, all while they danced in front of me.

Come.

An ache from deep within urged me forward.

They shifted from a large outpouring to a singular trail.

Follow.

We silently moved together, calling on my skills as the Hidden Henchman to sneak down the hall. Before we rounded the corner to get to Kade's room, the shadows halted.

Stay.

The shadows crept up my body, surrounding me just as they had when they'd protected me in a hallway similar to this back home. When they'd shielded me from Casimir.

A blanket of night stretched into the hall itself, no lights giving me away. Regardless, there was no doubt in my mind the shadows would protect me.

Click.

The sound of a handle made the faintest noise down the hall. I peeked around the corner to find King Dargan exiting Kade's room.

What was he doing in Kade's room at this hour?

The king glanced up and down the hallway, dropping a small object in his pocket, as he walked forward. Directly toward me.

I tried to run, but the shadows held me in place. A tendril of shadow stroked my back.

Safe.

I swore I practically heard them whisper, *We will protect you.*

So I stayed completely still. When the king rounded the corner, I held my breath and closed my eyes.

He moved past me without a second thought, passing through the archway, down a staircase past my room.

Releasing my breath, I waited a moment longer before attempting to move. The shadows shoved at my back and urged me forward once more.

Quicker.

We reached Kade's door, and I turned the knob. It swung open freely as the shadows spilled into the room. I lost sight of them in the dark, even though I still felt them around me.

"Kade?" I whispered, as I tried to find him. "Are you in here?"

Silently, I shut the door behind me. I received no response from the Fae.

"Kade," I said a bit louder this time.

Still nothing. I ventured farther into the massive room, out of his main entryway and toward his bed chambers as my eyes adjusted to the dark. Long beams of moonlight sifted through the windows along the far wall, almost as if they lit a path for me to his bedroom.

The door hung slightly ajar, and I pressed it open further.

I found nothing. No one. Just ruffled covers on his bed.

Suddenly, a shape sped through the darkness, slamming me against the wall next to the door. A familiar body trapped me.

"Careful, Little Rebel. The Monster of Mysthaven has been dying to get his hands on you."

Kade's eyes were so far beyond black they looked empty. Void. They were the darkest I had ever seen before.

"What are you talking about?" I asked. "Let me go."

"Sneaking about the castle in the dead of the night…is how shall we put this?" Kade laughed in a way I'd never heard before. The sinister chuckle twisted the normally bright feeling inside of me. "A poor choice."

My heartbeat quickened. He wasn't in his right state of mind.

This wasn't Kade. It was his monster.

Everything we'd been through rushed back. The touches,

whether I realized it or not, had helped him. I could help him now too.

Slowly, I reached up and touched his face, rubbing my thumb along his cheek, whispering, "Come back to me."

Kade's body jolted, yet his eyes didn't clear like they had before.

I wiggled my other hand free from the wall and grabbed his face with both hands now. "Kade," I said, my voice purposefully calm. "Come back to me."

He tried to pull his head away. "Why are you touching me like that?"

"Please, come back. I'm here, it's Lana."

His face slackened. His eyes shimmered, the void shifting as black swirled in his gaze.

My breath hitched as I watched the internal battle unfold.

Slowly, his eyes cleared to their normal grey hue. Instantly, his shoulders sagged as if a weight had been removed. He stumbled away from me without saying a word.

"Are you all right?" I asked.

"Yes." Kade took a few deep breaths and ran his hands through his hair. "Are you... Did I hurt you?"

I shook my head. He didn't look at me though, so I voiced it. "You didn't do anything to hurt me." I frowned, looking over my shoulder out of the room before turning back to face Kade. "What was your father doing in here so late?"

Kade's brow furrowed in confusion. "My father wasn't here. I've been in this room alone since I left yours."

I knew full well I didn't imagine the king earlier. "No, Kade, you were not alone. I watched him leave your room. Your shadows came and got me, and they led me to you. I saw him leave and found you like—" I paused, refusing to say *monster*. "Not yourself."

I could see the wheels turning in Kade's brain, the tick in his jaw, the furrowed brow. He took a moment before walking to his bed, sitting on the edge.

I gave him a minute to reflect before approaching him. "What do you think it means?"

He looked up at me, somber. "I'm not sure, but whatever it is, it's not good. As much as I don't want to believe it, I think it means my father is up to something more than just being a tyrant king. Whatever happened during the Blood Oath and whatever happened tonight are absolutely connected. He's desperate to have me under his thumb."

A knowing silence passed between us, and in that moment, I craved his touch. I wanted to soothe his anxious soul. Worry, guilt, frustration, all of it consumed him. It was almost like I could *feel* it rolling off of him.

As he sat there, looking defeated and confused, I wrapped my arms around him. He glanced sideways at me, and I reached for his face, bringing his head to my chest. Letting him hear my beating heart.

Even if the position wasn't the most comfortable given our size difference, he didn't pull away. Instead, he wrapped his arms around me. I held him there as his shadows wrapped themselves around my legs.

For as many times as this man had saved me, I could take a moment and provide him some comfort.

I had no idea how long I held him, but it still seemed too soon when Kade pulled away. He brushed a thumb across my cheek. "I'm sorry if I scared you."

"You didn't." I meant that. Even if he hadn't been in his right mind, I knew now he wouldn't hurt me. I trusted him.

I'd almost let him all the way back in. I'd told him the prophecy. Now I wanted to let go and trust him with all of it. I exhaled slowly.

Raya had told us Ian needed me to get to Valeford, which may have been news to the others, but not to me. If Kade and I were the key to figuring out this darkness, he needed to know everything.

"I need to show you something." I removed my father's

letter from the pocket of my training pants. I always kept it on me, never wanting to part from his final words. Too afraid of who might see it and lose the one piece of my father I had left. I handed him the paper as I sat down beside him.

He watched me for a moment before I urged, "Go on, read it for yourself."

Cocking a brow, he smirked. "Writing me love letters, Little Rebel? I'm flattered."

I smacked his shoulder. "You ass, just read the letter."

As soon as he was done reading, he folded the paper back up and returned it to me. I put it back in my pocket and couldn't help but shed a tear in that moment. I knew what that letter said word for word now, I'd reread it so many times. While it may have hurt slightly less with each pass, showing Kade something so personal made me feel vulnerable. I experienced the letter in a different way now that someone besides me had read its contents. It was harder than I thought it would be.

"I am so sorry," he said. "Receiving such news after what you saw, I—" He stopped talking and stood, moving a few steps away from me.

"It's okay—"

"It's not." He sighed, and though he made eye contact briefly, he looked away immediately. "It's not okay that you went through learning this alone. Having to read about your parents instead of having them there to tell you."

I swallowed, wiping away a tear that fell. "I'm not sure they would have told me."

He kneeled in front of me, taking my hands in his. "I'm sorry that chance was taken from you. I'm sorry for the role I played."

More tears fell, but neither of us stopped them. "I forgive you. I don't know if that's what you need to hear or not, but I don't hate you anymore for what you did. And for the record,

I believe you, Kade. If there had been any other way, I know you would have found it."

He squeezed my hands. "No matter what happens, we're leaving tomorrow. Whether Raya's plan works or not. I'm taking you and we're leaving. We'll get to Ian, then to Valeford, and wherever else we need to go."

"Cassandra made it seem like we needed to be here to solve the prophecies."

"I don't care," he said with fierce determination. Reaching toward me, his hand gently caressed my cheek. "I don't care about what anyone else needs or wants. I care about what *you* need. The rest, we can figure out as we go."

I nodded, not trusting my voice in the moment.

He dropped back, letting his hand fall from my neck, but remained kneeling in front of me. The sight of him between my legs, staring at me as if I was the only thing that mattered, did something to my soul. The pull between us strengthened, solidifying. His messy hair made me smile, and I reached for a strand.

I twisted it around my finger, and before I could pull away, Kade took my hand and kissed my palm. "If my father is sneaking around at night, it's not safe for you to be alone."

"It feels like it's not safe for me anywhere anymore."

Kade rose, his shadows dancing at his feet while he pulled me up to stand as well. "Stay here tonight." Brushing a strand of hair behind my ear. "Stay with me."

I knew I should say no, but my heart screamed at me to say yes. Just being near him made me feel alive. His shadows made me feel safe. He just made me feel.

I tilted my chin up toward him. "Using fear to get me into bed with you?"

His lips curved into a heart-wrenchingly beautiful smile. One I don't think I'd seen since Brookmere. He leaned down, his lips almost touching mine as a shiver ran over me.

"I don't think I need any tricks to get you into my bed, Little Rebel."

I started to pull away to try for a smart comment back, but he closed the space between us, capturing my mouth. He reached for my hair, his hand weaving into it as he moaned against my lips.

"I miss your taste. Every damn day," he murmured between kisses.

I reached my arms around his neck, deepening the kiss as I ran my tongue over his. *Fates.* I'd forgotten how perfect, how incredible his kisses were. My body melted into his, and he leaned down, lifting me by my thighs and wrapping my legs around his waist. He turned, falling back on his bed with me still attached to him, never breaking our kiss.

Groaning into his mouth, I didn't care how needy I sounded as I rubbed against him.

He chuckled. "If we're fleeing the castle, we need to sleep."

"We can sleep after," I whimpered against his lips.

"Little Rebel, when I have you again, it won't be rushed." He shifted his weight and then flipped me to my back. "It won't be used as a way to get you to sleep." He kissed my jaw, then down my neck as his hand trailed up my thigh, brushing over that sensitive spot where I craved his touch. "It won't be when I know you'll be riding hours on horseback and can't be sore from how long I spend inside of you." He buried his head in my neck, letting out a moan of his own. "It will be when I can linger on every sweet, delicious part of you."

Then he surprised me by sighing heavily, falling back and tugging me toward his chest.

"I don't like this responsible version of you," I huffed. "You only want me rested because our world is apparently riding on you keeping me alive right now."

He pulled the covers over my lower body before laying

back. Kade trailed his fingers gently over my shoulder in a soothing motion. "I'd destroy this world or the next to keep you alive, Princess, prophecy or not. No Fae or creature would be safe from my wrath should they touch one strand on your head. Your life and your heart are mine."

CHAPTER 26

KADE

Lana's body remained curled against me as a knock on the door sounded for the third time.

I didn't want to move, but I knew if someone persisted to this degree, it was on behalf of only one person.

The king.

I brushed the rose-gold hair away from Lana's neck and kissed her shoulder. Just because I fucking could.

Untangling myself from this woman might go down as the worst feeling in either kingdom. All I wanted to do was forget our troubles and be with her. Something shifted in her last night. She'd saved me from whatever the hell my father did to unleash my monster.

She always saved me.

Fates, I loved her. Looking at her one last time, I frowned, swearing she glowed lying there. Something ached within my chest, creating an indescribable drive to consume her. To make sure she knew she was mine. The swelling compulsion threatened to overpower me, but I forcefully shook it off. We'd have time.

I'd make sure of it.

I whipped open my bedroom door and moved to the main entryway of my chambers, throwing open the black doors.

"What?" I growled. A strong urge to destroy whoever disrupted us flashed inside of me. Fuck, I needed to get whatever this was under control.

Finn, one of my personal attendants, crossed his arms. If it had been anyone else, they would have cowered at the tone. Not Finn though.

"He wants to see you. Immediately."

I grunted in response and shut the door.

Finn's muffled voice came from the other side. "Shall I tell him you're coming? Or do you want me to be hung for my insubordination?"

Cracking a smile, I opened the door again. "Bring cook's hidden stash of pastries and juice to my rooms for my guest and I'll defer the hanging to another day."

Finn cocked an eyebrow. "He'll see you in the throne room."

I moved back into my bedroom, throwing on something more suitable to meet my father.

Lana turned, her arm sprawled across the bed where I had been all night. Like she reached for me in her sleep. Fuck, I wanted to be lying there with her.

Forcing myself to leave, I locked my doors, knowing Finn possessed the only other key to my chambers, and made my way to the throne room.

The dark, morbid hallways of the palace didn't seem as foreboding today. I had hope. Lana had instilled the strange sensation in me. Now that I'd experienced what she did to me, I would never let it go. Never let her go.

I inhaled, cracking my neck before pushing through the doors into the throne room. The king sat alone in his chair, but that hardly mattered. He'd sleep on that stupid throne if he could. Arrogant prick.

"Son, perhaps I should force you to stand vigil through the

night, then when urgent matters arise, I won't have to wait for you."

So, a foul mood today for the king. As always. I bowed my head. "How can I be of service, Your Majesty?"

He steepled his fingers in front of his face. "Something is brewing in Hemlock. A traitor rallying troops and followers far too quickly."

Raya had done it.

I frowned, knowing I must play my part well in case there was the slightest chance something backfired with her mind magic. "How many do you believe he has rallied?"

"I need you to scope it out and take care of it."

"Do you have a name?"

"No, my magic told me of the problem, but no specifics. You know how this works, the defiance will spread if it isn't handled."

I opened my mouth to ask more, but the king slammed his fist onto the arm of the throne, anger distorting his entire face. "I didn't raise you to ask questions. You are replaceable, Kade. I will find a new monster if you're incapable of following simple instructions. Get your people and take care of this. *Now.*"

Dark circles marred the king's face. For the first time, his usually predictable tyrannical rage seemed more unhinged. Normally, his orders were cruel and absolute but controlled. The delivery of this command bordered on manic.

I bowed from the waist down, attempting to curb his fury with my obedient facade before turning to leave the room. Adding a dangerous craze to my father's already cruel reign would make his orders heinous. I needed to leave before his directions included something worse than killing just one traitor.

"And Kade?"

I paused, looking over my shoulder as my hand reached for the door.

"Leave the princess here."

No. I pivoted, fully facing him. "She's coming with us."

The king's eyes narrowed. "No."

"Your Majesty—"

My father rose from his chair, an eerie calm descending in the room. "Your infatuation with that girl is finished. You will leave her here. You will take care of the traitors as it is your duty, and you will think twice before arguing again."

"That *girl* is a grown woman. A warrior, as proven at the festival. She is not a pawn for you to threaten me with." I stalked forward as an angry tempest inside of me thrummed. My shadows didn't explode from me, they crawled. Restrained as if they knew if they moved any faster they'd rip the king to fucking shreds. Purposefully resisting the temptation to do just that in order to maintain a sliver of sanity as my mind raced at Lana's fate if left in the king's hands. Leaving her behind would never be an option. "You may own me, my life, and the lives of my Guardians, but you do not own hers."

"Tread carefully, boy, you forget your place," he snarled.

I needed to get out of here. I couldn't threaten him while Lana remained here, the risk was too great. "She has a right to see what the darkness can cause. It affects her lands as well," I said, forcing the anger in my voice to calm. Emotion would only further paint a target on Lana's back. I had to be smarter with him, especially in his current state.

"It's not our job to help them rule." My father waved his hand, dismissing me, but I didn't move.

"She is a damn princess, Father," I said, knowing my use of his name may buy me some sort of listening ear. I loathed it, but I'd call him that for her. "It's of use to us to be on good terms with Brookmere's royals. It could be beneficial should our worlds ever combine. It is only a matter of time at this point, she knows we exist."

A smile played across the king's face, and he stepped down the three small stairs from his throne, taking his time striding toward me. "Do not think I am a fool, boy." His eyes grazed over me in disdain before a dangerous light flickered behind them. "Have your fun and take care of the traitors, my monster. We'll discuss this further upon your return."

The menacing tone did nothing to appease the worry I felt through every fiber of my being, but I refused to linger and allow him the opportunity to change his mind.

I bowed my head, pacing myself to slowly leave with my head held high. The moment the doors shut behind me, I raced back to my rooms. As long as I had eyes on her, she was safe.

Storm and Jax stood perched at the front of the wing that housed Lana's chambers along with my own. Waiting.

"Ready the horses," I said for the ears I knew could spy in the halls. "There's a new traitor to hunt."

I stopped, touching my chest at the throb there.

"Something wrong?" Storm asked.

I shifted, standing straighter and shaking my head. They exchanged a look, but I didn't linger.

The anxious weight in my chest accompanying the throbbing didn't lessen until I saw Finn exit my room and close the doors to my chambers behind him. "There won't be any breakfast left for you if that one has a say." Then he smiled. "I like her."

Relief was powerful knowing he had been with her seconds ago. "So do I," I said, grinning at him. "Thank you."

He nodded and left, not bothering to further the conversation. One of the many reasons he remained in my employ and a personal favorite in this castle.

I strode through my chambers, deliciously aware Lana remained in my bedroom. The door to the room already stood open, but she wasn't in bed. Instead, she paced by the window, brushing her hands over her clothes.

"Good morning, Little Rebel."

She jumped at my voice but relaxed once she saw it was just me. "Did it work?"

I nodded, the agitation inside of me soothing ever so slightly. "I'll walk you to your room. As soon as you've packed a bag, we'll be off."

She twisted her hands together, even though her shoulders sagged with relief.

I fought the urge to go to her. She'd saved me from the monster inside of me last night, and while she'd made it damn clear she wanted me, I didn't want to push my luck and believe her desire remained the same in the morning light.

"Ready?" I asked, daring to hold out my hand and leave the choice up to her.

She hesitated, pulling her hair over her shoulder, but then reached for me. I closed my eyes at the rush of our contact.

With that spark, I weakened in my resolve to approach this cautiously. I tugged her toward me, running a hand through her long hair and inhaling deeply as I let everything about the woman engulf me. "Thank you for last night," I whispered.

A soft smile crossed her lips as she stared up at me, leaning toward me.

Fates, I needed her. I leaned down, preparing to steal a kiss.

"Too bad you didn't give me anything to thank you for." She retreated, a playful gleam in her eye, as she left me behind in my own bedroom, high and dry.

Possessiveness had never been an issue for me before. Not once. Not until Lana.

If Jax hadn't diffused things with his incessant laughter as we readied the horses, I would have lost all the progress I'd made with Lana as I demanded she ride with me.

There were plenty of horses. She was a capable rider. Yet

the thought of her being on her own horse nearly drove me into a damn frenzy.

I stretched my neck from side to side, walking away before I said anything else to piss her off.

"What's going on?" Storm said, looping the reins around his own horse before tossing me my own supplies.

"A never-ending battle of wills." I sighed. "One I am currently losing."

Storm chuckled to himself as he adjusted his saddle. I rubbed my chest at the strange ache that hadn't disappeared since I woke this morning. It only increased when I looked over my shoulder at Lana mounting her own horse.

"Well, you better figure it out," he said, noticing my gaze. He slammed a hand on my shoulder. "She isn't the type to let someone lock her up in a glass cage and you know it."

I shrugged him off.

Instead of allowing myself to dwell on the whirlwind of emotions inside me, I mounted my horse, signaling for the others to move out.

We rode hard toward the border. The farther away we fled from the palace, the more my fear dissipated. As it lessened, this growing thing inside of me wholly focused on Lana finally settled in a way that made it more manageable.

I pushed us harder, frantically toward the border. The horses kept up, but I knew we'd have to stop soon for the night.

"A little farther," I encouraged Onyx, patting his side to encourage the beast.

Without hesitation, our steeds guided us through the barren lands. Obedient and grateful for the ability to run at full speed. Nothing stopped them from reaching their destination.

An eerie sensation of calm filled the air. Covered the space between us. We were Guardians on a mission. We'd trained for this. *Lived* for this.

No matter what happened, I had to secure Lana across the void and ensure she reached Ellevail safely. We had to rescue Ian, for I knew she wouldn't survive his death.

So we rode harder, faster, and with more purpose than ever before. Tomorrow Lana would return to Brookmere.

I just hoped her return didn't mean I would lose her forever.

CHAPTER 27

IAN

As I lay on the cold stone floor, I counted my breaths. One—*breathe in.* Two—*breathe out.*

Maria left me not long ago. Sent here by Andras, despite his empty threats of withholding her healing, mending me enough so he could continue his games. The torture, a never-ending loop of pain and healing.

With the guards present, Maria worked in silence, offering nothing. She managed to heal the superficial wounds and close the stab wound on my side, but a dark substance seeped from the closure. The scar resembled Lana's.

The assholes accompanying Maria down here dumped a pile of stale bread on the ground as they laughed their way out of my cell.

"Pathetic" they called me. Their once fearless leader now a lump on the floor.

"Lucien, if there was ever a time you could help with an escape, now would be it, buddy," I whispered into the abyss.

He didn't appear.

But someone else did.

"Ian?"

I groaned. The voice in my head had returned. Raya.

I'm busy. Go away.

She snorted. *"Trust me, if I could find a way not to enter your mind so easily, I would. Lana won't leave it alone now that she has access to checking on you."*

I'll work on keeping you out.

"Unlikely." She sucked in a sharp breath. *"Fucking Fates—"*

No wonder Lan likes you. You swear as much as she does. I smiled thinking of Lana finding another friend. Which was my first sign my mind needed rest to recover my logic—Lana didn't make friends often, and I was sure those who captured her would not make the short list. *I take that back.*

"Why aren't you healing? Anyone is going to be able to get into your mind if you don't heal. You must hurry." Raya's panic didn't help things. At all.

Apologies that the mind shield I didn't know how to use is failing. I've been busy trying to stay alive.

In the distance a stone skittered across the floor, interrupting the unending silence while footsteps scuffled closer.

"Now, Ian," Raya practically screamed. *"If someone is coming, shield now. We're—"*

As quickly as she'd appeared, she left. Or maybe I forced her to leave and blocked her out. I didn't need her around to see what was about to happen. Especially if she told Lana.

I didn't doubt my strength, but readying myself for another round of torture so soon would test even my limits.

"Psst," a voice called. "Ian?"

A second set of footsteps followed less quietly, and rapidly approached my cell.

"Who's there?" I asked as I rolled onto my side and stood. I steadied myself, taking a moment to allow the dizziness to clear.

"Ian."

I knew that voice but couldn't place it. No matter, the

figure came into my dimly lit view, and I instantly stepped back.

Hale Bardot. Joined moments later by Kalliah.

My heart soared. Maybe they knew how I could escape this Fates-forsaken cell.

"Kalliah? What are you doing here?" I asked. "With Hale?"

"It's time," Kalliah whispered. "We've come to break you free. We don't have a lot of time, but Hale has been helping us. He managed to finally steal a set of keys from a guard. We don't know how long we have till he notices they're missing, so we must be quick."

Hale fucking Bardot was part of my escape plan. I'd never pegged him for someone brave enough to go against anyone, let alone someone as evil as Andras. Always such a rule follower.

"Come on, Ian," Hale urged, "let's get you out of here before the guards notice. We have five minutes before their next pass."

"Well, what are you waiting for?" I gestured to the lock on the cell. "Let's get me the fuck out of here!"

Hale fumbled but removed a key from his pocket and inserted it into the lock. A small *click* sounded, and the door creaked open. Relief engulfed me.

I grabbed Kalliah into an embrace. "Thank you."

"Nonsense, this was all Hale." She let go, touching my face. "We'll make him pay," she said. "Now let's go before we get caught."

"Leif is in the kitchen staging a distraction. We'll grab him and then head to the stables, where Corbin is waiting for us." Hale handed me a dagger from his pocket. "It's not much, but it's the best I could get without raising suspicion."

I grasped the hilt of the small dagger and nodded. "Perhaps I was wrong about you all these years."

Hale rolled his eyes. "I never took you for a sap, Captain."

We rushed up the first stairwell and away from the dungeon door. Sure enough, the hall remained empty. Perfect timing. I never should have doubted my friends and their planning skills.

Kalliah ran through the palace in a way I'd never seen before. The confidence she'd gained during however long I'd been trapped appeared in every measured stride and the way she focused so assuredly on our goal. She'd gone from training because Lana forced her, to being truly in her element. I didn't want to think about what she went through to force such a change, but damn I was proud of her.

We snuck through the corridors, ducking at noises but successfully avoiding the wandering guards. The dungeon lay far below the main palace floor, requiring us to make our way up several more flights of stairs and cross to the southern wing to get to our destination.

Clearing the second staircase, we rounded the corner, heading to the next set of steps, but a guard was coming through the door just as we opened it. Before he drew his weapon, Hale jumped forward and slit his throat. I almost tripped over my own feet reaching for the guard before he fell to the ground. When the hell had Hale become a damn killer?

Kalliah and I advanced, catching his body and gently placing it on the floor. Trying to make as little noise as possible.

When we lived through this, I would have to absolutely eat many of my annoyed words to Lana about Hale.

Fortunately for us, the route through the southern wing of the palace was less traveled, as it held mostly the staff and off-duty guards.

As we continued our escape, my strength slowly started to return. Maria's powers had taken care of the large concerns, kick-starting my healing, but my magic flared since being freed from the warded dungeon, eager to escape. It continued to heal me, and I felt confident enough to take the lead, guiding my companions down the last hall.

Two guards spoke in low voices from the other side of the last remaining door we needed to breach before the kitchen hall.

I eyed Hale's blade. He bowed his head at me. Glancing at Kalliah, I noticed she, too, had pulled a small dagger.

"You're brilliant," I mouthed to her. She rolled her eyes and set her focus on the door.

I mouthed the words *one, two*. On three, I thrust the door back, opening it as Hale swung his blade forward, catching one guard. I'd slit the throat of the second guard before he had time to fight back.

I heaved. These men had been mine. Now I'd been forced to take their lives.

I closed my eyes tightly, only for a moment. I couldn't think about them right now. We had to get ourselves out of Ellevail so we could find Lana.

That was all that mattered.

We exited the doorway, all three of us running toward the kitchen through the empty hallway.

We skittered to a halt outside the kitchen and Kalliah took over, brushing by us. "Be ready to run out the side door."

The second she called Leif's name, chaos erupted.

Hale pushed open the door to find Leif in a cloud of flour, once again on Lucinda, with a false clumsiness mimicking his past transgressions. She screamed at him, raising a silver eggbeater above her head right as he ducked.

"Every time, Leif Ivans," she screamed. "You'll be fired now, mark my words."

Kalliah grabbed my hand. "You'll ruin the distraction if you stay to watch the show."

The bedlam in the kitchen grew as others scurried around in the wake of Lucinda's outrage. People tripped over each other, and I couldn't stop laughing at Leif's absolute success.

He shoved into us from behind as we exited out the side door of the kitchens. "Good to see you alive, now hurry up and run."

Hale held the door, only shutting it once Leif passed through. He slid his sword from his waist and glided it through the handles. "Should buy us a few more minutes."

We turned, fleeing across the gardens in the moonlight before a figure jumped in front of us. Hale held out his dagger, but I lunged in front of him when I recognized who approached.

"Your Majesty," I said, my heart stopping. What the hell was she doing out here? Alone?

A gruff bark sounded around us, and Lucien appeared from behind the queen's dress.

"He hasn't given me a moment's peace." She ran a finger along the head of the pugron before she looked at me. "I knew you'd succeed," she said watching Kalliah. Kalliah kneeled before her queen. "None of that now, you need to hurry."

"Come with us," I said, not bothering to hide the plea in my voice. If I could ensure her safety, everyone Lana truly loved would be together. Free.

The queen bowed her head. "I could never leave my people. I must stay here and fight for their justice. You are meant for bigger things, my dear. You must help Lana succeed so she is able to return home to her people."

I swallowed audibly. The pressure of the journey to come settled into my bones. "I will not fail you, my queen."

"We shouldn't linger," Hale said, glancing nervously around the garden, searching.

"I'll stay long enough to see you off," the queen gave me an encouraging nod.

Then I said the words I never thought I'd speak to someone else in this palace, let alone Hale. This wasn't my plan though, so I yielded despite the desire to take over. "Lead the way."

Without hesitation, Hale lead our group through the remaining gardens and toward the stables. I knew these paths well, knew the schedule of the guards, at least from when I had been charged with them.

No one stood at any of the usual posts. As if the garden had been deserted altogether.

"Something isn't right," I whispered.

Hale glanced over his shoulder. "Things have changed here in the time you've been locked away, Ian. I'm not going to spit in the Fates' faces now that they are with us again."

I frowned, hating that the palace had fallen into such disarray, and instead of protecting my home, I'd been trapped beneath it.

As we rounded the final corner, crossing the small bridge to take us to the stables, the wooden planks shook beneath us. I jumped off the bridge to the other side, extending my hand for the queen and Kalliah. They stepped off the bridge just as a handful of guards appeared out of nowhere before us.

Dread settled into the pit of my stomach. We were so close to escaping, our path to the stables clear. So much so that I stared at the saddled group, Corbin already mounted on one of the steeds. Only a short distance more and we would have succeeded.

I shoved the queen behind me, while holding firm in my footing. Whatever happened, she had to be protected at all costs. As of now, she remained the last hope for Brookmere until Lana returned to exact her revenge.

Leif and Kalliah also placed themselves in front of the queen while Hale doubled back so we formed a circle surrounding her.

"You dare attack your own queen?" I shouted at the group of guards who stood before us, weapons raised. Ten in total.

Not one of them appeared to hold a shred of doubt in their mind about their actions.

"Answer me!" I shouted, losing my patience. Lucien growled from my feet, his spiked tail swishing.

A sinister laugh echoed in the air around us. "Did you really think you could get away from me, Captain?"

Andras.

Andras was here.

He sauntered down the hill toward us, robes flowing behind him, as his wicked smile brightened the longer his gaze lingered on us. His teeth glistened in the full moon's light.

The guards in front of us shifted in formation, matching our circle with one of their own. Two held torches, the rest stood ready, blades in hands.

"The band of misfits reunited, so it seems?" Andras sneered. "Short one wayward princess. But then you've gained another one of her lackeys, I see?"

I narrowed my gaze on the man, refusing to allow anything else to distract me.

Andras glanced between each of us until he finally looked past me, eyes widening only slightly seeing the queen in our midst.

Queen Roxana pushed by me, fists forming at her sides. "Andras, this is enough. The time has come to end this ridiculous hunt. I am your queen and command you to cease your pursuit of Captain Stronholm." Her voice carried such firm authority, I wanted to get on my knees before her. Even after seeing how fiercely she battled Andras's mind magic, she still retained unwavering strength. "You are a traitor to Brookmere. Guards, arrest him immediately."

A pregnant pause filled the air before Andras cackled uncontrollably. "You think they answer to you? Roxana, how the mighty have fallen." Spit flew from his mouth as his rabid excitement grew. "You are the epitome of weakness, especially since your husband's death. You are not worth the ground you walk on."

"How dare you speak to your queen in such a manner," I seethed, stepping closer to Andras. "You will not win this war, Andras. I will make sure of that. Now bow before your queen."

Andras's eyes gleamed in a maniacal way. "There is no one to stop me."

Hale and Leif drew their swords. The beat of horses' hooves sounded for a few seconds before Corbin leapt from his animal and ran toward us, sword drawn.

For the first time since daring to position themselves against us, the guards appeared hesitant. Perhaps seeing the queen standing by me, with no intention of backing down despite Andras's taunts, jarred them out of his trance.

"Enough." The queen's voice echoed in the air around us as if she'd amplified it. Before I could stop her, Queen Roxana stepped forward, moving in front of me to come face-to-face with Andras. Andras held up a hand, and the hesitation I'd seen on my soldiers' faces moments before disappeared as they regripped their weapons and inched forward.

Queen Roxana merely lifted her chin and ignored the threat. "If you think for one moment I will surrender to you," she said, voice steady, "you are sorely mistaken. You will have to kill me before I hand over my kingdom to you."

The air thickened, tension palpable as Andras took one slow, calculated step toward the queen, bowing his head.

"As my queen commands it."

Andras's eyes glimmered as the smile plastered over his face widened so much, it looked painful.

He lifted a hand, signaling a guard behind him, and the chaos of the impending fight fell on all of us.

For our queen. For our lives. For the future of Brookmere, we'd fight and die here if we must.

The guard in front flicked his wrist, activating his earth

magic and commanding vines to sprout around us. They snaked and slithered, working their way up our legs. I hacked at them, but more guards stepped forward. Their magic unnaturally strong.

Lucien breathed fire out over them, trying his best to play a role, but even his flames didn't help.

I looked up, horrified as I continued to hack at the vines until I noticed movement behind Andras.

Casimir lurked from the shadows. He looked larger than I remembered him. His eyes as dark as night.

He'd siphoned magic. This was him, not the guards.

"Attack," I shouted to the others.

Corbin ran in front of me, blocking the queen from the guards, but she refused to leave the fighting to us. "While I honor your intentions, Ian, I am queen. I will not yield this kingdom without a fight."

She stepped to Corbin's side and I watched in awe as she raised an arm over her head, and summoned the guard's sword toward her into her own hands. She whipped her arms around, air swirling around the guard directing his earth magic until she lifted him from his feet, throwing him back. Her victory halted as a guard descended on her, engaging in a sword fight.

Corbin blocked skillfully where she missed, aiding her attack, but I couldn't let her risk herself.

I moved to join the two, but Casimir lunged and twisted his hands. Gleefully, he let out a dark chuckle as more thorny tendrils than I could count shot toward me. I kept my arms from being locked at my sides as blades hissed through the air and clashed around me.

The queen turned, shoving her air magic toward a patch of the growing vines, wrapping them around themselves. I shouted as another guard swung for her. She turned, blocking the assault and flinging air magic at some of the other guards nearby.

I'd never been gifted the opportunity to see her in action. Our queen, fighting alongside her guards. My chest swelled with pride for all she stood for. I wished Lana could see this too. She would be in awe of her mother.

I rallied, shouting and pulling my blade through two of the four vines constricting my legs. More and more sprouted to life, but I kept my fighting hand free as I used the dagger Hale gave me to slice through the vines attacking me. It wasn't enough. I needed a sword. My sword.

"*Ian.*" Raya's voice was back in my head, her presence popping into existence.

I sawed at one particularly thick vine around my thigh. *Your timing is shit. Don't distract me.*

"*Where are you? I can feel the man with the powerful mind magic nearby. Your shields are weak and—*"

Kind of busy at the moment, Raya.

The effort to block her out took my focus away from the task at hand. She lingered there, quiet, but I could fucking *feel* her.

"Damn it," I shouted as a vine wrapped around my waist while I finished hacking the one immobilizing my legs.

The queen's shout in front of me turned my skin cold.

Andras, though thrashing against the air the queen flung around him, had made it to her side. He grabbed her by her arm and pulled her toward him, producing a knife from the billow of his robes. He held her body out, facing all of us. "I'd stop fighting those vines, Captain. One more move, and she's dead."

CHAPTER 28

IAN

Immediately, I obeyed.

Sword fighting continued around me, but I froze, desperately trying to figure out a way to get the queen back. Andras ripped the knife down her dress, leaving the side of her ribcage exposed to the elements. The frayed edges of the fabric swayed in the breeze.

I gritted my teeth. "Unhand her."

"You're in no position to play hero," Andras said as he pressed the knife into her side. A small pinprick of blood pooled at the tip of his blade.

The queen didn't flinch, didn't move. "Let them go, Andras. I will stay, if they can be free."

"No." Kalliah ran up beside me.

"He's in her mind, Ian," Raya's voice whispered all around inside my head. *"I can feel it even from here. He's holding her in place, but she fights."*

"Ian," she said, not a hint of fear in the way she said my name. The queen's nose bled, starting small until a rivulet ran over her lip. The same way it had when she came to my cell. The sign of her internal struggle against Andras.

"Your Majesty." I moved, forgetting the vines clawing at

my legs, as I saw her face. That look would haunt me for the rest of my life if it meant what I thought it did.

She was willing to die for us to get out. The pleading gaze wasn't for me to save her. *No.* This look was a reminder of what I'd promised, what I'd vowed to do.

"You will finally be granted the death you deserve," Andras said, loud enough so we all could hear. His focus shifted from us fully to the queen. "Slow, painful. Your magic will be mine, and I will rule this kingdom."

Casimir lingered by Andras like a good lap dog, but the horror of what Andras had said hit me. He'd take her magic. Casimir would siphon it. If it worked as I had seen before though, it wouldn't last. Why would he be happy about a short burst of the queen's power?

Andras leaned into the queen, sniffing her hair before exhaling loudly. I strained against the vines, flipping my dagger downward to resume cutting through them as cautiously as I could. Careful not to raise suspicion, but I had to free myself while Andras remained distracted.

"How the people of Brookmere will falter when they hear of your treason," he continued. "So broken and fragile, locked away in mourning. The only one who remained steadfast and strong for the kingdom being the loyal advisor. I'll be the only logical choice as their new king."

"They will never believe you," Queen Roxana shouted as her body trembled, her inward fight physically showing more now.

Andras chuckled. "They already do. While you have been locked away in your '*room*,' mourning the tragic loss of your husband, I have been the one soothing their fears. Providing the stability they crave, the power they deserve."

This threat was real. Andras had passed the point of keeping the queen alive. He was truly going to kill her.

The wind whirled around us as thunder rumbled in the

distance. It was rare, so incredibly rare that the nature around us reacted to our lives here, but I would swear on the Fates it was happening now. Nature was not pleased at the scene before it.

"Andras, do not do this," I screamed at him, almost free from the last vine holding me.

Casimir put his hands on two guards nearby, inhaling and grunting until both of them fell to the ground.

I made my move, running forward, but Casimir had already claimed the magic from both of the drained guards. Vines, roots, and thorns shot out in renewed power. Two vines wrapped around my arm, and thorns sliced at my face, but I fought, running forward still.

So did the others.

A guard kneeled before Andras, throwing his arms out, and suddenly, we were trapped. Kept away by some sort of shield. I brought my sword down against it.

The guard's face strained, but the shield didn't break.

Not yet.

"Help me," I commanded the others.

"Any last words, Queen?" Andras asked.

Regret filled her eyes as she stared at me. I hesitated when I heard her voice.

"Tell Lana I love her. Tell her she was always my light. She will always be the light in the darkest of hours. Keep her steady on her path."

"Pathetic." Andras sneered as he slowly pushed the blade into the queen's side. He shouted, a happy, awful sound as he twisted it hard.

"No!" I fought against the bindings around me, but Casimir's power far exceeded mine after draining two earth Fae. I'd failed another woman in my life.

The queen screamed, but she still stared at me, swallowing her evident pain. "I love you too, my dear," she rasped through haggard breaths. "Don't lose hope."

Andras pulled the blade out. He thrust it into her stomach and stabbed her again. And again.

Casimir grabbed the queen with one hand as she fell, and reached for Andras with his other. My screams of utter rage echoed in my head. I watched in horror as a familiar ring on his index finger glowed brighter. They were siphoning her magic. Just like they'd tried on me. Casimir released the queen, and her body slumped forward. Lifeless.

Kalliah cried next to me, choking out unintelligible words of sorrow as she continued to fight against the shield despite the queen's death.

Voices shouted around me. I heard Leif's and Corbin's strangled sobs and looked to my left as they dragged their blades over the shield. Horror in every line on their face.

Tears flowed down Hale's face as he stood, his blade embedded in the shield.

A deafening sound of thunder clapped, and the skies opened. Lightning struck across the entire sky, illuminating the dark night as if it raged along with us.

It didn't happen often, but nature herself was here for this. Present and furious.

Andras stepped over the queen's body, not seeming to give a fuck about the clear sign from nature.

"How fucking dare you kill your queen." Rage coursed through my veins, but the damn earth magic holding me in place still hadn't receded. I wanted to kill him. I *would* kill him. The guard faltered, enough that I thrashed and pulled an arm free, slicing again at the vines. With no shield, I'd get to him and finish this.

He walked toward me, and I fought harder. Harder than I remembered being able to fight in a long time.

"Didn't you find it odd you didn't encounter anyone on your escape from the dungeons?" he asked with a sinister grin. "I *allowed* you to escape. And I will allow you to leave these palace grounds if you can fight your way out from the guards here and by the gates of Ellevail."

"Why?" I questioned. "Why would you *let* us escape?"

He tossed his head back, as rain pelted his head, slicking his thin black hair around his face until the crazed man within truly reflected outwardly as well. "Because no matter what happened here tonight, you will bring me *her.* Whether she is searching for you now or you find her and return to exact your vengeance. Illiana will return. I've made sure of it. And I will be ready and waiting for her when she does."

"I will *never* bring her to you." I spat in his face.

Andras wiped the spit off in pure disgust. "That is where you are wrong. The Fates have already decided."

"Nature has decided your fate. Do you see the storm raging around us? This is the response to you murdering the queen," I argued.

"This is the result of weak magic. Magic that has no idea what's in store for our land," he said, his lip curling in disdain. "Now leave, if you can make it past the guards."

Andras turned on his heel and grabbed a torch from the closest guard. A torch shrouded in magic, still burning brightly despite the rain. Without hesitation he dropped it on the queen's crumpled body. I watched in horror, but Leif and Corbin ran forward, trying again to get to her. Guards fought them, coming from dark corners we hadn't seen. The rain fell harder, but the flame still burned. I screamed against the restraints in agony, unable to control myself.

Andras didn't spare her a second glance. "Casimir, release him."

The vines fell away, and I bolted for them. But Casimir wiggled his fingers at me as Andras dropped some sort of smoky explosion, and they vanished behind it.

I shifted my focus now to the queen, not caring about the flames, or the grotesque smell of burning flesh as I tried to tamp them out.

The fire licked my skin, but I ignored the pain, throwing my body over hers. Thunder roared once more, and the rain pelted me angrily. My actions, combined with the increased downpour, somehow worked. The flames receded, smothered out.

"Thank you," I choked out to the nature around me.

Lucien jumped to the queen, licking her face, whimpering.

Pulling back, I kneeled before the queen as my friends fought around me. I touched her neck, delusional, like there might be a pulse. "Come on," I begged. We couldn't lose her. Lana couldn't lose her. She had already lost so much.

"Please," I whispered.

The queen didn't move.

I removed my hand from her neck, body trembling at the weight of what I'd just witnessed. At what we all just witnessed.

Without a thought for the battle still happening around me, I tilted my head back and yelled to the sky, shouting at the Fates themselves in a bellowing scream.

Our queen was dead.

Ellevail had fallen.

I placed my hand over her heart. "I want to stay. I want to fight. But I gave you my word. I'll never break my vow to you, Your Majesty. Never." Leaning forward, I placed a kiss on her forehead.

Tears fell down my face along with the rain. Lightning blazed around us again.

"I'm so sorry," Raya's voice whispered in my mind.

She hadn't left.

Don't tell Lana. Please. I need to be the one to do it.

"Where are you going now?" she asked. *"We'll meet you there."*

Valeford, I thought. *We'll meet Lana in Valeford.*

Corbin slapped a hand onto my shoulder as Raya's presence faded slowly from my mind. They'd handled the guards here. "We must go. I don't trust him not to change his mind and follow."

I looked up at him. Leif came to my other side and offered a hand.

Kalliah crashed into me and wrapped her arms around me. "Lana." I made out the one word as her sobs tore through her. Leif put a hand on her back, and she leaned into him next. I stepped away as he began whispering to her.

"Weapons?" I asked Corbin.

He nodded. "I grabbed the old Hidden Henchmen packs and additional weapons from the armory earlier today. We're ready to go."

A guard ran from behind one of the stables toward us. "Captain!"

I froze, whipping around as Corbin placed his sword in my hand.

"Wait!" the guard cried, stopping before me. "Andras has done something to nearly all of us. Only a few can fight it. I saw what happened."

"And did nothing." I stepped toward him, blade at the ready.

He lifted his hands. "I told you there is not much we can do. But when Andras left, his compulsion in my head wore off. Please, I'll bury the queen. With the honor and care she deserves. I'll do it before they can come for her body."

I eyed him warily.

"More guards are gathering. Some of them have enjoyed the darkness Andras thrives on, even if there are others of us who still fight. When Princess Illiana returns, there are those who remain loyal to her inside these walls."

I swallowed the growing lump in my throat. "Thank you."

I looked over my shoulder, Hale still pale in the rain, Leif holding an arm around Kalliah. "Let's go. We're not in the clear yet."

Lucien whimpered at my feet, and I kneeled in front of

him. "Hide. Find a place and wait for us. Lana will come home soon." He licked my hand before he trotted back over to the queen and sat beside her.

He breathed fire into the air before he let out a mournful howl.

We ran to the stables, mounting our steeds and proceeded to race through the city streets. The storm had driven most of the city inside. Almost no one lingered. The heaviness of an empty Ellevail hit me hard as we rode.

"People have been staying inside, especially the lesser Fae," Corbin shouted over the wind and rain. "Andras is building a city based on fear."

"He will pay," I said, not bothering to raise my voice over the storm.

"He said there'd be guards by the gate," Leif shouted from behind me.

We continued, three blocks from the city entrance. It wasn't until we were only a block away when I heard them. Even over the rumbling storm.

"They're coming," I shouted to the others.

This time, I drew my blade from the pack on my horse, feeling more prepared than before.

Some guards already stood defensively in front of the gates.

"For Queen Roxana!" I yelled, and the others chimed in behind me, shouts of comradery and a single purpose. We'd escape for her.

Fifteen guards surrounded the gates, and the hooves I'd heard a block before were heading our way.

I sliced across the neck of the closest guard, ignoring that they were once my men. If I looked too closely, I'd never get us out of here. Escape was all that mattered now.

Despite our exhaustion, we pressed on. The storm didn't help.

As if sensing our diminishing reserves, the rain lessened to a pitter, but the thunder and lightning refused to cease.

Corbin shouted, a blade slicing his arm a few feet from me, but he quickly corrected for it, flicking his sword to the other hand and stabbing it into the guard who'd gotten a jump on him.

I lost track of the others but trusted them to hold their own. Soon, only two guards remained, fighting Hale and Leif.

"Go," Leif shouted to Hale. Corbin was the first to the gate, shoving hard and finally opening it. He mounted his steed.

"Open!" he yelled to us.

We rode toward him as the last guard fell. The sound of hooves grew, and my head twisted as my gaze shot toward the center of the city entrance. A group of guards on horseback rode straight for us.

"Go!" Leif shouted again.

They couldn't follow. None of them could know where we were heading. We needed time to find Lana. To form a plan, before anyone alerted Andras to our location.

Leif rode up to me. "Get out of those gates now."

"We can't let them follow," I argued, but Leif reached across my horse and grabbed my arm.

"I know, Ian," he said. "They won't."

I frowned, looking between him and the approaching horses. Corbin, Hale, and Kalliah had already cleared the gates.

"I can't let you stay." I couldn't lose someone else tonight. Especially not Leif.

Leif shifted his horse, circling me in a way that caught me off guard. As my horse turned to follow, it faced the gates. Leif drew a hand back and smacked my horse. "Ya!" he shouted.

My horse bolted forward. I drew on the reins, but Leif

dismounted his steed and was already pulling the gate closed, remaining inside.

"Leif!" Kalliah yelled, riding toward me. She dismounted, running and thrusting her arm between the metal bars to grab him. "Don't do this."

"I swear to you, Kalliah Brennan," he said, reaching his hand between bars and stroking her cheek. "Nothing will keep me from your side. I'm merely buying you time."

"Swear it again," she cried.

"I swear it. You will see me again. If Lucinda hasn't killed me, they certainly won't." He smiled.

"Stay alive, brother," I commanded. "Kalliah," I said, hating the fact that I had to say anything to her. "We must take the time he's given us."

"No," she said. "No." She grabbed the collar of Leif's shirt and yanked him toward the bars, kissing him fiercely.

Corbin moved faster than I did, pulling his horse forward to Kalliah's side. He grabbed her arm, dragging her back to her own horse. "I'm sorry," I saw his lips say but didn't hear him.

"Don't you dare die, Leif Ivans," she yelled.

He saluted us and turned to face down the approaching guards.

Alone.

Lightning split the sky as we fled into the night. Into the storm. Into the unknown, lying vast and ominous before us.

"To Lana." I clicked my tongue, urging my horse faster. "We ride to our queen."

CHAPTER 29

LANA

The flames of our campfire crackled, but I couldn't take my eyes off Raya.

She sat across from me, her eyes white, body completely still. We'd stopped an hour ago for the night, eager for sleep before the rest of our journey in the morning.

A white-hot pain raced down my spine, and I muffled a cry.

"Lana?" Kade's urgent tone sounded in my ear, and he moved closer to my side.

I gripped my thighs, trying to breathe through the ache, but the pain disappeared within seconds.

Raya's eyes shot open, and her body lurched forward. She placed a hand on her chest, gasping for air. Tears fell from her eyes before she blinked, taking in her surroundings.

The sadness didn't fade from her gaze.

"Raya!" Jax sounded truly concerned for the first time since I'd met him. He kneeled next to her, resting a hand on her knee.

"What happened?" I jumped up, rattled at what could have made Raya, of all people, cry. "What did you see?"

I tried to fortify my heart, building as much protection

around it, as I prepared for whatever she'd say. I desperately needed to know Ian was all right. I could not bear it if something happened to him. The sympathy in Raya's gaze made me *know* her news wouldn't be good.

Raya inhaled deeply. "Change of plans," she said. "We are going straight to Valeford."

I frowned, looking at Kade. He tried to give me a reassuring smile, but it didn't meet his eyes.

"What happened, Raya?" I asked a bit more sternly. My fingers curled into fists, my nails biting into my skin so hard they drew blood. A shadowy tendril stroked over my hand, begging it to loosen.

It didn't.

Raya would need to start spilling some of the more intimate details of what she'd seen before I completely spiraled out of control.

Raya didn't move. "Ian escaped along with some others I don't know. They are on their way to Valeford."

I walked over to her and kneeled, resisting the urge to mimic Jax's touch on her leg. We weren't that close, but I needed more information. "I know that's not everything. I may not know you well, but I know you would not cry for no reason."

"There were a few dangerous moments during their escape. Ian's fine." She refused to look me in the eye.

Irritation clawed at me. "You're hiding something."

"I checked in on your friend as you asked me to, *Princess*," she bit back. The venom took me by surprise. Immediately, she softened. "I'm sorry, being in the minds of others isn't easy."

"You were out for a considerable amount of time compared to before," I pressed. "That can't be all. Is he all right? Who else is with him?"

"Lana," Jax said softly.

I ignored him. My barrage of questions wouldn't stop

until I got answers. I watched Raya take a deliberately slow breath, as if she were calming herself.

"No, you swear to it. Right here, right now." The anger of not knowing raged like a beast inside of me. "You tell me Ian survived and is in one piece. That my friends are okay."

"Ian is fine," Raya yelled. She paused, closing her eyes and taking a few measured breaths. "I swear, Ian is fine. Now, I am exhausted. I'm going to sleep, and you should too. We've got a long day ahead of us tomorrow."

With that, Raya stood abruptly, forcing me to lean away from her. Without a word to the others, she fled the fireside and retreated to her tent. I couldn't help but notice her hand wipe away another tear.

Jax slapped his knee as he stood. "Well, for once, Raya's right. We need to rest."

He said his good nights to Kade and Storm, both of whom stayed strangely silent during the exchange, and headed toward his tent. I still kneeled, staring at Raya's tent, knowing I wouldn't get more information. A swell of jealousy rose in me that she'd seen them, which was absurd. If she spoke the truth, I'd see them tomorrow, if we pushed the horses hard enough.

A hand touched my shoulder. "We'll see him tomorrow, Lana." Storm squeezed reassuringly. "I'll take first watch. Rest. As much as you can."

He stepped away from me, settling by the fire.

I stared into the depths of the sky, the stars glistening so beautifully, though they did nothing to quell the worry filling every fiber of my being. My thoughts spiraled, wondering what Raya wasn't telling me, knowing it could not be good—whatever it was. But she did say Ian was all right, and he had others with him. Which meant Kalliah could be with him too.

A soft tendril of shadow caressed the back of my head, turning me to face Kade, who stood behind me. "Come on, Little Rebel, let's get some sleep."

He reached his hand toward me. I looked up and as soon as I saw his face, I let the tears pooling in my eyes fall. His compassionate expression broke the fragile hold I had on my emotions. Relief, mixed with a heavy fear at what Raya left unsaid, poured out as my hand touched his.

I grasped it firmly, willingly, needing his comfort in this moment, as he led the way to the tents.

"Pick—mine or yours," he said quietly. "But you are not sleeping alone tonight."

"I want you with me," I whispered. The truth settled in my chest. After last night, I realized the times in his arms in Brookmere hadn't been flukes. Being with him made me feel safe, and I needed to cling to that feeling. I wasn't sure I could give it up again. Certainly not right now.

He tugged me toward his tent, and I answered the question in his gaze with a slight nod.

As soon as we entered, he sat on his oversized bedroll, pulling me close. I let him wrap his arms around my center as our bodies burrowed into each other. He brushed my hair down from my face, over my neck.

"I'm sorry for bringing you here," Kade whispered in my ear.

I didn't know what to say, so instead of answering, I clasped his hand around my waist and squeezed.

"I'm sorry for everything, Illiana. For kidnapping you, for exposing you to my terrible father, bringing you to Mysthaven, taking you away from your friends. For what happened to Ian, your father. All of it. I should have been more truthful with you sooner about my prophecy."

I rolled over to face him, pushing a strand of his hair out of his face. "I know you are." I paused, realizing I needed to say these next few words out loud. For Kade as much as myself. I'd told him I forgave him for my father, but we hadn't discussed everything else. "I forgive you for all of it. I didn't tell you about my prophecy, and I know firsthand the burden of carrying one."

He ran his fingers over my face, then my neck. "I don't know how to open up to others well. But the minute you became more than a line in a prophecy, I should have tried to find a way."

I intertwined my fingers with his. "I forgive you," I said again.

His eyes closed and he inhaled. "I don't know if I deserve your forgiveness."

"You can have it anyway," I whispered before cradling the back of his head and bringing his mouth to mine.

Though the ever-present spark ignited at our touch, he kept it sweet and tender. The kiss did not last nearly as long as it should have before he broke our connection and placed his forehead against mine.

"I promise myself to you. To only you. Whether you want me or not is your choice, but I swear to you there will be no more lies, no more secrets." He stroked his thumb across my cheek. "You have every part of my heart. Every part of my being, Little Rebel. To do with as you wish."

My lip quivered as I soaked in the feelings swelling inside of me. The words he spoke hovered in the air like an unbreakable vow, swirling around us as if sealing something bigger than both of us.

"I think—" The tremor in my voice made me swallow. "I think there are quite a few things I wish to do with that declaration, Kade Blackthorn."

He huffed out a laugh, his chest rumbling against my body. "Dirty girl." He squeezed me tighter to him. "Prepare yourself for everything you wish for and more. When I take you again, Little Rebel, you had better be sure it's what you want. Because there will be no coming back from it after."

I shivered in anticipation. "I'll hold you to that."

"You need to sleep," he cleared his throat, promptly

changing the subject even though I could feel how hard he was as he lay next to me.

I sobered. "I don't know if I can. I'm so grateful Ian escaped, but something's wrong."

"I know." Kade ran his hand through my hair. "But if Raya said Ian's safe, then he is. She wouldn't lie."

"She's not telling us everything."

Kade hummed in agreement. "We're going to get through this. You'll be able to see Ian tomorrow."

"In Valeford." I chewed on my lip. The weight of what awaited lay heavy on me.

His lips touched my cheek. "I will help you get every answer you want. Even those you don't. You won't face this alone."

Kade shifted, positioning us so my head lay on his chest. It was a damn perfect fit, and I sighed, feeling his lips again as my eyes turned heavy. His calming scent mixed with the comfort of his arms was intoxicating. For a brief minute I worried if I did this much more, Kade would be right. There would be no going back.

"Tomorrow," I said, almost to myself, before drifting off completely.

———

The five of us stood facing the dark, misty void. The ominous heaviness of the vast dead area loomed like a silent threat.

"Everyone has to be touching me, understand?" Kade said.

The group muttered their agreements. Jax held the reins of three horses behind him, Raya held the other two. With the need to touch Kade to pass through, we couldn't all be on horseback.

A shadow brushed under my chin, tilting my head toward Kade. "No running from me this time, right?"

I smirked, despite the tiny amount of fear in Kade's eyes. "I don't know. I kind of enjoy making you chase me."

The comment erased the fear and turned his gaze darker. "Careful, Little Rebel."

"I think I liked it better when she wanted to stab you," Jax said. "Don't we have somewhere to be?"

Kade blinked a few times, as if to clear his thoughts before returning his focus to the task at hand.

We all reached out, Raya and Jax behind him, Storm on one side, me on the other. The tug in my stomach as we crossed the barrier felt familiar this time, and when we made it into the void itself, I shivered remembering the lifelessness of the place.

One of the horses reared, and Jax cursed.

"I hate it in here," I said, rolling my shoulders back.

"Same," Jax agreed. "It's why Storm always went with him instead of us."

"Baby," Storm tossed over his shoulder. He drew his blade as we marched through the mist.

"It's quieter," Raya said.

The sound of her speaking in the deathly silence made me jump. They were the only words she'd spoken to anyone this morning. She'd barely acknowledged my presence, her eyes trained anywhere else, never meeting my own. The silent treatment she gave me did nothing to quell my nervousness.

Before long, we reached the barrier on the other side. Kade instructed us to grab hold of him again, and we traveled through.

Finally, I was home.

Even though it had been less than a week, I inhaled as if it had been years, breathing in the crisp air. The lush green of Brookmere's vibrant environment stole my breath. The contrast between Brookmere and Mysthaven stood out even more now that I was back.

"This part will never get old," Storm murmured, standing

at my side. "The first time we came through the void I thought maybe I'd died, and this was the afterlife. The beauty here is unlike anything we knew growing up."

I smiled. "There is beauty in your home too, just a different kind."

Kade approached with Onyx, holding the reins to my horse. I cocked an eyebrow. "No temper tantrum about me riding alone? I'm shocked at the growth you've shown in one short day."

Storm laughed and bumped into me. "I had to give him a pep talk this morning so he could do it. He's still…him."

"Not true," Kade grumbled, but I noticed the slight upturn of his lips.

I took the reins of my horse, mounting as I joined in his laughter. It felt incredible to genuinely laugh.

A giddiness raced through me as I sat atop the horse, taking in Brookmere. Soon I'd see Ian. He had escaped. He was free.

And I was *home*.

Without a word spoken among us, I took off. Straight ahead, farther into my lands. The wind brushed against my face and swirled around me, making me swear nature welcomed me home.

The warm sun against my face brought forth a smile, and I threw my head back, raising it toward the sky.

No one spoke, even after an hour of riding. On the horizon toward the left of us, a forest came into view. There was only one it could be, based on where I imagined we crossed to get to Valeford.

We weren't far now.

The silence here felt almost as strange as the silence in the void. Like things moved too easily for us. Before, we could barely leave Ellevail without being attacked by dark ones. Yet we hadn't seen anyone, let alone dark Fae.

"What's Storm's first name?" I suddenly asked the group, breaking the uncomfortable silence radiating from my home.

Jax laughed, throwing his head back. Storm grinned at me, and Kade shook his head, even as a smile played over his lips.

"I'm shocked you even know he *has* a name other than Storm," Jax said. "Count yourself lucky in that alone and know that none of us will break."

"It's just a name, it cannot be that bad," I grumbled.

A shriek from overhead chilled me to the bone, halting our conversation.

I tugged the reins, stopping my horse completely as I shifted my entire focus to the sky.

"What is it?" Storm asked, pulling up beside me. Kade, already there, followed my gaze.

"A strox," I whispered. The beast's midnight blue hue stood out against the light blue sky.

"One of them fought in the last trial," Kade said, no question in his voice.

I nodded. The beast circled above us, cawing a few more times. My heartbeat quickened. "They're deadly. The deadliest creatures in our history. Hundreds of years ago, rumors of their brutality circled Brookmere. I've only seen one once before the marriage trials, and that was from afar."

I didn't take my eyes from the beast ahead.

The others remained still, just as I did.

"Deadly how?" Jax asked, his voice a whisper.

"Shred-through-armor-and-flesh-and-devour-bodies-whole kind of deadly," I said, raising a brow.

The strox called out another cry and deviated from its path, flying directly to the forest I'd noted earlier.

The Southern Forests.

I shivered.

"That was…" Jax paused. "…fun."

Tentatively, we moved forward on our horses. The forest in

the distance drew closer for a bit as we rode, but we veered right slightly, in the direction of Valeford as I led the way.

"What is it?" Kade asked.

"As children, we were told the beasts of Brookmere resided in the Southern Forests. It's so remote that no one really travels there. Dark, nightmarish tales threatened those who were naughty about being dumped there for the creatures to deal with." Though it had been children's bedtime tales, I smiled remembering the way my father told them. "I wonder now if there's some truth to it."

"Let's avoid the woods, then." Jax shook atop his horse, exaggerating the movements. "Just in case."

I looked toward Raya, but her gaze remained ahead, not engaging with any of us. I frowned. Jax followed where I stared briefly before he met my gaze. He shook his head once, then flashed me a reassuring smile.

Pursing my lips, I continued our ride. I didn't need his silent reminder to let her be. I hadn't tried to talk to her again since last night. But I worried nonetheless.

Smoke and the first few scattered homes came into sight in front of us, and I leaned forward. "Faster," I whispered to my horse, knowing who waited for me there.

We flew, galloping across the field closer to Valeford.

A familiar caw broke through the sky. Ian's hawk appeared moving toward me as quickly as my horse took me toward him.

My hands shook. I leaned forward, desperate to see if this was real.

Please, I begged the Fates. *Please do not let this be a dream.*

Ian cawed again and I sobbed.

Raya was right, Ian was here. She'd told me the truth.

I cried harder, choking and blubbering until I could make out the feathers of his wings in his dramatic dive. I barely slowed the horse before I jumped from him, running the distance to where Ian hurtled to the ground, transforming out of his hawk form.

I wanted to call his name, to shout it as I tripped over myself, desperate to get to him. I couldn't get a single word out though as he ran to meet me.

I threw myself into Ian's arms, crashing into each other, and I shattered.

I held onto him tightly, crying into his neck.

"Lan," he choked out. I felt his own tears falling on my skin.

I shook as uncontrollable sobs escaped. "Tell me it's real," I managed to say between sobs.

"Real as roses." He pulled away and cupped my face in his hands. "I'm here. You're here. Real as roses."

He said it like he needed to hear those words too, so I said it back. "Real as roses."

I hugged him fiercely and we fell to the ground. He held me, rubbing my back. I knew the others finally caught up when they dismounted around us, but I didn't care. Ian was here. Safe.

Slowly, but too soon, he made the first move to separate our bodies from each other. Tears still streamed down my face, my nose running. I sniffled, staring into his vibrant blue eyes.

Eyes holding untold pain, and my heart broke all over again. "Ian."

My heart constricted as I assessed him for injuries. Though none were visible, I knew he hadn't been treated kindly. Part of me could feel the anguish radiating off him. But it didn't matter. Whatever he'd experienced, I'd be there to help him through it. Just as he'd spent our entire lives helping me.

He took my hand, pressing it to his face as he held it there, trying to give me a smile, even a broken one.

We rose from the ground, neither of us looking away from each other yet. There was so much to say, but I couldn't find any words through the absolute joy of knowing he was all right.

I felt Kade before I saw him as he approached us cautiously, Storm at his side.

"Captain," Kade said, bowing his head slightly.

Ian's face fell the moment he looked at Kade. Without warning, he shoved me behind him, took two strides toward Kade, and punched him square in the face.

LANA

"I will kill you," Ian shouted, lunging forward, wildly taking another swing at Kade.

I scrambled toward them. "Ian," I yelled, but my voice caught in my raw throat. "Wait!"

Ian landed another blow to Kade's jaw, one he should have easily deflected but didn't.

I stepped between them, holding my hands out in an effort to quell the fight.

"Please, Ian," I said at the same time Kade spoke.

"I deserved those," Kade said to me, standing with his chin lifted. A sly smile forming as he turned to Ian. "But I won't hold back should you come for me again."

"Tits and daggers you're an idiot." I shoved him, turning to face my best friend. "Ian, he can explain, just give him a chance—"

"An explanation?" Ian's eyes flared. "An explanation? He murdered your father. Do you not remember? Then kidnapped you, which allowed your kingdom to fall without you there."

I wobbled. I knew Andras had won the moment we'd discovered Ian trapped in the dungeon. But to hear the words of defeat from Ian's mouth as if my presence could have changed things was unbearable. I ignored the rising guilt.

Yet I said nothing.

Ian lowered his voice and reached for my hand. "You cannot trust them. Whatever lies they told you, let them go."

"Ian," Storm said, finally speaking.

The malice in Ian's gaze surprised me. Only once had I ever seen such hatred seep from him, and that was toward Andras. He pointed his finger directly into Storm's face. "Don't even think about spewing your deceit with me. I will never trust you again."

"Maybe we should all take a breath." Jax emerged from behind Storm and Kade, followed by Raya.

"Great, there's more of you?" Ian asked.

Raya scoffed. "There's always more of us."

Ian's gaze drifted to Raya and his body stiffened at her appearance.

Raya ran her cool, appraising gaze over him once and then dismissed him by looking elsewhere.

"You." Ian's eyes flared. "She has mind magic. We cannot trust them." He didn't take his gaze off Raya as he spoke. "Do not *ever* enter my mind again."

Raya scoffed again. "Gladly."

"Jax is right," I pleaded, trying again to get through to Ian. "We need to talk."

He shook his head. "We do need to talk," he agreed, lacing his fingers with mine. "But not with them here." He turned to face Kade and Storm once more. "You've returned her, now you can go."

Shadows unfurled around us. "I'm not going anywhere," Kade said through gritted teeth. His gaze lingered on where my hand joined Ian's until it rose to me.

I cocked an eyebrow, daring him to say something. His expression softened, but barely. Storm observed the whole interaction as he always did. Only this time, his lips twitched as if he found it amusing.

"You've done enough," Ian seethed, turning his back on the group to leave.

"We need them," I said, slipping my hand from his.

Ian turned on his heel, facing me. "We don't need them. Not them."

I didn't say anything else, just stared at him, trying desperately to convey that he could trust me, even if he didn't trust them. There was no doubt in my mind we all needed to work together to conquer the evil facing both of our worlds. Especially with both prophecies. Ian would come around. He had to.

He ran a hand through his hair, through heavy breaths. "I refuse to fight with you the second I have you back. These assholes nearly cost me your life, Lan. Mine too. I will not trust them. I cannot. Don't ask that of me."

"Fair enough," I whispered, closing the space and taking his arm. "But for now, I need you to trust *me*. And since I trust them, I need you to have faith in me."

Ian looked over my shoulder toward the others. "One toe out of line, Blackthorn, and I will not hesitate to end your life with my blade." He led me back to my horse and climbed on, grabbing my arm in his and hoisting me up. The others remained close, mounting their horses as well.

I turned to see Kade and Jax riding side by side. Jax wiggled his fingers in a wave before turning back to face Kade.

"I think that went well." Jax's playful tone made me believe this could be okay. Eventually. "Twenty coins says Kade's shadows toss the shifter from behind Lana," he added, loud enough for all of us to hear.

"Fifty." Storm didn't bother hiding his amusement.

"We arrived only an hour ago and set up camp outside Valeford," Ian said, ignoring the others and bringing my attention back to my best friend. "We believe it's important to keep our presence quiet."

"Who is here?" I asked.

Ian turned in the saddle slightly, looking over his shoulder, and I followed his line of sight to Raya. But she didn't look back.

"Kalliah, Corbin"—he paused—"and Hale are with me."

Hale's name came as a surprise. Ian never liked the man. "Leif?" I asked, not understanding why he didn't mention him.

Ian sighed. "Remained behind to buy us time to flee."

I clutched his wrist "Will he make it?"

"I don't know, Lan." Ian quieted. "Andras is more deranged than ever before, and the guards were about to attack Leif as we left."

I trembled. Leif had thrown himself in front of me at the castle when Andras and I fought during the final trial. Damn him for playing the hero. My heart ached thinking of the lesser Fae who continued to prove braver than most of the Royal Guards with three times the magic in their veins.

Ian tightened his hold on the reins and breathed in deeply. I silently thanked the Fates he was free from the dungeons and with me. "What did he do to you?" I whispered.

I looked over my shoulder when I heard no response, but Ian shook his head. "Later."

"Are any of the others hurt?" I asked.

"No."

His answers were short. Hopefully once we arrived at the camp and we all had a chance to talk, he would open up more. I knew how the dungeons affected us before. To know he had been back in them, and alone, made me sick to my stomach.

We rode down the lush hills, and speckles of black figures appeared in the distance.

I let out a sigh, seeing one break into a run.

"Kalliah." I grinned.

Ian urged the horse forward, galloping across the field. Moments later, he helped me down from the steed, and I collided with her too.

"Fates, Lana," she cried, tears in her eyes.

"I'm so glad you're safe," I whispered.

Ian's arms wrapped around both of us, and I looked up to see Corbin and Hale approaching too.

When Kalliah let me go, I walked toward them. Hale bowed, but Corbin kneeled in front of me.

"I'm so glad you're safe, Your Majesty," Corbin said first.

I couldn't help but laugh. "You know how I feel about kneeling and titles, Corbin. Plus, you've elevated my status a bit."

His gaze jerked up, looking from me to Ian. I caught something passing between him before Corbin swallowed and rose.

I didn't stop myself from giving him a hug, shaking off the uneasy weight that settled on me. "I have to tell you about the flowers in their homeland."

He remained stiff but brought a hand to my back, patting it twice. "I look forward to it."

"Illiana," Hale said next, kissing my hand before pulling me into his own embrace. "It's so good to see you safe."

"It's thanks to Hale we escaped," Kalliah said as I pulled away.

Hale shook his head, red coloring his skin. The boyish features I remembered seemed to have disappeared completely from his face. "Illiana needed Ian. Needed all of you."

"Thank you." I squeezed his hand.

Jax cleared his throat from behind us. "Princess, I'm appalled at your manners," he teased. "How dare you ignore us."

"You're impossible to ignore," Ian grumbled.

"Kade and Storm you all know." I pointed to where Kade stood, arms crossed and defenses clearly up. "This is Jax and Raya." Pointing out each of my friends, I ran through those here. "Jax, Raya, this is Hale, Corbin, and Kalliah. Ian you sort of met already."

"What are they doing here." Kalliah's hands clenched into fists as she spoke. Ian flashed her a proud smile.

"We're going to work together," I said, then sighed. "There's a lot to discuss."

The stillness overcoming my friends brought back the feeling of uneasiness I'd been trying to ignore. Kalliah attempted a smile, but her eyes welled with tears.

"What is it?" I asked, looking between each of them.

No one answered.

Ian's face fell, but he took a step toward me.

"I can show you all where we set up camp." Corbin moved to the Mysthaven group, but Raya stilled.

I didn't take my eyes off Ian, even as the others shuffled around me. Kade's presence loomed at my back as shadows sprawled around me in the grass.

"Ian?" I whispered. All the fears of the unknown, some awful atrocity occurring, crashed into my bones so hard, it could no longer be ignored.

Kade's hand squeezed mine before he stepped back to give us a moment.

Ian still hadn't spoken a word. Kalliah stood slightly behind him, tears falling freely now.

"What the hell is going on? You're acting as if someone —" I froze. Icy dread prickled down my back. "Ian?" I asked again, my voice cracking.

"Lan," he mustered, his voice hollow, "your mother—"

I shook my head. "No, no," I begged. "Do not say it." My stomach dropped, and I took a small step back. I could not lose anyone else. It couldn't be true. I refused to believe the words about to come out of their mouths. What would I do if I lost my mother too? I would have no one.

My family would all be gone.

"Lana, I'm so sorry," Kalliah said, stepping forward, closing the distance between us. Her green eyes brimming with tears.

I stretched my arms in front of me as I looked between the two of them, like keeping them at bay would keep the truth from reaching me. "Please." It came out as barely a whisper.

When they didn't continue, both with tears falling down their faces, I turned away from them, coming face to face with Raya. I clung to a feeling separate from despair.

Clenching my hands to stop them from shaking, I whispered to her, "You knew."

"I'm so sorry, Lana," Raya uttered, barely audible, unable to hold back her own tears. "I couldn't."

Grief, hard and debilitating, hit me. I stumbled back, knees giving out. Kade lunged forward, but another pair of arms had me first. Ones I'd escaped into since childhood.

I screamed, as Ian held me from behind, arms wrapped around my waist. When I ran out of breath, Ian slowly allowed my body to fall to the ground.

I screamed again, this time at the sky. I screamed at nature, at any Fates listening.

"Please," I begged them. *Begged.* "Please don't let it be true."

My screams turned to sobs. Ian stroked my back, holding my head against his chest as I wept. Kalliah kneeled beside me, whispering words that didn't reach my ears, even with her soothing tone.

Together, the two of them held me as the fragile shards I had so carefully reconstructed broke again, shattering into a million pieces.

A few hours later, I sat with a blanket over my shoulders in front of the campfire Storm easily kept alive.

The others handled erecting the tents in the small meadow, though they maintained a clear division. Those from Mysthaven on one side, and those from Brookmere on the other.

Stew warmed over the fire, but my body rejected the idea of eating.

My silence lingered long after the tears stopped, and I had been unable to ask the question burning in my throat. "How?" I finally croaked out.

Ian sat, arm around me, but Kade's shadows hadn't left my side either, wrapped around my ankles, touching whatever skin they could access.

Numbness threatened deep, unreachable parts of me, and I knew if I succumbed I might not climb back out of the bliss it promised.

"Andras killed her," Ian said, his unwavering presence enveloping me. His reassurance constantly crashed into me, despite knowing he suffered greatly from my mother's loss too, in addition to the horrors he'd experienced at Andras's hands.

"She fought alongside us," Corbin added. "She moved like the Fae old stories are written about. She fought for our freedom. She was a true queen."

I hung my head before leaning against Ian's shoulder.

"We will kill him, Lan," he whispered before placing a kiss on my head.

"No," I said, my head jerking up as I stared straight into Ian's gaze. "I will kill him. For killing her. For touching you. For myself. He dies by my hand. Understood?"

No one spoke, but their silent nods acknowledged my declaration. I once again rested my head upon his shoulder as I struggled to find any other words. Starting and stopping a hundred times in my mind, yet nothing came out. My mother had fought to free our people. She knew our purpose was greater than the pain I'd face without her. Just like my father knew. Her mate.

I knew it too.

At least my parents were together again in the afterlife. It was the only small piece of comfort I could latch onto.

Lifting my head from Ian's comforting embrace, I wiped my eyes, sitting straighter. In order for Andras to pay, I had to keep moving.

Though my voice quivered, I didn't stop. "What happened after I left?"

"After you were kidnapped," Ian corrected, shooting a glare at Kade.

Kade didn't take the bait, flipping a dagger between his fingers with his focus on me. The heaviness of his attention bothered Ian, maybe the others too, since they shifted uncomfortably watching the exchange. It didn't bother me though.

The comfort his gaze, his presence brought me was too great for me to care what anyone else thought of it. I could only wonder how my life had turned upside down so fast. I shook my head.

"We'll get to that at some point," I said. "What happened?"

Clearing her throat, Kalliah spoke first. "I was sequestered in your mother's tower initially. We were not allowed to leave unless with permission only from Andras and in the presence of multiple guards. It was terrible, Lana. Living in that state of constant fear of what he'd say or do. Andras is out of control. But the queen—she was so strong. She fought him. Fought his mind magic."

Another piece of my heart chipped away, threatening to turn my soul into black nothingness. The shadows stroked my calf where they rested.

"He left me alone, unless he wanted to use me to taunt Ian," Corbin said, adding to the story. "I quickly learned pretending to hate Ian meant I'd be granted the tasks that would send me to the dungeons, allowing me time to map out an escape route."

"Clever," Storm said.

Corbin grunted. "Hale and I connected, and we were able to form a plan—not to Hidden Henchman standards but good enough."

"He let us escape," Ian said, staring at the crackling fire. "I don't know why, but we would be fools to think otherwise. He told us, after he killed—" Ian swallowed, closing his eyes. I slipped my hand in his. "He told us after, if we could get past the guards we could go. He knew you'd come back for revenge."

"It was too easy," Corbin agreed.

"Were you followed?" Kade asked, looking away from me for the first time this evening.

"No," Ian said. "I shifted a few times to backtrack and check. We weren't followed."

Kalliah rose. "I think I need to lie down," she said. Walking toward me, she pulled me into a hug. "I'm so happy you're back."

"Me too. I love you." I didn't want to let her go, so I held her until she pulled away. "He's going to be all right. We will go back for him," I assured her, knowing her thoughts were on Leif.

Tears pooled in her eyes as she nodded and went to one of the far tents.

Hale stood next. "Perhaps we should all rest."

Everyone shifted, moving and packing up. Everyone except Ian and me.

I needed to talk to him, needed to hear he would be okay. He knew it, too, because he didn't move at all.

Kade approached, standing next to me for only a moment, leaning down and placing a small kiss on the top of my head. "I'm here if you need me."

I nodded at him, watching him retreat until even the shadows reluctantly followed.

Then, only Ian and I remained.

"What can I do?" I asked.

He took my hand again. "Sit with me. Remind me what's real. The same as we've always done for each other, and I will be okay."

"Always, Ian." I wiped away another tear, so grateful to be by his side again. "How did you know to come here?" I asked.

"Your mother visited me in the cells." Ian paused. "She told me she knew you had to come here. That something was here, something you needed to do. Your father made her promise to make you come if anything happened."

"I have so much to tell you." I let out a deep breath, pulling out the letter my father wrote me. "About me, and the Forgotten Kingdom."

Ian snorted, smiling a real smile. "What does your favorite book have to do with anything?"

"Because it's not just a fairytale. It's real. Actually, it's where Kade and his friends are from."

Ian ran a hand down over his face. "Next you'll tell me he's the king."

"Prince," I corrected.

"Fucking hell, Lan," Ian said. "I'm listening."

CHAPTER 31
LANA

The pit of my stomach continued to drop, as an anxious ball of energy buzzed in my veins the closer we got to my parents' home.

My real parents.

Ian and I talked long into the night, his shock as heavy as mine had been the more I revealed, both in letting him read my father's letter and discussing Mysthaven. Though I didn't give away all Kade's secrets, I did tell him about the prophecies. That brought out a string of expletives, which eventually turned into Ian reluctantly conceding the Fates must want all of us together.

Though he made it clear he still did not trust them.

Ian handled organizing everyone this morning, revealing only some parts of our plan. We knew we needed to find my parents' home. Once we did, I had to find the journal my father said lay buried with my mother.

Now faced with the purpose of coming to Valeford, my slick palms were not merely caused by the summer heat. The anticipation of walking where they walked, seeing what they saw rattled me. My boots thudded on the ground with each step, pounding to the beat of my racing heart as I realized I would be face-to-face with the last place they ever lived. I would be able to have a glimpse of what my life might have looked like had they not been brutally murdered the night Vivienne and Elisabeth rescued me.

I closed my eyes and took a deep breath as Kade's shadows whispered up my sides.

We're here, they seemed to say.

Ever since the night they came for me in Mysthaven to help Kade, I swore I could understand the thoughts of his shadows.

"I'm here," Kade whispered, echoing what his shadows physically showed me, "every step of the way."

I nodded once, too afraid my voice would fail me.

Kade steered our horse down a narrow beaten path, riding directly behind Ian as Valeford came into view. The rest of our cadre followed close behind in a single-file line.

Every few minutes, Ian glanced over his shoulder, as if to remind himself I was still there, not allowing me out of his sight for long. Though a part of my heart felt the same desire to check on him, I knew his unease stemmed from his lack of trust in Kade and his friends. Understandable after everything that had happened, but I trusted him. He would too... eventually.

I hoped.

"Ian if your horse keeps stopping so close to mine, I cannot ensure you will not be bit," Kade tsked. "It would be a shame for you to have come all this way to be bested by such a simple beast."

Anger emanated from Ian. He was my oldest friend, and I didn't need to look at him to know the daggers he shot with his eyes toward Kade. I reached out, shoving Kade's shoulder.

"Harder next time, Princess," Jax encouraged from behind us.

I winked over my shoulder, grateful for Jax's keen ability to distract when we needed it. Maybe Jax's teasing nature would settle the thick tension around us once and for all soon.

"You mean *Queen*," Corbin snapped.

A pang of pain seared my chest. Corbin's intention was good, based on loyalty, and yet I couldn't help but hate that the title belonged to me now.

Ian ignored the side comments around us, focused solely on Kade. "If you think for one moment that I will trust your intentions simply because my queen, who you kidnapped, does"—Ian's voice trembled, an obvious attempt to contain his rage—"you are sorely mistaken, Kade Blackthorn."

Kade chuckled but said nothing else. Ian eventually heeded his words, relenting and allowing his horse to keep a few paces ahead of ours.

We crested the shallow hill, and I took in the small town of Valeford. I'd been here once with my father many years ago, not knowing then the significance of the town as I did now—at least for my personal history. Homes clustered along tree-lined roads. Small quaint cottages dotted the land in front of us. Most contained beautiful gardens lined with white picket fences. Birds and other wildlife buzzed in the abundance of flowers, unperturbed by the disturbances of darkness to our land.

Being back in Brookmere provided a sense of relief in some ways, like breathing in its sweet air again. But at the same time, the looming suffocation of complete dread lingered at the task before us now that I had returned.

Ellevail had fallen.

Andras undoubtedly had stolen the crown for himself.

Fucking asshole.

I repeated the words I swore I would continue to say until they actually rang true.

I am Illiana Dresden, and Andras Braumlyn will die by my hand.

Slowly, painfully, and without regard for proper decorum normally afforded a member of the royal court.

I put a hand over my heart, fighting back the fresh new wave of grief washing over my soul.

The anguish over my mother's death.

A warm hand swept over my cheek. Kade's knuckles brushed away the falling tear, and I leaned into the compassionate touch.

"You will have your retribution, Little Rebel," he said, low and ruthlessly.

I let myself believe his words as Ian led us down the small hill.

The last few paces toward the main entrance to the town felt like time stopped and sped up all at once. A whirlwind of emotions flooded my body, leaving me desperate for air.

Riding silently down the main road, we searched. Neither Ian nor I knew how we'd find my parents' house, or the journal my father wanted me to obtain.

I figured I would merely ask someone. It might give away that we were here, but unless clearly marked, the idea of finding a home from twenty years ago seemed impossible.

People appeared content as they pushed wooden carts covered in dirt along the road. Children ran across yards, darting in and out of the small homes and onto the streets.

Despite the horrors gracing Brookmere, happiness filled the air. A joy that would be destroyed if the threats from not just the dark ones, but Andras continued to spread unchecked.

I dismounted and approached an elderly Fae tending to his front garden. He hummed to himself, his tan trousers caked in mud with a blue shirt billowing in the summer breeze.

"Excuse me?" I asked.

The man turned with a bright smile on his face. "Can I help ye?"

"I'm sorry to disturb you," I said. "We're looking for a cottage that belonged to the king's sister. I'm not sure—"

"Yes, yes." He wiped his dirt-covered hands on his

trousers, though with the dirt already on them, it didn't do anything other than cake more on him. "It's still just as he requested. Come on now. Not far."

I blinked, surprised he knew the place so easily. Ian remained on his horse practically on top of me, but Kade dismounted and hovered with his shadows.

"He doesn't know what you look like? That you're the princess?" Kade asked.

I shook my head. "I wouldn't expect them to. I didn't travel outside of Ellevail often. Unless he had business in the city, he wouldn't know my face."

Kade relaxed. "I suppose that's good to keep our presence quiet."

We all followed the elderly Fae. His hands in his pockets, he kept on humming, not at all bothered with small talk.

He stopped suddenly and turned to face me. "Not my business, I know, but I'm assuming he requested someone check up on the place in his absence. We heard about his passing."

I frowned, not sure how to respond.

"The king held a lot of unwarranted guilt about his sister. Terrible thing, the dark Fae. Especially killing the babe. But his sister and her husband, they were happy until the end. Kept to themselves, but always had a smile and lent a hand whenever someone needed it. Remembering their life rather than their deaths might be a better way to honor them."

I frowned. "I'm not sure I know what you mean."

The man nodded toward the end of the road, where a cottage sat in disrepair.

"Oh," I gasped, a small sob escaping.

The man patted my shoulder. "I don't mean no disrespect, young lady, especially with our king just passing and the princess missing. I thought I'd simply speak my piece. I disobeyed him and trimmed the hedges last year, just so the place was still visible. But like I said, none of my business. It's his family matter."

"Thank you," Ian said for me, since I stood in silence a few moments too long for comfort.

I nodded at the man, and he gave me a sad smile before turning and leaving us.

My hand came up to my mouth in pain and anger, shocked at how neglected the cottage had become.

My parents' *home*.

It took less than a heartbeat for me to decide my next move. I took off running the rest of the way, leaving the others behind.

"Lana!" Kade and Ian shouted simultaneously.

I ignored their shouts. One of fear and one of warning.

"Give her a minute," I heard Kalliah say to the others.

I slowed, stopping in front of the overgrown white fence and broken trellis. Before me lay the ruins of my parents' home. A small gold plaque, barely visible through the overgrowth, glinted in the sun, posted near the entrance to their garden. I brushed my hand over it. "To remember what we fight for. Always. By decree of the king, this home is designated a historical monument. Never to be touched."

They could have at least cleaned it up, not left it as some abandoned piece of property.

Falling to my knees in their garden, I placed my hands on the earth. Feeling the overgrown grasses intertwine between my fingers. I inhaled, as if I might feel my real parents somehow.

I could have run through this yard, playing games with my father. Picked flowers with my mother. Instead, I'd been robbed of the innocence of my childhood. Thrust into the chaos of life in the palace without a choice. Without a voice.

Into the hands of Andras.

I didn't know until this moment the anger I held at the king and queen for allowing what he did. Even knowing they allowed it by sheer ignorance. The overpowering guilt that followed when thinking anything bad about them after their deaths wrecked me further.

The others remained silent behind me until Ian kneeled next to me.

"Come on, Lana, let's do this. Let's find what your mother left you."

Standing, I turned to the group, wiping my hands along my pants. Resolve washing over me. "I'd like to look inside."

Kade sent his shadows in ahead of us, slipping in through the cracks of the windows and doors. He had been adamant that he examine everything first, wanting to make sure we weren't walking into an ambush. The moment his shadows returned, he nodded.

"Storm and Raya will remain outside to keep watch. If anything appears amiss, leave. We don't want to disturb any unnatural forces here."

Kade spoke like a commander. A leader. Even Ian nodded in agreement.

I stopped at the front door, knowing everyone was standing behind me. With me. I tentatively placed my hand on the knob. After one more deep breath, I turned it, allowing the door to creak open.

Unlocked.

I frowned, until I looked at Kade. He gave me a wink while his shadows danced at his feet.

Was there anything his shadows couldn't do?

As I stepped inside, my breath caught in my throat. Stumbling backward, my hand flew to my chest.

Kade caught me before I fell. His hardened glare, focusing on the house, softened instantly as he looked at me.

"Breathe," he whispered. "It's okay." He cradled my head to his chest.

"What is it?" Ian ran forward and abruptly halted at the door. "Fucking Fates."

He'd seen what I had. Not only had the outside of my parents' home been left alone, but the inside had been as well.

It had never been cleaned from the attack that took their lives.

I'd walked in the front door of my parents' home only to witness the bloodstained walls perfectly preserved from the night they were murdered.

CHAPTER 32

LANA

"I'm sorry," I apologized, stepping from Kade's firm grasp. "It just caught me off guard."

Kade tensed beside me, but instead of pulling me back to him, his shadows closed in around me. With him by my side, I stepped fully into the living room.

The furniture in the home lay scattered and broken, disheveled from the obvious fight on that night. Nothing remained upright or whole. A thick layer of dust covered the home and shifted with our steps.

I walked up to a long-crusted bloody streak and gingerly touched it.

Tears silently fell down my face as I placed my hand on the wall.

"Why?" I asked to no one in particular. "Why leave it like this?"

"Sometimes grief makes people do horrible things." Jax stood beside me, closer than he normally did. I looked at him to find his focus solely on me and not the mess around us.

"Horrible things?" I asked.

"When I was a boy, dark ones murdered my mother. I

"

grew up on a farm, and my father had been working in the fields when it happened."

"Oh Jax." I brought a hand to his arm.

He smiled softly. "He refused to move anything in the house. He stopped working, started drinking. The grief consumed him. So much so that a year later, he dropped me at the palace gates to be taken in as a Guardian, sort of like Raya. He couldn't bear the sight of me, because it reminded him of his failure to protect her."

I squeezed his arm.

"The guilt he felt for not being home, for leaving my mother there alone—it was too much. It didn't matter that it wasn't his fault, he held on to the blame and never moved past it. I haven't seen or heard from him since. But as someone who has seen what guilt and grief can do together, perhaps the king couldn't do any more than leave this place alone. If I had to guess, I would say he loved his sister very much and never quite came to terms with her death."

"The man knows," I said. "The one who led us here. That's what he meant by preserving their life."

"I have a feeling you'll be the one to do just that. In more ways than simply fixing up a home, Lana." He didn't say any more, but walked away, back toward where Hale and Corbin stood.

I held my palm to the wall. "I will make your deaths, *all* of your deaths, count. Andras and the darkness will not win. I will be the queen the four of you raised me to be."

The small cottage didn't take long to walk through. A small library alcove, a dining room table, the kitchen area, a sitting room, and two bedrooms made up the entirety of the home. Imagining what it looked like originally remained difficult, and didn't give me much of a picture of the lives my real parents led.

I climbed a small set of stairs leading to two bedrooms. Corbin stood in the doorway of the smaller room.

"I found this," Corbin says quietly. "I think you should take it with you."

He handed me a small folded-up piece of paper, and I looked at him quizzically, furrowing my brows. All he gave me was a soft smile in return. I gently unfolded the paper and gasped when I saw its contents.

I stared down at a painting of my mother and father, holding a baby. Holding *me*. My knees wobbled, threatening to give out.

I held the painting to my chest, taking measured breaths.

"Thank you, Corbin. Just…thank you." It was all I could get out without completely losing it. I wrapped him in an embrace. He awkwardly patted my back. He never was one for physical touch, but especially not from his princess.

Though he hastily pulled away, a faint smile graced his lips before we returned to the others, who were waiting for me in the backyard. I had seen everything I could bear to see in this home. The thought of seeing where my parents slept. Where I slept… It would have to wait for another day.

I took one more steadying breath, determined to regain my composure and accomplish our goal here today. Ian turned as soon as I stepped outside and immediately approached, noticing my tears. I shook my head indicating I was all right.

Behind the house, a small outbuilding sat untouched, but in surprisingly good shape considering the rest of the property.

Silently, Kade's shadows entered the outbuilding, feeling for any disturbances, and unlocked the door upon their retreat.

Everyone waited, allowing me to open the double doors.

"Fates above," Kalliah breathed out from behind me.

Beyond the entryway lay grass trimmed to perfection. A beautiful archway of roses accented a small space with three gravestones. One for my mother and another for my father. And one for me.

The others remained silent as I stared at the etchings in the marble.

There were floral arrangements everywhere, of all colors and shapes. Magic pulsed against my skin. The area must have been warded in a way to allow it to stay in such pristine condition.

I approached reverently. Tracing the carved words of the headstones as I dropped to my knees on the small ivory runner lying between the graves. Two to my left and one to my right.

"Hi," I whispered.

I kneeled by myself for a few minutes, until one by one my friends joined me.

"Are you ready?" Ian asked, his hand slipping into mine.

I nodded. "Ready."

"Corbin?" Ian called. "We need to get the journal and go. Andras may have let us escape, but the last thing any of us needs is him learning of our position."

Corbin stepped forward, followed immediately by Hale.

"I can use my summoning magic on your mother's coffin, so we don't have to disturb too much of the earth or the magic here," Hale said. "If there is any risk to the grave being destroyed, I'll stop."

"Thank you." I gave him a small nod.

"I'll use my earth magic to get through some of the extra layers on top," Corbin explained. "As gently as possible."

The care and respect the two of them displayed for my birth mother warmed in my chest. Their love of a woman they didn't know was because of me. Because of what this moment meant for me.

The numbness I had been worried about seeping into me and staying didn't stand a chance. I knew that now. Grief would not consume me. There were too many people to live for.

Corbin rarely displayed his magic in front of others. As a private person who preferred to work alone, it had taken most of us years to witness him at work. I had only recently seen him in action in my garden the past few years. I knew he hated being a lesser Fae, but his magic was extraordinary in my eyes. His attention to detail and care for nature always made me appreciate his talents.

Concentrating on the ground, Corbin carved shallow lines through the earth, moving clumps to the side. After a few moments, he nodded toward Hale, who took it as his cue to summon the coffin.

They moved carefully, respectfully, as promised. Hale's body strained with his magic, as Corbin continued to move mounds of dirt. Suddenly, with a loud *thud*, a massive double-wide white marble coffin appeared.

"They're together," I said, my voice cracking.

Ian and Kade moved forward and stood on the left side, readying to use their combined strength to open the tomb.

"Are you all right?" Kade asked. When I nodded, he instructed Ian as well as Storm, who joined him by the coffin's lid. "On three," Kade instructed. "One, two, three."

They pushed the top cleanly off.

I prepared myself for the stench of death to fill the air, but instead, the scent was masked. I stepped forward. Even if it was only bones, I would see my parents.

The skeletal remains of my mother and father lay together, hands clasped side by side, in purple and gold robes. The colors of Brookmere. While only bones lay before me, whoever buried them did so with care and compassion. I could feel their love of each other, and the way they were positioned so delicately side by side.

I let out a shaky breath and stepped forward, falling to my knees beside the coffin. Resting my head on the side, I whispered a prayer to the Fates, hoping their souls remained together in whatever came next. A gentle breeze swept through the room, caressing my neck in response. Willing myself to stand, I knew I must continue the journey started for me at their deaths.

Raising my head, I searched the coffin for the journal. It should have been plainly visible.

Only there was no journal there.

"What's that?" Kalliah asked.

Storm reached into the casket and pulled out a small scroll. Not a journal, but it was something. He handed it to me, and I unrolled the delicate paper, reading it once to myself first.

My heart sank. It didn't make sense.

"What does it say, Lana?" Kalliah asked.

I looked up at all of their expectant eyes, so eager to find an answer, even if we had no idea what answer it was.

Anger coursed through my veins as I gripped the scroll in my fist. I thought this path would lead to something of value, something to save Brookmere. Instead, we got a dead end on the only lead we had for this ridiculous mission.

"Are you okay, Little Rebel?" Kade whispered, sending his shadows to my waist in an embrace.

I took a deep breath and read the words so hastily scrolled upon the weathered parchment.

"I must protect the secrets of Atheria. Only one shall be brave enough to end our blight, and she must always look to the light. Search in the realms of nowhere and nightmares for answers you seek, for the royal blood's journal cannot be obtained by the weak."

The stupid text sounded like a riddle and reminded me too much of Vivienne's or Cassandra's nonsense. It reminded me why I loathed seers.

"Well, that is less than helpful," Ian stated. "Let's take the parchment and get out of here before we attract too many eyes. We can regroup once we are out of Valeford."

Everyone murmured in agreement. Hale, Ian, and Storm

shifted to move the coffin lid back when a flicker of gold flashed in the corner of my eye. "Wait," I said, stopping them. Squinting, I peered into the casket once more.

Again, a small flash of gold flittered in my vision, on top of the regal robes.

"Kade, do you see that?" I asked quietly, as the rest of the group spoke among themselves.

He peered into the casket. "See what?"

Summoning all of my bravery, I reached into the casket and moved the robes of my parents, right where the gold reflection had caught my eye. I reached out and grasped the golden shimmer, which turned solid at my touch.

I inhaled sharply and wrapped my fingers around a solid hilt. When I pulled back, a white dagger lay in my hand. A wave of energy raced down my spine, and the dagger thrummed in my palm.

My eyes widened in disbelief.

"How?" Kade murmured.

I stared at the dagger in my hand, humming with a kind of power I didn't recognize. The consistency wasn't metal, at least it didn't look like it. "This feels unlike anything I have ever held," I said. I turned the blade in my hand again. The weapon quieted, the hum settling. I tucked the dagger into an empty sheath along my thigh. I needed to keep this safe and out of sight for now. Daggers didn't have a habit of appearing out of nowhere, even from powerful magic.

The men returned the lid to the casket, and both Hale and Corbin replaced the coffin and land to its natural state, as if completely untouched.

Corbin kneeled in front of the graves, touching the ground. When he stepped back, a small ring of purple and yellow roses rested at the headstone. A parting gift in honor of my parents, who'd died protecting me. Protecting Brookmere's future.

Despite all the troubles that still lay before me, I couldn't help but feel an unknown weight lifted. Even though they were dead, I'd met my parents. Stood in their home. I would carry the pieces of them with me through this fight, whatever battle awaited.

Corbin turned, still on his knee, and remained bowing before me. "I know you hate the reverence, but you are my queen now, Illiana. What you had to face here today and the dignity with which you did it reminds me why I'm proud to be your humble servant."

I touched his shoulder. "You are no servant, Corbin. You are my friend."

He shook his head and rose before leaving me behind. Corbin, the unsung hero of today.

The others left, but Kade lingered by the doors when Hale stood beside me next. "Did you know, after Andras caught us in the gardens the first time we tried to fool around, your mother came to visit me?"

A low growl escaped Kade's lips, but I shook my head and flicked my hand at him, dismissing him and his protectiveness.

My gaze shifted to Hale's face. Somehow in the past few weeks he had transformed into something harsher. More determined.

"How terrifying was that?" I smiled thinking about our younger selves and how discussing a tryst with my mother would feel.

He grinned back at me. "She asked me my intentions." He raised his eyebrows.

"What did you say?"

He sighed, putting his hands into his pockets. A warm smile remained on his lips. "I told her you were too good for me, but I would spend time earning your love."

"Hale," I breathed out. How many times had Ian and I joked about Hale as a mere distraction? I told him during the marriage trials that he would always be my friend, and I had no intention of going back on that now, but a nagging guilt puttered in my chest. I couldn't help but wonder if I'd missed out on years of having another close confidant.

He took my hand but didn't turn from my parents' grave. "I told your mother that if you wanted me, I would bask in your presence forever. If you didn't, I would serve by your side however you saw fit. Whatever you chose, I believed I might love you until I died."

I squeezed his hands. "What did she say?"

Tears pooled in Hale's eyes. "My mother was— Well, you saw how important appearances were. I never quite lived up to her expectations, neither in the strength of my magic nor my ability with a blade. But your mother cupped my face and kissed my cheek. She said my belief in you was all she needed to see, and I was worthy no matter what your heart chose." He looked over at me. "Then she told me if I did anything more serious than romping around in her rose bushes before you were ready, she'd banish me."

I couldn't help but laugh. "I can hear her saying that."

"My point in telling you is that your mother saw the good in everyone. She had an ability to make people feel seen when she spoke to them. She made people feel as if they mattered. You have that ability too. Your heart for your people is exactly like our queen's was, and your tenacity is like the king's. I obviously didn't know your birth parents, but I can only imagine the force they were to have created someone like you, Illiana. Meeting them would have been an honor."

I leaned my head against Hale's shoulder, and he kissed the side of my head before he spoke again. "You carry the traits of four parents who left their mark on this world not only in their actions, but in you. Our queen."

Hale squeezed my hand once, then walked away, leaving me privacy at my parents' grave. This time, I looked at their headstones with a smile on my face. A new stirring blossomed in my chest.

One of hope and pride. One of determination.

I looked at the headstone one last time. "For Brookmere and for you, I will fight."

CHAPTER 33

IAN

I stared at Lana across the fire as she spoke to Kalliah in hushed tones.

Kalliah always helped her to process her thoughts through their conversations. I didn't realize how much I missed the sound of their voices together until now.

Exhaustion from recent events looked like it threatened to take all of us under. The anticipation of finding the journal, then not finding the journal crushed most of our spirits. Another obstacle to overcome in this war we didn't understand that we'd already been fighting for years. On top of already being behind, anyone who may have had any answers to aid us was dead.

My body still ached slightly from the numerous rounds of torture, but being out in nature significantly improved the healing process. The scar on my side remained, and I wondered if it would ever fully heal.

Kade's shadows lingered around Lana's ankles. A pool of swirling mist. He had been particularly quiet since our groups joined forces, but always watching. He never let Lana out of his sight, not even for a moment. Those shadows too always stayed near her. I didn't remember them being so present

329

during our time in the trials. It was unnerving, but he had kept her safe. And he'd brought her home. For that, I would be forever grateful.

Ugh. How could she stand him after everything he did to her? Prophecy or not, that Fae remained full of too many secrets.

A dark anger filled me just watching him. Black circled my vision, like it had in the dungeons, and I shut my eyes hard, shaking my head.

When I opened them, the feelings were gone.

Jax strutted toward Kalliah with a wink. "Care for any more stew? I'm not sure if you heard, but this was my catch today."

She promptly rolled her eyes. "Not interested."

Jax chuckled. "What? You are gorgeous. And since that one"—he pointed toward Lana—"is taken, and that one," he continued, this time pointing to Raya, "is angrier than a panther in heat on any given day…well, you can't blame a Fae for trying."

"Still not interested," Kalliah said again. "But no, I can't blame you for trying."

"I knew I liked you." He smiled, taking the seat right next to her.

Raya sighed heavily. "Some things never change."

Storm laughed, and even Lana let out a small giggle at Jax. I had to give it to him, he seemed to be trying to bring us together. I imagined his penchant for humor in darker times alleviated some of Lana's anxieties too.

Returning my attention to the fire and those around it, Lana finally spoke. "I'm sorry this did not work out how we hoped. I wish I knew what to say, but I don't know what to do or where to go from here. This note is just words, nonsense. Though we know someone clearly stole my birth mother's journal, there's nothing else to go on."

Kalliah rubbed Lana's arm. "We'll figure it out."

"I am supposed to be queen, and yet I have no answers." Lana stared at the fire, disappointment clear on her face in the way her nose wrinkled, the weariness in her eyes. All the signs were there, and I knew what she heard right now in her head.

Andras's words.

Worthless. Magicless.

"This burden isn't yours to bear alone." I stared at her until I knew she felt my gaze. When she finally gathered the courage to meet it, I tried to convey everything I normally did in these moments. "We are a team. We always have been."

"He's right," Kalliah exclaimed. "All of us. Together. The fact that there's an entire other kingdom, and two prophecies bringing us together? That's fate. Even if you hate it. We're meant to do this, and so we shall."

Lana squeezed Kalliah's hand in silent appreciation. "Too bad Vivienne can't produce visions on command," Lana said almost absentmindedly. "What good is being a seer if you can't even predict important things when necessary?"

I glanced at Kade, whose brows furrowed as if he were deep in thought.

I stood, cracking my neck. My muscles still ached from the past several weeks. "It's too dangerous to return to Ellevail to get to her, you know that, Lan."

"We're not going to figure it out tonight," Raya butted in. "It has been a long day, and we are sure to have longer ones ahead. Rest now, for battles are in our future. I can feel it in my bones."

"Did your mind magic tell you that?" I scoffed.

Raya glared across the fire at me. "I thought we weren't speaking?"

I held up my hands. "Just making sure you remember to keep those magical abilities to yourself."

Her lip curled and I swore I could hear her muttering unmentionable curses at me in the recesses of my mind.

I couldn't name the reason for my viciousness toward her,

but I swore it still felt like she was in my head. Even though she helped me against Andras, knowing her magic worked the same as his put me on edge. Whether that proved fair to her or not.

Kade stood abruptly, reaching a hand toward Lana like she was his. "Come on, Little Rebel." His eyes darkened for a brief moment before he rolled his shoulders. An obvious attempt to right whatever flared within him. I hadn't missed the way his eyes changed every so often. "Raya is right, we will regroup when we can think more clearly in the morning."

Lana's eyes darted among the faces surrounding the fire. She settled on mine, searching for an answer to her silent question of whether I was all right. I'd given her that look more times than I could count growing up. Fates, I'd missed her so damn much. I wanted to let the others go and talk to her more about everything, but instead, I gave her a quick nod. She was losing too much too quickly. There would be plenty of time to talk and process this new hell together later.

"I'll take the first shift," Hale offered. "Jax, I can wake you in four hours for the next rotation, all right?"

With the plan in place, Lana and Kalliah walked toward their separate tents, escorted by Kade and his inky shadows. The others broke off as well, while I entered mine. Alone. I was sharing with Hale, but with him on watch, I would at least get a few hours of peace and quiet before he returned.

My head weighed heavily on my shoulders, and the exhaustion from escaping Ellevail, riding for days, and searching for the journal hit me harder than I cared to admit.

Last night, knowing Lana slept safely nearby allowed me to rest better than I had in a long time. The thought of her here still made the weariness easier to succumb to.

Lana was safe.

We were all together.

With that knowledge allowing a semblance of peace to

enter my mind, my eyes were closed before my head even hit the ground.

I couldn't be sure how long I slept, but a crushing, lingering weight tugged me from my dreams. My eyes flew open as hands closed around my throat, choking me.

My attacker wore a hood over their head, but I bucked my hips and thrust them forward. A surprised male voice grunted. His elbow landed next to my head as he balanced himself on top of me again, but I wasn't that easy to disarm. I wrapped my leg around his and flipped him onto his back, slamming my forearm into his throat.

The hood fell to the grassy ground.

Hale.

"What are you doing?" I seethed. "Have you lost your mind?"

I released the pressure at his neck to allow him to gather himself, but as I searched his expression for some sort of answer, his gaze collided with mine.

Hale's eyes glistened in midnight black.

"Hale?" I swallowed, knowing immediately something was off. "What is wrong with you?"

Hale stilled beneath me, and I leaned back slightly, giving him space to speak. But he jolted and caught me off guard, landing a punch square in my jaw.

"The fuck is wrong with you?" I asked angrily, standing and putting some distance between us.

Hale stared at me, wincing, his eyes flickering as the black lightened, revealing a sliver of his usual brown coloring. He fisted his hands by his side, clearly fighting some internal battle.

"I'm sorry," he admitted hoarsely. As soon as the words were out, his eyes returned to the solid state of black.

Suddenly, a powerful magic washed over me, making it impossible for me to move. Another set of darkened eyes and red hair appeared before me, surrounded by full moonlight in the slit of the tent flaps.

Lord Casimir West chuckled eerily softly, only loud enough for me to hear.

"My, my, my, Captain Stronholm." His eyes narrowing as a sly smile crept up his face. "We meet again."

My lips remained sealed by whatever magic he used to overpower me. My shifting ability vanished. Without having to touch me, somehow my magic evaporated, leaving me unable to reach for the string of power connected to my soul.

Casimir crept the few paces toward me and kicked my paralyzed body to the ground. He ran his tongue over his teeth.

"Healers are a fascinating thing," he said.

I could do nothing. I lay there, half on my bedroll, my arms and legs in an awkward uncomfortable position as he peered over me.

"Do you know how your precious Elisabeth helped the king?" he continued.

Even if this magic had not been keeping me paralyzed, I would have frozen. I wanted to scream at him. Tell him to keep her name out of his mouth.

Hale stood, dazed, barely present.

"She created a potion that dulled his magic." He laughed humorlessly. "Without magic to feed on, Andras's control faltered. She kept him alive years longer than should have been possible. But that potion is ours now." He turned to Hale, slapping his shoulder. "Delivered in the package of a friend."

"What a good dog," I hissed, using all of my final strength. My body may be immovable, but I would have him know he had not completely succeeded in dulling my magic. "Obeying your cowardly master."

"Throw your words at me all you want, *Captain.* Your time has come," he sneered. "Your power, your magic—it's mine."

The words I spoke were my last. For now. Unable to do anything, my scream remained lodged in my throat as Casimir clutched my neck, draining me of my magic. I stared into his eyes as he did it, vowing silently this would be the last time he stole from me. Or anyone I loved. The second I could get to him, I'd end this Fae.

"What a pity you will miss all the fun. Stuck here, helpless."

A jeweled ring on his hand glowed a brilliant emerald as he siphoned my magic into the piece of jewelry.

Unable to fight, to do anything against this evil, I lay there fucking helpless. A failure once more. I had to warn Lana and Kade. Jax and Storm. Everyone.

"Pathetic."

The last word I heard uttered by Casimir as my world blurred, but the oblivion of fading into darkness escaped me. Instead, I lay there awake, bound by a magic stronger than me.

How many more times would I fail?

The thought haunted me while I lay paralyzed, silently begging the Fates to wake the others before I had to face the nightmare of losing Lana again.

This time, perhaps forever.

CHAPTER 34

LANA

"Talk to me," Kade said, rubbing his warm calloused hand over the back of my neck as we lay in his tent together.

The tingle against my skin mixed with the soothing way he kneaded the tension from me felt like bliss despite my lingering fears.

"I'm worried about Ian. I'm worried about what's next," I admitted, leaning into his touch. The other fears I wanted to keep to myself. Not voicing them made me believe I could store them in the box I tried so hard to keep them locked in.

Kade kissed my shoulder. "Give me whatever it is you're holding on to, Little Rebel. Let me help you carry it."

"I feel like everyone has been handed an incompetent, worthless Fae to lead them. How can I help Brookmere when I have no magic? How do I stand a chance against Andras as weak as I am? All of this comes down on the shoulders of others. How can a queen ask that of her people, let alone the people she loves most?"

"Look at me," Kade demanded. I rolled over on the bedroll to face him. His eyes completely clear of any darkness.

I sucked in a sharp breath at their intensity, at the adoration staring back at me.

"You have never needed magic to prove your worth. You have never been weak." He rested his hand over my heart. "In your darkest moments you survived, and then chose to not only continue but to throw yourself into caring for your people. You inspire loyalty for *who* you are, Illiana, not what magic you can offer."

My lip quivered. "They're beautiful words, Kade. But at the end of the day, it will take someone extremely powerful to do whatever is needed to take back my kingdom."

"You *are* powerful," he whispered. "It will take *you*. Magic does not determine a Fae's worth. I know you believe that. You treat lesser Fae exactly the same as nobility, if not better. You don't let their worth be determined by their magic. So why allow your mind to use it to condemn yourself?"

I shook my head, but he gripped my chin tightly, forcing me to look into his eyes. "Hear me, Little Rebel. You are worthy. You have always been worthy. There is no one else I would follow into any battle, any fight so willingly as you. There will never be a moment when I doubt what you can accomplish." He kissed my forehead, lingering there.

I shuddered, soaking in his words. "What if I fail?"

He pulled back, not allowing me to look away. "Then I will tell you the Fates had something else in store for you to rise again. You will never fail because you will never give up. And when you think you cannot continue, I will carry you until you stand beside me once more." He brushed his fingers over my face. "There is no kingdom, no world where I am not kneeling before you as queen. You will not fail."

I swallowed as the ferocity of his belief in me ignited all the dark corners of doubt. I may not know where to go from here, but I would never have to determine it alone.

"You're not holding back anymore, are you?" I smiled,

unable to stop the grin from spreading at his utter confidence in me.

He leaned in and yanked me toward him so no space lingered between our intertwined bodies. "You have ruined me, Little Rebel. Completely ruined me. I refuse to go back to acting as if that isn't the truth."

"Prove it," I said against his lips.

A low sound rumbled in Kade's chest as his lips crashed into mine. Gone was any hesitation, and I relished it. I ground my hips into him, whimpering at how hard and ready he was for me.

I reached down, stroking him over his pants. He nipped my bottom lip. "I don't want to take advantage, so do not tempt me."

"It's not taking advantage when I'm asking nicely," I practically whined. "I need this. I need you. Make me feel whole again. I cannot be consumed by grief anymore."

I reached inside his pants. This time he groaned but didn't pull away. "I'm holding on by a very loose, unstable thread."

"Break for me."

Kade lunged, hovering over me, and flipped me to my back. His fingers trailing down my throat and over my thin shirt, running between my breasts. He traced his fingers over my pants, slowly rubbing until I arched into his touch.

"More," I begged.

"Greedy girl." He smirked, removing his fingers from my body to lift my shirt. He dipped his head, tracing his tongue along the line of my pants.

I jerked at the divine sensation of the heat from his mouth. Running my fingers through his hair, I tugged, forcing him to look at me. The satisfaction dancing over his features drew out a moan from deep inside of me.

"I haven't even touched you yet, and look at you." He slipped my pants off with his shadows. "Perfect. Beautiful. *Mine*."

I arched again when his lips caressed the inside of my thigh. I tugged his hair, desperate to pull him to my core, but he simply laughed against my skin. "I warned you the next time I had you I would not be rushed."

"I need you," I said, breathy and urgent. Fates, I had never been so desperate for anyone, and I didn't care that he saw it. That he heard it.

He moved lower, farther from where I wanted him. He raised my ankle to his lips, kissing my skin before slowly running his tongue up my leg. When he finally reached my clit, he pulled away, retreating to the other side.

I let out an anguished moan.

"I better shield our friends from all the filthy things about to come from your mouth." Kade smiled as his shadows arched outward around the edges of the tent.

"Fuck me, Kade," I demanded.

"Are you wet for me, Illiana?" He kissed my thigh and slipped a finger inside of me.

"Yes," I managed to hiss out.

He pressed deeper into me, taking his sweet time. His shadows curled toward me and suddenly pulsed outward. "They had their turn. You're all mine now."

He pressed into me steadily with his finger, and he added another, building a toe-curling rhythm. He curled them upward inside of me until I thrust my hips up for purchase.

Kade controlled my body like a damn musician, gradually coaxing the crescendo of pleasure further toward his goal.

"Please," I begged.

He let out a satisfied sound and ran his tongue along my clit right as he curled his fingers again, thrusting inside of me.

"Beg for me again, Little Rebel."

"Please," I obeyed, willing to say anything to get more of this. More of him.

He sucked my clit hard, and I knew I was headed for oblivion. The skillful stroke of his tongue in time with his fingers brought me closer and closer, until suddenly I exploded.

He groaned, slowing his movements. "Fates, I'll never have enough of you on my tongue." He licked and kissed and refused to relent, even when I squirmed from the sensations.

Too much.

Not enough.

The orgasm did nothing to quench the desire building these past few days. A tugging inside of me flared at his touch, refusing to be sated. I knew I needed him deep inside me if I had any hope of quelling this uncontrollable urge to have him.

Have him completely mine.

Kade lifted his head, like he knew my very thoughts. He moved, crawling to his knees before spreading my legs wider as he rested between them. He pulled his fingers from me and put both of them in his mouth, licking them slowly, before leaning over me and kissing me.

His tongue swirled over mine, demanding my submission, and I was all too willing to give it.

He leaned back and removed his pants, stopping to stare at me as he stroked his cock once. Twice.

I leaned up, tugging his shirt. "Off." Full sentences were impossible. I wanted to see all of him.

He tugged his shirt over his head and gave me the sexiest smirk as he went back to his cock. "Better?"

I shook my head. "Not yet."

His smile widened, and he ran the tip of his cock over my slit. My eyes fluttered shut and he stopped.

"No," I cried.

"Then look at me," he said. "Watch me take you or I stop."

My eyes flew open, meeting his, and he triumphantly smiled and lined himself up against me. I thought the torture would continue, but he gave me what I wanted, sliding into me.

I tensed when he made it halfway in and looked down to see where he was inside of me. Fates, watching him pressing into me. I was undone.

His body shook as he ran his hands over my thighs. "Relax your body, Little Rebel. I don't want to hurt you."

I reached for him, and he intertwined his hands with mine, bringing them over my head.

As my body relaxed, he slid farther in until he was to the hilt. Everything stopped. Nothing existed outside of Kade and this moment. His breath against my face came out shaky. He rested his forehead on mine. "The soul-searing memories of being inside of you did zero justice to the real thing. You were made for me, Illiana."

He kissed my lips, my entire body melting into him. He slid out of me, and when he didn't thrust back in right away, I almost cried at the loss of him.

"Say it," he whispered.

"Mmm." I choked back the plea. "Say what?"

"Tell me you were made for me."

"I was made for you," I answered, as reverently as a prayer.

He slammed into me, then torturously slowly pulled out again. "Again."

"I was made for you," I said louder this time. The words were barely off my lips when he dragged us upward to rest on his knees. He wrapped one hand around my throat and another around my back.

"You are mine," he growled before taking my bottom lip between his teeth. He nipped at me, and it snapped that tugging, deep tether inside of me.

"Harder," I demanded, no longer satisfied with his speed. I needed this at my pace. As much as he claimed I was his, Kade Blackthorn was mine.

He obeyed, his own control slipping as he took me over

and over, holding my body on top of his and demanding every pleasurable sound that escaped me.

His hand squeezed around my throat. "I can feel you, Little Rebel. You're so close."

"Yes," I said. "Don't stop."

"Never."

I wrapped my arms around him, letting my tongue take the lead as I took control of his mouth, using my arms to drive myself downward harder on him. I swallowed his own groans until the frantic way our bodies moved begged for that final release.

"Now come for me," he ordered, and my body obeyed. Instantly.

His words flooded my senses as I screamed his name, throwing my head back.

"Fuck," he bellowed. "Fucking Fates, Lana."

As he spilled inside of me, another orgasm ripped through my body. Kade's tremors coaxing it out of me until I thought I'd never stop. He held me in place, forcing my body further onto him somehow.

"Don't move," he whispered, pulling back and looking into my eyes. He brushed my hair back, holding me in place. He opened his mouth as if he planned to say something, but closed it again quickly, replacing the look of reverence with a stunning smile instead. "I missed you. I didn't think I could miss anything. But fuck, I missed you, Little Rebel."

I wanted to say something back, but I hesitated. These feelings were dangerous. They were exactly the sort of thing Andras would use against me. Andras or the king. I couldn't risk it. Instead, I kissed him gently, trying to convey the words I remained too fearful to say.

Kade laid me down on the bedroll before rolling over and grabbing something from his pack. He took out a cloth and wiped between my legs, trailing kisses up my chest.

"If you keep that up, we'll be going again," I said, unable to stop my smile.

"If you go to sleep, I'll give you more in the morning," he chuckled.

My grin spread at the warm sound of his joy.

When Kade curled up next to me, he pulled my body firmly into his, wrapping around me until no space existed between us.

I soaked in his warmth. His shadows hovered, welcomed back and allowed to touch me again.

"Sleep," he whispered.

I closed my eyes and allowed my heart to crack open enough to let in the scent of fresh rain and the safety of Kade's arms. This time, I knew there would be no coming back from him. From us.

And that was one fate I realized I might not mind.

CHAPTER 35

KADE

My body jerked violently as I shot straight up in bed. Beads of sweat lined my brow from the humid summer night. My breath came in short, quick successions. I reached out to feel Lana on the bedroll beside me to calm this unease.

But the bedroll lay empty.

Lana was gone.

A sense of foreboding permeated the air.

Yanking my clothes on took seconds before I shoved my feet into my shoes. I secured all of my daggers, pushing them into their respective sheaths before grabbing my sword. I exited the tent, desperate to catch a glimpse of her rose-gold hair in the moonlight to prove to me I had nothing to fear.

I stumbled away from the tent, clumsy for perhaps the first time in my life as panic swelled, blocking out my finesse. "Illiana!" I shouted.

How had my shadows not even noticed her absence?

She wasn't sitting near the extinguished fire, nor wandering between the tents. "Lana!" I yelled again.

Deep in my soul, I knew something was wrong. I rubbed my chest, feeling the throb of the new shadowy tendril inside of me. A tether had further solidified after last night, a connection to Lana that now dimmed.

I dug my fingers into my skin, as if I could reach the core of the feeling at my center, admitting to myself the words I hadn't yet said out loud. Fates, I remained unsure if I even *could* say it with the curses forced upon our kingdoms.

Kalliah, Corbin, Raya, Storm, and Jax all appeared from their respective tents, groggy and confused.

Turning to Kalliah, I moved to her side in a few strides. "Is she with you?" I asked desperately.

"No, she went to bed with you." Kalliah put her hands on her hips. "If she's not with me, then the next logical conclusion would be Ian."

We all looked between us before Jax asked, "Where *is* Ian? And Hale?"

I scrambled in an uncharacteristic panic toward the remaining tent. Jerking the flaps of the tent, I yanked them open and saw Ian lying face down on the ground, hog-tied.

"What the hell," I bellowed, quickly removing the ropes from his ankles and wrists. "What happened? Where is Lana?"

My heart raced. I would not lose her now when I just got her back.

"Hale," Ian choked, his hands shook hard as he tugged the gag out of his mouth. "Poison."

His eyes held an untapped rage alongside fear. I helped him up, but his body went limp. "Raya," I shouted.

She was inside the tent as her name finished rolling off my tongue.

"No." Ian tried to pull away, but Raya took his face in her hands, closing her eyes.

They opened a second later. "I can't access my magic." She frowned, her gaze wandering over Ian's form. I noted her concern, something she rarely showed, but pushed it aside.

"Poison," Ian repeated. "It's wearing off. I still can't feel my magic, but I'm not immobile anymore." He stepped away from me, wobbling on his legs, but he remained standing. "Hale poisoned the stew. See if you can tap into your magic."

I didn't need him to say any more. I became instantly aware the dimming connection to Lana had nothing to do with her distance. My shadows hadn't sensed she'd left because they weren't with me. I staggered back, realizing my terror over Lana's loss eclipsed the fact that my shadows were silent.

We stepped out of the tent. "Check if you can access your magic," I demanded of the others.

One by one they met my scrutiny with furrowed brows. No one had their magic.

Ian rubbed his wrists and hurt lined his face. "Hale betrayed us. They took a potion that stifles magic, one Elisabeth created when she was trying to heal the king, and he used it on us."

"Hale wouldn't do this," Kalliah said.

"Well, he did," Ian snapped.

"Then something is controlling him—" She froze, staring at Ian wide-eyed. "He is the one who got us out of the palace. It was his plan. He came to us."

Ian rubbed his forehead. "I agree he wasn't himself. His eyes shifted in a way I've never seen before."

I paused. "The darkness." Storm met my worried gaze, coming to the same conclusion I did.

"Andras planted Hale with us and sent Casimir as well." He looked at me. "You were supposed to be with her. Why isn't she with you?" he demanded, as if this were my fault.

"She was gone when I awoke," I confessed, dread leeching my common sense from me. "I will murder him if he touches a hair on her head," I growled. "Jax, you know what to do."

Jax nodded, and stood beside Ian, sniffing his shirt.

"Hurry up," I snarled, unable to temper my raging emotions.

He glared at me over Ian's shoulder. "It's a bit more difficult without full access to my magic." He sniffed again.

"What in the Fates are you doing?" Ian asked, but he didn't push Jax away.

"My senses as a shifter are heightened regardless of magic," he responded, taking a step back from Ian. "As are yours if you would learn how to train them properly."

I noticed the captain frowning, no doubt unappreciative of Jax's comment about his own abilities.

Jax approached me next, winking. "Fates, I should have started with you—"

"Not another damn word," I said through gritted teeth. I couldn't handle his teasing, the way he wanted to diffuse some of my anger. Not when it came to Lana's safety.

Jax stepped away from all of us and stretched his neck, turning slowly until he froze, eyes opening. "To the woods." He pointed off to the right.

"He can track them by scent much faster than we can search on foot," I explained to Corbin and Kalliah. "You have a choice. Stay here and guard the campsite or join us for whatever we are about to face."

I looked back toward my tent. Where Lana had been with me just hours before. The ball inside of me tightened in response to my agitation again. If I had been able to access my shadows, there wouldn't be a campsite left. Perhaps the poison was a blessing at this moment.

Corbin and Kalliah looked at each other for a moment and nodded. "We fight," Kalliah responded, unsheathing the dagger from her side. A glimmer of vengeance twinkled in her eye.

"Let's go."

Following Jax's lead, we ran. Every so often, he paused, sniffing the air again.

He cursed, a frustrated snarl escaping him. "It's harder without my damn magic. Give me a minute."

I should comfort him, reassure him the way Raya did, instantly going to his side. But my mind churned too fiercely to be of any use. I left the encouragement up to the others.

Harder, faster we ran. We jumped and dodged low-hanging branches and rocks, forcing ourselves through the wooded area at a speed defying what our diminished magic should allow.

The love each one of us had for Lana pushed us forward. She may be mine, but she was also theirs. All of theirs.

A woman who brought together two kingdoms just by being herself.

"Ahead!" Jax's shout spurred us on the last few feet. As we cleared a row of trees, and entered a small clearing, Kalliah gasped.

All of us stopped dead in our tracks.

Dark ones littered the open area like locusts. Hundreds of them stood behind a tall, hooded figure. There were more than we could ever defeat alone. But I would not be deterred. From the way the others stood their ground, neither would they.

An evil laugh cackled loudly from the figure, as they stepped to the side, revealing Hale holding a dagger to Lana's throat. Fear etched into every part of her body, and my heart stopped.

"Hale," I screamed. "If you have harmed her..." Fury engulfed my entire body. "You will pray for death."

"Release the queen," Corbin yelled beside me. Thorny vines shot out from around his feet toward the closest group of dark ones.

The figure removed his hood, and the midnight hair beneath shone glossy, reflecting in the moonlight. *Andras.*

He cackled loudly again. "Release her? Never. She is *ours.*"

"I swear on the Fates themselves, if you harm her, there is nowhere you can hide where I will not find you," I said furiously. "Whether in this world or the next." My hand twitched at my side, and instinctively I drew my blade from my back and over my shoulder. "It will not just be your body I destroy. It will be your very soul."

Andras's eyes narrowed as he stalked forward a few steps, braver with the army of dark ones behind him. "I am a loyal servant. One who has no fears for the words of a Fae so easily swayed by his heart. Come, Kade Blackthorn, try to make good on your threats."

He raised his arms above his head as lightning cracked in the night sky. The dark ones jumped from foot to foot behind him. Agitated and waiting for a fight. Crazed.

I ran forward only to abruptly slam into a solid invisible barrier. My eyes went wide, staring the short distance to Lana while realizing I couldn't reach her.

"No!" I tore at the barrier, the impossible wall I couldn't see.

Andras laughed again. "As you can see, my loyal devotion is rewarded with gifts, like shields. Shields from weak men before"—he twirled his pointer finger around in a circle, staring like a starved man at the gem on his finger—"now made strong when multiplied."

I shouted, an unintelligible sound coming from the base of the tether inside of me. "This is your last warning. Release Illiana now, or prepare to die."

He grinned in response. "Idle threats don't look good on you. I was just going to take her and leave, but it would be so much more entertaining to watch you fight my dark ones. You can watch while I play with her."

I slammed a fist against the barrier with a force that shook the ground. An inky shadow spilled from my fingers, and I smirked at the man in front of me. "Looks like your poison is wearing thin."

"It won't matter," he taunted. "Attack," he shouted at the dark ones behind him.

On his command, they raced forward, having no trouble

getting through the shield from their side. They descended on us. Swords clashed and clanged, but my sight remained trained on Andras except for the brief moments I took to ensure Hale hadn't hurt Lana.

He stood there, arm shaking so badly I could see it from here. Lana's concentration focused solely on the man she called a friend at her side.

I needed her to look at me. Just once. Darkness tapped at my mind, knowing how easily I would let it seep into me if it promised her safety.

Extending my arm, I called forth my blade of shadows and sliced at the barrier. I heard it before I saw it. A tiny crack. A feral smile overtook me as I watched Andras's glee falter.

"Casimir, reinforce the shield," Andras bellowed.

Hale twitched next to where Andras stood, his dagger lowering to his side. Lana made a move to run toward me, but Andras grabbed Hale's shoulder. "Keep her here at any cost."

Casimir threw his arms to the side, grabbing two soldiers who collapsed momentarily under his touch. Then two more, until strands of visible magic coiled around him. He touched Andras next, the magic seeping into the ring, and the shield pulsed.

The triumphant smirk returned.

"Do you think there is any magic in this kingdom that would keep me from her?" I yelled, hitting the shield again. "You will never have her again."

"Kade!" Lana yelled, and I saw Hale tug her back to Andras's side by her fucking hair.

The control I barely held on to snapped. A darkness I had never given into willingly seeped through my shadows, curling around them inside of me. The fight they normally put up against this darker magic evaporated, as even they welcomed the fresh new power into them. Fusing with them.

All for her.

Illiana Dresden was mine. No Fae in this Fates-damned world would keep her from me, especially not a conniving coward like Andras.

A familiar heat flared at my back, and I pulled my attention away from Andras and Lana for the first time since arriving. My gaze collided with Storm's.

"I'm here," he yelled over the fight with the dark ones. He knew.

He noticed, as he always did, the warning signs of danger those few moments before chaos spilled from me. He would protect the others.

I sliced my shadow blade down in one final stroke, opening another crack in Andras's shield.

Then I reached for the power nestled inside of me. I unleashed my magic alongside the darkness I always feared. Freely. Unhindered.

And let myself erupt.

CHAPTER 36

LANA

"No, Kade!" I shouted, desperate for my cries to reach him.

Unlikely given the battle around us, and whatever shield Andras had in place, but I had to try.

Storm yelled to the others, flinging his body toward Ian, and created a circle of fire around them all as darkness exploded from Kade's body. The blast tore through the clearing even stronger than it had when we had first crossed into Mysthaven. A deafening roar accompanied the darkness surrounding us, and the barrier cracked.

The darkness dissipated and every single dark one on the opposite side of the shield lay lifeless on the ground. I held my breath, searching for my friends.

Storm's fire receded, revealing that they'd remained safe.

Kade ran forward toward the shouts, engaging the new wave of dark ones ready to pounce through Andras's broken shield. He fought with ferocity, a wildness, unlike any other fight we'd previously encountered.

Hale's grip on my arm loosened, the dagger at my neck wavering momentarily at the blast. I looked toward my friend

—the man I thought had been my friend. Hale's face slackened in disbelief as he met my gaze.

Andras approached my other side, but his expression held no fear. Despite Kade breaking through his defenses, he watched unimpressed. He reached down, yanking my hair back. Hale's blade nicked the skin of my neck, and I winced.

"Look at them fight," Andras whispered in my ear. I struggled against him, but the power of his grip along with Hale's kept my fight in vain. "They come for you so eagerly. Especially him."

Andras gripped my chin in his fingers, jerking my head slightly to the side to watch. He didn't need to though. My gaze already rested on Kade, breaking through Fae as though they were nothing. Coming for me.

"I will have Casimir drain them one by one." His nose brushed against my cheek, and I jerked away from him as best I could. Bile rose in my throat at his unwanted touch. "I will have you watch the life fade from their eyes as each of their magic becomes mine."

"Get off of me," I gritted out.

He laughed, continuing. "Kalliah looks as though she is about to collapse." He turned my head toward her. "Ian will be one of the last. But Kade…" He inhaled, as if greedy for air itself. "Kade will be the grand finale. I won't drain him completely; he wants him alive. But it will be fun to watch him suffer alongside you."

"He will slaughter you like the pig you are," I promised.

Andras clucked his tongue. "Pretty words, Princess. But they're for nothing. Your friends have come to die because of you. You have never been strong enough to save them, and now you'll see it firsthand."

I elbowed Hale in the gut, sending him stumbling back. Andras was only caught off guard for a moment before he waved a hand at me. Searing pain ripped through my body, and a yellow gemstone on Andras's robe flared as I sank to the ground.

"I cannot kill you yet." He shook his head. "He has plans for you. But he never said I couldn't play with you."

He has plans for me? Who the fuck is "he"?

"Illiana." Kade's scream tore through the clearing, and like the coward he was, Andras pulled back.

"Get her," Andras hissed at Hale.

Hale obeyed immediately, wrapping his arm around my chest, but I saw my opportunity. It was now or never to escape their clutches.

Grabbing Hale's wrist, I pushed out and up and stomped on his foot, as I ducked beneath his arm, pushing him away from me. I yanked a blade from my boot, grateful to have thought to grab it when Hale had led me away wanting to talk. The white dagger I'd discovered in my parents' grave rested on my thigh, but I left it alone for now, opting for the dagger I knew so well.

"You were my friend," I fumed at Hale. "I trusted you. How could you?"

Hale let out a garbled laugh, but it was broken. A drop of blood rolled from his nose as his body jerked.

No. Those jerky movements... I recognized them now. The same way some of the dark ones moved.

Hale whipped his dagger around and bent his knees, readying himself for an attack. "When the darkness...calls..." More blood flowed from his left nostril. "You must answer." The last of his words escaped from him forced and breathy.

He lunged toward me half-heartedly, and I blocked his attack with my dagger. He grunted as I easily lashed his own out of his hand, the momentum of my swing forcing it from his grasp.

Even with the battle raging around us, in this one moment, I saw a broken man, eyes shifting from dark to light. His shoulders sagged, and his arms hung limply by his side as he panted. Straining against an invisible force I could not comprehend.

"Lana." His voice tried to sound angry, but it fell short. Hale jerked his head to the side, eyes squeezed shut. He wiped the blood flowing freely from his nose with his arm. Streaks of crimson remained on his face. He leaned down, reaching for his weapon, and his arm shook.

An idea struck me. If this didn't work, I would surely be dead by Hale's hand. Watching him though, I knew this was not him. No matter how my heart ached at his betrayal, leading me into the hands of Andras—this was not the Hale I knew. Cautiously, I approached him. He turned, staring at me, but as that black darkness seeped into them, I closed the distance fully between us and placed a hand upon his cheek. A warmth filled my insides.

"I know this isn't you. Come back to me, Hale. Be the man I knew in the gardens. At Millie's Café," I begged him, the battle sounding like it crept closer and closer. "You are stronger than the darkness within you."

His gaze met mine, and he shouted, roaring loudly but not pulling away. I didn't let go. A moment later, his eyes cleared, the black returning to their normal amber hue.

"Illiana," he whispered, clutching the hand that held his cheek. "Lana?" he asked.

"I'm here," I said, watching as his expression transform to a look of horror.

"I'm so sorry."

"I know," I answered too quickly, glancing to the side. "But I need you now. Kind of in the middle of a battle."

His eyes flared.

"You're all right?" I asked, needing to know if I let go, he wouldn't go back to that darkness.

"Because of you." He nodded. "Thank you."

"Then we need to fight." With a resurgence of strength, we turned to greet the battle around us.

Casimir stood a few feet away, draining the magic from several dark ones, channeling it into various gems sewn onto Andras's cloak. A brilliant rainbow of gems glittered in the moonlight as they filled with the magic from any Fae Casimir touched.

The bodies formed a pile next to them as he continued to siphon more and more magic.

At least it was fewer for us to kill, but the amount of magic Andras hoarded scared me. No one should have that amount of power. That kind of magic. He had to be defeated.

"Little Rebel," Kade yelled across the clearing, like he needed to continue to remind me he was coming, battling his way toward me. Storm shot fireballs across the night sky, making it glow as brightly as if it were daylight.

Hale and I continued our own battle toward our friends. Together, we engaged the dark ones, whose jerky movements made it almost impossible to predict their next move. But we powered on. Using every trick and strategy taught to me from Fae on both sides of the void, I cut my way through any enemies who dared cross my path.

Hale struggled to keep pace, struggled to fight the dark ones. It appeared to take every ounce of effort to fight against the ones he'd stood next to mere moments before. As if the darkness drained him now that it no longer controlled him.

Andras bellowed gleefully over the sounds of battle, and I turned to see what caused such a sound of pleasure.

"Lana," Hale shrieked. "No!" He threw his body in front of mine.

Stepping back, I fumbled only for a moment as Hale landed on his stomach, not moving.

Rage coursed through my veins, and I instinctively flung my blade, landing straight between of the eyes of a dark one who'd stood immediately in front of Hale as he fell. Dropping to my knee, I rolled Hale onto his back and gasped when I saw the dagger protruding from his chest.

"Oh, Hale," I whispered, resting my hand on his chest. "You idiot. Why would you do such a thing?" A tear formed in the corner of one of my eyes, waiting to drip down my sweaty face. "I can stop the bleeding and…and…you can heal yourself."

He brought a hand over mine as his blood seeped onto my skin. The cough forced out of him, accompanied with the sound of gurgling blood in his throat made me want to vomit. "I had to save you," he declared. "I love you, Illiana. It has always been you."

The tears flowed freely at his admission. "I am going to take the blade out," I said, gripping the handle of the dagger. "You're going to be okay, do you hear me?"

He shook his head. "The darkness drained most of my abilities. They aren't strong enough yet."

"They will be," I said, refusing to let doubt clog my voice. "They will be. I'll leave pressure here as soon as it is out while you heal."

He gave me a sad smile and nodded. I pulled the blade quickly, pressing my hands hard over his chest as blood spurted out. "Now, Hale," I commanded. "Right now, start healing."

He closed his eyes and tightened his grip on my hands.

"I didn't know what to do," he whispered, breathing heavily. "When you were missing, taken by Kade and Storm, I tried to find you, but nobody knew where you were. I thought if I gave in to the power they offered, I would be strong enough to fight it. That I could defeat Andras from the inside to protect you. To protect all of you. I only ever wanted to protect you. If I could never have you to love, the least I could do was keep you safe."

"Hale." I barely choked out his name.

Blood leaked from his mouth, and his breathing became labored. "Lana, listen to me. The marked dark ones accepted the darkness willingly. They are stronger than the others who fight it. Do not underestimate them."

"Hale, hold on. I can save you."

"Did you hear me?" he asked, the words choppy and fading.

I nodded vigorously. "Yes, yes, I heard you. The marked ones are more dangerous."

He sighed, his chest caving into his now fragile-looking body.

I shouted, looking up to the sky, praying to the Fates they would give me the opportunity to save the man who'd saved me. We needed a healer. I hated being on my knees again beside someone dying for me, with nothing I could do.

"I love you, Lana," Hale said, barely a whisper. "I have loved you for longer than you know, but more importantly…" Hale breathed in, a rattling, shaking sound, and while I kept one hand with pressure on his chest, I brushed the other against his face as he spoke. "I believe in you."

Squeezing my hand one last time, his head rolled to the side, and his arm fell to the ground, revealing an inky black circular dark-one mark on his forearm.

Dead.

I stared at the mark. The sign that Hale had tried to take on a force none of us understood, all to save me. I wasn't worthy of that kind of sacrifice. He had taken on evil for me. And died because of it.

A heart-wrenching scream left my lips, echoing throughout the meadow. "Come back," I begged.

I brought my head to his unmoving chest as I closed my eyes. My bloodied hands trembled against his body. I could not keep doing this. I could not watch those I cared about falling, slaughtered, over and over. I stood, anger coursing through me.

A shout called my attention to a dark one running toward me. Good. I would kill them all. Realizing my weapon remained lodged in the head of a dark one several feet away, I reached for the white dagger at my thigh.

I screamed right back at the man, diving over Hale's body, and thrust my blade deep into the gut of the attacker. Reckless and with abandon.

A sooty black mist erupted from his body with a loud crackle, as he crumpled to the ground instantly. The dark one's expression, once wild and crazed, now appeared relieved.

"Thank you," he whispered.

Eyes wide, I stared in disbelief, not understanding.

What in the actual fuck?

It was as if the darkness left his body.

An eerie silence fell as my immediate surroundings quieted.

Gripping the blade tighter, I pivoted toward Andras, who stared at me with unmasked rage. Piles of bodies lay littered beside him, and his cloak glowed from the gems powered by the magic of the lifeless dead surrounding him.

"You are next, Andras Braumlyn," I swore at him. A surprised, pained sneer deformed his lip as he stared at the man kneeling in front of me in complete disbelief.

"Casimir!" Andras shouted. The worm had not ventured far from Andras. With his eyes on the dead man beside me, he pointed and whispered something to Casimir.

I bolted into action, running toward the pair of them. They would die. *Now.* A dark puff of smoke appeared, and in a feat of magic I had never seen before, they were gone.

Vanished into thin air—and they weren't the only ones gone. The previously overwhelming number of dark ones we thought we were battling disappeared too.

His army had been almost completely an illusion.

"No!" I screamed, reaching the spot where they just stood. "Come back and fight me, you cowards!"

A pair of strong hands grabbed me around my waist,

lifting me into the air. I didn't need to look to know it was Kade, the whispers of his shadows caressing my skin.

"Not now, Little Rebel." Kade turned, throwing me over his shoulder, and ran toward the safety of our group. The few dark ones remaining, left out in the cold by their master, looked around and saw him gone. They fled, retreating into the woods.

I fought against his hold. "Let me go. We have to get them."

Kade didn't stop until we reached Storm, Raya, Corbin, and a limping Kalliah. Jax lay on the ground, his arm bloody, but not so bad that he didn't give me a smile.

"Where's Ian?" I asked in a panic.

Kade set me down and grasped my face in his hands. "Look at me," he commanded. "Ian's fine. We have to get you to safety." The heat of his touch sent sizzling waves of energy through me. Energy I was so used to feeling that it had become second nature for the thrum to never stop.

"But look at the destruction he has caused. Look at the death surrounding us." I pointed to the bodies littered across the battlefield. "We have to stop him. I refuse to let anyone else die in my name. Hale—" I choked. "Hale is dead."

His eyes softened, but he remained firm in his stance. "This is not the final battle. His time will come, I promise you. But for now, we need to regroup. We need to come up with a plan so we are not caught unsuspecting again."

"We can't leave him," I whispered.

Kade kissed my forehead. "We will bury him before we go."

Corbin placed a hand on my shoulder as he walked past me. "I'll take care of it."

I looked away from him, finally seeing Ian jogging toward me. "Fuck, Lan, you're all right?"

I buried my face in his neck and cried. I cried for Hale, for the boy who loved me enough to try to take on the darkness alone. And for the long journey we had ahead.

Kade did not shy away from keeping us moving. "Get your weapons and return to camp. We need to gather our things and make our way to The Knotted Willow as quickly as possible."

Each member of our group acknowledged the command and picked up extra weapons discarded across the ground. As I bent down to pick up a dagger from the hand of a dark one, I noticed a symbol on his arm. A symbol I had seen before on Andras and on Hale.

"What do you know of these marks?" I asked Kade.

He exchanged a glance with Storm before he responded, "We aren't quite sure. We haven't figured out exactly what they mean, but we noticed them on the dark ones in Brookmere. We tried interrogating them previously, but they refused to say what it meant."

"As far as we can tell," Storm said, "it seems to be on those of the dark ones who are less frenzied. Less crazed."

"Like a branding?" Ian asked.

"Andras has one," I told them. "I saw it in the palace during the last trial. Hale had one too. He told me he took on the darkness believing he could help from the inside." I closed my eyes, thinking of how he had clutched my hand in his final moments. "He said the marks show those who accepted the darkness willingly. Those without the marks are fighting it."

Storm breathed a heavy sigh. "So, they're not crazed, they're battling something inside of them."

"But from who?" I whispered.

"We will add it to the growing list of things to figure out," Ian said. "For now, we should go. Kalliah needs to see a healer, or at the very least needs to get off her ankle. Let's go somewhere safe."

I moved toward Kalliah, who favored her right leg, her left

ankle already swollen, and let her wrap her arm around my shoulder.

Jax slid next to Kalliah's other side and picked her up in his arms. "I've got this." He winked at me.

"I told you I'm not interested," Kalliah muttered.

"No, but I'd rather not die tonight, waiting around here for the cackling wannabe king to return and find another way to surprise us." Jax snorted. "So let's go."

I turned to face the battlefield once more, vowing to myself to avenge the death of yet another Fae lost to this monster.

Facing the western sky, the white dagger in my hand heated. I hadn't set it down, even as I gathered the other weapons. I had no idea what had happened when I used it against the dark one, or what happened to the man after.

I stepped forward, the heat growing, and the dagger glowed in response. "What are you for?" I whispered to it, as though it would provide an answer. I knew this dagger was important. What it meant, I wasn't sure, but as we trekked north back toward camp, the glow of the dagger dimmed. As did the heat.

The blade called to me, a song begging to be sung. I just had to figure out what it called me toward, and what it meant for us in the war we had been thrust into.

CHAPTER 37

LANA

Kade's shadows caressed my arms as we rode hard toward The Knotted Willow.

They didn't leave my side the entire ride. The way Kade had acted once he'd reached me during the fight, I couldn't be sure they would leave me again until this war ended. One way or another.

When I might have demanded space before, the words died before ever becoming strong enough to say. I accepted knowing I needed their comfort too.

Everyone around me was dying.

I glanced over my shoulder at the small group of people I loved most in the entire world. Though Leif's absence hurt, I couldn't help but wonder if he remained the safest because he was farther away from me. Everyone here was at risk of being used. Being destroyed.

Yet I believed if I acknowledged out loud what Kade meant to me, the focus of all our enemies would hone in on him. The losses we suffered broke me. But if I lost him? It would destroy me forever.

Everyone rode in silence. Hale's loss, along with witnessing the power Andras wielded and the way he so carelessly took the lives of his own followers without the blink of an eye, lingered among us. We all needed rest. A small reprieve. Even though I feared none of us would feel safe enough to allow ourselves that moment.

We slowed, calming both ourselves and our horses when the inn came into view.

"One thing is bothering me," Raya said, once we were all riding close enough together. "Why didn't Andras take Illiana once he had her? Why stay and let us find her?"

Kade jerked his head to look at her. "Watch what you say."

She held a hand up defensively. "I don't know what is wrong with you, but relax for one moment and listen. He had her. He could have taken her away but chose to stay for what? To fight us? And then lose her again?"

Storm ran a hand over his jaw. "Between letting Ian escape the palace and this, there is something we are missing."

"Andras referred to a 'he' twice tonight," I said. "He told me *he* has a plan for me. But who could he be talking about?"

"Whoever told him about the magical dream coat, maybe," Jax muttered.

"He spoke in the dungeons like someone else was out there," Ian added. "Like someone gifted him his extra abilities."

"Which aligns with the idea that someone else is marking Fae with the darkness," Storm said.

"Your father?" I asked Kade. "Could he be referring to him?"

A crease formed between Kade's brows. "I don't believe my father has a way to communicate with anyone in Brookmere."

"Great, so Sir Cackles-A-Lot has someone worse than him calling the shots." Jax snorted. "This day just keeps getting better."

"We will figure it out," Kade said, leaning toward me and brushing a knuckle down my cheek.

We had barely slowed the horses to a stop to dismount when Kade's name rang out, bellowed across the trees.

"You better be dismounting quicker than that, Kade Blackthorn."

My eyes widened, and despite it all I snorted, trying to stifle the laugh at the brash tone from the innkeeper calling Kade by his full name.

"Someone is in trouble," Jax said in a singsong voice.

William, who I last saw when he gave me no aid while being kidnapped, had his hands on his hips. His face reddened in anger, or perhaps frustration. I didn't know him well enough to read it.

We dismounted our horses and Kade approached the angry Fae.

"There's a mad woman here. I didn't sign up for crazed Fae walking around my rooms, scaring off my patrons." He shook his finger at Kade.

"I'm unaware of sending any crazed women," Kade said, calmly eyeing William.

Storm laughed. "Since when do you have patrons?"

The innkeeper threw up his hands. "Fine, I will leave you to figure it out without a warning." William shoved the front door open, storming through it and leaving us out front, bewildered.

Kade ran a hand over his face. "We shouldn't push him much further. Let's board the horses and get inside."

Corbin took the lead once we drew close to the barn, from habit, I supposed. I watched him brush a hand over each animal. He caught me staring, and I decided he had been pushed to his limits with warm words and affection. I gave him a soft smile and turned away, leaving him to tend to the horses in peace.

We entered through the door William had slammed

earlier. As Storm predicted, there were no patrons, but he had been right about a crazed woman. Grey wiry hair peeked from around the corner among a flutter of tattered robes. Unintelligible nonsense spilled from her lips as she paced back and forth, her path evident by the disturbance on the dusty floor.

"Vivienne?" I cried out, running across the room.

I approached, standing in front of her, but she didn't see me. Or if she did, she refused to acknowledge my presence.

She stopped her pacing, taking a few steps back until she sat on a wooden bench. Drawing her knees to her chest, she rocked back and forth. Her wild hair was worse than I remembered, the strands jagged and frayed.

She chanted, "Blood of the heirs," repeatedly.

"Vivienne." I said her name softer, as I kneeled and reached a hand tentatively toward her.

Shame rushed over me. I wasn't sure how to comfort her during one of her episodes. I'd never stuck around long enough before to see how it played out before I ran away. Even during the last trial, I was too consumed by what was happening in the arena to see what happened to her.

Yet Vivienne had saved my life. My father's letter told me so. She saved me and Elisabeth. I'd repaid her with years of loathing and bitterness.

As if sensing my emotions, Kade stood closer to me. But it was Ian who crouched down next to me, taking my hand.

"The past is the past, Lan," he said. "There is still time to make it right."

He knew how I'd despised Vivienne for most of my life. He also knew what the words in my father's letter did to me, knowing her role in my life. Ian didn't judge me. For any of it. Even if I wished someone would.

"We're here, Vivienne," I said, this time not hesitating to touch her skin. "You are safe."

Her body paused, still for a moment as she blinked a few

times. A smile curved her lips when she finally registered my presence. "Beautiful little babe."

"How did you escape?" I asked. "Are you hurt?"

She shook her head, resuming her steady rocking. "Evil didn't linger. Time to flee arrived. Flee to the feeling. Flee to the pull. Blood of the heirs."

I turned, looking over my shoulder, asking the group instead of any one person. "Can you get her water? Something to eat?"

"Of course." Kade responded first, touching my shoulder. Though he moved toward William, his shadows stayed with me.

Vivienne smiled as she rocked. "The time has come. Fear, yes. Fear. But light. It's coming."

"Everything is all right now," I said, brushing her arm. Her skin felt cold to the touch. Instead of asking someone else this time, I wanted to do something for her myself. It didn't make up for the past, but Ian was right. I could treat her with kindness now.

William stood at the bar, lining up mugs by slamming them down on the counter. I tried not to jump as the last one cracked with the force he put behind it.

"I hate to bother you," I said. "Do you happen to have a blanket I could borrow?"

His hard stare softened the minute I smiled, and a blush crept up his cheeks. As if he suddenly realized who he was speaking to. "I mean no disrespect, Your Majesty."

"I understand. I used to be uncomfortable with the ramblings myself."

"I'll be right back," he huffed under his breath. When he returned from the back, he carried a quilt in his hands.

"Thank you," I said, touching his arm before returning to Vivienne.

I wrapped the surprisingly soft blanket around her shoulders, and she stilled once more.

Kade held up a spoon, blowing on the steaming soup delicately before offering it to Vivienne. She shifted her attention to him, a smile breaking through again, just as it had with me. "You listened well."

He grinned back at her. "I know when to heed a seer."

Vivienne leaned forward, allowing Kade to feed her the brothy soup. My chest tightened. A prince on his knees before an old woman, caring for her despite the hell he had just experienced. A woman he barely knew. She wasn't Cassandra, even if he told me once she reminded him of her, but he treated Vivienne with the same respect.

A respect I'd failed to give.

A sharp breath behind us made me jump, and I swiveled.

Raya's body stood stiff, her eyes white.

"Raya?" Ian pushed past me, going to her side. Before he grabbed her, Storm cut him off, holding him back. "Get off," Ian argued. "Don't you think she needs help?"

"She does *not* need help," Storm said. "Give her a minute. You can't touch her when she's like this."

We waited, watching Raya, and I knew before she spoke that Kade's father was infiltrating her mind.

She lowered her head, color returning to her eyes. "We've been ordered to return now. The length of time is unacceptable for handling the traitor."

She did a double take at Storm's arms wrapped around Ian, but then stepped away toward an empty bench. She brushed her hands over her arms. Storm loosened his hold, and Ian moved back toward me.

"He's angry?" Jax asked.

Raya looked fearful briefly, then masked it back to the emotionless mask she so clearly preferred wearing. "There was something in his tone." She swallowed. "We need to be prepared when we return. I don't know for what, but"—Her gaze shot to Kade—"he feels different. Excited."

Kade leaned back on the bench, setting down the soup he

held in his hands. Closing his eyes, he inhaled slowly. "Storm, Raya, Jax, we leave in three hours."

"No," I said, stepping forward, between his outstretched legs, blocking him from looking anywhere but at me.

"Raya is second to none at gauging his moods, and she has never been this rattled. You are not going back there," he said, jaw grinding.

I glanced over at Vivienne. "We need answers. Cassandra is the only option for getting ones not laced in riddles. The dagger, the journal. If we don't figure out what it means, this is all for nothing. It's worth the risk to talk to her."

He gripped my waist. "Then I will talk to her. I will return when I can."

I pushed his hand from my waist. "And what are you going to say when you return without me? I hardly think your father will believe that you left me behind somewhere."

"We can all go," Ian suggested. "We'll keep Lana somewhere safe."

Jax scoffed and Kade moved my body to the side like it was nothing, rising from his seat. "There is no hiding in Mysthaven. I can't protect all of you."

Ian's eyes narrowed on Kade. "The last time Lana was left in your hands, mere hours ago, she was taken.

I let out a breath. Kade's shadows darkened, swarming the space around us. Ian's mouth twitched. "I am not afraid of your shadows. No need to try to intimidate me."

"I met the king, Ian." I put a hand to his chest. "He barely tolerated me, and I have the threat of a crown with my name, should he try to hurt me. I refuse to put you in harm's way unnecessarily, which is exactly what will happen."

"Lan—"

"No, listen to me. I lived knowing you were in danger in those dungeons, and I will not be the one to put you in that position again," I argued. "Which is exactly what could happen in Mysthaven. This is the right thing to do."

"Your people need you both here." Storm's arms were crossed. "You need an army. You have to raise them up."

"Ian is capable of raising an army in my name," I said.

I would not back down. I would not allow Kade to go to Cassandra with my questions. My gut told me I needed to be in Mysthaven as much as it told me I would be returning sooner than I thought to Brookmere.

"Little Rebel." The way Kade said my name nearly broke my heart. The desperation.

"Ian, you know who to ask." I focused on my best friend. My best friend who I just got back and was leaving again. He hated this idea. "Track down those we aided with the Hidden Henchman. Every time we completed a drop, they wanted to know how they could help. You, Corbin, Kalliah—you can rally them."

"Rally them where?" Kalliah asked from Corbin's side. "We don't have access to the palace, to weapons."

"We provided weapons on many of the drops," Corbin said. "We always added extra. They've been defending their homelands from dark ones for years. Once they know the Hidden Henchman was their princess, we'll have their loyalty."

He sounded so sure.

"Fates, we could even reach out to Ryland. He was an excellent swordsman and may be able to help," Ian said as he rubbed his finger over his lips in thought. I smiled at the motion. It had been the same thing he did when I first approached him with the idea about the Hidden Henchman runs. He was onboard. "Can we stay here? Train here?"

"Not a bad idea," Storm agreed. "The location is close to the void, which means easy access to and from Mysthaven. It also remains off the main roads enough that we might have a chance at hiding our actions from the palace." He looked over at William. "But I'm not the one asking William for permission."

I walked straight toward the bar, giving my best princess-worthy smile to the old innkeeper. "William, I have a favor to ask."

He watched me warily, eyes narrowing.

"I'll pay you three times what you made in the last three years for allowing us to set up camp on your property for my army."

William sighed. "Hosting an army?"

I didn't miss the flicker of light in his eyes; whether it was the money or the prospect of an army, I didn't know.

"Throw in making some of them cook and helping around here and it's a deal."

I bowed my head and shot out my hand toward his. "Deal."

I turned triumphantly back toward the group. Kalliah smirked, shaking her head. Corbin nodded reassuringly.

Ian sighed. "I don't like this."

"I need you to take care of Vivienne too," I said.

"Illiana," Kade said again. "You cannot—"

I marched up to him, taking his face in both my hands. My time for indecision, for second-guessing things was over. No longer would Brookmere's princess—no, queen—sit idly by and do nothing for her kingdom.

"I will be with you in Mysthaven. We will get the answers we need from Cassandra and we will come back here. Away from your father."

His shadows enveloped us. Ian and Corbin shouted, but I heard Storm mutter, "Again?" under his breath with a clear tone of exasperation.

"Do you think I want to leave you?" The gentle way he cupped my face was so at odds with the harshness and fear coating his tone. "My father could harm you in ways I cannot even begin to think about. Do not ask me to bring you back to a place where you are not safe."

I leaned into his touch. "I will be in danger here or there.

There is nowhere safe for me to be. You know that. But I will find the answers we need at your side. Do not put me on the sidelines in a misguided effort to keep me unharmed. I refuse to live that way. I will not ask for your permission, for the decision is mine to make."

He pulled back, the argument strong in his gaze, but instead, Kade shook his head. Taking my hands in his, he kissed my fingertips as his shadows fell from around us. "I suppose I'm at your command, Little Rebel." He straightened. "We ride in three hours."

CHAPTER 38

KADE

The near-constant worry about returning to Mount Legion clung to me as thickly as my shadows.

The exhaustion I should feel from keeping everyone atop their horses through the night barely registered. We all agreed getting to the palace expeditiously might allow me to rest and recharge my magic before seeing Cassandra at first light and facing my father. Dusk crawled through the pass as the last rays of sunshine crested over the peaks of the mountains.

We spent our time traveling, planning, and scheming. Exploring all possibilities for what Lana's mother's journal could contain and where it may be. We repeated both our prophecies so many times, I never wanted to hear them again. We only stopped for a few hours to allow the horses, and ourselves, to rest. Otherwise, we rode furiously back toward my father's home.

It would never be mine again.

No, my home now remained firmly wherever Lana was.

Raya and Storm agreed to go straight to the king for an update, stalling him to allow Lana and me time to speak with Cassandra. If anyone could possibly push us in the right direction, it would be her. That is, if she decided her input would not harm the Fates' plan.

I doubted I could force her, but I was on edge and willing to give anything to get the answers we so desperately needed to save our worlds.

Arriving late in the night would grant us a few extra hours to make our strategy work. The plan was solidified, and while I knew it was good, my hands clenched Onyx's reins as another bout of terror coursed through me. The tether to Lana bordered on painful if I lingered on thoughts of my father too long.

"Do we need to go over the plan one more time?" I dismounted, looking at the others who did the same. We planned to arrive on foot, Jax taking the horses through the side gates opposite where the rest of us would enter. He swore to me he'd leave two saddled in case Lana needed to escape. She refused, but one look at Storm and I knew I had the silent promise from my brother that he would get her out.

No matter what.

I could practically hear Raya rolling her eyes as she spoke from behind me. "Storm and I will go meet with the king. Tell him of the troubles with the traitor. Make up some bullshit excuse why you can't be the one to tell him yourself. Exhaustion perhaps?"

"And I'm going to be looking pretty—" Jax started but was cut off by Raya.

"For once, could you be serious?"

Jax laughed as he reached for the reins of our horses. "It's not in my nature, but for you, since you asked *sooo* nicely, I could try." He gave her a wink. "I'll be finding those we trust and ensuring their loyalty."

I could sense the unease spilling from Lana. She drew closer to me, and I wasn't sure if she was even aware. I welcomed her presence, letting it soothe the unsettled worry in me. There was too much at stake, and all of this going wrong seemed a probability instead of a mere possibility.

Lana checked the dagger hidden in the sheath of her tunic, and the newly added white one at her thigh. "Come." I took Lana's hand, clasping it in my own. I had meant what I told her in my tent—I refused to act as if I didn't need her. Not even here at the palace would I hide my feelings for her anymore.

She offered me a small smile and handed the reins of her horse to Jax to return to the stables.

"Go get a few hours of sleep after doing your respective tasks," I reminded my friends. "We will meet after breakfast in the training ring, just like normal."

I led Lana through the palace halls with fervor. I needed to be alone with her. I needed to feel her beneath me. Preferably naked and writhing.

I jolted into my bedroom, desperate to have a moment with Lana to reassure myself of her safety. The sinking feeling from waking up alone and finding her missing had not fully subsided.

We hadn't taken much time to eat over the last few days, so I grabbed a pitcher of water and bowl of berries from the antechamber of my rooms as we finally settled. Ensuring Lana had some sustenance while also keeping her to myself would hopefully help calm the frazzled thing inside my chest. We both devoured the fruit and drank two glasses of water before speaking again.

"Are we sure this is going to work?" Lana asked as we moved toward my bedroom.

I eyed her as my shadows slinked over her, desperate to touch her, to be near her. "It will work, Little Rebel."

I watched her enter the bedroom as though she did this all the time. The ease with which she settled in here calmed me.

"We only have a few hours before we have to meet with Cassandra and then the others," I said, moving toward her.

"You were almost taken from me. I'm not sure you understand the absolute terror I felt when I realized you were gone and I wasn't able to protect you."

Lana sat on the end of the bed. "Kade, it's not your fault —you were literally poisoned. I'm here now. Safe and in one piece."

Approaching her, I wiggled myself between her legs, resting my knees on a pillow fallen on the floor. I reached for a strand of hair that had come loose and twirled it in my fingers. "I need to feel you, Little Rebel. I need you everywhere. I want your scent all over me so there is no mistaking who you belong to." I ran my nose along her jaw, her soft skin begging to be touched. "I promised you the next time I had you completely, we wouldn't be rushed, or in the middle of a field. We can worry about saving the world in a few hours, but for this moment, you are mine, and I am going to worship you like the queen you are."

Pink hues blushed Lana's cheeks. "We've been riding for days, I need to bathe."

"Shh." My shadows caressed her lips, silencing her protests. "I am a Fae on my knees, craving the sanctuary only you can provide. One I desperately desire."

The shadows receded and I leaned forward, my lips lightly brushing against hers as I barely contained the unsated beast coiled up inside of me, still consumed with thoughts of losing her. Within a breath, her lips parted and welcomed me inside. Our tongues danced, swirling in a hot, heady need.

My hands clasped the back of her neck and angled her chin upward, allowing me a deeper reach into her mouth as a soft moan escaped her lips.

I moved along her jaw, stopping at the bottom of her ear, nipping at the lobe, as my hand palmed her breast. "Let me make you mine," I whispered.

Lana pulled back and looked directly into my eyes. Her playful gaze did nothing to hide the longing. Her lips parted as her breathing grew heavy. Even the Fates themselves couldn't ignore the pull between us. The absolute inferno of desire. "Do your worst, Kade Blackthorn."

Without another moment's hesitation, her arms were above her head, signaling for me to remove her tunic, which I gladly obliged. I followed suit, kicking off my shoes. Lana did the same as she removed her pants but lost her footing and had to grab the edge of the bed for support.

Chuckling, I couldn't help but admire the sheer beauty of the woman before me. She was smart, brave, and beautiful. And she was *mine*. Even without magical abilities, she was more of a queen than any who came before her. In either kingdom.

I pressed her against me and picked her up by her ass as she let out a yelp in surprise. One I cut off as our mouths met again, desperate for each other.

I walked us over to the small wooden desk in the corner of my room, covered in maps and other papers I had haphazardly strewn over the years. I plopped her on the edge and with one flick of my wrist, the shadows sent the papers careening onto the floor. Perhaps I would reward them later for removing the obstacles by feeling Lana come around them. Come around us both.

Letting my shadows roam her body would have to do for now. They tweaked and palmed her nipples as her hands raked down my back.

"Now, Kade," she whispered in a demanding tone. "Don't make me wait."

Trailing kisses down her body, I licked and tasted her inch by inch. She arched her back, placing her hands on the desk behind her, pushing her breasts toward me, teasing me and begging to be played with.

"Patience, Little Rebel," I teased. "Good things come to those who wait."

She smacked my arm playfully. "And you'll have a dagger in your side if you don't fill me with your—"

My shadows tweaked her nipples, and she inhaled a sharp breath, as I plunged my finger into her entrance. My Little Rebel was already soaked with need.

She moved her hand, bracing it against the wall, pressing her body down onto my hand. The walls inside of her throbbed, begging to be massaged.

Our breaths mingled, intertwining as hers escaped in short pants. Her head fell back as she rolled her hips to meet my finger coaxing the pleasurable moan slipping from her lips.

"So close," she whimpered.

Grinning, I sucked on her nipple, flicking it with my tongue in tandem movements with my finger, while I slipped a second finger inside of her. "Come for me, Illiana."

She jolted at the sound of her name and crested over into waves of pleasure as she rode my fingers, grinding herself into them.

My cock throbbed in need. Watching her come undone made me feel like nothing else would ever be as hot or turn me on as much as she could. Lana would be the end of me. She would destroy me, and I would allow it. Willingly.

"I am not nearly satisfied," Lana drawled, as she slid off the desk, pushing me back gently. Slowly, she moved me toward the edge of the bed. "Sit."

My mouth watered. I loved when she got bossy. Demanding my obedience and rewarding me with earth-shattering oblivion.

"Yes, my queen." I tilted my head in a bow, and she rolled her eyes at me. I obeyed her though, my hands resting on my knees, ready and waiting for her next command. She ran her fingers through my hair, and my cock twitched. One simple touch, one fucking touch and she owned me. The inexplicable pull grew stronger every time our bodies touched. That little spark craved her, demanded she be near.

"Good little shadow prince," Lana murmured. "Just where I want you."

Fucking Fates, this woman.

She dropped to her knees, and I moaned in anticipation. Knowing my cock would be in that perfect mouth of hers sent shivers up my spine. She looked up at me, her icy blue eyes piercing my very soul as she licked me from balls to tip before wrapping her mouth around and taking me completely inside of her.

"Little—"

She pulled off and tskd. "No talking. Let me take you."

All I could do was nod in response, hesitant to disobey her wishes again in case she decided to punish me for my transgressions.

Lana smiled and cupped my balls in her hand, gently massaging them as she took the top of my cock in her mouth, licking and swiping the tip. It felt so damn good. I wanted more, needed more.

When she took me deep and I felt the back of her throat, I gripped her hair. "I am not ready to come, Little Rebel."

Her gaze seared into me as she stared from her knees, licking the length of me as she pulled away. She didn't stop though. A groan worked up my throat as I stared at her taking me so perfectly.

She swirled her tongue around my tip. "I want to taste you."

She took my length again, and I couldn't stop my hips from moving in rhythm with her. "That fucking mouth," I ground out.

Lana hollowed her cheeks, sucking all she could take while wrapping her hand around the rest of me.

I thrust, feeling her gag slightly. Then she moaned, and it was too much. Her hands, her perfect mouth, all of it threw me over the edge, and I shouted her name prayerfully as I came.

I loosened my hold on her hair, rubbing small circles on her head as she took every drop. Her tongue flicked out, licking her bottom lip, and I lost it. Shadows poured into the room from me, and I leaned forward, tugging her upward and kissing her.

She stood between my legs, arms wrapped around my neck. "I love you," I whispered against her mouth. "I am yours, Little Rebel."

I cupped her face, searching hers as tears welled in her eyes. Somehow I knew she wouldn't say it back, yet I also knew she felt it. I would show her every damn day what those words meant to me and earn them from her. I didn't care how long it took.

"Say you're mine," I whispered, letting my lips touch hers, too lightly. She tried to press herself into me more, but I shook my head. "Say it."

"I'm yours." The words barely left her mouth as she pressed her lips against mine again. This time I let her in. She grasped my body like she thought I might disappear, and I took her delicious moans into my mouth.

"I will beg if I must, but I need to be inside of you," I said, not recognizing the sound of my voice.

I barely registered her movements, as she stood and straddled my lap. I grabbed her hips, watching her lower herself onto my slickened member.

"Fuck," I hissed.

A cocky grin spread over her beautiful face as she stared at me. I memorized the sound of every breath, every angle of her face as she slowly moved up and down, rocking her hips while she lowered herself again and again onto me.

It was fucking divine.

"You're so tight around me." My hands gripped her hips tighter as she moved, arching her back. "Made for me. You're made for me."

Lana's body clenched. "More. I need you deeper."

I gripped her hips and leaned back slightly, thrusting into her, letting her maintain her illusion of control while I lost mine beneath her.

"You are amazing," I praised, thrusting harder. "So perfect."

All she did was moan in response, her hands roaming her breasts as my shadows supported her back so she wouldn't fall. I didn't trust myself not to completely lose myself inside of her and tip us over the edge of the bed.

I slipped my hand between us, rubbing against her clit.

Her breaths grew shorter, quicker, and I could feel her starting to reach her peak.

"Come with me, Kade." A desperate plea.

"Anything for you, Little Rebel."

I gripped her hair, tugging her head back and licking along the column of her neck. I slammed her body into mine, and as her hips rocked harder, she sent us both into oblivion, her screaming my name while we came down from the electric sensation of pleasure.

I pulled her in close, not allowing her to move. Not ready to release her and have our bodies separate. I nuzzled my face into the side of her neck, surrounding myself with her beautiful hair.

We sat there silently, trembling in aftershocks, joined in an embrace that spoke more than words ever would. Our kingdoms would have to find a way wherever we ended up, because I would never again be parted from her side. I would not give her up. I couldn't, even if I tried.

The ache in my chest, which remained after Hale kidnapped her, finally ebbed enough that I took in my first full breath. Her scent surrounded me, soothing every corner of my soul.

I loved Illiana Dresden, my Little Rebel, and whether in this world or the next, she would forever be the compass that pointed me home.

CHAPTER 39

KADE

The early morning light streamed on my face, waking me from our brief slumber.

Lana remained curled into my side, and I would give anything to stay in this bed for hours—no days longer. The only thing pulling me from this heaven was the need to protect her and our kingdoms.

I planted sweet kisses on her forehead, trailing my lips down her neck and between her breasts until she woke. It would only take a few words for me to say "forget it" and risk the wrath of my father, and I was shockingly close to allowing the thought to come to fruition.

"We need to get to Cassandra," she whispered, running her fingers through my hair.

"And if I say no?"

She laughed before claiming my lips. "Let's go find a way to save our kingdoms."

I grumbled but pulled myself from her side, a monumental effort. Ten minutes later, we made our way through the castle, not speaking more than absolutely necessary. One could never be too careful in palaces, especially this one. I trusted no one here except Finn. There was always someone listening, trying to get in the king's good graces.

We ended up outside Cassandra's door in record time. I squeezed Lana's hand once. "Ready?"

She nodded. I knocked at the large door. Letting out a slow, measured breath, we waited. I knocked again.

"We don't have time for this," I grumbled, sending my shadows to her lock. The contraption clicked, and I pushed through.

Cassandra's living room was eerily dark and chilly. The flames that should still be simmering in the fireplace, even at this hour, were absent. A small, barely visible light flickered from underneath her bedroom door though.

"Cassandra?" I called out as Lana shut the main door behind me. I pointed toward the back rooms. I had only seen Cassandra's personal room once, but I'd recovered in her guest room on more than one occasion.

I strode across the room and knocked on her door. It opened with the force of my hand, and Lana gasped.

Cassandra didn't turn to look at us. She wrote frantically over and over on the wall from a perched position on the corner of her desk. The entirety of her room was covered in a garbled mess of words.

"Kade?" Lana whispered.

I felt her fear as my own. What happened here?

Cassandra didn't flinch at Lana saying my name, or at our presence. Instead, she hummed and muttered to herself.

The words haphazardly scratched into the walls didn't make sense.

Light.

Dark.

Thames.

Mate.

Mate.

Thames.

Mate.

Traitor.

Destruction.

Blood of the Heirs.

Listen.

Listen.

Listen.

"Cassandra," I said more firmly, trying not to let my gaze linger on the words too long.

Her head tilted to the side, and she looked over her shoulder, her eyes completely white.

I rushed to her, grasping her by the shoulders. "Cassandra, it's Kade. Can you hear me?" I shook her once. "Cassandra," I shouted.

"The traitor will rise. He comes with fury." She twisted her hair around her finger, winding it and unwinding it. "Light. Light. It is not ignited."

Lana tried next, but she approached Cassandra differently, with the same calming tone she used with Vivienne in The Knotted Willow. She took her hands. "Cassandra, we need your help."

"Time runs thin. You need to trust. You need to give in."

"Give in to what? What time is running out? Does this have to do with my mother's journal?" Lana pressed, but not gruffly. She stroked a finger over Cassandra's whitened knuckles.

The seer fell away from Lana, taking a few steps and bumping into her desk. A hand flew to her chest and her eyes cleared.

She blinked, her breathing returning to normal over the next few steadying breaths.

"How can I help?" I asked. Cassandra comforted others but usually loathed being touched or shown any sort of compassion in return, so I remained back.

She shook her head, looking over Lana and me. "Time runs short," she said, her voice raspy.

I grasped her arm gently when she swayed, leading her toward her sitting area, away from this room holding so many jumbled thoughts.

"Tea?" I asked her.

She swatted my hand. "No time, dear. No time. Fate draws near."

I pulled a chair up for Lana before taking the farthest one. The same spots we sat in the last time we were with Cassandra.

"We went to my parents' grave in Brookmere," Lana said. Cassandra's gaze flicked toward her. "I am going to assume you know what I'm about to say, but stop me if you do not."

Cassandra nodded once.

Fuck. I understood Lana's loathing for seers. A flash of anger welled in me, knowing Cassandra could help Lana and me keep our kingdoms safe but instead chose to remain silent.

She jerked her head up at me. "Do not throw your rage my way. I am telling you what I can. Fate cannot be changed. Too much has been sacrificed. I will not risk everything because you feel afraid to face what comes next."

I leaned back, not daring to look away until Cassandra saw whatever it was she needed to.

"Continue, child," she said less sharply to Lana.

"My mother's journal supposedly contains answers, but it was missing," Lana said. "However, we found this." She pulled the white dagger from her thigh and Cassandra smiled.

Not just a smile—the seer beamed. "I knew it was you who was worthy."

Lana blanched, but when she met my gaze, I desperately tried to convey the truth of Cassandra's words. They were the same words I'd said to her. The world would fall to their knees once this woman believed in herself.

"Do not ever let that go," Cassandra instructed.

"I used it on a dark one back in Brookmere, and the darkness erupted out of him. Like the dagger itself destroyed it."

Cassandra cocked an eyebrow. "A funny thing, darkness. Willingly accepted or not, it does not do well when brought into the light."

"Please," Lana said, touching Cassandra's hand. The woman did not shy away from the touch. Something I would have surely been smacked for. "There was a note, a riddle with the journal—"

"As much fun as it would be to discuss the riddle and your journey, I fear there are truths you must hear now. I can feel your questions swirling around the room, and I do not have long."

"Long for what?" I asked.

"Never you mind that," Cassandra said. She stood, throwing a hand toward her fireplace and lighting it.

My jaw dropped. She healed. She prophesized. There was no way Cassandra should possess another power. It wasn't possible. Two had seemed beyond belief. But three? Impossible.

She glanced back at me and winked, but the teasing look faded from her expression as a frown crept along her brow. Her face fell, and for the first time I realized how haggard Cassandra appeared. More so than any other time I could recall.

"I'm relieved to finally be able to speak these words," she started. "I have been trapped here for a thousand years. Without my family, waiting to find the light of fate capable of ending our eternal night."

I frowned, staring at her. "I don't understand." A statement, not a question. I clenched my jaw, barely masking my frustration.

She smiled at me sadly. "More than a millennium ago, an evil walked this land, threatening to destroy it." The fire flared as she spoke, and she turned away, her eyes closed. She gripped the back of the chair she stood behind, knuckles whitening. "I was blind to the atrocities he committed because he was—he is…" She stopped, opening her eyes. "My mate."

"What?" I leaned forward, not comprehending what she said. "That's not— It doesn't—"

She cocked a single eyebrow at me. "You of all people know better than that," she scolded.

I pursed my lips, touching my chest to feel the bond I had noticed. The bond connecting me to Lana.

"How?" I asked.

Lana glanced between the two of us, a crease forming between her brows.

"So much of this story is not mine to tell, but there are things I believe you need to know that will not influence your fate." She walked around the chair, falling into it.

"Thames was a gifted Fae. Charming, cunning, he wrapped people around his finger and bent them to his will. When we met, I felt the bond and wanted to make all of his dreams come true. All of my dreams come true. So I excused the things he did to gain such immense power. I used my own power to help him." She brought her fingertips to her lips, swallowing audibly. "I helped him and am guilty of many things the Fates will never forgive—things I cannot forgive. You know I can heal and see. These abilities should not coincide together. But I was special, and he made me feel exceptional. I was the only one of my kind—a seer and a sorceress. I was his."

"There's no such thing as sorceresses," Lana whispered.

"Not anymore, no. And not then either, save for my mother and me." For the first time ever, Cassandra shed a tear. "Thames twisted my love, our mating bond, until I foresaw my sister dying to save me. I saw the destruction of our lands. I saw the withering of life, crawling in an eternally blackened land. So I fled." The fire again sparked behind her, almost as though it reacted to the emotions in Cassandra herself. "I approached Thames's enemies, Queen Evelyn and King Jasper."

Lana sucked in a breath and Cassandra chuckled. "Yes, your Queen Evelyn. Together, we trapped Thames, creating the void. It separated Atheria in two, creating Brookmere and Mysthaven, the worlds we live in today."

She stared at the fire, silent for a few moments, but neither Lana nor I spoke. The woman who'd wiped blood from my back, who encouraged me to keep going every time I faltered under my father's reign, was more powerful than I'd ever imagined. After a thousand years, she'd spent her time caring for me, leading me to this moment.

"Such magic required sacrifices," she whispered. "Sacrifices greater than you could ever imagine. We may not have been strong enough to defeat Thames for good, but we trapped him, containing him to the void to protect our world."

She focused on Lana. "You, sweet girl, will learn more truths when you find your mother's journal. As you know, the rest of Brookmere is unaware of Mysthaven, or even King Jasper." Her face softened into a smile as she looked at me next. "Your father should have told you all of this by now, but he has been consumed by his own greed for power. The amulet he wears uses the power of your line to keep Thames trapped in the void. Contained. It requires each king to sacrifice himself at the end of his reign, feeding his magic into the amulet before passing it to his heir."

I froze.

"Kade," Lana whispered, her breath heavily exhaling from her. "That sounds like what Andras is doing with magic."

Cassandra's gaze darkened. "Thames is growing strong again. I have felt it these past few years. Your father is not containing him but feeding him. He has ruled too long, Prince."

"How would Andras know about this?" Lana asked.

Cassandra rose again, rubbing her arms. "He has come to me in dreams. Our mating bond not yet severed. His power has spread, infecting and festering in the hearts of the broken. The darkness spreading and feeding on your Fae is him. His power. He must have a way to get through to others willing to give him their blind faith."

"If you weren't enough to stop him—" I started, but one look at Lana stopped those thoughts, and I ignored the seed of doubt growing inside me. "What must we do?"

Cassandra walked up to me, cupping my face. "Ask yourself, Kade Blackthorn, why Fate decided—after years with no guidance, no prophecies—to grant two?"

"Us," Lana said, standing as well. "You think we are the ones to defeat him? I have no magic." She looked at me, panicked, and in a few strides I stood by her side, taking her hand in mine.

Regardless of if my Little Rebel saw it, Fate had chosen wisely with her. Compared to her, I was the one who wasn't worthy. Yet as the tether in my chest throbbed, igniting at the feel of Lana's hand in mine, I knew Cassandra spoke the truth.

The man Lana made me, the man who fell in love and refused to lose it. That man would burn the entire kingdom down for her—*his mate.*

That's what she was.

There was no longer any doubt in my mind, in my soul. This thing with Lana was a gift I may not be worthy of, but one I would *never* let go. I would face this evil for her. For a future with my fucking queen. Without hesitation.

"You are more than whatever magic you believe you lack, Illiana," I whispered, kissing the palm of her hand.

Cassandra let out a moan and fell to the side.

"Cassandra," I cried out, reaching for her as she fell near the fire.

"I'm fine," she hissed, rising as she smacked at my hands.

Just as I predicted she would. "Today has taken a toll on us all. I don't need to warn you to be careful. Thames may be trapped for now, but he has been starved of the power he craves for a thousand years, waiting to be set free. Something has changed, even if the Fates have kept me blind to what exactly that something is." She rubbed her forehead. "Thames is cunning, and underestimating him would be a mistake for all of us. I have seen firsthand how desperate evil men get when they feel their power slipping. Stand together, and the Fates will guide you. As will I, when my interference will not hurt our survival."

Lana blew out a shaky breath.

"Let me at least help you to your room," I offered the seer, but she refused me. Again.

"I am capable without your hand, my prince." She patted where she had just smacked me away, but then, in an uncharacteristic move, wrapped her arms around me. "I never meant to love you as I do. If the Fates had blessed me with a child, I would have wished for them to be just like you."

She rubbed my arm and turned away from me. I stared, dumbfounded at the sweet words from a woman who I, too, had loved like family. I didn't dare want to acknowledge that the way she spoke sounded too much like a goodbye.

At her bedroom door she turned to face us again, but only looked at Lana. "I am not the only one who heard Fates call when the dagger returned home to you." She lifted her finger and pointed directly at Lana. "Illiana, find my sister."

CHAPTER 40

LANA

Kade's hand tightened over mine as we left Cassandra's room.

"Are you all right?" I asked, knowing the moment between him and Cassandra at the end got to him.

He paused and smiled at me reassuringly. "I am." He brought my hand to his lips, pressing a gentle kiss on my knuckles before pulling me alongside him again.

Neither of us spoke as we walked the halls with purpose. I knew it would be too risky to repeat anything out loud. Inside though, my mind churned.

Cassandra's words to find her sister immediately made me think of Vivienne. The only other seer I knew of in either kingdom.

She had found us though, showing up at The Knotted Willow after I found the dagger, even if she had been trapped in one of her usual episodes.

I ran my fingers over it at my thigh.

Kade squeezed my hand again. I stared at his profile, focused and unyielding as he led us through the halls of the palace.

Cassandra's comment to him about mates burned over my

skin. An ugly, jealous rage blossomed inside of me at the mere thought of Kade having a mate. He hadn't denied her words though.

No.

That didn't matter right now. Even if the thought pulsated in my chest, threatening to knock me off my feet. The strange thrum of energy present around Kade now lingered as a constant buzz.

I inhaled deeply, rubbing my chest as if I could relieve the knot inside the center of me. It had grown last night, only settling when I awoke to Kade's lips kissing up and down my body.

We burst into the training room, walking to the ring.

We were alone so far; the others hadn't arrived.

"Well," I breathed out, blowing the air purposefully.

Kade ran his other hand over his face.

"This Thames has to be able to communicate with Andras," I said, the words Cassandra spoke replaying in my head. "Using Casimir to siphon magic into gems? It sounds like your father's amulet is essentially the same thing."

"Thames is trapped, according to Cassandra." Kade frowned. "But it's that or my father communicating with Andras, and I don't believe that's possible."

"Let's hope he's trapped for now. We don't know what your father is doing. The darkness *is* spreading with similar magics on both sides of the void."

Kade nodded. "I think you're right." He pulled me close to him, kissing the top of my head. "Whatever is happening, it's you and me, Little Rebel. We will figure this out together."

"The end of your prophecy." I swallowed the lump in my throat. "Say it again."

"Fuck, I know," he answered. "Though evil will free and be bound no more, Fate still awaits one final war."

The doors opened, and Jax and Raya jogged in.

"Storm?" Kade immediately tensed, shadows swirling around him.

"Fine, checking on something for the king," Raya answered. Her eyes bounced back and forth between the two of us. Dark circles marred her face.

"How did it go?" Kade asked, and she turned her attention to him.

She shrugged. "He seemed angrier in my mind than he actually was. In fact, he barely cared for the details." She closed her eyes and shook her head like she wanted to rid herself of her thoughts. "He's too calm."

She balled her hands into fists once, twice.

"I say we take that as a blessing. Maybe the Fates decided to let us catch a break for once," Jax grumbled. "There's nothing here. No rumors. No curious inquiries about where we were. Everything is merely continuing on as usual."

Kade released a sharp breath. "That's good. So right now, everything is okay."

"What did you learn?" Raya asked.

"Nothing good," I said. "Apparently there's an evil being, worse than we've ever seen, trapped in the void. Desperate to take over the world."

"Excuse me?" Jax asked. He rested his hands on top of his head. "We have our hands full with your mad man in Brookmere and our king here. Please don't tell me we now have another evil creature to battle."

"We don't know," Kade said. "Though we gained information, none of it is particularly helpful yet." He paced a few steps. "We'll go about our days. See what comes up. We need to think about trying to gain more Guardians to our side and discuss what to do about Brookmere."

I stroked a hand over my chest, rubbing at the tiny ball of tension there. Kade stepped closer, staring at the movement. His nearness helped.

"You hear that, Princess?" Jax smirked, winking from across the ring. "You're stuck with us now."

Raya let out a grunt and her eyes whitened. But she came to quicker than the other times the king had contacted her.

"He wants to see you." She stared straight ahead at Kade. "I would take Jax."

"Did he ask for both of us?" Kade questioned.

Her nose crinkled, almost in disgust. "No, but he's in a mood. You need a buffer."

"Fuck," Jax muttered. "Where's Storm when you need him."

Kade brushed a thumb along my jaw. "Stay with Raya. Don't trust anyone else." He looked at Raya. "Take Lana to her chambers, and wait with her, please."

"Of course," Raya agreed. "I've got her."

I grabbed Kade's arm. "Be safe."

His lips turned up into a breathtaking smile. "You don't need to worry about me, Little Rebel."

I nodded, his confidence reassuring me. Still, an uncomfortable feeling returned the moment he and Jax left the ring.

"Let's go," Raya urged, pressing her hand against the small of my back as we left the training ring.

"He wasn't angry last night?" I asked.

Raya shook her head, walking beside me. "No."

I frowned. She seemed more approachable in Brookmere. Now it appeared she returned almost fully to her standoffish ways. "If you need to talk, I'm here." I touched her arm.

She looked down to where my hand lay and inhaled. "Thank you."

I walked straight at the first break in hallways, but Raya pulled me to the right. The opposite direction from my suite.

"I need to get more weapons," she stated when I started to protest. "I'm not comfortable with only what I have. We'll be quick."

"You're uneasy." It wasn't a question.

Raya sighed. "Be on guard." She froze, her body trembling once like a chill raced through it. Then, kept walking.

"What did he say to you?" I asked, knowing the king had to have said something to create this tension in her.

"He doesn't need to say anything. I'm a Guardian. I'm always worried."

I smiled. "True. You merely seem more worried than usual."

We turned and two guards eyed us carefully as we walked by. I hadn't been to Raya's room, but if she resided in the barracks, I assumed we'd see more Guardians along the way.

Once we passed, the two peeled away from the wall, following behind us. Raya glanced over her shoulder before locking eyes with me. She looped her arm through mine and continued walking. We didn't change our pace, but still, she held my arm tightly.

My pulse quickened. The heavy boots of the guards behind us echoed in the hall.

We took a few more turns, until I realized I had no idea where we were in the palace. Not that I had it mapped out in my mind perfectly, but I knew enough to know we were getting far from the safety of my chambers.

"Raya?" I asked as quietly as I could.

She shook her head once.

The guards behind us made no effort to stop us or speed us up. We turned again, a shorter corridor greeting us. The windows lining the hall overlooked the magnificent gardens. Yet I had no time to admire them.

Raya slowed, catching me off guard. I looked at her as her grip tightened on my arm. "Illiana," she said, my name coming out of hers slowly. She grimaced and a trickle of blood pooled under her nose.

"Raya." I tried to pull my arm back to help her, but she didn't let go. "Your nose is bleeding. I don't have anything—"

I froze. Her hand grasped my forearm too tightly.

The bleeding. It came from fighting mind magic.

She stared at me unwavering, blood falling in a slow drip from the edge of her lip onto the stone beneath us.

I tugged at her, pulling to run, but the guards behind us closed in. Raya yanked me forward as a single tear formed in her eye.

She opened the door at the end of the corridor, forcing us through as the guards positioned themselves behind me.

Raya fought the king's mind magic, but still, she led me along to whatever awaited me.

Fates above.

"Raya, please," I begged. "You can fight this."

She pulled me through, and the archway opened into a massive circular stone room. Half of it was lined with bookshelves, while the other half contained open windows. In any other situation, it would have taken my breath away.

Now though, I had no choice but to ignore the cavernous views from the window in favor of what lay before me.

Because along the far wall, next to the bookshelves, hanging from a pair of chains with blood pouring in rivulets down his body, was Storm.

Storm barely raised his head, but it was enough to see the terror in his eyes when he noticed me.

The man in front of him turned, even though I knew who it was already. The obsidian crown gracing his head remained firmly in place despite the evident signs that he'd been delivering brutal torture.

"Ah, the guest of honor has finally arrived." King Dargan grinned wickedly, and Raya dutifully tugged on my arm, leading me straight to him.

CHAPTER 41

LANA

I struggled against the restraints tying me to the chair that faced Storm's bloodied body.

The king stood across the room, murmuring to Raya.

Raya, who had betrayed us.

Even if it was outside of her control right now. Kade's biggest fears were coming true. No wonder they never told her everything. The king's ability to push past her defenses and see her thoughts was just as dangerous as they all suspected.

"Storm?" I asked.

His eyes were trained on mine, and he gave me a strained smile. "I have endured torture before, and he will have to try harder than that to break me," he said calmly.

"Why are we here?" I asked.

Storm shook his head. "I don't know. We'll be okay though."

I winced because there was no way he spoke the truth when his body appeared as mangled as it did. He had endured far too much in such a short period of time.

"Go stand guard outside of the door." The king's voice echoed through the large room. I glanced over my shoulder, locking eyes with Raya as a small rivulet of blood fell from her nose. Her eyes hardened as she walked out of the room, obeying the king.

"Sorry to keep you waiting." The clap of his hands made me jump. He brought those hands down hard on my shoulders. "Shall we continue?"

Nausea churned in my gut hearing his voice and the glee dripping from his lips for what was to come.

I met Storm's gaze, refusing to look away as the king approached him, standing at his side. When he circled behind him, as if he needed to admire what he had done to him, Storm mouthed two words to me: "Be strong."

Then he schooled his expression into a stone-faced stare.

King Dargan stood on the other side of Storm, his focus shifting entirely to me. "The time has come to set him free."

Him? Thames.

I tried to relax my breathing. We were out of time and completely unprepared to face the threat of Thames's wrath.

The king backhanded Storm across his face so hard his lip split. The rings on his fingers left imprints on his skin.

"I will be the one to do it and will be abundantly rewarded." He shifted in front of me and smacked Storm again on the other cheek. "Oh, I didn't mean to block your view of my handiwork." The king gave me a smug smile. He grabbed Storm's chin in his hands. "Hmm, this one didn't leave enough of a mark. We'll have to try that again. Ready?" he asked. "Of course you're not." He smacked him harder this time, splitting skin to match the other side of Storm's face.

"Stop!" I cried out, tugging at the restraints futilely.

But the king didn't stop. Instead, he grabbed a candelabra resting on his desk only a few feet away. The large three-pronged decor dragged across the table. My stomach clenched watching the king wield the dense matte black weapon. He heaved it sideways, crashing it into Storm's side. The crunch of bone ripped through the air, and I gagged at the sound.

I was going to vomit.

Storm's eyes widened in obvious pain, but he didn't dare utter a sound.

This torture *was* real. Unlike the torture Andras used against Ian, where it was all an illusion, this was actually happening. And there was nothing I could do to stop it.

I pulled harder at my wrists, still bound to the chair. "Let him go. Stop this. What do you want from us?"

The bite of the rope burned my skin. I had to get free. I had to save Storm. I couldn't do this again.

Storm's head hung low, and his breathing rattled, labored. He surely had a broken rib, and I hadn't been here for his initial torture to see what else might be broken. Even if we could escape, I wasn't sure if I could move Storm's body. He was a strong Fae, but was he strong enough to walk out of here after everything he'd endured?

I prayed to the Fates, begging with all I had for Kade to appear. His shadows could save us all, and then Dargan would be outnumbered.

King Dargan flicked his wrist and a *whoosh* sent the air swirling in the room straight down Storm's throat. Stuffing it into his body, essentially choking him.

Storm tried to close his mouth, but the force of the magic was too strong.

"Stop!" I yelled again. "Please stop." Pure desperation laced my pleas. I had to do anything and everything to draw attention to myself and away from Storm if he had any chance of survival.

Dargan turned, narrowing his eyes as he stalked toward me. "Apologies, dear," the king said, smoothing back his hair. He flicked his hand again and Storm gasped, falling against the chains holding him up. "I merely needed to ensure I had your attention."

He kneeled in front of me. "It is time to free Thames."

I schooled my features, forcing myself not to react.

"He promised me power, even more than he has already gifted me. I will never have to make a sacrifice to the amulet again." He grinned, knocking me underneath my chin. "I can live forever."

I jerked my face away, but he didn't allow it for long, grasping my neck.

Storm's head rolled to the side, and he spit a mouthful of blood onto the floor before choking out, "Who the fuck is Thames?"

"Someone you can never defeat." The king laughed mirthlessly.

My eyes flicked over the king's shoulders to Storm. He hadn't been in the training ring when we relayed what Cassandra told us earlier. "Thames is trapped."

A sly smile spread over the king's face as he watched me argue. "Ah," he chuckled, "you know about Thames, Princess? But what you obviously don't know is there is indeed a way to set him free. There is always a counterspell."

I didn't dare say a word. I refused to reveal anything in case my knowledge would help the king. Even if I barely possessed any about this threat.

The king stood and walked to his desk. He ran his hands over the candelabra, stroking it with his fingers like a pet. "Even a sorceress cannot defy the Fates, Illiana Dresden. Thames told me all about a sorceress's attempt to interfere with fate's calling. She may be powerful, may have trapped him temporarily. Yes." He hummed. "Despite her meddling, her time is coming to an end. Her hold over this kingdom. This world. It will soon be over.

"Imagine my reward when I find her after I free him. Deliver him the sorceress who trapped him all these years." King Dargan spoke almost to himself.

He had no idea Cassandra was the sorceress. I held on to hope that his desire to free Thames was just that: a fool's yearning for power.

Storm groaned and looked like he struggled to maintain consciousness. His body beaten to a pulp. "Stay with me, Storm," I begged quietly. "You can do this. Fight."

"You can save him, you know," the king sang.

I snapped my attention away from Storm over to the king.

"All of this can be over in a matter of minutes. You have the power to choose, Illiana. You have the power to save your —" He spat at the ground near Storm's feet. "Friend. All I need is your blood. Offer me your blood willingly, and all of this can be forgotten. You can take him and go."

I sat there in shock, trying to remember anything about blood in Cassandra's words. "My blood?"

My heart rate increased, wondering if there was something we missed.

King Dargan slammed the candelabra into Storm's gut. He shouted, crying out in pain for the first time.

"No," I cried. My eyes watered, shedding tears for the warrior who had become a friend.

King Dargan approached my chair again, gripping his makeshift weapon. He ran a hand over my hair and licked his lips. "All I need is your blood and I promise not to touch Storm again."

"What could my blood do?" I asked, trying frantically to move his hands off me.

"Though locked away a thousand turns, the final battle has yet to burn. When light and dark unite, prepare—freedom is granted with the willing blood of two heirs," the king chanted prophetically.

I dragged in a shaky breath. That sounded too close to a prophecy. But how? Cassandra hadn't told us of a prophecy about Thames being freed.

The king smiled, as if he could taste my panic. "If you don't want to see Storm die a slow, excruciatingly painful death, you will hand over your blood." He brought my face closer to his and he whispered in my ear, "The choice is up to you."

"Do not break, Lana," Storm muttered. "This world can survive without me, but it cannot survive without you."

Vivienne's wild ramblings at The Knotted Willow replayed through my mind. She knew. She had a vision and knew my blood was needed. Those exact words, "blood of the heirs," had spilled from Vivienne's lips. They were also written on the wall in Cassandra's room.

Our blood. Kade's and mine. What did the king say though?

Willingly.

That was the key. If we refused to give our blood willingly, Thames would never be free. He needed the two heirs to make their own sacrifices in order to be free.

Deep lines formed between my brows. "I will *never* give you my blood." I prayed the king didn't hear the tremble in my voice. I wasn't sure I could watch him kill Storm and not succumb. I had to try though.

King Dargan chuckled, barely audible. "I think you will."

He threw out his hands, fire spurting from his palms. He had the power of too many elements. Wielding magic that couldn't all be his, just like Andras.

He sent his flames to Storm's body, and although he maintained his composure at first, the pain eventually became too much and Storm cursed, spewing at the king.

"Do not say anything, Lana," he shouted through his agony.

I closed my eyes. It was Ian all over again. But this time I had what the king wanted to make him stop. I may not possess magic that could have saved Ian from Andras's torture, but my blood I could give. I pursed my lips, holding back with everything I had. I could end his pain though. I sucked in a breath and the flame receded.

The king narrowed his eyes. "Interesting. You may not do

it for Storm. But I've seen how you look at my son. I bet you would do anything to save him. To save Kade."

Panic coursed through my veins. Pure terror. I *would* do just about anything to save Kade.

The king smiled. "I will give you time to decide. When I return, loosen your tongue or prepare for Storm to die. Then we'll move on to my son." He glided around me, his hand dragging across my collarbone before he left.

I didn't speak until the door shut behind him. "I'm sorry, Storm," I sobbed. "I'm so sorry."

"Don't you dare apologize," he groaned. "But you can tell me what the fuck is going on."

"Kade and I learned that a thousand years ago, a Fae named Thames had grown too powerful, threatening the entire world. With a sacrifice from a queen and king, he was trapped in the void, splitting the world in two. Apparently, now he wants to get out." I tried to recap quickly without saying Cassandra's name, knowing the king had no idea his own seer was the sorceresses he sought. "We thought there was no way to free him, but apparently, he has his own prophecy just as Kade and I have ours. Fucking seers."

"You can say that again."

"What can I do?" I asked.

"You're as trapped as I am right now, Lana." Storm coughed. "Kade will come."

I shivered, and even in pain, Storm noticed.

"He won't kill Kade. Not if he needs his blood willingly too."

I looked up and met Storm's eyes. There was so much courage there. He hung, bloodied, burned, and beaten. Yet he still sought to reassure me, and perhaps himself too.

"You're right." I inhaled an unsteady breath. "Are you able to access your healing abilities despite what he's done to you?" I tried not to let my voice crack.

Storm nodded once. "It will take time in this state. But yes,

I can heal the major injuries to make them bearable with this reprieve."

"Good." I nodded back, letting his words comfort me. Hopefully Dargan took his time coming back.

"When I was younger, Andras tortured me to try to get my magic free," I said softly. "He would bring Ian down and make me think he was hurting him, even though Ian's pain was all in my mind. If there had been a way to fake having magic, I would have done it to save him." I sighed, emotions clogging my throat. "But this time, I *can* save you from the pain. I don't know that I will be able to deny him if he comes back."

"You can and you will," Storm commanded. "He knows if he kills me, Kade would never cooperate. You wouldn't either. You must stay strong. I can withstand this, and so can you."

I didn't respond, but I refused to look away from him. Holding eye contact right now grounded me, reminded me he was able to handle it.

"I was right when I said you would care for me as much as Ian one day," he laughed.

I smiled through my tears. "Never."

"If you repeat what I am about to tell you, I will deny it." He sighed dramatically, but I noticed the rattling had lessened in his voice. "And then find a way to retaliate."

I widened my stare, waiting for the rest.

"My first name is—"

He paused, watching me just as I watched him. "Tell me!"

"Chester."

I laughed, my entire body shaking as he shook his head at my reaction.

"A little torture and you are spilling your deepest secret," I teased.

He smiled before wincing. "Never speak of this weak moment."

The door flung open, startling both of us from our conversation. The sound of the door creaking on its hinges was the only thing I allowed to pull my gaze away from Storm.

Raya stumbled forward, falling to her knees.

"Raya!" I shouted.

The chains holding Storm clinked and I saw him fighting against the hold. He didn't fear the king, but right now, his determination told me he was worried. "Whatever he's doing, fight it, Raya," he shouted across the room.

Raya crawled, slowly inching forward. Her haggard breathing was evident, but she didn't stop. Even as she barely made progress, she continued.

She looked up, tears streaming down her face, and still, she moved toward me.

"You're all right," I lied, trying to reach her with my words. The pain etched on her face was too much. "Raya, it is okay."

She pulled herself up on her hands and knees in front of me. Her body convulsed, shaking uncontrollably.

Then she let out a terrifying, blood-curdling scream.

CHAPTER 42

IAN

Corbin and I stared at the makeshift map we'd made from mugs of ale and utensils, courtesy of William. I rubbed my temples, taking in the sight.

It only struck me now how many people we'd helped over the two years of Hidden Henchman work. Pride swelled in my chest at what Lan had accomplished in such a short time, just because she loved her people.

"Oh, and here." Corbin set down a spoon up toward the coastal towns. "It was out of the way, one we completed a year in. Leif and I ran it."

I nodded. "I remember. Good work. This is—" I paused.

"Incredible," Kalliah finished, setting down plates of food for both of us. "Now eat something before you get back to it."

"There's too much to do. We have no idea how long we have," I argued, rubbing my temple. A headache had formed an hour ago, only growing stronger as we worked.

"You won't accomplish anything if you starve yourselves. They only just left last night. According to Raya's estimate, they should have arrived in Mysthaven not too long ago."

"Raya's estimate?" I pressed. Hearing her name clawed at my brain, raking over my spine, and not at all in the disgusted way I pretended to believe. Spending time with her in my head had been strange. In person, awful.

Kalliah glared at me. "She was nice to me. Even when you were a dickhead to her."

"I was not," I argued.

Corbin wiped a hand over his mouth, coughing as though covering a laugh. I shoved his shoulder. He stepped away from the map with his hands up. "It was intense. Your behavior. I've never seen you treat someone so poorly before."

"Her magic—"

"Saved your life and told Lana where to find us," Kalliah huffed. "I knew you could be dense, but I never took you for an inconsiderate idiot."

"You don't understand," I sighed.

Kalliah refused to back down, cocking her right eyebrow the way she always did when determined to get to the bottom of Lana's or my lies.

I grabbed the plate of food on the table and moved to the bench Corbin and I had dragged away earlier. Before I could take my seat, I stumbled. I heard the plate clatter to the floor, but I was no longer in The Knotted Willow.

I was in my own mind, like I had been in the dungeons.

And someone was screaming.

A hazy form took shape in front of me and screamed again.

Raya.

I rushed over to her like I could touch her somehow, even though we were merely illusions.

"*Ian,*" she shouted. Her body jerked, and she crumpled forward on her hands and knees.

What's wrong? I reached out, but the illusion flickered, and she was gone.

She screamed my name again, screamed it like there was something I could fucking do, and my heart pounded in my chest.

I couldn't see her in my head anymore.

I turned frantically, wondering where she could have gone. Another scream.

Raya! I demanded more forcefully.

She appeared again, back on the floor. She looked up at me, blood running from her nose, from her ears. Fuck, from everywhere, all while bloody tears streamed down her face.

I reached for her, startled when my hands actually touched her shoulders. She shuddered once as I made contact. I could feel her, even in my mind. The pain coursing through her threatened to break me. *I'm here,* I promised.

Fuck, I didn't know that to do. What she needed.

"*Help,*" she whispered.

And then she was gone.

CHAPTER 43
LANA

I watched Raya scream until her voice gave out.

Her screaming continued to ring in my ears, even after she stopped. I don't know if I'd ever heard such a tortured sound before.

She pulled herself to my chair and worked to untie me.

"You can do this," I said, my voice low. I didn't want to startle or scare her.

Fates, her crestfallen expression was so unlike the strong woman I'd come to know.

"We're with you," Storm added. "You aren't alone."

"You should hate me," she whispered. "He is too strong."

"You're fighting now," I said as the rope dropped away and my hands fell forward. I rubbed my wrists, begging the circulation to return.

She moved to Storm and produced a key from her pocket, leaving me to untie the ropes at my feet.

"I don't know how much time we have. I haven't been able to release his hold until now," she murmured. "He must be distracted."

"You need to be careful," Storm said as she reached up to work on unlocking his chains.

I stepped out of the ropes, my muscles locked up from sitting with my hands behind my back.

Raya didn't answer him, so he pressed harder. "We don't know the damage fighting his mind magic causes, and I can barely see your face through the blood."

"I'm fine," she snapped. The lock clicked around his wrists.

"But you won't be." The king's voice came from behind us.

I turned as guards poured into the room.

Followed by Kade. The second he saw us, he shoved forward. Guards approached Raya, Storm, and me, circling and blocking us from Kade.

"What the fuck is going on here?" Kade shouted. "Lana?"

Storm struggled to undo the last of his chains behind me.

"I'm okay," I answered, unable to look away from him.

"Oh, not for long, my dear," the king said. He flicked his wrist as he ordered his guards. "Seize them."

Kade stepped closer. "I don't think so," he said, his tone menacing and dark as he stared down his father.

The king showed no sign of concern. "You will stand down, son."

"You will not touch her. You will let all of them go."

The king stepped around Kade. "I said, take them."

Kade turned, shuddering, and I knew what was about to happen. I pivoted throwing myself at Storm and Raya. "Hold on to me," I shouted.

Kade's shadows cocooned around me, and I gripped them tightly. Darkness covered the room. I clung to the others, too nervous to let go without knowing if we were safe.

But I heard silence.

There was nothing.

Arms wrapped around me, tugging me away from both of them. Only then did I open my eyes. Storm and Raya stood unharmed in front of me.

Kade spun me around, touching my face, my neck, my arms.

"I'm not hurt," I reassured him. "I'm okay."

He pulled me into a hug, and I saw over his shoulder. The deadly explosion from Kade hadn't even given the guards a chance to scream before the shadows destroyed their bodies.

Except they hadn't killed everyone. Laughter echoed freely in the room, and I tensed, making eye contact with the king.

Who stood unharmed.

Jax ran through the doorway, taking in the destruction as he entered the room. His eyes flared wide as he took in the four of us, and then the king.

The king who should have also been destroyed and yet stood untouched by Kade's shadows.

He laughed again. "Did you think the darkness I molded could destroy me?"

Kade's lip curled, and he gripped me by the waist, holding me close to his side. His shadows relentless as they frantically jerked around him, spidering out in the room.

One of them curled around my leg, and the others calmed slightly at the closeness but didn't retreat.

"What are you talking about?" Kade asked.

The king ran a hand over the front of his robes, walking toward a pile of dusty ash on the floor and kicked it.

He ran his foot through the resettling ash. Bile rose in my throat. That pile had been one of his loyal Guardians. Kade had not hesitated to destroy all of them.

All because they tried to come for me.

"You dare to defy me when I *created* you," the king snarled. "I spent years feeding the darkness into you. It worked so easily to control my Guardians. They fell to my will after a dose or two."

"We would have seen that," Storm argued, limping forward. Kade's shadows reached out to him, supporting his friend.

"I am not stupid enough to turn them here," the king snapped. "My true army lies safely elsewhere. Away from the eyes of any disloyal. Who knew my own son was one of the traitors I needed to weed out. But my monster will return to me. You can't fight the darkness already in you."

"You have no power over him," I shouted, surprising everyone in the room. "You have tried to control him for years and failed. He is stronger than you will ever be." I tried to step forward, reaching for the dagger at my thigh, but Kade's shadows held me back. I glared at him, wanting us to charge the king now. To end this.

The pride on Kade's face reassured me, but he shook his head once, keeping me from continuing the struggle against him.

"If you knew I was disloyal, why wait until now to say something?" Kade asked, crossing his arms.

"I wasn't sure, of course. With no proof, I didn't want to make any hasty decisions," the king responded. "Until I got into Raya's mind last night. Finally weak enough to infiltrate completely as she spent too much of her energy giving to others, leaving her defenseless."

She sucked in a breath and her head fell back. A whimper was all we heard as she stumbled forward.

"Fight it, Raya!" Jax shouted from the doorway. The king threw a hand in his direction and Jax flew backward, slamming against the wall.

I ran over to him. "Jax," I whispered. His body seemed limp, but his pulse remained strong.

"Go get my Guardians, dear," the king instructed Raya. "Bring them here. Then we can discuss your punishment."

She bowed her head, in a complete trance as she left the room. I stared back at the true Monster of Mysthaven. The king.

He moved toward Kade, arm outstretched. Kade's eyes bulged, and he gasped.

The king curled his hand around in the air, like he was using an invisible hand to choke Kade.

I ran forward, but Kade's shadows blocked me from reaching him.

"Did you think you could lead a rebellion behind my back without my knowledge? How foolish," the king said. "You will willingly submit to your punishment, or I will use you to destroy everyone in this room."

"I would never," Kade choked out.

"Ah, but you know how you lose yourself to that darkness sometimes. Do you think I cannot make that permanent?" The king grinned, loosening his grip on Kade.

Raya returned, guards coming in and flooding the room around the king. Around us.

"Now." The king smiled. "You will submit to a whipping here, willingly."

It clicked. If Kade submitted, the king would have his blood. *Willingly*.

"Kade you can't, he's going to—" A guard grabbed me, covering my mouth with his hand.

"Let her go." Kade moved forward, drawing his sword and stabbing the guard standing in front of him with no remorse.

"Kade," Storm shouted as two guards pulled him closer. "You can't submit—"

The king turned his power on Storm, and I watched in horror as he pulled our friends off to the side, trapping them behind some sort of magical barrier. We could not hear their voices, despite their mouths moving frantically.

The king laughed, turning his attention to me as an invisible hand covered my mouth, taking me from the guard as he pulled me to his side.

"Think about this carefully, son," the king said. "You drained your power in your earlier display. You are not strong enough to defeat me."

He ran a hand over my hair like a damn pet as he beckoned a guard over to take his place. The guard slapped his hand over my mouth as the king removed his magical hold.

"I'll submit to whatever you deem necessary," Kade shouted. "If you let her go."

I shook my head. The second the king obtained his blood, he would be one step closer to releasing Thames.

And Kade had no idea.

I had to do something, warn him in some way. I bit the guard's hand, and he yelped in pain as I thrust myself forward. "Kade—" But the king shoved me backward, sending me careening into a line of guards behind him.

The force of the motion caught me so off guard, I landed at a Guardian's feet, who forcefully picked me up underneath my arms. He wasted no time, his hand clasped over my mouth and a dagger held to my side.

For the first time since I'd met Kade, he looked terrified. His cool demeanor cracking at the sight of me struggling before him. I would be dead in an instant if the king willed it.

"I said I will submit," Kade growled. "On the condition Lana and my friends go free."

All I could do was shake my head, unable to communicate that Kade would be giving the king exactly what he wanted.

The king's eyes glimmered in giddiness as he readied the whip he'd picked up. "On your knees."

Kade started to drop to his knees where he stood on the other side of the study, but King Dargan stopped him. "No, boy, not there." He pointed toward me. "There."

I screamed against the guard's palm as I fought unsuccessfully to free myself from his grip. His armor too thick for me to do any damage, more likely to injure myself in the process.

Kade slowly stood to his full height and made his way across the room, cautiously lowering himself once more, this time at my feet.

King Dargan strode toward Kade as he removed his shirt. It had to be an automatic response from his past. He placed his hands on his knees and his back remained as straight as board, ready and waiting for his punishment.

I tried once more to scream at him, to tell him not to do this. His father has no intention of letting either of us leave here. At least not alive.

Kade looked me straight in the eye and mouthed, "I love you," before schooling his expression into a blank stare.

The sound of the whip cracked in the air as leather met flesh. My whole body revolted at the sound, flinching as the aroma of copper filled the air. Kade didn't even flinch as the second crack echoed in the silence of the study. Droplets of blood laced the darkened leather and splattered across the stone floor.

"You dare defy your master?" the king whispered as he stalked from one side of Kade's body to the other. "I created you. I made you the Fae you are today, and this betrayal is how you repay me?"

Tears streamed down my face as I watched while Kade was whipped three more times. Blood freely flowing down his back now. The king collected the flowing liquid into a vial.

The blood of an heir, willingly given.

Kade remained unmoving, his eyes staring straight into mine.

"I have been feeding the darkness into you for years." Dargan was brazen in his explanation. "Haven't you ever wondered about your little blackouts? The way your magic intensified?"

Kade didn't say anything, but I could practically see the wheels turning in his mind. Replaying every interaction with this newfound knowledge.

"You are my monster, and once Thames is released, you will not be able to ignore darkness's call. You will stand by my side."

"Never," Kade grunted through gritted teeth.

The king scoffed and pivoted to face Raya, Storm, and Jax, still trapped behind his magical barrier. I had almost forgotten they were even here because I was so focused on Kade. Tears still flowed down my face. Dargan flicked his wrist and the barrier fell away, their screams now audible in the once quiet study.

"Thank you, Raya. Your assistance in this matter is greatly appreciated. You will be rewarded for your loyalty to your king."

All their heads turned to look at Raya. Everything they had done to safeguard their plans from the king was for nothing.

Raya let a single tear fall down her face as she stood there, unable to move despite the dispersion of the magical barrier.

"Now the time has come!" King Dargan started. "Thames has waited a thousand years. It is time for him to be released."

He still needed my blood, and I would not give it up willingly. There was no way I would be the cause of the release of this murderous void monster living between our lands, sucking it dry, infecting our people.

"Why?" Kade asked.

A single word. The power of the question unmistakable. The king froze and pivoted to face Kade.

"Why? Power of course." The king stated it so plainly. Like it was such a simple answer. Like we were all idiots for not knowing.

"You already have power. You already rule all of Mysthaven. What more could you possibly want?" Kade probed further, keeping the king talking. Hopefully the others were devising a way to get us out of this situation, preferably alive.

"I have power in *this* world. But he has promised me more. No more sacrifices. No more being bound to this desolate land. Brookmere is ripe for the taking. And all I need now is the willing blood of the second heir."

King Dargan dangled the vial of Kade's blood in front of us. "One down. One to go."

I bit down hard on the hand covering my mouth, the guard wincing in pain and loosening his grip. I screamed at the king, "Never! You will never get my blood."

Dargan frowned and waved his hand at several guards standing by the door, making sure we couldn't escape. "Then Kade is dead."

The guards hastily moved toward Kade, drawing their blades before thrusting them against his throat.

"Give me your blood," Dargan stated once more. "It's really quite simple. We can sacrifice your friends too. It really doesn't bother me either way how many we kill to get your blood."

"No. I'd rather die than release that evil into this land," I spat.

"Pity." Dargan sneered. "We'll see how you feel in a few hours, after you watch him being torn to shreds by each and every one of the guards in my command. You will give me your blood before the day is over. Guard, take her to the dungeon. We'll let her wait there."

Terror threatened to overtake my entire body. I could not leave this room if I ever hoped to see my friends in one piece again.

The guard moved to take me out of the room, but he only made it one step. Kade's shadows snaked up the bodies of the guards at his side, and snapped their necks, killing them instantaneously.

Dargan stumbled back, appearing flustered, but only momentarily. He removed the amulet from its resting spot against his chest and uncorked the vial of Kade's blood, pouring it onto the stone.

And then all hell broke loose.

CHAPTER 44

LANA

Kade's palpable rage strengthened as two more guards joined the other four at his feet, all snuffed out by his shadows.

I slammed my elbow into the guard pointing a dagger at me, and he winced in pain. He hadn't expected me to fight back, and he stumbled enough so I could twist out of his grip.

Storm and Jax fought side by side, aiming their attacks at the guards that lined the room. We had survived worse odds before, we could do it again. I ran toward Kade, needing a weapon of my own, but was yanked backward.

"Enough," King Dargan shouted. He reached forward, grabbing me by the neck with his free hand and hoisting me back in front of Kade.

He froze immediately, but the fighting around us didn't stop.

Kade leveled his sword at us. "You will put her down now or I will destroy you, Father."

"My boy, you have no idea who you are up against. I will drain you like your worthless mother," the king spat.

Kade's eyes widened, shock slacking his features.

His father grinned. "Ah, I am surprised you didn't put that together. I hadn't bent you to my will yet, so when the time came for the amulet to be reinforced with magic, I was hardly going to give up my life. I gave her life instead. Fueling Thames's prison for just a while longer."

Kade let out an anguished cry, charging his father, but the coward used me as a shield.

He held me to his chest, hand tightening around my throat. A shadowy tendril inched past me, snaking around my side, curling toward Kade's father.

"When will you learn that allowing your heart into situations only causes pain," his father hissed, squeezing my throat.

I couldn't breathe. I kicked my legs.

In Dargan's arrogance, he didn't see Kade's shadows until the moment they attacked.

Thrashing out and entangling with the king, he had no choice but to drop me to the ground. The fighting around us closed in as battle waged. I searched for where I could grab a weapon, not daring to take out my white dagger for fear the king may see it.

A dead guard lay feet from me, and I crawled forward, nicking the palm of my hand as I pulled his sword from his limp hand. Turning, I ran back toward the king and Kade. Raising my blade over my head, the king turned his head and threw his hand out in my direction, sending me sideways—not hard, but enough to push me from his fight with Kade.

"Lana!" Kade shouted, but more Guardians moved toward him purposefully. A group surrounded him, reaching to hold him back, but his shadows took them out. Yet the minute one fell, another Guardian stepped forward to take his place. They were pouring in from the door as if they were waiting in a never-ending supply.

"You cannot defeat me," Dargan yelled excitedly.

A sword came toward me, and I blocked it vigorously, engaging my threat. I refused to back down. This would not be our final stand.

I lost sight of Kade in the chaos.

Stabbing my attacker in the stomach, I continued, trying to get close to the others.

Raya shouted my name. I whipped around to find a lumbering giant of a Guardian whipping his axe in an arc directly over my head. I jumped out of the way, spinning to shove my sword into him. In the time it took him to dislodge his axe from the floor, I had gotten a good hit into his arm.

The wound did nothing.

Raya met me at my side, looking pale and unsteady. She squeezed her eyes closed and grunted as if under pressure.

The giant paused, his eyes glossing over.

A whimper came out of Raya's mouth before the man toppled over. She opened her eyes but immediately fell slack against me.

"Tell them I'm sorry," she whispered.

"Don't do that," I said, dropping my weapon to drag her toward the side of the room. "Do not act as though this is the end."

"I can't—" Her eyes rolled as her head lobbed backward.

"No, no, Raya." I laid her down, slapping her face. "Wake up. Wake up right now. Raya."

Nothing I did mattered.

A boot kicked me hard at my waist, sending me flying sideways. I snarled, lifting myself up despite the arduous effort it took. The Guardian lunged, continuing his onslaught. As if I weighed nothing, he lifted me and slammed me against the wall.

His dark eyes gave away where his extra boost of power came from.

He was a dark one.

Far more in control than the crazed Fae. This Guardian had willingly turned.

I thrashed against his body, but it was no use. My vision blackened at the edges. I couldn't lose consciousness. Not now, while everyone I loved fought around me.

A caress against my cheek came a second before I could breathe again. The guard collapsed, shadows pulling away from him as I gulped in air.

I fell to my knees. Kade stood feet away from me, still fighting his father.

Kade. I needed to get to him. To fight by his side.

Storm charged toward where the king and Kade faced off, taking Kade's place as if planned, and Kade ran from the fight to my side.

He flung a wall of shadows around us, blocking the room as much as possible.

"How are there so many Guardians?" I asked.

Kade shook his head. "There are dark ones too."

"We have to get out of here with the amulet or he is going to release Thames."

Kade looked around, catching sight of his father, still clutching the amulet in his fist. It hadn't stopped glowing since Kade's blood touched it earlier.

"If I can kill my father, his magic will be sacrificed into the amulet. It should be enough to ensure Thames remains contained, and the responsibility of keeping him that way falls to me," he said quickly.

"He'll kill you if he knows your plan," I argued, frantic, knowing he would sacrifice himself to save us all.

Kade cupped my face. "If that happens, you run. Flee the palace."

"No." I shook my head. "We fight him together."

"Our world needs you, Lana," he whispered.

I slammed my fist into his chest. "It needs both of us. I don't have magic to fight the king."

Kade crashed his lips to mine, tugging me in. The room fell apart around us in a bloody, never-ending battle, and yet my world calmed in this moment with him.

"It doesn't need your magic. It's you. With or without magic you will be the one to save our kingdoms."

"No, Kade." I fought to hold onto him, to keep him with me, but the bastard winked, pulling away.

"If I fail, grab the amulet and find a way out."

I yelled after him again, uselessly. He jumped back into the fight with Storm against his father.

Kade landed an easy blow to the king, slicing down his arm. Dargan cursed, swinging for his son.

Guards flocked to him, piling on top of Kade. He'd used too much of his magic already.

His magic weakened as he did, even his shadows sputtered in and out.

I gripped the sword, running toward him, but the king's magic wrapped around me, flinging me to the back of the room.

My head slammed against the wall, and I crumpled to the ground. I heard Kade cry my name. Scream it across the room. The noise rattled in my mind but sounded so distant.

I looked up from where I lay, my body feeling broken. Raya lay unmoving where I had left her at the side of the room. I wasn't sure if I imagined her chest rising and falling or not.

Storm's injuries from his torture hadn't slowed him down, but as more Guardians fell into the room, hope sputtered out.

Jax was in his panther form, ripping and clawing at his fellow soldiers.

And Kade.

I lifted my head to see Kade held in front of his father, losing as he fought, outnumbered.

"Kade," I shouted, pushing up from the ground where the king had tossed me.

The king laughed, five men pinning Kade as he thrashed in their arms, his shadows keeping three other guards at bay.

He'd run toward the king to stop him from this nightmare. To try to get that damn amulet to keep Thames trapped. Without hesitating, he'd risked himself. I couldn't take it. The world quieted around me. My body shook, trembling.

Kade would live. He had to. Which meant I had to get up.

Determination clenched its claws around me, sparking, igniting, fueling something deep within that hadn't existed before.

Get up. Get to Kade.

Or maybe it had always existed. Locked away.

With lover's touch, she shall ignite.

I couldn't lose Kade.

Kade, who stole my heart too easily. Kade who protected me, even if it killed a part of him to do it.

Mine.

He was mine.

A well inside me filled, brimming with fury, rage.

With light.

Get up.

Storm shoved a guard away from me, and I rolled onto my hands and knees.

You are Illiana Dresden. The voice inside of me spoke, and I didn't know if it was my own, or something more.

You are stronger than the darkness within you. You are stronger than any darkness.

I shook, straining to get onto my knees. I would rise here to fight the king. To save Kade.

But I would also stand on my own feet, even in pain, because I was worthy. I may not have magic. I may not ever have magic like those clashing before me, but I was strong in my own right. Never again would I allow the desires of powerful men to cause me to feel weak. To feel less than.

"I am Illiana Dresden," I whispered to myself, rising off one knee.

"You will die here today, son." The king swung his blade back, lashing out with a flame toward Kade at the same time.

He couldn't have him. The king, the darkness, nothing could have him. Because he was mine.

Kade Blackthorn loved me.

I was worthy of that love and so much more.

I screamed, standing fully again. The noise exploded from a place deep within me, finally breaking free. A place where darkness could not touch. The hairs on my arms rose as time slowed around me.

With guards holding him back, Kade looked at me and I knew. What I'd known in the dark recesses of my soul yet hadn't spoken aloud.

I loved him. Kade Blackthorn was mine.

My mate.

The realization dawned on me, and I detonated from the inside out with power, with love, with a fury I didn't dare deny any longer.

With *magic.*

Light burst out of me, and my screams for Kade echoed around us as it sliced through the guards.

The others shouted my name, but I knew my light, my power wouldn't harm those I loved.

It would, however, devour any who hurt them.

Any who hurt *him.*

I stood on steady feet, unable to see anything but white around us. When the light faded, the guards in the room lay dead. Scattered around, their limbs at unnatural angles. No more entered through the doorway either.

Kade stood alone, unbound by anyone now, hovering over the king.

"I have waited a long time for this," he said, his voice dripping with hate and malice. "This is for what you did to my mother." He stabbed his sword into the king as his shadow sword formed in his other hand.

"For this kingdom," Kade shouted, stabbing his father again and yanking the shadow blade out, leaving the steel one rammed in his chest.

My body, so filled a second before, drained. I wobbled and fell to my knees.

Kade looked at me, eyes widening before he turned back to his father.

"And for ever thinking you could harm my mate and live." Kade slammed the shadow blade down into the king's chest with a sense of finality, his father not even coherent enough to utter a word in the end. Not even begging for his worthless life.

Kade turned, meeting my gaze. I wanted to run to him. Touch him. To ensure we were both okay.

The amulet lay toward my right, flung haphazardly in the chaos of our battle. I reached for it, wanting to secure its safety before whatever came next.

Before Kade or his shadows reached me, the ground shook, throwing us sideways.

"What the fuck?" Jax shouted from somewhere behind me.

My hand burned and I dropped the amulet in horror. I stared at the blood on my hand, realizing what I had done. Willingly.

The earth refused to yield. A sound like a bellowing roar, louder than anything I had screamed moments ago, surrounded us. I covered my ears, struggling to keep upright.

Kade crawled, feebly inching across the ground, desperately reaching for my hand.

A light smoke coated the room, swirling and hissing, making the roar even worse.

"Get away from it, Lana," I heard Storm call.

I kicked the amulet across the room as I cried out in

horror. It teetered on the ground before breaking into two pieces. Smoke billowed out of it, coating everything.

Thames. With the amulet destroyed, Thames would be free.

If Cassandra had been right, and the amulet kept his evil trapped, the magic holding Thames at bay in the void was now gone.

A shape formed in the misty haze.

Kade didn't look at the amulet like the rest of us. Instead, he still tried to crawl toward me, calling my name as the earth shook, preventing him from making progress.

I had to get up. I tried to stand but couldn't keep my balance as the earth trembled beneath us. The power shifting the world around us was too strong.

A laugh replaced the roar as the smoke solidified into a tall figure. A man.

His black hair hung in greasy, almost wet stringy clumps over his head. His thin face too sharp and angular.

He laughed again, finally blinking more fully into existence.

"What in the Fates' names…" Storm made it to me, grabbing my arm.

"I need to get to Kade."

"Stay there—" Kade shouted as the figure's arms developed. "Don't leave Storm's side."

"Do listen to your mate," the figure said, his voice haunting and old. "Though they are such tiresome things. Mates." He spit the word out like it left a bad taste in his mouth.

Kade's shadows froze, going rigid as the lighter smoke surrounding the ominous figure lurched forward, wrapping around him.

"No," I yelled, desperate to dig into my power. A magic I knew I now possessed. But there was nothing left. The initial burst had been too much too fast, and now that well I'd hoped to be endless sputtered. Empty.

I had no idea how to access it again.

"Kade!" I screamed. The world stopped shaking and I ran forward, Storm close behind me. I reached through the shadows, pain lancing up my arms as I did.

Thames's power poured into Kade. I touched his exposed chest, his shirt ripped and torn.

"Fight it," I screamed.

His eyes, even from here, darkened and grew wide as the shadows that weren't his lifted, swirling around him. His own darker shadows clashing with the gray ones.

"Run," he choked out. "I can't fight off his power. Not this much."

I shouted as I forced my body closer to his, ignoring the burning sensations on my arms threatening to consume me. "Please," I begged.

Why wasn't it working? My touch always worked before. He'd said it had. Why not now?

"Get her out of here," he shouted to Storm through gritted teeth. Storm locked his arm around my waist, dragging me halfway out of the shadows.

Storm's grunts let me know he wasn't immune to the pain resulting from Thames's magic, which meant Kade was suffering too.

The man laughed. "He's mine."

Storm removed me completely from the mist.

"I love you, Illiana." Kade's body was almost fully covered, only his dark eyes visible through the mist.

I tried fighting back. I needed to get to Kade. We couldn't let Thames take him.

One second of stumbling. One weak moment from my own damn legs and Storm took over, throwing me over his shoulder and running for the door.

Kade's face blipped out, and his shout from his own battle within broke me: "Run, Little Rebel."

As Storm hauled me through the doors Jax held open,

carrying Raya over his own shoulder, I heard Kade's voice again, now a mere whisper in my soul.

"Please don't let me catch you."

Read the Exciting Conclusion to *The Broken Prophecy* Series in
Crowns of Fate (Book 3)

WHERE TO FIND
ANNA & HELEN

We're most active on Instagram & in our Facebook Reader Group! We'd love to hear from you there!

Facebook Reader Group:
Anna & Helen's Enchanted Society

Anna's Instagram:
https://www.instagram.com/authorannaapplegate/

Helen's Instagram:
https://www.instagram.com/authorhelendomico/

Acknowledgments

Here we are at the end of another book! Every week, every day on this journey keeps getting better and better.

A year ago, we never could have predicted being where we are today. What started as something fun to do with each other has transformed into something we hope to live out for many series to come.

Not only have we forged incredible friendships over the past year, but we've also grown and become women who take more chances and believe in the goals we set for ourselves daily. We believe in the power of "why not" and use that as our personal mantra. We feel so lucky to do this together and are so incredibly grateful to all of you who have been a part of this with us.

To our Beta Readers: Maria, Danielle, Katie D., Katie B., Mims, Megan, Cara, and Shanni: Thank you so much for all of your help, time, energy, and input. We are forever grateful for all of your comments to make Shadows what it is today. You didn't hesitate to jump in and not only cheer us on, but also provided feedback that helped evolve the story and the characters into the best book 2 we could have created. Thank you for loving our characters, and us, so much. We couldn't have done this without you!

To our Little Rebels Street Team: We will never be able to say thank you enough. You have no idea how much you impact us on a daily basis. Thank you for all of the absolutely unhinged conversations and for being our best hype girls. You have made this experience surreal. We live for the unhinged fun and joy each and every one of you brings to our lives. Thank you from the bottom of our hearts.

Thank you to Christie Stratos at Proof Positive Editing: Thank you for your time and love on our manuscript!

Jessica Allain at Enchanting Covers: Your work is unparalleled. We adore working with you on all of our covers and love how you bring our visions to life.

To all of our friends and family, who continue to listen to all things Broken Prophecy every single day: Thank you for supporting us on this journey. We are so lucky to have such massive support systems in place.

And finally, thank you to YOU! To all of the readers who took a chance on Blooms of Darkness and loved it as much as you did, we wouldn't be anywhere without you. We hope you enjoyed Shadows of Ruin and we can't wait to bring you the conclusion of the Broken Prophecy series with Crowns of Fate.

Until next time ... Happy Reading!

About the Authors

Anna Applegate is a USA Today Bestselling Author. She writes fantasy romance and lives tucked away in rural Maryland surviving on coffee, champagne, and an unchecked book addiction.

Anna is an avid reader, especially if it involves morally grey love interests. She enjoys escaping into the fictional worlds she creates - filled with strong heroines, surprise twists and turns, and "destroy the world for her" leading men.

Helen Domico published her first romantasy in 2024 and has no plans on stopping. Writing a book was always a bucket-list item, but when the opportunity knocked on her door to do so with one of her best friends, she couldn't say no!

When not writing, you can find Helen reading, spending time with her family, and sneaking in a glass of cabernet. Helen resides in central Maryland with her husband and two children.

Anna & Helen love hearing from their readers! Find them on their social media or website to connect!

www.ingramcontent.com/pod-product-compliance
Lightning Source LLC
Chambersburg PA
CBHW061042310726
48969CB00004B/1045